I0450907

SINCE ETERNITY, 'TIL ETERNITY

GITANJALI NANDA

All Rights Reserved
Copyright - 2018 Gitanjali Nanda

~~~

No part of this book may be reproduced or transmitted in any form or by any means, graphic, electronic, mechanical, including photocopying, recording, taping or by any information storage retrieval system or device, without the permission in writing by the author.

Any resemblance to actual people and events is purely coincidental.

This is a work of fiction.

Paperback-Press
an imprint of A & S Publishing
A & S Holmes, Inc.

ISBN-13: 978-1-945669-44-6

DEDICATION

Maa, Savitri Nanda, for being the strongest woman in my life. Sisters, Sheetal Nanda and Ashtami Nanda, for their support. Brother, Shivam Nanda, for always teasing me. Kishan Mansukhani for being my brother from another mother. Friends, especially Yogita Rane, Isha Chaudhary, Ankit Saini, Navni Shrivastava, Shikha Mali, Ghata Chauhan, Nandini Meena, Shubham Jain and Archana Yadav for their love. Ankita Dutta for the disaster she is. Shikha Ankit Khare for her faith in me. Aryika Tripathy for being my grammarian and what not. And last but not the least, Syed Shahab Ali for whatever I am today, this wasn't possible without you.

In memory of J S Nanda. I miss you, papa.

ACKNOWLEDGMENTS

Rakhi Sharma for letting me use her laptop when I was having none. Aishwarya Rede and Tarika Phalak for motivating me to write. My publisher, Sharon Kizziah-Holmes, for her patience, kindness and support. You are a rock star, Sharon.

CHAPTER 1

She has had a breakup, few said. Few others were not interested in the reason behind it. They were only making stories about my new look. I had returned to Pune from one of my best friend's, Shikha's, wedding, and just as I had warned everyone before going for her wedding, I got a haircut. Earlier, I had long wavy brown hair and once I returned from her wedding I cut them short like those of a boy. Since then, Abbu was very upset with me. According to him, being a girl, and belonging to Muslim community, I was not allowed to do these kinds of things and that, day by day, I was turning irreligious for which Allah would not forgive me.

The first day of my office after I changed my hairstyle, I wore business formals to complement my look. It was a maroon shirt paired with black trousers. I also applied a lot of kohl on my eyes. I was tired of answering people that I like changing my look very often and it has nothing to do with my relationship status but they were not ready to believe me.

"Maybe you should have tried a wedge cut. But this one is also cool," Kishan looked at me.

"You never agree with me, *dada.*" Kishan was like a brother to me. We both belonged to the same city, Bhopal, and had done our graduation from the same Government College, but I did not know him at the time. I came to know about him when we started working together. He had a huge muscular body and stood five feet eleven inches tall with spikes on his hair. Almost all of his hands and neck was inked with so many tattoos, mainly related to Lord Krishna, of whom he was a great devotee.

"Who is she?" Akhtar shouted from a distance.

Soon I was surrounded by all my office friends. We were working in the same account and eventually became friends. Most of them were genuinely shocked that I actually cut my hair short.

"On one hand, there are people who are afraid of even touching their hair, and on the other there are people who are playing around with them," Hemant burst into laughter.

Hemant used to crack jokes on every possible thing around him and he could die for food. That's why he was fat I guess.

"So on this occasion of Gul's new look, Gul will throw a small treat for all of us and I will have my favorite sandwich," Kishan said.

He had a habit of asking for treats from others.

"Let's go to D-Mart. We will buy some cold drinks and I will ask canteen staff to make *rabdi-jalebi* for us," Hemant said.

Rabdi-jalebi was the trademark sweet dish for our events and as D-Mart was close to our office, it was easier for us to enjoy the same with other beverages at a lower cost.

"I only had a haircut. It's not Akhtar's wedding for which we should celebrate," I turned towards my desktop, ignoring them for the treat they were asking from me. Akhtar was the next candidate from our group to get married and we all were eagerly waiting for that day. In spite of the fact that he was ageing, he was the most eligible bachelor among us. Soon the topic changed from my haircut treat to Akhtar's wedding.

"Akhtar sir, you are at the age of playing with your grandchildren. You must get married," Meenal said without taking any breath.

We all laughed but on Meenal this time. We would tease her that we don't understand what she says as if she was speaking while chewing something.

"We should head back to our desk and must start our work," I said when my cell phone rang. It was Sohan who was calling me.

"By the way, you look beautiful this way too," Akhtar whispered into my ears and disappeared.

I received the call and blushed after listening to him.

"Where are you? Why don't you want to meet me?" I asked.

"Listen, are you in office?" Sohan ignored my question.

"Yes."

"Good, I am sending you an email; you have to do all the research related to it and inform me discreetly. I think it is a big issue and I want to highlight it."

"Fine, but when are we meeting?" I had not seen him since the day I left for Shikha's wedding.

"Possibly tonight, if there will be no work pending. I will inform you. Listen, I am getting another call, I will call you back," he disconnected the call.

Sohan was also working in my account but he was our customer. My organization was providing services to his organization. He was one of the finest gentlemen I had ever met. Five feet eleven inches of slim and fit body, fair complexion, naughty eyes and a perfectly shaped nose which I always wanted to pinch. His hairstyle was the only thing I ever wanted to change. He would always prefer a little long hair but I would find him cuter when they were short. Though, I knew him for only a year, he was my best friend. I was hanging around with him almost every night. He would call me multiple times a day asking everything about my office and updating me about everything from his side too. But these days, if he was calling me frequently, it was for things related to work only. Now he was less interested in things going around me. Still I used to call him every now and then.

***

"*Bhaiya*, please give two Kooka with chocolate crush," Sohan said to the shopkeeper. He searched for seats where we could sit.

I wanted to ask Sohan how I looked after my haircut but I knew he was indifferent to my appearance. He was least bothered about the dress I would wear, my heels, my kohl or my hairstyle. Though once he said-*nice* to the pair of sandals I was wearing and once he was laughing hard because of the *kameez* I wore, which had a pocket but he would never appreciate me for anything good.

We both grabbed our Kooka which was the default beverage we would order every time we would meet. Kooka was a type of cold coffee served in various flavors. Our favorite was Kooka served with chocolate crush. I would ask for extra tissues which he would use to aim at the distant dustbin from the place we would sit. Each shot he would miss would make me earn a hundred rupees from him and till now he owed me a few hundred rupees. But, he had never given me a single rupee for the shots he had missed otherwise it would be me giving him a lot of money for the shots he had made.

"Look, they are not husband and wife," He signaled to a girl and a boy sitting perpendicularly next to us.

"How do you know everything? They look like husband and wife." The girl was wearing *shadi ka chuda,* which are bangles that, according to tradition, married women would wear for a certain period after their marriage, and both of her hands were full of beautiful henna designs. She was also wearing a beautiful red *saree* and a golden blouse. I was not able to see her face as she was facing the boy, who was facing us.

"He is not making any eye contact with her. He is continuously gazing at you."

I immediately looked at him. Sohan was right.

"I will tell you one important thing, if a boy is only concentrating at his girl while there are other beautiful ladies around him, it means that he is serious for her. Here the girl is definitely married, but not to this boy."

"Oh! Then you should not look at me."

He smiled. I would love to see him smiling; his naughty face would turn even naughtier and his eyes would reflect his charm.

"What happened to that issue?" I changed the topic.

"The issue I have raised today has been accepted as a functionality gap. This is a big one. I have got a higher level of appreciation for highlighting this issue."

"I know. I saw your email." We used to keep each other in bcc whenever we would play something big in office. "You should thank me for this."

He smiled again. He would never thank me for any such kind of support I would give to him. For him I was the undercover agent deployed in our organization who would provide all the detailed information to him, as and when required. But he would have never called me for such things, provided that they had access to the details. But then we wouldn't have ever discovered such a great friendship with each other.

"What did they say?"

"Akhtar said that I am looking beautiful," I understood that he was asking about the reaction of the people from my office to this new look, but I only cared about informing him what Akhtar said.

"Someone is blushing."

I blushed even more. "I heard rumors. They think that I have got a breakup and that is why I have changed my look to start with something new."

"What? You had a breakup? When? Why you did not tell me? Who is your ex?" he managed to ask many questions while laughing at the same time.

I too began laughing. He knew that I was single, and moreover, if I would get committed with someone, he would be the first one with whom I would like to share the information. He would also be the first one to come to know about my breakup if I would have one.

"Let's go," he interrupted the laughter.

We both moved out of the Kooka shop on his bike and went to the nearby vegetable shop, with a small cigarette and *paan* counter next to it. It was around 10 PM; the road was full of vehicles.

"Why everyone is out today?" He parked his bike near the vegetable shop.

He placed his bike on main stand, making sure to arrange a seat for me to sit, and went to bring a *paan* and his cigarette. This was usually our second destination after Kooka shop where he would have a few puffs of cigarette; meanwhile I would enjoy his dramatic stories along with the sweet *paan* which he would bring for me.

As usual, the vegetable shop vendor had an eye on us and we ignored him for the rest ten minutes and then Sohan dropped me home. My home from that vegetable shop was barely half a minute away by walk, still he used to drop me home each time we would meet. Previously when we both were staying at Magarpatta City, he used to make me comfortable by his pick up and drop facility.

"Bye," he was in a hurry when I got down from his bike at my apartment. "I have a lot of work lined up to finish today."

"No," I held his bike's handle. "Stay for another fifteen minutes; you will hardly take five minutes to reach your apartment." Sohan was also staying in Baner and his apartment was hardly five minutes away from my location. He moved to Baner three months after I moved here from Magarpatta City. *My office is close from Baner,* was his answer when I asked him why he moved. I was happy as he was again staying close to me. It was almost eight months of daily Kooka meeting since then.

"I can't. I will meet you tomorrow," he started his bike.

"Ok. Bye," I called the elevator and he went.

I took out the keys and entered my apartment. Chaudhary, my flatmate was waiting for me for dinner, but most importantly, she was waiting for me to have gossip with her. We were three girls staying together. Apart from Chaudhary, I was sharing the apartment with Dutta. Dutta was in Bhopal these days, so only Chaudhary and I were present at our apartment. While having dinner, I told her everything about what had happened today. She also told me how her manager was making her work after the office hours and how she managed the situation.

"Still two more days are left for the weekend to come."

"I love to go to office," I teased her. "We have to plan so many things for our trip and we can do that in office only."

"Yes, your trip to Leh. So, did you finalize any package?"

"No, nothing is finalized yet. Hemant and Akhtar are following up with travel agencies. They want the best deal. We will get another itinerary tomorrow. But Vikram is still not able to make up his mind for the trip. If he and his wife will join us, we will be seven people for the trip. We can get a better deal in that case."

"Vikram is your team leader, right?"

I nodded.

"So you, Hemant, Akhtar, Vikram and his wife want to go. Who else is going?"

"Meenal and Aditya will also join us."

She smiled. "It is nice to hear what you people are doing. Mark my words; it is going to be a memorable trip for you."

"Yes, we will make it so."

CHAPTER 2

I pinched Akhtar's arm. He and I were wearing same color combination, white shirt and black trousers.

"You both are wearing matching clothes with each other," Meenal said from her desk.

"Yeah, he always copies me," I stood near Akhtar's desk.

"Why are you here? Go back to your desk. Meenal, please call her."

"*Arey*, tell me what that travel agency said? I am here to discuss our trip."

"Hemant will call the agency after noon. By the way, Gul with long beautiful hair will go with us. Not you. I don't even know your name."

"What happened? Who is not coming with us to Leh?" Hemant proceeded towards Akhtar's desk.

"Akhtar doesn't want me to come with you people," I complained about Akhtar. "He is saying that he doesn't know me."

"Yes, what is your name Miss?" Akhtar looked at me with naughty eyes.

"Ok. I will not come then," I started to leave his desk.

"Wait." He held my hand.

Akhtar would always tease me like this; in return I would show him some attitude as I knew that he would pamper me for all this.

"You think we can leave without you?"

"When will you finalize the trip? It is February and we only have three months left to plan every other thing," I removed my hand from his grip.

"Yeah, you have to shop, right?" Hemant taunted me.

I said nothing. It was not the shopping that was bothering me. I was forcing them to finalize the trip soon, so that I will get to know the amount I have to arrange for all the expenses. Abbu was not ready to finance me for this trip. *I don't have money for your debauched life,* he told me when I asked his permission. He was right. Being a peon, it was very difficult for him to offer a lavish life to us. He had already struggled a lot to save some money which was spent on medicines to save my mother's life. He was broken when she left us. It was only me and my younger brother Shahid he had left with so many unpaid bills. The moment I got the job, I settled all his bills by taking a personal loan. Now all of Abbu's and my salary were spent in paying EMI of that personal loan, Shahid's college fee and other expenses. Taking personal loan was one of the worst decisions I had ever made. We were clearly not in a situation to enjoy such expensive trips. Still, I wanted to go because I knew that I would cherish this trip throughout my life.

"We will finalize it today. But before that we need to confirm it from Vikram." I was lost in the thought of my money crunch when Akhtar interrupted.

"It is 11:45 AM. He will be here soon," Hemant said. "See, there they come."

Vikram entered with Aditya.

"Look at you!" Aditya shouted looking at me.

"How am I looking?" I said to him in a childlike tone.

"You are looking younger," he pulled on my cheeks.

"Yes, I agree. She is looking younger and hot." Akhtar winked at me.

"Stop flirting with me," I blushed. "Vikram, did you finalize anything? Are you coming?"

"Yes. We are coming. Sonia wants to come. I cannot say no to her."

It was good for us that Sonia, Vikram's wife, was also excited for this trip, otherwise Vikram wouldn't have agreed for it.

"Cool," Hemant said. "I will get the deal finalized today."

"*Kashmir jaungi, ice-cream khaungi, sholo me bhadke jiya.*" I sang one of the bollywood songs and danced. Meenal and Aditya started singing with me. Everyone else laughed.

"Gul, Meenal go back to your desk," Vikram said as he saw our manager, Gopinath coming towards us.

Meenal and I went back to our cubicle but we were unable to hide our excitement.

Aditya came toward us. "Wait, I am also coming. What have you brought for me to eat?"

"Gul, where is Kishan?" Vikram interrupted us.

"He had a flat tyre. He will be late today."

"I am fed up with Kishan and his bike."

A moment later Kishan arrived. Vikram scolded him for coming late and gave him a last warning.

***

"The package is of thirty five thousand rupees per person for eight days and seven nights." We were back from lunch when Hemant came and informed us about the package one of the travel agencies offered to us. "And the dates are from 9th June to 16th June."

"Oh, can't we negotiate more?" Akhtar asked.

Hemant signaled a no. "He is not ready; he has included the best hotels, food, vehicle and sites for us. He also gave us the option to pay at any time before the date of our journey and our seats will be confirmed."

"That's great, but thirty five thousand," I got worried.

"I know, but it also includes the to and fro flight tickets between Delhi and Leh, so I guess it's good."

Akhtar asked about the travel agency name. "This one is Ghumo.com, right?"

Hemant nodded.

"Is everyone ok with this plan?"

Everyone else nodded in agreement but I was still worried. *How will I arrange thirty five thousand rupees?* -was the only question which was troubling me but, other agencies were asking even more.

"Don't worry; we will look for other deals also. Meanwhile, we will stick with this one," Akhtar said. "But we are reaching Delhi two days before. What shall we do there?"

"We will visit a few places in Delhi," Vikram suggested. "Some of my relatives stays in Delhi, I can arrange accommodation for us."

"Delhi will be on fire those days; I don't want to burn my skin," I rejected their proposal. I did not want to get tanned wandering around in Delhi but no one listened to me.

***

"Hello madam," Sohan said as I answered his call.

"Do not talk to me."

"I was busy yesterday with hell lot of work. You know it well." He understood that I was upset because he did not call me yesterday.

"I understand that you were busy so you did not meet me. But why didn't you call?"

"Ok hmmm hmmm."

He would always end the conversation like this. I would not like him all those times.

"Where are you?"

"I am standing behind you. I came to your office regarding yesterday's issue."

"Are you here?" I turned around. He was standing at Akhtar's desk wearing a light blue T-shirt with black jeans. We exchanged quick smiles with each other so that it would not get noticed by other people. He would never publicly show his friendship for me. I didn't know the reason behind it. I had never asked, I noticed he would never take me out with his friends from office or flatmates but on the other hand his childhood friends knew me well.

"I have so many things to tell you." I was excited to see him in my office.

"Let's see. If I will go for smoke, I will call you."

"I am sorry but I will not come."

"Why?"

"First, I want you to quit smoking. And second, there will be rumors about you and me here in my office. After all, why would any female associate accompany their client for smoking; it's not considered a good business here."

He laughed. "True." He moved toward the cabin where he was settled today. "Ok then, if I leave early we will go together. I will provide you an update on this."

I agreed to go back to Baner with him because I had no plans this weekend, otherwise most of my weekends were spent here in Kalyani Nagar as all of my office friends were staying nearby. We would hang around at Kishan's apartment mostly. We would cook, watch horror movies which would turn into comedy. Some of us would booze and later when nothing would be left to do, we would go to Chandani Chowk and return early morning. In Pune, Chandani Chowk was the well known place to people who loved to hang out late at night. CCD, there had the license to provide service throughout night. Most of the crowd, especially young people could be seen there. And it was also our prime location for after parties.

***

I asked Akhtar if there was any chance that we do something this weekend, but he was not available as he had to attend some of his family functions. I asked him because I wanted to spend time with him. I liked it when he was around. Akhtar was tall and slim with round face and silky hair. He was an average looking man but I was attracted towards him. And the way he was treating me was giving me a hint that he also had some feelings for me.

I waited till 7:15 PM and then called Sohan.

"I am not sure how much time I will take to finish my work. An important meeting is also scheduled next week; I need to finish issues pending in my To-do list," he said to me and then I went home which was the only option left for me.

I reached home after an hour. Chaudhary was studying. Without disturbing her, I went to my room, changed the skin tight grey jeans and black top I was wearing and made myself comfortable in pink shorts and white T-shirt.

After I was done with my dinner Sohan called me.

"*Turant se bhi pehle aao.* I am waiting for you at the Kooka shop." he asked me to meet him before the snap of the moment.

"I will take minimum five to ten minutes."

"Ok. Come fast."

I looked at myself in mirror to make sure that I was looking good. I also confirmed the same with Chaudhary.

"Yes, you are looking good. Go, enjoy your Kooka."

***

"I am waiting here for you since eternity."

I hardly took five minutes to reach the Kooka shop still Sohan complained that I was late.

"And I am already here since eternity; you were busy in your mobile."

Making use of the word *eternity* was one of the most common things we would do. And *waiting since eternity* was number one in our list. The shopkeeper was already ready with two *Kooka with chocolate crush* when we were talking. Sohan picked up the glasses while exchanging smile with the shopkeeper.

"I am worried."

"What happened?"

"We have finalized the package," I told him about every other detail I had regarding our trip.

He smiled. "Nice itinerary. Why are you worried then? Akhtar will be present with you."

"It's the money which is making me worried. The trip will cost thirty five thousand rupees. Additionally, there will be flight tickets, hotel stay in Delhi and other expenses. I need a minimum of forty five thousand rupees to suffice."

Sohan was aware of my money crisis. Nothing was hidden from him.

"But you want to go," he knew about the best part of the trip.

"Yes, I know. This will be a lifetime experience for me," I smiled.

"You already have twenty thousand rupees with you, right?"

"Yes, but I cannot spend all of it. I need to save some money."

"Hmmm. Tell me how much money you need?"

"No no. I will try saving some money from my salary. I will tell you if that will not be enough."

Then as usual we went to the cigarette counter, after which he dropped me home.

CHAPTER 3

Dutta and Chaudhary had gone to their hometown for the celebration of the colorful festival, Holi. Sohan also went to his hometown, Lucknow, for same reason.

"Holi is on Friday and my roommates are gone, so I will stay at your apartment," I told Kishan when he came at my desk. It was not a big issue for a girl to stay at their apartment.

"Why don't you come on Thursday? We will plan a secret Holi Thursday midnight."

Meenal was sitting behind us. "I will also join you guys."

"What about Deepak and Nitin, will they also join us?" I asked about the other two friends staying with Kishan at his apartment.

"Yes. We will include them as well. But Meenal, make sure that you don't have any issue in staying overnight at my place."

"No problem at all."

"Ok then, buy as much color and water guns as possible," I smiled. During last year Holi, Kishan and I were staying in Magarpatta City and Kishan and his roommate surprised us a night before Holi. They came with so many water guns. My entire apartment was filled with colorful water; we were all drenched and made so much noise that the guard came and told us to behave properly as it was late. Kishan fired his water gun at the guard and shouted- *bura na mano Holi hai,* which was a common expression of happiness and forgiveness used for the festival Holi. A moment later they were dragged out of the building. Next day

Kishan took his revenge by coloring that guard again as it was very hard to recognize any of us. We all were looking same; drenched and enshrouded in so many colors.

I winked at Kishan as a thought came to my mind. "Dada, let's have coffee."

"I can sense that something is going in your mind," Kishan knew I would never wink at him unless there was something funny.

"It's obvious that we will play Holi at your place, right?" I smiled mischievously. "Let's make *thandai*." I suggested him to make a local beverage which was made from milk, some dry fruits and sugar.

"What is so unusual about it? Holi without *thandai* is incomplete."

"I know that, but what about adding bhang to it," I smiled again as he filled his cup with coffee.

"Are you serious?" He raised his voice. "It sounds interesting though."

I patted his muscular shoulder. "Now you are sounding like my brother. You need to make arrangement for bhang and I will prepare *thandai* on the occasion. And remember, no one should ever come to know about it."

"We have only one day left, let's see if we get the bhang."

We moved back to our desk.

"I will arrange it but please bring all of your required stuff tomorrow only. I don't want to hear that you forgot something at home and you need it on SOS basis. I will not go to bring your stuff."

I was very particular about things; I wanted everything in my own way. He knew that. If I want saffron shade lipstick with black dress, it means that I want saffron shade only; I would not adjust with orange or other similar shades.

"You surely have to save my soul," I laughed.

"This time I will not. Four days of your tantrums will be a big torture for me."

"Ok. But then tell your maid to clean the kitchen and washroom properly," I showed my biggest concern towards the cleanliness of these two places. "I will not adjust there."

"I will tell her in advance that Gul is coming, so clean the house properly."

Each time I had visited their house, I would fight with their maid, scolding her for not cleaning the washrooms properly. Many times Kishan would take me to the nearest super mall as I would deny using their washrooms.

***

I brought everything required for my stay at Kishan's house. I did not tell anything about this to Abbu. Otherwise he would have scolded me to death. According to him, I should not hang around this much with boys. *I am a girl and I should maintain a fair distance with them. They are not good when it comes to a girl so foolish like me*, he said to me once when I was at home in Bhopal. For him I was still a naïve child who trusts everyone easily. I wanted to tell him that everyone was not bad, but then I thought that everything was right when it comes to a father who cares a lot for his daughter. He just wanted me to be safe all the time.

During dinner, we planned that we would start playing Holi from the night only like previous year. Kishan and I told others about what we did last time and how Kishan was dragged out of the building by the guard.

Around 11:00 PM we got ready with all the color and water guns and started for Akhtar's place. I was sitting on Kishan's bike, Meenal was coming with Deepak, and Nitin was coming alone. Deepak offered Nitin, his new Royal Enfield bullet, so that he wouldn't feel bad for coming alone. After Akhtar joined us, we headed for Hemant and Aditya. We made sure not to disturb any married friends of ours.

We laughed and colored each other. When colors finished, we started playing with the garden pipe which was kept to water the plants.

"Let's move out of here, we should not disturb other people, they must be sleeping," I said and we all moved out making noises on the roads. We were drenched and tired at the same time as we fought a lot to grab the color and water guns from each other. It was around 1:00 AM, and the road was filled with the cold breeze of air when Akhtar noticed me shivering.

"Let's go home now."

"Yeah, I am feeling cold." I was wearing a black ankle length leggings and a long pink T-shirt. My T-shirt was wet and dripping.

"It seems that all of your color is used tonight only, you will be attacked by us tomorrow," Aditya gave a high five to Hemant.

"Picture abhi baki hai mere dost." Kishan said that we were not done yet and started his bike.

"Gul, I will drop you. Are you staying at Kishan's house?" Akhtar looked at me and asked.

"No, it's ok. I will go with Kishan."

"Come with him. You are feeling too cold," Kishan went.

"Let's take Meenal also," But Deepak and Meenal already went when we were talking with each other. Akhtar unlocked his car and I settled myself in the seat next to him.

"Thanks," I was a little nervous as this was the first time when I was alone with him.

"Thanks for what?" He started his car. "If you will get cold, how will I color you? I need you to give your best performance tomorrow, as it will not be an easy fight for you against me."

I smiled. "Sure, but I am really feeling cold," I rubbed my hands together.

"Are you?" he took my hand and started rubbing them.

I felt the warmth of his body through his hand and remained silent.

"It's ok. Drive," I took my hand back after sometime.

"When will you come tomorrow?" I asked him when we reached Kishan's place and stepped out of his car.

"I don't know. I will come after meeting my other friends."

"Ok. Bye, see you then. Ping me, when you reach home."

"Sure. Bye."

***

Akhtar messaged me on Whatsapp, which was one of the mostly used applications for chatting purpose, when we were settling ourselves to sleep.

Akhtar: I am home.

Me: Good. Thanks again.

Akhtar: The pleasure was all mine.

Me: It was mine too. ;-)

Akhtar: Sleeping?

Me: Yes.

Akhtar: Sleeping with wet clothes. ;-)

Me: No, I changed my clothes.

Akhtar: By the way you were looking hot when you were wet.

Me: Really?

This was the first time when he said something to me which couldn't be heard by anyone else. Otherwise he would do it publicly, which I would have to ignore.

Me: You are making me shy.

Akhtar: I wish I could be there.

Me: Don't worry, we are meeting tomorrow. Sleep now, it's late.

Akhtar: Yes, goodnight.

Me: *Goodnight.*

I placed my cell phone on one side. I was smiling while thinking about him.

***

Early morning I called Sohan to wish him on the occasion of Holi. I knew that once he would start celebrating it, he would get busy with his friends and family and would not be able speak to me. He asked me what I was doing today. I told him about our plan, I also told him what had happened last night, how Akhtar asked to drop me to Kishan's place and how easily he took my hand to warm them. *I will call you in the evening again,* he said and disconnected the call abruptly without listening to me.

I dressed up in white T-shirt and sky blue Jeans. Kishan and I secretly added the bhang in to the *thandai* and kept it inside refrigerator. Before starting to play Holi, we took a group photo to compare how bad we would look at the end of the day.

Akhtar was dressed in white *kurta pajama* and was looking smoking hot. He equipped his car with so many colors and parked it to a location which was easily accessible. But he kept the keys with him so that no one could claim the colors which he had brought.

We were playing badly; coloring everyone and protecting ourselves from getting colored when Deepak brought the *thandai.* Kishan and I looked at each other. We did not decide when to offer the *thandai,* we left it on others so that no one could blame us for the effect it could create. Some of them had two three glasses of it, Kishan enjoyed only one glass and I on the other hand, had none as I was not allowed for any kind of intoxication. I told Akhtar about it so that he too would not consume it.

"Are you mad?"

"Just chill, it's a festival. We can have a little fun."

"Like this?" He poured a bucket full of water on me.

I shouted and ran after him to color him. He used all his man power, grabbed me with his hands and colored me instead.

"I told you, this will be tough for you." He laughed as I helplessly watched him.

After sometime, *thandai* started showing its effect. Everyone was laughing without any reason. Some of them complained about getting headache. They were the ones who had more than one glass of it. Kishan told them that we had added bhang to it. He was also laughing, losing a little control of himself. Then instead of going anywhere we decided to take rest at Kishan's apartment for the rest of the day. Everyone adjusted themselves according to the place available.

"They are fine now," Akhtar examined everyone and sat next to me.

"Don't worry." I laughed, resting my head on his lap.

He pinched my cheeks. "Such a bad girl you are."

This time I was not afraid of showing my affection to him in front of others, maybe because others were sleeping. He was playing with my hair. I looked at him and he smiled. We kept silent and enjoyed the moment for the rest of the time.

CHAPTER 4

"Someone pulled the chain." Sohan said over the call.

He was returning to Pune in Lucknow Pune Express train and called me to complain about the train and the people who were travelling in it.

"Oh, did they stop the train at some area other than railway station?"

"*Arey*, I told you multiple times, Bhopal is a small town and people belonging to this place believe that this train does not stop here, so they just pull the chain every time," he said playfully.

"Sohan I will kill you. Bhopal is not a small town. It is a bigger junction when compared to Lucknow." He would always tease me saying Bhopal was a rural place and that it was still struggling in terms of good roads, electricity, education and everything else. On the other hand, he would say that his city Lucknow had grown far beyond Bhopal could ever reach. We would fight with each other to prove that our own city was the best.

"You don't know anything. You come from a rural place."

He would always jest on me and he would do it in such a way that I would always like it but without showing my likeness about it, I would lively debate him.

"Sir, the place you are calling as rural has its own international airport."

He laughed again. "You are funny. That is the other thing you don't understand. International Airport is like a lollipop for the citizens of Bhopal, so that they will not complain about other things, feeling proud about it."

"*Chup be*," I told him angrily to shut up. Becoming angry would be the only option left to me when I would not be able to confront him.

"Calm down. You know that I am kidding. Bhopal is a big city; Lucknow is nothing compared to it."

"Yes, you are right," I felt levitated from his predictable gesture. Whenever we would fight, I would either go angry or upset and he would persuade me. He would never hesitate to do that. "I will come to the railway station to welcome you. What is the arrival time?"

"No, it's not needed. Don't you have to go to office tomorrow?"

"I do have to go to office tomorrow, but I can come to welcome you."

"No," he ordered me.

I would never argue with him when he would order me something, because in those conversations he would never persuade me. He would be right in almost all those times, and he would convince me why he was right.

"The train will reach at around 10:00 AM and it will be your office start time, I don't want you to be late for office just to welcome me back."

I had observed over these years that he would be late for everything but not for office and the same thing he expected from me as well. "But I want to meet you, *turant se bhi pehle*."

"We will meet *baboo*."

I could imagine that he must be smiling because I used another common phrase of ours, *turant se bhi pehle*, to show the urgency of meeting him.

"When will we meet? Can we meet tomorrow evening, after office?"

"Yes, we can meet, but only if it is possible for me to come."

He would never commit anything to me, neither for a movie show nor for a dinner. *Commitments when broken hurt a lot. Open up for surprises though*, he told me once when I was fighting with him, asking for a Friday night movie show, and he was not ready to commit anything.

"Ok, as you say." There was no point in asking him anything again and again after knowing that it could irritate him a lot.

"Good, train has also started and the electricity also came back," he teased me again.

Bhopal was not a rural place which couldn't even supply electricity to the trains when they cross its railway station.

"I will block your calls, Whatsapp, Facebook and every other thing if you will say so," I warned him.

"No please, don't block me," he requested and laughed. "I will hang up the call now; I will talk to you later."

"Bye. Take care."

"Bye."

The moment I hung up his call, Dutta entered the house. I hugged her as she saved my Sunday evening; I did not know that she was returning to Pune. Dutta and I started working together in this city with Shikha as we all got placed in the same company during the campus recruitment drive conducted at our college. All three of us were best friends since we were in class eight. After her marriage Shikha was settled in Bangalore and then Chaudhary joined us.

For the rest of the night Dutta and I told each other about everything that happened around us. She also told me that her parents were seeing another family, and now, as she was also there in Bhopal, her marriage had been planned.

"What? But why do you want to get married so early, Dutta?"

"If not now, then when?" She read the slogan written on my T-shirt. "Also I will be moving to Mumbai this May. That boy is working there."

"No Dutta. First Shikha went and then you. I will be left alone here," I felt the loneliness I would feel, when she would move to Mumbai.

"Mumbai is not too far from here. And if we talk about the loneliness, then I know how much alone you are here in Pune," she said sarcastically knowing that I had many friends including Sohan in Pune. "So don't play this loneliness game with me."

"Anyway, I am happy for you."

"You should also get married. I also want to be happy for you."

"*Ho nai paaega*," I told her a thing Sohan would say to me when he would not be willing to do anything. I meant that I cannot marry just to make Dutta happy, as we went to sleep after the long awaited talk.

***

"Are you coming from office?" Sohan asked me when I met him.

I was dressed well today for Akhtar and as Sohan was on leave today, he came directly from his apartment, so he was under dressed as compared to me. He was wearing dark blue track pants and a black t-shirt with Captain America printed on it, along with slippers, which he would usually wear at home. Unlike other days, today he was looking tired even after taking rest for the entire day. But the moment he saw me, he smiled and everything was changed.

"Yes. What happened?"

"Nothing, you are just full of makeup."

"Ok hmmm hmmm." Sometimes I would use some of the words which he would use to end conversation or to change the topic of discussion.

It was around 11:00 PM; I was telling him about all the things that happened around me when he wasn't here. He also told me about his trip. We babbled for hours and I did not even realize that it was getting late as I was feeling alive with him; I would always feel something magical when he would be around.

We would talk about every irrelevant thing, laugh on each other's joke and examine the couples around us. Sometimes, we would turn serious and discuss some of the topics like money, career, marriage and the education of children and other related things people face after their marriage. We would also share some of the best moments from our school time. We knew that we would understand it and would not get bored, as we had done our schooling from the Kendriya Vidyalaya, a well recognized CBSE school. He had done it from KV Lucknow, and I had done it from KV Bhopal.

Some other times, he would share some of his experiences with me, which he had enjoyed a lot with Harish and Kunal, his best friends since he was in school. I would listen with the same eagerness irrespective of the number of times he had told me the same story. I would enjoy his excitement while he would narrate any such incidents to me. Later, when I would guess the end of the incident, he would say, *how do you know about it?* I would just smile. *I already told you*, he would say smiling back with his tempting smile.

Maybe that's why I knew Kunal and Harish. I had never met them but it seemed that I knew them for a long time. Sohan would always tell me about all the escapades he, Harish and Kunal had done in their school and college life. I was aware what they did when a cyber café was opened in their city; how they have performed rituals every KVian was bound to do; how many cricket matches they have played together; how many fights they have fought for each other, and about the scooter, which belonged to Kunal's father, which was their only hope if they had to travel within city. He would tell me about their tripling stories related to that scooter.

When we finished our Kooka, he picked up a tissue paper and aimed it towards the dustbin, giving me a naughty smile as if he was saying that I would lose the bet again.

"No," I shouted. I stopped him because I knew that it wasn't possible for him to make a successful shot, rather it would hit the fat uncle who was sitting near the dustbin. He was wearing much gold jewelry and was looking much like an angry politician.

"Don't challenge a cricketer," Sohan was over confident.

He had been playing cricket since his childhood and he had won many trophies and titles in various cricket tournaments for which I had always appreciated him, but this time he was over judging himself.

"As you wish, but be careful." I hid my face with my hands. He made a shot but not in the dustbin. It was that fat uncle who got hit. He looked at us angrily; we both apologized to him and left the Kooka shop, keeping our last activity in mind.

Our second destination, the *paan* counter, was closed, so Sohan purchased his cigarette from a grocery shop which was next to a wine shop. That fat uncle came to purchase liquor from that shop. We both looked at him and laughed without coming into the notice of anyone. And then Sohan started telling me that whenever Kunal, Harish and he would go for any trip, how Kunal would fool them by sleeping in the middle of the bed when no one else would be sleeping. Later, when all three of them would sleep, Kunal would fight for the corner of the bed saying that he had already slept in middle, so now it's not his turn.

I was already laughing hard, as he was being so humorous and was narrating to me many funny incidents from his life. But I couldn't bear to control my laughter when suddenly while narrating those incidents he jumped abnormally. That was the funniest stunt I ever saw. Moments later we saw that the fat uncle, who was by mistake hit by Sohan at the Kooka shop, was standing next to us and he was again angry as Sohan's slipper hit him when Sohan jumped.

I stopped laughing. I had to because this was something which could cause us trouble.

"What is happening? Do I look like a fool?" that uncle shouted in a heavy voice.

He was looking furious and as he approached us, many people started gathering to see what would happen next.

"Sorry uncle, that was unintentional." Sohan grabbed his slipper and I moved closer to him.

"We are extremely sorry, Uncle. Please forgive us." I turned to Sohan and noticed two men coming toward us. "Let's go," I whispered in his ear.

"Sorry." Sohan started his bike and I immediately jumped to sit behind him.

Then, he rode his bike and stopped only when we reached my apartment.

"Was that intentional?" I asked him, getting off his bike. I wasn't sure what just happened.

He laughed. "No, are you mad? Why would I do that?"

He was cackling on it.

"Then what made you do that stunt?"

"*Arey*, a cockroach went inside my pants. I did not understand what had happened but jumped."

I laughed even more. We tried to copy the move he made a moment earlier and laughed till our stomach and cheeks ached.

"It is late now, you must go. I cannot laugh anymore," I held my stomach which was hurting because we were laughing madly.

"Madam, do you know what Marilyn Monroe said?" he asked, with naughty eyes and smiled in a way giving me goosebumps.

"No, will you tell me?" I was curious thinking that it was the time when he would tell me another of his learnt lessons.

"If you can make a woman laugh, you can make her do anything." His smile turned endearing.

I remained thoughtful. I knew Marilyn Monroe was right. So was he.

Leh Trip Day 1

The clock was showing around four in the morning, I was not able to sleep. I was worried and excited at the same time. Mixed type of feeling it was. I tried many things to gain some sleep but ended up awake. When I totally gave up on sleep, I picked up my phone and found Akhtar online on Whatsapp and messaged him without thinking.

Me: Hey

Akhtar: Hey, good morning.

Me: GM. I am not feeling sleepy.

Akhtar: What happened, why are you not able to sleep?

Me: I don't know, maybe because we have to start for the trip today.

Akhtar: Feeling excited?

Me: Obviously yes, but I am also feeling nervous. This is the first time I am going for such an outing. I want everything to be alright.

Akhtar: Don't worry Gul. I will take care of you.

Me: Will you?

I smiled when I read his message. He was one of the reasons I was going on this trip.

Akhtar: Do you have any doubt on me?

Me: Not at all.

Akhtar: Good. Now try to take some rest, I will also sleep.

Me: Hmmm

I felt good after having a conversation with him and thought of calling Abbu when Akhtar went offline; Abbu was not talking to me since last two days. He was furious and this time I was not able to console him. He was right at his place. To be able to go for this trip, I had arranged money by asking Shikha, which he never approved of. He was also upset thinking that I was so shameless to go out with boys. I would have called him but he would not respond.

***

We were playing cards, making fun of each other and enjoying the back to back meal services of the railway. All the people who were settled around us were enjoying our conversations and were impressed that we were to going to Leh for holidays.

"We can go to India Gate, Bangla Sahib or maybe Connaught Place," Hemant suggested what we could do in Delhi.

"Yes we can go but not during the day time please," I said.

I was aware that Delhi's temperature during summer crosses every limit; I knew that if we would wander during the day time, I would surely get sick. Sunburn was another reason I was continuously requesting them not to make plans during the day time.

"Tomorrow morning after getting fresh, we will go to Bangla Sahib Gurudwara," Akhtar ignored what I requested.

I signaled a no.

"Listen to him first," Vikram looked at me.

"In the morning we will go to Bangla Sahib and then we will decide which place we can visit in nearby area. But at night I would like to take you all to one of my favorite places, Essex Farms."

"Ok, Akhtar *bhaiya*," Vikram's wife said.

"We are ok," said others agreeing with the plan that Akhtar suggested.

Akhtar was the one who had spent maximum time in Delhi, so we trusted him. But I was worried because I knew that it was not a good plan.

"Listen to me, please," I said, but no one was paying attention to me.

"Next day we can hang out in any super mall and we can go to India Gate or Connaught Place at night," Hemant said.

Everyone nodded a yes as they were finding this plan good.

I raised my voice. "I will not go out in a sunny day; don't you know that it is Delhi? We can get sick due to its high temperature."

"Will you please shut up? Why did you come if you don't want to go and visit places?" Akhtar shouted on me.

Everyone else went silent. I did not expect that Akhtar would react in such a way as if my opinion was countless. I raised my voice again. "I want to visit places but not when it is burning hot temperature outside. Our main goal is Leh; I don't want to get sick in Delhi itself and spoil rest of the days." This was the first time Akhtar and I were having harsh conversations.

"Shut up Gul. I will not eat this, I will not go outside. We are not here to pamper all your tantrums." Hemant stopped him.

Maybe Hemant sensed the anger on my face. No one had ever spoken to me like the way Akhtar was speaking.

"I show tantrums sometimes but there is a way to handle me. Why are you shouting on me? Go easy I am not stubborn."

"I don't want to discuss any plans with her." He turned away from me, referring to me as a third person.

I did not say anything and took out a novel from my handbag and pretended to read it. I was furious on Akhtar. It was only today morning when he was saying that he would take care of me, and this was how he was taking care. I remembered Sohan. He would never explicitly express that he takes care of me, but on the other hand he would always make things comfortable for me, be it any small thing like getting on his bike or crossing the road.

Few minutes went with same angry vibes all around, and then the dinner was served by the railways authority.

"Will you eat or do I need to console you?" Akhtar asked me when dinner was served.

"Why wouldn't I eat? I don't show tantrums in wrong places," I did not look at him.

"Good, and don't worry, we will reconsider the plan."

I nodded slowly.

We had dinner without making much chaos, I was not speaking and no one dared to speak to me. After having dinner we all moved to our respective seat. I was about to sleep when Akhtar messaged me on Whatsapp.

Akhtar: No harsh feelings.
Me: Then what kind of feelings do you have?
Akhtar: You are naughty.
Me: And you are bad.
Akhtar: Bad is the new good. ;-)
Me: Ok hmmm hmmm. I will sleep now.
Akhtar: Fine, good night.
Me: Good night.

Though he forgot what happened and behaved in a normal way, I tried to end the conversation, as I wasn't in any mood of talking to anyone. I was certainly missing Abbu who would always treat me like a doll. I was missing Sohan, knowing that I had a lot of fights with him but he never happened to disrespect my opinion.

CHAPTER 5

Leh Trip Day 2

"Wake up," Akhtar said.

"Let me sleep, please."

"Wake up Gul. We are about to reach Delhi."

"Wake me up when September ends," I smiled.

"It was a bad joke."

"Bad is the new good, I learnt last night."

"Hmmm, can I sit here?"

"Sure," I made space for him by moving my legs.

"You look like a small innocent child while sleeping."

"I am sleeping like a pupa sleeps inside its cocoon," I covered my face with the blanket. *Sleeping like a pupa inside its cocoon,* was another dialog I learned from Sohan. He would always say that sleeping is an art similar to what a pupa does, which sleeps inside its cocoon.

"Really? Wake up," he tickled me from outside the blanket.

I immediately jumped out of the seat and he laughed. Soon we reached Delhi railway station and headed towards Kalkaji, a place where we had hotel reservations for our two day stay in Delhi. It was around nine kilometer journey from the railway station to our hotel which we covered through an auto, enjoying the sunny morning. Aditya and I were continuously taking pictures of each other; we had decided that we would take at least thousand individual pictures throughout the trip, so

27

we started to achieve the target from Pune only. I was his cameraman and he was mine. We checked in the hotel where three rooms were already prepared for us, out of which one room was taken by Vikram and Sonia; another was taken by Akhtar, Hemant and Aditya. Meenal and I made ourselves comfortable in the third one. After some time we went outside for breakfast as we were all hungry. And as it was burning hot outside, we came back fully exhausted and drenched with sweat. The moment Hemant opened their room's door, we jumped into their bed. Akhtar, Hemant, Aditya, Meenal and I adjusted us in that double sized bed while Sonia and Vikram went to their room.

"I told you people, it is so difficult to go outside." The AC was running at a very low temperature, still it took more than half an hour to feel the cold.

"Really, we need to reconsider the plan," Meenal said.

"Yes." I was lying between Akhtar and Meenal. Aditya was lying beside Meenal and Hemant was speaking with his fiancée on phone.

"Let's take rest for the day and then we will go to the Essex Farms in the evening," Akhtar said.

We agreed with the idea of staying at the hotel room and only moving out in the evening. By 5:00 PM we decided to get ready to go to Essex Farms. I took bath and wore a dark blue top having cream color on its neck and sleeves with a cream color plain georgette skirt ending above my knees. I applied black eye shadow and a lot of kohl on my eyes and to give a cool look to my appearance I took out my knee high boots to wear. After I was satisfied with my own look, I moved into another room where the boys were getting ready. I knocked and Aditya opened the door.

"Oh my goodness." He whistled after looking at me from top to bottom.

Akhtar and Hemant, who were applying deodorants, turned towards me.

"Stop it Aditya, it doesn't suit you." I turned towards Akhtar and asked him. "How am I looking?"

"Good."

"You are looking handsome," I said to him, even though he said one of most common words to praise me, which was not even considered as praising.

"If you both are done praising each other, shall we go?" Hemant interrupted us.

We went to Essex Farms located near IIT Delhi Flyover. The ambience of the place was soothing and vital. It was built in a large area, out of which most of the part was converted into a garden, created with many trees and bushes and decorated with dim but inviting lights. The seating area was equally promising from everything including table cloth to ceiling which was designed in its own way. There were a lot of people from various age group seated inside, most of them coming from a high class society. We ordered food while Akhtar started sharing some of his memories when he was staying in Delhi, which gradually changed to memories when he was in school. Akhtar told us, how he and his friends used to bunk classes to watch movies. He told us that once when they were not attending classes but came to watch a movie, their headmaster caught them red handed outside the movie theater when the headmaster himself had come to watch the same movie. It was only then I came to know that he had done his schooling from Kendriya Vidyalaya Ajmer. Then we started gossiping about our school days and things related to it like summer vacation trips conducted by the school and the experience related to it, social science and science exhibitions where students would only participate to find the love of their life, sports day which was another platform to impress girls and boys of another Kendriya Vidyalaya, fees structure of the school and the four houses namely Shivaji, Ashoka, Tagore and Raman.

"Ahem ahem," Aditya cleared his throat to signal us that other people were also present.

"You can also talk to each other. Why are you listening to us and getting bored?" I taunted him.

He made a sad face. I pulled his cheeks and asked him few things from his school days. He and other people shared some of their experiences while having dinner. We came back from dinner, overeaten and tired. Before I could do anything, I called Sohan to talk to him. He asked me how the trip was going and I told him what we did today. He suggested me to visit Connaught Place without fail.

"Indian flag has been hoisted there at the maximum height across Asia," he informed me.

Like always, as a mentor, he guided me through his experience and knowledge and I was again determined to do what he had suggested me.

***

Leh Trip Day 3

We woke up early in the morning and while having breakfast we decided to go Gurudwara Bangla Sahib which was located near Connaught Place, and I did not oppose considering everyone's interest to visit this place. While we were on the way, we laughed, giggled and made noises discussing what would happen in Leh, but the moment we entered the Gurudwara, we went taciturn. As if we had found the eternal peace we were looking for. We spent around one hour sitting inside the Gurudwara and listening to the Gurbani, after which I gained a little confidence and decided to call Abbu once again when luckily he responded to my call.

"Abbu," I said happily.

"How are you Gul?"

"I am fine, Abbu. How are you?" I broke into tears.

"I am also good. Why are you crying my dear?"

"I never wanted to hurt you Abbu. I am sorry," I sobbed. I genuinely never wanted to hurt him in any case but at the same time I wanted to live my dreams as well.

"It's ok. At least you are doing what I can never do for you."

"Please don't say so, Abbu. You are the best father anyone could ever get," I proudly said wiping my tears.

"Hmmm, where are you?"

"I am in Delhi, tomorrow morning we are flying to Leh."

"Ok. Take care my child."

"Sure. You too," I disconnected the call. I felt better as if the guilt of hurting Abbu was taken away from me. While I was speaking to Abbu, Akhtar noticed me crying but did not ask anything until we went back to our hotel room and settled in their room.

"Tears don't suit you," he turned towards me.

We were again resting on their bed. I was watching TV and he was lying beside me.

"Did you see me crying?"

"Yes, I did. What happened?"

"There is nothing serious, I was speaking to Abbu. He was upset with me since the day we started for this trip, but now everything is good."

"How can anyone be upset with such a cute girl?"

"I did not want to hurt him," I turned towards him placing my head near his chest, almost touching him.

He moved closer to me. "You are a good girl with beautiful heart."

We were so close to each other that if he could have wanted, I could have landed under his arms but we maintained the little distance present between us.

"Do you really mean that?" I looked at him.

"Yes," he tucked my hair behind my ears.

"Can we go to the Connaught Place this evening?"

"Yes, we can go. We can also go to the India Gate."

***

By 7:00 PM we got ready to go the India Gate and Connaught Place. The weather outside the hotel room was full of humidity and the places were crowded with many people. We also met some of our colleagues who were also working for same account, but from Delhi location, and then by 10:00 PM we returned to our room.

***

Aditya, Meenal and I were fighting with pillow with each other in our room. Aditya was against us and even though he was alone, he was giving equal competition to both of us. We decided that we would not sleep and whoop it up the whole night while others were already asleep.

It was late and we were playing cards when Hemant knocked the door. He warned us to get some sleep as we had to check in to the airport before 7:00 AM tomorrow.

"We will start from here by 6:00 AM," Hemant said. "You must get up by 4:30 AM to pack everything that belongs to you."

"It is only 11:45 PM. We will sleep in fifteen to twenty minutes," I said.

"Sleep at whatever time you want, but wake up on time. That is all I want to say, otherwise you will be responsible for whatever happens," he warned us. "And Aditya, shall I keep the door open for you? Akhtar and I are sleeping, and I don't want you to disturb us later, knocking the door late at night and expecting us to open it."

"Can I sleep here?" Aditya looked at Meenal and me.

"Yes," I hit him with the pillow again. He hits me back. The pillow fight was again started.

"I am sure you will be late tomorrow morning," Hemant said and went.

CHAPTER 6

9th June Leh Trip Day 4

We checked in at airport at around 6:45 AM. Our flight was scheduled at 9:30 AM from domestic terminal of Delhi airport. We got our boarding passes and proceeded for security check. There were only two window seats allocated to us. Aditya and I won the fight for it. Aditya was seated with Akhtar, Vikram with Sonia whereas Hemant and Meenal were sitting with me and finally the day had come.

Soon we were flying above the huge mountain series covered with snow. It felt like we were entering a new world, full of scenic beauties where we could lose ourselves to gain something eternal. We were quiet, enjoying the outside view from window. It was the first time I was seeing such a place. I came to know that I made the right decision when I agreed for this trip. I thought that I would once again arrange a trip to Leh with Abbu and Shahid. After one and half hour of the beautiful journey, our flight landed at the Leh airport. The moment we stepped out of the flight, we felt the change in atmosphere. The sky was shining blue and crystal clear with no signs of clouds.

The cutting cold wind was striking with a very high frequency against the glowing sun. We took out our jackets and sunglasses and posed for the first group picture in Leh. We thought of checking in to Facebook, in order to inform our friends that we landed in Leh but there was no network coverage in our cell phone. We checked out of the airport; one man was standing near a cab asking for a person named Hemant. He was our driver and guide for the trip and his name was Ahmed. We loaded the cab with our luggage and sat inside it. Aditya and I were seated in the front seat next to Ahmed, Akhtar, Meenal and Hemant were in the middle and Vikram and Sonia in the rear seats of the car.

Ahmed took us to our hotel through the narrow wavy roads of Leh, telling us about every aspect of their life. He was very humble and informative. Aditya and I were asking him so many things related to the culture and places of Leh, and he was answering us with all the minor details possible.

After twenty minutes, Ahmed stopped the car outside Shingee hotel and the hotel manager welcomed us. It was a huge hotel with its doors and windows engraved with small and beautiful wooden flowers. We were given three rooms out of which again Vikram and Sonia took the most beautiful and biggest one. As this trip was like a honeymoon for them, we did not oppose. Meenal and I kept our luggage in another room and immediately went to the next room where Akhtar, Hemant and Aditya were settled. As we entered, we saw that Aditya was playing some song on their TV while jumping on the bed. Their room was provided with one double bed and a single bed. He was jumping on the double bed.

"Come on girls," he shouted.

I joined him while Meenal remained dancing on the floor.

"It's so fluffy, I am going to die," I shouted one of the famous dialogs from the animated movie, Despicable Me. We were jumping over the bed, dancing on the floor, fighting with pillows and blankets when Hemant and Akhtar entered the room. They were following the hotel check in procedure until now.

"What are you doing? What a mess you have created here," Hemant shouted.

"Stop," Akhtar said.

I went down on the floor and hugged him.

"What happened?"

"Thank you for planning this trip," I looked at them. I was again dancing on the floor.

"Let's go to Vikram's room," Aditya said and we ran to their room.

"It is going to be difficult for us if they are going to behave the same way," Hemant closed the door behind us.

Vikram was lying on the bed and Sonia was looking outside the window when we entered and told them about the excitement we were having.

"Yes darling. I was also thanking Vikram for this trip. I cannot imagine how much fun we are going to have here."

"Look at the bed; it is so soft and comfortable," Aditya jumped to their bed where Vikram was already relaxing.

"Even a choke slam will not hurt on this bed," I said and immediately regretted it.

"Oh yeah, let's try it on you," Aditya gave an evil smile to me.

Vikram took out his camera to shoot this WWE fight between Aditya and me.

"No," I shouted but Aditya did not listen and lifted me to give a chokeslam on the bed. Though it did not hurt, I kicked him back lightly. He was also kicking me and I was trying to defend myself with my hand when I broke my nails. Sonia ran towards me to examine the injury when she saw blood coming out of the wound.

"I hate you," I looked at Aditya.

"Sorry, I didn't mean that."

"Don't worry. I will put a bandage on your fingers then it will be fine," Sonia said.

Vikram, Meenal and Aditya were laughing looking at the video Vikram had filmed. After Sonia bandaged my fingers I went back to Akhtar's room in order to gain some sympathy from him, I entered their room and started a fake cry.

"What happened?" he asked me while adjusting their luggage in their room.

"Aditya, he is so bad, he broke my nail," I cried.

"Show me," he took my hand. "But you, too, are not innocent, I can guess that."

I laughed. "We were playing WWE."

Vikram entered the room and showed them the video he had made.

"See, I told you earlier, you are not innocent," Akhtar said after watching the video.

"Get ready. We will start the sightseeing today. Ahmed will come by 02:00 PM," Hemant interrupted us like he was being appointed as our headmaster to keep an eye on us.

"Yes. It's 12:30 PM already and we must get fresh before time," Akhtar added acting as the other headmaster.

"Ok boss," Vikram said as we moved towards our respective rooms.

"Vikram, please inform Meenal and Aditya too," Hemant closed their door.

Meenal and Aditya were still in Vikram's room. I came back to my room and took out the stuff I was going to need to get ready when Meenal entered the room. I told her that I am going to take a bath, so meanwhile she can carry some other work.

"How much time will you take Gul?"

"It will take around twenty minutes for me to take bath. And then you can bathe."

"Ok, Gul," she started taking out her clothes from her bag.

After taking bath, I dressed myself and went to check on other people. Hemant and Aditya were ready while Akhtar was still inside bathroom. Sonia and Vikram were also getting ready in their room.

After having lunch, Aditya and I went outside the hotel. We saw that few Royal Enfield Bullets were parked in the parking area. We started taking pictures around those bikes. Soon Akhtar and others also joined us. After taking few pictures, we sat inside our car, following the same sitting format when we had arrived at the hotel. It was our first day in Leh. Aditya and I were handling the music system as we were seated on the front seats while the rest of the people were sometime enjoying our playlist and complaining the other time.

"Where are we going Ahmed?" Meenal asked.

"I will take you to Shanti Stupa, Tsemo and Leh Palace today," Ahmed handed over the itinerary sheet to us. "We will go to the Shanti Stupa first, as it is closest from here."

"How far is it from Leh?" I asked.

"Around five kilometer."

He told us that it was a Buddhist white-domed stupa located in Changspa, a steep hill, which was inaugurated in 1991 by His Holiness the Dalai Lama. He asked us about the two ways we had to reach to the stupa. One was by road and another one was by climbing some five hundred steps. We chose the earlier option. The stupa was located at an altitude of around four thousands meters so that the whole city could be seen from there. Due to its altitude it was colder as compared to the city Leh. We enjoyed the peace and prosperity of this two level structure and clicked some memorable pictures. Our next destination was Tsemo Gompa, a monastery. It was around five in the evening when we reached the monastery. We enjoyed the scenic beauty offered by the gumpa and examined some of the rich collection of ancient manuscripts and wall paintings. As the day was ending, weather was getting colder and our woolens were not helping to keep us warm against it. It was also getting very difficult for us to walk and breathe as we were not properly acclimated to the new climate. Even a small physical activity was making us lose our breath. We started feeling a little headache and restlessness. But still we headed towards our last destination for today, the Leh Palace.

Ahmed told us to visit the location fast, informing us the reason behind it. "The city would be closed after sunset, so we need to reach the hotel on time and then the dinner would be only served till 9:30 PM."

We were exhausted and wanted to go back to hotel as soon as possible, but we were excited as well, as there was going to be no second chance to visit such a place again. Akhtar, Hemant, Aditya, Meenal and I went to see the former royal palace while Vikram and Sonia remained resting inside the car. The palace was a nine storey building made from stone, mud, wood and sand. Local people around the palace told us that it has been renovated by the Archaeological Survey of India. As we entered, we saw that there was not much remaining of the palace. The thick wood and mud walls were keeping the heat from entering the palace. We visited various compartments, rooms and corridors inside the palace and then returned to Vikram and Sonia.

"It's a nice palace," I told Vikram.

"Yeah, you should have joined us," Hemant showed them some of the pictures we took inside the palace.

"It's ok, both of us are suffering from headache. Let's go back," Vikram requested as we were getting inside the car.

"Let's have hot tea first," Akhtar suggested. "It will help reducing the headache a little bit."

"Yeah it's a good idea. Ahmed can you please take us to any nearby tea stall?" Hemant asked.

Ahmed took us to one of the local tea shop. Around 8:00 PM after enjoying the hot tea in the cold weather of Leh we came back to our hotel. Ahmed asked us to be ready by eight tomorrow morning, as we had to go to places outside Leh which would take the whole day.

"I will come on time. Jhuley," he greeted us in their local language.

We came back to our room and changed into some comfortable dresses and wore as many woolens as possible to protect ourselves from getting cold. We also wore scarf and socks so that it would help us to feel warm. Then we immediately went for dinner knowing that dinner would be served for a limited time. Later when we came back from dinner, we were gathered in Akhtar's room. We discussed the whole day and shared our experiences. When the conversation proceeded, we started looking for the funniest pictures of the day and made fun of them. Akhtar, Hemant, Meenal and Vikram were settled in the double bed while Aditya, Sonia and I were inside the huge, heavy blanket of the single sized bed.

"Honey, let's go. It is getting cold and I am feeling sleepy," Sonia said to Vikram.

"No. I am settled here. It is warm; I don't want to get outside the blanket and feel cold again."

"Let's go please."

"Vikram why don't you leave before Sonia orders you. Sonia, please do that." Hemant asked Sonia to order Vikram instead of requesting him.

Vikran laughed. "Let's go."

Being a husband he had to follow what his wife orders.

"Can we sleep here?" Meenal asked as Vikram and Sonia went.

"Do you really want to?" Hemant looked at Meenal.

"Yes, if you people don't have any problem."

"There is no problem at all."

"Cool, our room is colder compared to this room," Meenal stepped inside the blanket of their bed.

Akhtar was already asleep. Hemant, Meenal and Aditya were talking slowly and I was thinking about the people back in Pune and Bhopal. I thought to call Abbu, but again there was no network in my phone. I had got a few missed call alerts from Abbu, Dutta and Sohan when we were out. I thought to call them whenever I would get network in my phone and fell asleep.

CHAPTER 7

Leh Trip day 5

The wind was sharp, almost cutting the edges of my body but I wasn't feeling any pain or cold. I wanted to go as high as possible, up above in the sky. I stopped for a while to look down. The valley was looking even more beautiful from such a height. I stretched my hands, which were covered with feathers, and tried to cut the winds, flying like a bird, above the beautiful valley of Leh. I felt happy, free from all the rituals of this fake world. For the moment I forgot everything- my name, my identity, my financial crises and everything else. I thought to go even higher. I tried to push my wings against the wind but I wasn't moving. Something was holding me from escaping from their world. Then I saw that Akhtar was holding my leg and he was pulling me down.

"No, let me go," I shouted struggling even more trying to cut the winds with my feathers.

"Wake up," Akhtar smiled.

"No, please let me fly," I requested him to let me fly higher. Soon I heard a sound of laughter. Vikram and others were standing near Akhtar and were looking at me with amusement. Suddenly my wings turned into hands and I found myself lying on bed. I immediately stood up.

"What happened?" I asked them still feeling like a bird.

"That would be you telling us what happened. Why were you moving your hands in that fashion?" Akhtar was perplexed. Others were still giggling me.

"I had a dream where I was a bird flying high in sky. That's it," I smiled.

"When you were flying in your dream, you were actually hitting me with your hands. I got scared." Aditya looked at me.

"Shut up," I stepped out of blanket feeling a little embarrassed. It was early in the morning and after Aditya asked others, they gathered around my bed to see the funny moves I was making. Vikram even filmed it on his camera. Hemant acted to make me understand how I was moving my hands in order to fly. Embarrassingly I went to my room and Meenal came with me. I narrated to her how I was flying in the sky and how good it feels to be free like a bird. She nodded while listening to me. While taking bath, I remembered how everyone was laughing on me but I was helpless to do anything. When Meenal went to bathroom, I thought of playing a prank with others. I immediately took out a packet of gems chocolate and a pink colored medicine, which looked exactly like gems chocolate, from my hand bag. I opened both packets, emptied gems chocolate from its packet and transferred the medicines into it. I took one chocolate in my hand so that I would not be the victim of my own prank and then I went to the next room where the boys were getting ready. I knocked their door and Akhtar opened it.

"You smell like a rose," he took a deep breath and said.

Aditya was making spikes on his hair and Hemant was wearing his jacket. I waited for the right time to play my prank. Soon Vikram, Sonia and Meenal entered. I ate the chocolate I was holding in my hand. I made sure that it was noticeable.

"I also want that," Aditya moved towards me, looking at the packet I was holding.

"No, it is mine," I moved away from him, hiding behind Vikram. I knew that if I would not share any eatable with them, they would definitely fight with me for their share. And, the same thing happened. Aditya snatched the packet from my hand and took the chocolates out, which were actually medicines, and without noticing their common color, they shared it among themselves. As I expected they ate those medicines immediately. *What is this?* They shouted spiting the medicine out of their mouth. Their face turned bitter. I knew that within few seconds of taking that medicine inside their mouth, they would come to know that it was not any chocolate but something else, as we all had the human tendency of chewing chocolates the moment we took them inside our mouth. I laughed while their mouth tasted something acidic. I told them that I replaced the packet of chocolates with medicines to fool them, and then as a generous person I offered them the original chocolates which first, they resisted to eat, but then enjoyed a lot.

"That was clever," Vikram said as he ate few chocolates.

"Let's go for breakfast now. I want to eat something good. My whole mouth tastes like the medicine," Hemant drank lots of water.

I laughed and we locked the door behind. While going towards the dining hall Akhtar came near to me and placed his hand across my shoulder. "From where did you get such ideas?"

"My mind is working all the time."

"I need to stay away from you. You are dangerous."

"Like this?" I asked holding his hands and he laughed.

We finished our breakfast just in time, and as Ahmed was before time and was waiting for us, we immediately settled inside the car. According to today's itinerary, we were going to visit Sindhu Ghat, Druk white Lotus School and Hemis Monastery. We moved outside the city and reached Sindhu Ghat which was located ten kilometers ahead the upstream of Indus River in Shrey. It was one of the most peaceful river banks inaugurated by the former Prime Minister of India Mr. Atal Bihari Vajpayee. The water of the Ghat was crystal clear like a mirror and cold like ice. We clicked few pictures on the Ghat and then went to the *Druk White Lotus School*. As we entered the school, we were given a brief description about the school by one of the school teachers. She told us that the school had been inaugurated in 2001 to provide cultural learning to local children. She also told us that the school totally runs on charity and they are always open for the same. There were two options through which we can do the charity. One was by purchasing handmade item by the school children or by directly donating the money. After purchasing the handmade items by the school children, we proceeded to visit the school.

"Only limited area of the school has been opened for visitors," the school teacher told us while we moved out of her cabin. "That's the area where one of the scenes from movie, Three Idiots starring Aamir Khan has been shot."

"Yeah, I want to see that area," Aditya shouted.

I ran with him. Then we went to the small ground of the school where the movie was filmed. All the boys posed like peeing on the wall, exactly like one of the scenes from the movie and the girls clicked them through camera as they wanted.

After some time, the school teacher informed us that the visiting time had ended and we must leave. "This is the lunch time for students."

We left the place as we did not want to disturb them. Our next destination was Hemis Monastery. It was located at a distance of around forty five kilometers from Leh. We entered the never ending long roads of Leh which was accompanied by huge mountains from both the sides. During our journey to the monastery, we saw so many army troops located at every ten kilometers distance. As we proceeded, the sky turned dark and heavy winds started blowing. It was getting very cold. We saw few groups of bikers overtaking us.

"I also want a bike ride," I turned towards Akhtar. He was shooting the mountains from his camera.

"We cannot travel on bikes, we are odd number and I don't know how to ride a bike," he replied without looking at me, still shooting the mountains.

"I need a ride, it is such a romantic weather."

Vikram suggested that we could take bikes on rentals from the local market so that at least we could visit the market on bike. We decided that after going back to the city, we would enquire about it.

"Ahmed, can we sit on top of the car?" I looked at Ahmed.

"Are you mad?" Hemant asked.

"Yes, I am mad," I replied excitedly. "Please Ahmed."

Ahmed agreed. "Ok, but not for a very long period as this area belongs to army and it will not be good if they will catch us."

He then pulled the car on one side of the road and helped us get on its roof. Soon Aditya, Meenal, Hemant, Akhtar and I were seated on the roof of the car. Vikram and Meenal remained inside the car as Meenal was not feeling well because of the cold. Ahmed started the car, drove over the beautiful roads of Leh and we felt like a roller coaster while seated on the roof. Now the wind was striking with even more frequency. But we didn't care. We were shouting and all the people who were passing by were looking at us while Aditya made an unforgettable video.

After two kilometers, Ahmed stopped the car and we stepped inside it. We started feeling even colder when we stopped, so we took out the extra woolens we were carrying and wore it to warm our frozen bodies. We reached the monastery after some time. It was much colder as compared to other places as it was located at the foothills of Indus Mountain at Hemis. Hemis Monastery was one of the wealthiest monasteries in India which was famous for its rich collection of ancient remnants including the big statue of Buddha made of copper.

We were hungry and cold. Headache was by default associated with every kind of feeling we had. While returning, we told Ahmed to stop in the local market so that we could shop, have some food and enquire about bikes on rentals. Meenal, Akhtar and I were resting inside car only while others went to the market. After an hour, they came back from the market and told us that the shopkeepers were charging very high for bikes on rents, so we dropped the idea and stuck to our car only. We rested for an hour after coming back to our hotel. Ahmed, in advance, informed us that tomorrow we have to go to Nubra Valley, so we must start early in the morning. He also told us that it would be a night stay at camp in the valley, so we should carry a lot of woolens and thermals. Later when I was resting in my room before dinner, someone knocked the door.

"Gul, few bikers are staying in a room which is next to mine," Vikram said as I opened door. "Why don't you come and check?"

"Really? They must be the bikers whose bikes were parked in the parking yesterday."

"Come fast. Out of all those, I have found one who is suitable for you," he winked at me.

"Ok. I will come in few minutes."

Later when I was going towards Vikram's room, Aditya told me that everyone had already went for dinner and I should also join them. He also informed me that the room next to Vikram's room was also locked so there was no point in waiting. We proceeded for dinner. Vikram, Sonia, Hemant, Meenal and Akhtar were already seated on one dining table with one empty chair on the right side of Akhtar. They did not notice us coming. On the opposite table, I saw a group of gentlemen having their dinner. I looked at them, and a boy who was the most handsome among them all looked back at me. Till the time I reached our table, he was continuously staring at me and I was also giving him equal competition. His friends were smiling, murmuring something which was difficult to hear.

I was lost in the thought of having a bike ride with him when Akhtar shouted. "There she comes, my girl."

Soon that handsome man looked at Akhtar breaking his eye contact with me. I immediately sat next to Akhtar after grabbing food in my plate.

"Why did you call me that?" I asked Akhtar angrily.

"What wrong have I done?"

"It was not wrong, your timing was wrong. I was having an eye contact with that boy. You ruined everything. I lost my bike ride."

"You ruined my dinner. I was so happy to see you, but you don't care at all," he raised his voice.

He was angry. Other people present in the dining table remained silent.

"What happened?" Vikram asked when he returned after refilling his plate and sensing that something was not right. I explained him everything.

"It is ok, Gul. You will find more ways to get a bike ride."

"Will I?" I looked at Akhtar.

"Do not talk to me," he shouted angrily and went away taking his food plate.

I felt bad even more than the previous time when he did not want to talk to me in the train. A drop of tear came out of my eye and I tried to hide it from rest of the people. I finished my dinner fast and without facing anyone, came back to my room. The moment I entered my room, I closed the door and burst into tears. I was wondering why Akhtar shouts on me every time when I was not even accountable to him. I remained in my room for rest of the time. I wanted to call Abbu and Sohan and feel a little better, but the network coverage in my cell phone did not help. I remembered that Sohan was also sometimes rude to me. He was also efficient at blaming me for things which would happen to him. But then he had that right on me. I would never feel bad when he would blame me that as because of me he forgot to have an important conversation as I talk a lot. I would never cry when he would blame me when he would not be able to cut his nails on time or when he would not be able to go somewhere, as it would be raining outside, and I would have predicted it. I remembered that during the days when he had recently moved to Baner, they did not get any servant. It was the main reason why we were meeting daily. He had to take his dinner and I would accompany him. Eatsome, one of the fast food restaurants, was the place we would frequently visit before the Kooka shop was opened. Once, I was late and he was waiting for me at Eatsome. I arrived talking to someone over phone and noticed that he had ordered three wraps instead of two, which was his daily consumption. I gestured a no with a shock assuming that he had ordered third one for me.

"Even if I am hungry I will not eat," he moved his plate away from him, discarding it.

I abruptly disconnected my call as I was not able to understand what happened and it was the first time I saw him disrespecting food.

"You know that I don't like people restricting me for anything, especially for food. Why did you make that face at me that three wraps are not my appetite?"

His face was red out of anger and he was looking away from me.

"But I did not say that you can't eat three wraps, I made that face because I wanted to say that I will not eat any wrap. I thought you ordered one for me."

He was still looking away from me whereas other people present there were looking at us.

"This is enough. You always restrict me from smoking too."

"That's because smoking is bad for health. Anyway, I am sorry," I apologized but deep inside I was myself hurt as he misunderstood me. "Please eat," I requested him showing off a fake smile. Throughout the time when he was eating, we did not have any conversation. He was eating and I was figuring out why he thought that I want to restrict him from eating. Comparing cigarette with food was totally unacceptable. I knew him as a very soft spoken man, but on the other hand, I had seen him talking very rudely to me even when I wasn't guilty. This thought was disturbing me and I was feeling shocked but I did not react and pretended to be busy in my mobile phone.

"You were right, I am done with two. I will ask them to pack the third wrap," he broke the silence with a naughty smile.

I did not say anything, looked at him and lowered my eyes immediately.

"Let's go, I will drop you home."

"No, I can go by myself," It was my time to show tantrums.

"Let's go, it is enough for today," he started moving towards my apartment whereas I followed him silently. "Please don't be upset now," he looked at me for the third time. I did not say anything.

"Gul."

"I don't want to talk to you. You always shout at me and why do you think that I don't want you to eat whatever you want? Do you think cigarette and food are equivalent? I want you to stay healthy, that's why I ask you to quit smoking and you always take me wrong," I burst out.

"Baboo, I was already angry, so I lost my temper on you."

"That is what I am saying, that I have become a punching bag for you."

He burst into laughter. "Do you know that you are a comedian?"

I smiled which indicated that everything was now normal between us. I had always loved to bicker with him. It would always be a sweet and salty memory for me. But it was not the same with Akhtar. He was behaving as if I was not a good human being. After about an hour at around 10:00 PM when I was missing Sohan, someone knocked door of my room.

"Who is there?" I shouted.

"It is me, Gul. Please open the door," Aditya replied.

"Please go away Aditya, let me sleep," I did not open door. I was angry enough that I wanted to spend the whole night alone.

"Please."

I did not reply. I was crying even more after Aditya attempted to console me, thinking that Akhtar did not even care for me. That was why he had sent Aditya to talk to me. After half an hour when I was still weeping, my door was again knocked.

"Gul, open the door," Vikram ordered.

"Open the door, Gul, it is cold outside," Aditya politely requested.

I opened the door. Vikram, Aditya and Akhtar were standing outside my room.

"Come. Let's go, everyone is waiting for you at Akhtar's room," Vikram said.

"I don't want to come," I sobbed.

"You are a mature girl; it was a very small incident for which you are overreacting."

"No, it was not a small incident. He shouts on me every time," I looked at Akhtar. He was looking at me but was not saying anything.

"Please come. You have ruined your kohl because of crying," Aditya said innocently.

I smiled and everyone laughed expect Akhtar.

"Do your kohl and join us," Vikram combed my hair, believing that I would join them as I smiled.

When I entered their room, few things were changed. On the double bed, Meenal was sleeping between Hemant and Aditya. Sonia was sitting on one corner of the same bed. The single bed was occupied by Akhtar and Vikram, so I adjusted myself on the chair which was kept at the maximum distance away from the single sized bed where Akhtar was resting. Sonia complained about her headache so I offered her a head massage.

"Thank you Gul. It is so helpful. I can sleep now."

"You can ask me anytime Meenal. Abbu always says that my hands have the magical power to heal every pain. Whenever his body hurts, he asks me for a massage."

Vikram and Akhtar were talking some project related issues and Meenal was telling Hemant and Aditya about her childhood stories, they were making fun of her.

"Your dad is so right. Vikram, let's go to sleep, otherwise I will have to sleep here only. She is making me comfortable."

"Yes, let's go. We have to wake up early tomorrow," Vikram came out of his blanket.

"Can we go outside for a walk?" Akhtar asked the moment Vikram and Sonia went.

"Do you want to go now for a walk? It is late," Aditya was shocked.

"Yes, we can go to the terrace only."

I was sitting on the chair listening to their conversation without saying anything.

"Ok. Will you come with us, Gul?" Aditya looked at me.

I did not say anything but went outside with them. Meenal and

Hemant rested in the room itself. As we stepped outside their room, we saw that it was dark everywhere with no signs of light on the roads. The city was quiet, only wind was making noise like someone was whistling slowly. We were shivering because of cold. Aditya and Akhtar discussed about the serenity of the place and I remained silent. As it was getting hard to bear the cold, we came back shortly. As soon as we entered their room, Akhtar opened the door and stepped inside the single bed without asking anyone.

"Will you not sleep here?" I looked at Aditya.

I was still angry on Akhtar. I did not want to share the bed with him.

"No. I will sleep here. I have a lot of space in this bed," Aditya stepped in the bed where Meenal and Hemant were sleeping.

Akhtar was not saying anything but was watching us. I did not say anything further and got inside the inner side of the bed where Akhtar had created some space for me. The single bed was provided with a single blanket, I had to share it with him. We both were lying on the same bed, sharing the same blanket. We tried to move as less as possible so that we would not touch each other while sleeping. He was lying straight and so was I. Soon my anger was gone and my thoughts were filled with nervousness. *Why is he sleeping here?* I thought. *And why he is not talking to me? Oh my god, we are in the same bed.* The room was quiet, no one was speaking but I was continuously talking to myself. I did not know how to react. After sometime, I turned my back towards him and rested on my left shoulder, creating a lot of space between us. He then moved himself towards me and placed his right hand over me to grab me closer to him.

"Are you comfortable?" he whispered near my ears.

I felt his warm breath.

"Yes, much more comfortable now," I whispered, holding his hand and pulling me back towards him, leaving no space between us. I started breathing with him.

"Good."

Are you comfortable? Huh, you are sleeping inside the arm of a man who made you cry a moment earlier. Ask him why he behaved like that? The inner Gul was talking to me. *Why don't you turn yourself and kiss him? I must not.* I said to myself and concentrated to sleep. *You are getting goosebumps. You like him.* I was really getting goosebumps.

"Is there anything wrong?" Akhtar asked.

"No, everything is alright."

"Try to sleep then. We have to wake up early."

"Hmmm," I turned towards him, resting my head on his chest, sleeping under his arms.

"Now you are sleeping like a pupa sleeps inside its cocoon," he whispered.

I said nothing, went even closer and fell asleep feeling protected under his arms.

CHAPTER 8

Leh Trip day 6

Akhtar slept holding me without turning to the other side for the whole night. I did not sleep thinking about him. I was trying to recall when it started. I knew him since last couple of years but never felt like this before. And though he had flirted with me many times, he never committed his feelings for me. On the other hand, he was getting intimate with me. I was a bit confused about my feelings for him, but I was sure I wanted to get closer to him.

My heart was beating fast as if it would come out of my chest when he took his hands from me and went to bathroom. I adjusted myself straight in bed resting on my back. I pretended to be asleep when he returned. I did not want to face him so I did not move, totally covered with blanket which we were given to use. He came back and got inside blanket. He placed his head on my chest, wrapped his right hand around me and started playing his finger near my abdomen. Almost half of his upper body was resting on me. I felt seduced. I did not resist, but I was not able to hide the shiver I felt because of him.

"Are you awake?" he asked in a low voice so that no one else would hear.

Hemant and Aditya were snoring and Meenal was sleeping quietly. *How did he know that I am not sleeping?* I thought. *And why is he sure that I would not protest what he is doing?*

"Wake up," he tickled near my belly button.

I laughed and held his hand. "Stop," My laughter was loud enough to be heard by others.

"Why? It is so fluffy," he removed his hand from my grip and moved it upside towards my breast.

It is so fluffy, I am going to die, was one of my favorite dialogs, and I would make sure to use it in case of super excitement. Sometimes other people would also use it in front of me to show the same kind of feeling.

"I will die, stop," I stopped him again before he could touch my breasts. He went back to his pillow. *Why is he going away from me? I said no because it's not the right place, not because I did not want him to come closer to me. Instead, I want to take off my t-shirt and get naked in front of him,* I thought. He was making me excited. "Sorry," I moved on my right shoulder facing him. I then placed my hand on his chest rubbing it lightly.

"It is ok, don't be sorry." He turned towards me kissing me on my forehead.

He moved his hand on my back, adjusted my t-shirt and tucked it inside the pants I was wearing as if my open body was encouraging him to touch me. The rest of the time, we rested under each other's aura without speaking. I was almost asleep when around 5:30 in the morning, Vikram knocked and Hemant opened door. Akhtar immediately stepped out of bed breaking my sleep.

"Not so early," Meenal wrapped herself with blanket.

I did not want to waste a single second of my sleep so I said nothing. Aditya was also not showing any sign of being awake. It was early and cold.

"We have to get ready by seven, and that includes breakfast and packing our luggage too." Vikram said.

I knew that I would need time to get ready. I would not compromise on my appearance, so I woke up and started leaving to brush my teeth and take a bath. I took the keys of my room and rubbed my eyes. "Meenal you have thirty minutes more to sleep."

I was smiling for no reason while unlocking door of our room. I placed my left hand on my abdomen to check if it was fluffy and burst into laughter thinking, how foolish I am. I sat on bed after taking bath, covered with a bathrobe, giving a deep thought on what happened since last night, when my phone rang. It was Dutta.

"Hello madam," I picked her call.

"Oh, finally I have reached you. How are you? How is the trip going?"

I told her everything, including what had happened last night. I knew that it had happened because of mutual understanding between Akhtar and me, but still I was seeking a second opinion on it. Irrespective of the level of confidence a girl has, she would always need expert advice about things, be it her dress, color of her nail polish, her feelings, her dates, her boyfriend, her relationship and everything else. And that second opinion has to be given by another girl only; a boy would not be trusted over that. Dutta was the right person in this case. She told me to be calm, not to hurry as that could ruin the moment between Akhtar and me. I listened to her and told her how much I miss her. She had already moved to Mumbai a month ago.

"First enjoy your trip and then we will meet soon," she said and disconnected.

I called Abbu immediately and informed him about everything, and then I thought of calling Sohan. *Its 6:05 AM, he must be sleeping,* I thought but still dialed his number because I was not sure when my phone would latch in the network again. He picked my call after one ring.

"Good Morning," I said.

"Good morning. What is happening?"

I told him that the trip was going awesome so far. I also told him that we would go to the Nubra Valley today and would stay there for a night and return tomorrow.

"You will go via Khardung La. It is the highest point on the earth where road exists," he said.

He would always share such information with me as if he was always using Google. Since the time I met him, I was less frequently using Google. I would simply ask him and he would right away solve my problem.

"Why are you awake so early?" I asked.

"I am going to gym in the morning and working late in office. After all, I don't have to meet anyone for Kooka."

"Take your dates to the Kooka Shop," I said, but I did not want him to take anyone to Kooka shop except me.

He smiled. "How is Akhtar?"

Maybe he was sure that my feelings for Akhtar would definitely grow in this trip, and that's why he was asking about Akhtar. I wanted to share every detail with him but I was not sure how he would react.

"Good. We are getting closer to each other. He is trying to seduce me."

"Enjoy. I will call you later."

"I will call you, we don't get network here."

I didn't understand context of the word- enjoy, he used. I wanted to ask him about Akhtar and me. I wanted to ask him whether I should continue getting closer to Akhtar. *What does Sohan mean by enjoy? Why doesn't he express himself?* I was disturbed with what Sohan said when Meenal knocked. I opened door in a confused state and came back to take out my clothes. I bent myself to open my suitcase and felt acute pain in my chest.

"Meenal, my chest is hurting," I held my chest and rested on bed. She ran towards me.

"Gul, I have told you multiple times to visit a doctor, but you don't listen at all. Is it hurting a lot?"

I had complained to her about my chest pain earlier.

"Nothing is serious. It comes after physical stress and goes right away," I stood next to her as the pain was gone.

"It is good that nothing is serious Gul, but you should consult a doctor."

I just looked at her as I did not know what to say.

"Are you ok now? Or should I call someone?" she asked me.

I smiled and she left to take bath after a while. *You need to look different.* I told myself and dressed for Akhtar. Though there was no point in wearing anything classy, because we had to always cover ourselves with woolen, which would ruin any attempt of looking good, I still tried to catch Akhtar's attention. My hair was short but I managed to pin a small section of my hair from the front side of my head on the left side just above my ears. That was giving me a cute look. The coal black kohl I applied on my eyes, the sweet rose perfume I used to fragrance my body, the matte red lipstick on my lips; everything was used in the name of Akhtar. I could not deny the fact that though I was excited to see him, I was equally scared of what would happen next. So I remained in my room and waited for Meenal to join me.

"Why are you still here?"

"I am waiting for you. We will go together." I was feeling nervous to go out and face Akhtar. After she was ready, we both went to the next room. I was walking slowly behind her, anxious like never before when we entered Akhtar's room.

"Are you ready?" Akhtar looked at me and ignored Meenal.

Unlike other days, he was ready before Hemant and Aditya. His eagerness explained that he was waiting for me to come. I did not look at him, but from the corner from my eye I saw that he was checking out on me. I felt more nervous.

"Yes. Let's go for breakfast," I came out of their room. I was standing in a balcony in front of their room facing the panoramic view of the city, resting my hands on the railing. Soon Akhtar came outside, stood just behind me, and placed his hands above mine.

"Why are you hiding?" he whispered into my ears.

"I am not hiding." I turned towards him, placing my hand around his shoulder. The nervousness inside me was gone. I felt confident knowing that I had the power to entice him. He was standing very close to me; I was looking straight into his eyes.

"Rose," he held my waist coming closer to me.

I said nothing even though he called me with a different name. I was waiting to hear from him, but we were interrupted by Vikram and Sonia as they came out of their room and we immediately behaved.

***

After finishing breakfast, we came outside the lobby where Ahmed was waiting for us. We quickly settled everything and started for Nubra Valley at around eight in the morning. We were running late.

"We need to take the travel pass. So we will go from the market," Ahmed took a right turn which could lead us to the market. "As Nubra Valley has been located near the Line of Actual Control we need a line of permit to enter the area."

I looked at other and smiled as everyone was as excited as I was. From last one hour we were travelling through the humongous mountain faces reaching higher and higher altitudes. The temperature was decreasing as the travel time was increasing. At a distance of about a kilometer we saw that few vehicles and bikes were parked on both sides of the raw road, and after reaching there we saw that huge trucks were cutting down the mountain which was the reason everyone was waiting. *What is happening?* We asked as we got out of our car.

"Sorry for the inconvenience. We need to cut the mountain to make it wider. It will take around twenty to thirty minutes," One gentleman answered, who was dressed like an army, standing above one of the trucks.

"No problem sir, you must be from Indian Army," Aditya said.

"We are from Border Roads Organization, BRO."

"Oh, so you maintain road networks across Indian borders?" I asked. "Can we also get up on this truck?"

"Yes Madam," he extended his hand towards me so I would climb up.

We waited above the truck, watching how they were cutting the mountains and discussed about their life, appreciating them for their efforts, when I felt tiny drops of snow falling on me. It was disappearing the moment it was touching any surface. When the snowfall started, temperature decreased even more. We started shivering but did not forget to click pictures of our first snowfall in Leh. Then the BRO gave us a green signal to continue ahead. We were again back to our car. As we proceeded we saw huge mountains covered with snow. The brown altitudes were now replaced by white snow. This was the first time I was crossing through such mountain series. I kept silent and watched the view. I started believing that this was the place where one could really live. The peaceful view was simply turning me crazy. There was no comparison of this place with any other city and as we proceeded further, we found it even more beautiful.

"The journey is halfway done," Ahmed parked our car at one side of the wet muddy and curvy road. "This is Khardung La Pass."

I took a deep breath. "Khardung La Pass! Is this the world's highest motorable road?"

"Yes, you can see by yourself, meanwhile I will take the permit." Ahmed pointed towards a board.

Khardung La Pass. Height 18380 feet. Please do not stay for more than thirty minutes was written on the board. We ran towards it to click some pictures. We felt so uneasy and hard to breathe that it was difficult to even move. All of us complained about sudden headache and felt ultimate cold because it was snowing at such an altitude. So we went to our car to take out the extra winter wear we were carrying, which was kept in our luggage. A man from army was standing near the board surrounded by so many civilians. He was telling them about the Pass. He advised people not to exert and inform immediately in case of heavy breathing problem. He also told that till now the roads were gaining altitudes, but from now on, it would descend and the uneasy feeling would pass. After listening to him for a while, I turned toward the edge of the road to live the view which was breathtaking. All I could see was fog. There were white colored mountains touching sky. The cold breeze was serene in its own way.

There were a lot of people. Some of them were capturing the scene in their cameras while some others were struggling to find something hot to drink. Few other set of people were asking for public toilets to use. Some people were coming to this place and turning as amazed as we were while some others were leaving us behind. But the place was different from all. It was alluring like nothing else. Hemant was not feeling well, so we had to move from the place, which I never wanted. Within fifteen minutes, after getting the permit, we moved from that location. And as we moved we discussed about how hard it was to stay at such a place, and appreciated our Indian Army who was staying in such areas for years.

***

After travelling for seven hours from the huge mountain faces, crossing ultra wide landscapes, lovely trails, wide variety of colors and musical Shyok river, we reached Diskit which was the main headquarter in Nubra Valley. Ahmed parked our car near the area where Shyok River meets Siachen River and forms the large Valley. For the next one hour, we forgot where we were. The valley was so huge and beautiful that it was the perfect place to be called heaven. On my one side, there was a Shyok River, melodic as it was, surrounded by a wide variety of trees and yaks, which were as lively as the river. My other side was covered with mountain ranges as if they were guarding the valley. And between the mountains and river, there was a huge landscape covered with sand.

It was difficult to imagine all of the prepossessing beauties in one place. We could do nothing but behaved as a bunch of crazy people who had never seen such place before. And as we had descended to normal altitude, the headache was gone, even though the cold remained, but it could not have stopped us from turning fanatical. And then when we were overwhelmed with the view, we proceeded towards our camp which was located in an open area. There were so many small tents located at small distance from each other covered with many local trees. The camp in charge showed us our tents and told us that after eight, electricity would be cut off so we should finish everything on time. After coming to our tent, I told Meenal that I was not feeling well.

"Wash your face, maybe you will feel better."

"I can try that," I went to examine the bathroom so that I could use it.

"You know what Meenal, you are a girl and you cannot feel excited."

"What are you trying to say, Gul?"

"I am trying to say that being a girl if you feel excited about anything, your periods will ruin your feelings."

She laughed. "You got your periods? But it was not supposed to come today, right?"

We had discussed about the common problem of a girl before coming to this trip when I told her that I would be safe.

"Yes, but I don't know why they are early, maybe because of exertion and excitement."

"Do you carry sanitary pads?"

This was such a remote area that it was hard to find anything.

"Yes, I do. I was prepared," I took out the required stuff from my bag. Then I went to bathroom. I wanted to clean myself so I took head bath with cold water without imagining its consequences. I changed my dress and then went to the next tent where others were settled. As I entered, everyone shouted on me. *Are you mad to bathe with cold water?* They said and I said nothing. I was not feeling well. I looked at Meenal who was resting under a big white blanket on the double bed. Hemant, Aditya and Sonia were sitting next to her. Vikram and Akhtar were settled on the single bedding which was kept on the ground.

"It's ok. Warm yourself," Meenal said.

"Come," Akhtar made some space for me.

I said nothing and sat between Akhtar and Vikram inside their blanket. They were talking to each other and I was not able to pay any attention. My eyes were burning, chest was paining and headache was crossing every limit.

"Can I lie down?" I asked Akhtar.

"You want to sleep?"

"Yes," I said in a low tone. *I had not slept since last night, maybe after sleeping for a while, I would feel better,* I thought and rested my head on his lap. After few minutes he took his hand inside blanket to pull my cheeks.

"Oh my god, she has fever," he touched my neck and head. "Gul, are you alright?"

Soon they were again shouting on me. *Who told you to take bath? Why you never listen to anyone?* But I was not in any mood to explain to them why I took bath.

"Let's get something to eat, I have medicine which she can take," Hemant said.

"Don't worry. You will be fine," They went to get something to eat.

Meenal, Sonia and I remained inside tent. Then I told Sonia that I got periods and that's why I took a bath. A moment later they came back with a biscuit packet and soup made from local vegetables. I ate that, took medicine and again slept on Akhtar's lap while he covered me safely with blanket. After some time my chest pain and fever was gone but I was still feeling uncomfortable because of the periods I got.

***

After dinner we were resting on Akhtar's tent. We were provided with a lantern which would suffice the minimum requirement of light. All the boys were settled on double bed whereas all the girls were resting on the bedding which was kept on ground. We gossiped for hours and then somewhere close to midnight; we decided to go to sleep. I told Meenal that I would sleep with her. I did not want to feel embarrassed because of my periods, and that was why I wanted to avoid Akhtar. I hated the feeling because I wanted to sleep with him.

"I will come back after getting fresh," I said coming out of the tent with Vikram and Sonia.

"Please don't take a bath again," They all laughed on me.

"Good joke," I took out a torch and went.

When I came back I saw that Aditya had moved on the floor, next to Meenal. And on the double bed a place was left for me next to Akhtar. Hemant was sleeping on the other side.

"What is this? I will sleep there," I said to Aditya.

"No, I will sleep with Meenal, Hemant snores a lot."

I waited for five minutes but no one was saying anything. So silently I slipped inside Akhtar's blanket wanting nothing to happen this night. He was already asleep. The bed was not strong. It was shaking with every movement, and the white bed sheet and blankets were slippery. Also there was only a single pillow between Akhtar and me. Hemant was using two of them. Akhtar woke up the moment I got inside the blanket. He held my waist and pulled me towards himself as if he was waiting for me to sleep with him. I felt nervous not because he had touched me but because of the periods I was suffering from. I tried to move as less as possible. It was my first day which was heavy flow day, so after every fifteen to twenty minutes I was checking whether the pad was in proper position to avoid stains. *Don't panic,* I thought, but nothing was helping. I was in fear of getting exposed during the menstrual period of mine. I hated being a girl for the moment. I was disturbing him too.

"I am not able to sleep properly." I said to Akhtar. I was feeling irritated. I wanted to have a separate pillow from him. I wanted to ask Hemant for a pillow so that I could use it and sleep a little away from Akhtar.

"Me too," he came closer to me.

Why can't he sleep a little away from me? I thought irritatingly. And then I turned towards him, taking his hand off me and keeping it on his own body, creating a lot of space between us. Now my head was closer to his chest, my knees were touching his legs and my abdomen was in a fair distance away from him. He again placed his left hand on my back moving it upward and downward, touching the hooks and strap of my bra and examining every curve on my waist. I forgot everything when he touched me and went away with the feelings of having him so close. Soon I placed my right hand around him and went closer to him almost touching his chest with my face. I sensed that he was breathing fast. So was I. He then moved his hand towards my thigh and tried to take it inside my t-shirt. I got a shiver with his touch on my naked body. But I held his hand, looked at him and signaled a no through my eyes. He stood up immediately.

"Can we go to the other tent?" he asked in a low voice, which only I could hear.

I cannot, I thought. *Why is he asking so? What does he want? I cannot have sex with him right now. I am in periods. Otherwise, do I want to have sex with him? Does he love me? Oh god, what is happening?* So many thoughts were coming into my mind.

"Am I creating any problems?" I said in a calm tone. "I can ask Aditya to swap his place with me."

"Don't disturb him. Can we both go?"

"No," I knew that we would not be able to control ourselves after moving to the other tent alone. I did not want him to know about my periods, I had never shared that information with any boy.

"Such a stubborn girl you are," he came back to sleep.

"Please ask Hemant for one pillow. He is using two."

"You are already disturbing me and now you want to disturb others also. You would never adapt yourself according to situations. You need your own pillow, your own blanket; you can never share anything with anyone. On the other hand, when I am offering you more space in the other tent, you don't agree to that as well. Take this pillow," he pushed his pillow towards me.

"It's ok. I don't need your pillow. I can sleep without it," I silently moved to the corner of bed, leaving ample amount of space between us. But still I was sharing his blanket, which was the only option left for me. On the second night when I was unable to sleep, I kept wondering why he got angry on me. *Maybe because I said no to him when he asked me to move to the other tent. But we could have ended up having sex with each other. Do all men behave so when a woman says no for sex? I made him upset. We need to talk about it,* I thought as I slept.

CHAPTER 9

Leh Trip day 7

I woke up with the sound of laughter. Sonia had come to our tent. Hemant was explaining to her the splendid view of the valley he saw early in the morning. He woke up before sunrise and went outside for a walk.

"I did not sleep for the whole night," Akhtar complained.

I was listening with my eyes closed.

"What was the issue?" asked Sonia.

"*Arey*, this bed is so slippery; it was difficult to sleep in here. And then her tantrums," he signaled towards me.

"We all are a great victim of that," Hemant laughed.

I was still quiet.

"But I have faced it maximum times. I have to share the bed with her."

Are you serious? Then why do you share your bed with me? And yes, because you have extra benefits over me, you must handle my tantrums also, I answered Akhtar in my mind.

"We must find someone who can handle her, she is going difficult day by day."

You are that person, I thought getting shy.

"What did she do?" Hemant asked.

I wanted to hear what Akhtar would say in return. After all it wasn't me who was doing anything.

"She was asking for a separate pillow in the middle of the night."

I was stunned. *The whole fight was for the pillow only? What about rest of the part? Who would tell about your proposal of moving into another tent?* They all burst into laughter after listening to him.

"Yes, I asked for a pillow because it was difficult for both of us to manage in one. We both were not able to sleep," I got out of the bed. I too did not want to mention about other things that had happened. Akhtar looked at me; I saw a little anger on his eyes. "Anyway, I am going to get fresh."

"Gul, Aditya is using your bathroom." Sonia informed me.

"What? But why is he using our bathroom? They had been provided with their own."

It was my time to be angry. All these days in our trip, I was waking up early before Meenal so that I would get enough time to get ready and most importantly, I would not have to use a used bathroom. They knew I cannot adjust in terms of sharing a bathroom, especially in periods.

"She has started throwing her tantrums again," Hemant laughed.

"Hemant, I am serious. I don't like using already used bathroom. Now Aditya will spill out water everywhere making me uncomfortable to use it."

"That is the process of using a bathroom. How can anyone use a bathroom without using water?"

"I don't find it hygienic and I can never make you understand this, so please let's not discuss it anymore," I came out of their tent. I was wandering here and there out of anger.

"Gul, you can use our bathroom, I will tell Vikram to use it wisely. Or wait; let me check if he is there in the bathroom, otherwise you can go first," Sonia came out of the tent.

"It is ok Sonia. I will use mine. But I don't want them to make fun of me without even knowing about my situation," A tear came out of my eye.

"Don't cry, darling. I know you are in periods. It must be difficult." she came close to me.

Others were watching us without saying anything. Akhtar was a part of them. Soon Aditya came out of my tent.

"Can't you control yourself? Don't you know Gul? Now she needs the bathroom clean," Hemant said sarcastically.

"Everyone was sitting there, so I used their bathroom."

I understood Aditya's point, but still waited for a while before using the bathroom.

***

While having breakfast Ahmed told us that there would be no special sightseeing today apart from visiting few monasteries and returning back to Leh. We chose going back to Leh directly followed by a little shopping in the market. Akhtar was not talking to me. But I observed that he was staring at me every now and then. Many a time we had eye contact also without any visible facial expression. It seems like a cold war was started between us. I wanted to talk to him but said nothing as he was saying nothing. I was quiet throughout our breakfast time and while visiting local places near Diskit. And then we started coming back to Leh. We saw that all the vehicles coming to the Valley from Leh were covered with snow, so we guessed that we could experience the snowfall again. When we proceeded, heavy snowfall started. The whole area was covered with thick white layer of snow; it was getting difficult to differentiate between the roads and the mountains. Keeping the surroundings in mind, Aditya played songs from one of my favorite movies, Rockstar. I was already having a feeling for Akhtar and now after listening to songs from this movie, I was feeling crazy for him.

"I need a bike ride. Vikram you promised me one," I looked at the bikers who were crossing us. Aditya was sleeping on my shoulder.

"Yes, but I cannot help you right now."

"I don't think that it will ever happen," I was disappointed. No one said anything. Everyone was lost in their thoughts. After nine hours we reached Leh. We took two hours extra as compared to the time we had taken to go to Nubra Valley, but it was understood that it was difficult to drive in such weather. Leh, on the other hand was clear and shiny, though still cold. We stopped in market to spend some time. Everyone was buying some of the local things as a memory to keep. I controlled myself on spending money. I was happy to take away the experience. And then we returned to our hotel rooms. It was a normal day today as we had only returned to Leh without any sightseeing. We went to our respective rooms to get fresh and changed to normal dresses and gathered in Akhtar's room as usual. Everyone was energetic. Aditya and Hemant were again making fun of Meenal; Sonia was sharing her college experience with Vikram and Akhtar. I was sitting on the chair looking outside window.

Sonia and Meenal were thinking that I was low because of my menstrual cycle, whereas Vikram, Hemant and Aditya were continuously asking me reasons for my weird behavior. Akhtar was not saying anything. He was the only one knowing the actual reason behind my behavior. He was the reason.

I came out of their room. I did not want to talk to anyone. I wanted to go in my room and spend the time alone. I wanted Akhtar to go away from my thoughts. He was continuously disturbing me, and his stare was making me uncomfortable. I wanted to hide myself, I felt as if something wrong was happening. And as I was feeling insecure, I wanted Sohan to be around. I knew that he would make me laugh anyway. I knew that he would never ignore me for any reason. I was certainly missing him.

"Where are you going?" Sonia asked me.

"I need a little time for my own. I am not feeling good."

After coming back to my room I called Sohan. Luckily the network helped.

"I was thinking to call you," he received my call.

There was a charm in his voice, he seemed happy. Half of my tension went away after listening to him. He would unknowingly act like a medicine to my spoiled mood. Whenever I would be sad, or stuck in any dilemma, I would call him. He might not solve my problem, but would surely help me take a better decision by cheering me up.

"I heard your telepathy. Now tell me what happened?" I ignored my own concerns.

"There is this girl, she is driving me crazy."

"Which girl are you talking about?"

"This girl, I cannot name. She is new in our office."

"Try to approach her," I suggested him. Whenever he would tell me about any girl and even though he would do things in his own way, we would discuss how to take the next step in order to impress her. I would never doubt his skill here.

"Jokes apart, the news is, I have been selected as a captain for a cricket match organized for charity purpose."

"Wow, that's great. When is the match scheduled?" I knew that he was crazy for cricket. His father was one of the reasons behind it. His father was a cricket coach in a sports institute in Lucknow and his mother was a housewife. Sohan was their only child; his father had always motivated him to play cricket, although cricket was in his blood.

"16th June. I am working hard for it."

"Oh. That's why you are going to gym."

"I want to go to the gym since eternity but you know I have a lot of work pressure which always stops me from doing so many things. Because of that I am not able to pay attention to cricket too."

"Yes I know, because of your work pressure you are not taking me out for dinner also." Once Sohan asked me to do something, and in return he said that he would take me out for dinner, which never happened.

He laughed. "Don't worry, I will take you to your favorite restaurant."

I too laughed with him. He was talking about one of the restaurants which was located in Baner near the vegetable shop where we used to go, and Sohan knew that I had a bad experience in that restaurant. Whenever we would discuss about dinner he would ask to take me there and I would simply deny. "I would die but not go to that place."

"I am ready to take you for dinner but you don't want to go, and then you would blame me."

He knew that I would never go to that place.

"This way the dinner which I am expecting will never happen."

"It will. Just give me some time; I will take you to some very nice place."

"I am waiting for that day. By the way I want to tell you something."

"What? Are you pregnant?" he laughed.

"*Chup be*. I don't have that much courage to get pregnant."

He laughed again. "Tell me what happened then?"

"He is not talking to me," I told him without taking Akhtar's name. It was obvious to both of us that I was referring to Akhtar here.

"Why? You said something to him?"

"No, I did not say anything. I just said no. Now he is not talking to me, but on the other hand he is continuously gazing at me. I am getting disturbed. I don't know what to do now; I want to talk to him."

"It is ok. Let it be. Always remember to look like a girl, act like a lady and think like a man."

I tried to understand what he was teaching me this time. "I already look like a girl I guess. What do you mean by act like a lady and think like a man?"

"Act as if he is not bothering you. Don't give him so much of your attention."

"Ok. And how should I think like a man?"

"Don't think at all. Simple."

I smiled. "I will try," I felt good after having a conversation with him. I knew that he would surely provide some of his out of the box idea to overcome the situation, and he did.

"I will leave from office now. We have to go for a practice match tomorrow early morning."

"Hmm. Shall I wake you up?"

"By five in the morning, if possible."

"Ok, I will call you, but it totally depends on the network so set your alarm also."

"Hmm, bye," he disconnected.

The moment he hung up the call Sonia and Meenal came. Sonia told us that she was happy to come with us. She never went for such trips so she was enjoying it a lot. She also told that whenever some of her college friends would go out for such trips, one or two girl and boy would end up having sex with each other.

"Are you serious?" I remember about last night when Akhtar asked me to go to the other tent. *He surely wanted to have sex with me* I thought.

"Yes. But we don't have to worry. We have come with gentlemen."

I don't agree, I thought. *I need to stay away from Akhtar.* Now I was afraid of him. I thought that he was only coming closer to me because of physical attraction. He doesn't love me.

"The girls and boys are getting divided into gender specific groups. May I know the reason behind it?" Aditya entered our room.

"It is not like that. We were just talking," Meenal replied.

"Let's go for dinner then," We went for dinner when Sohan messaged me on Whatsapp.

Sohan: I have reached home.

Me: Good.

Sohan and I would inform each other after reaching home whenever we would not meet for Kooka.

Me: Thank you, I am feeling better now.

Sohan: Just remember, yahi sab toh life hai.

He used another of his dialog, *yahi sab toh life hai,* to state that all the ups and downs are part of the life.

Me: Yeah, I agree. Love you.

Sohan: Love you too.

We would endear each other by saying love you. We would feel loved for the moment but would not take it seriously. I was smiling while having dinner thinking of Sohan and after coming back from dinner when we were settled in Akhtar's room as usual, I behaved normal as Sohan told me, but I was still confused to share my bed with Akhtar.

"Let's go brother," Akhtar said to Hemant.

"Where?"

"We will sleep in their room and they will sleep here," he signaled towards Meenal and me.

"Why? What happened?"

It was likely possible that if we would sleep in their room, he had to share his bed with me, so I knew why he was asking for sleeping in another room.

"It's not needed, Meenal can we sleep in our room?" I looked at Meenal.

"Sure Gul, but what had happened?"

Akhtar and I went silent.

"Did you people fight?" Vikram asked.

"No. Why would we fight?" Akhtar said immediately. "It is just like I need a little more space to sleep. Two people sleeping in a single bed is congested."

I did not say anything and came to my room. *I will not think about him,* I thought. Soon Meenal came into the room. I did not talk much and before sleeping I set an alarm for five in the morning, *I have to call Sohan.*

CHAPTER 10

Leh Trip day 8

"Gul, your phone is ringing, wake up," Meenal said.

My alarm was ringing. It was five in the morning and I had to call Sohan to wake him up for his practice match, but there was no network in my phone, so regretfully I went outside our room and sat in the balcony after wrapping an old shawl around me, which my Amma used in her days. The balcony was common for all guests staying in the hotel, with many comfortable wooden chairs placed to sit and enjoy the splendid view of the city. I sat there thinking about Sohan and his cricket practice match. Hemant joined me after some time. As usual he was already awake early in the morning. He and I sat there for around half an hour and then went inside to get ready to go to Pangong Lake. I did not talk to him much during the time I was with him. Pangong Lake was around one hundred and seventy kilometers away from Leh and it was one of the most mesmerizing lakes of the region. We were told the journey would be harsh and difficult so we need to be prepared for it.

***

At around eight, after taking breakfast we started to reach Pangong Lake. I tried my level best to behave normal. As there was again going to be a night stay over camp near the lake, whose temperature almost drops to zero even during the nights of summer, we carried all the woolens which were possible to carry. I did not pay much attention on Akhtar. I wanted my relationship with him to grow even stronger but it was not happening. He was going away from me which disturbed me.

Unlike the roads to Nubra Valley, roads to Pangong Lake were really harsh and raw. After travelling for around two hours, we were stopped by BRO. They told us that due to heavy snowfall, roads ahead near Chang La had been closed and snow cutting process was going on, so by that time we need to stop here only. And if the process would take time we might need to go back to Leh. So hoping for the best we stayed there. There were other people also waiting for the next information to come. We came out of our car and searched for toilets. A local man guided us, and then Sonia and I went to get fresh. After coming out of washroom I saw that few bikers were standing on the opposite side of road, with few bikes labeled as Royal Enfield parked nearby. After giving a concentrated look, I figured out that one of the bikers was looking similar to the man I saw in the dining hall of our restaurant back in Leh when Akhtar misbehaved with me. I asked Sonia to confirm on my doubt.

"He is the one."

"Should I talk to him?" She was the only one present with me at the moment. Others were resting near our car which was parked around three hundred meters away.

"Go ahead Gul, you are pretty and young. You might get a bike ride."

"Yeah, I only need a bike ride," I was filled with confidence. While crossing road I took off my sunglasses so that I could flatter him with my eyes. Playing with eyes adorned with a lot of kohl was the one graceful thing I believed I could do, which worked almost all the time. I gazed at him continuously till we reached them; he was standing with two of his friends who were speaking to a local man. They also pictured us I guess, because they were smiling looking at us. I thought that I would not fool him and would directly come to the point of having this conversation with him.

"Hello. Do you remember me?" I extended my hand for a handshake.

"Yes of course, the beautiful lady from Shingee Hotel," he turned towards me. He took my hand and kissed it.

I felt admired. These types of tricks would always work for girls, especially when they are seeking it. I wanted to be praised by Akhtar. Even though I was not sure how he had touched me emotionally, or how much I would need him when I would be sad or tensed, but I definitely wanted to be physically close to him. I would prefer Sohan over Akhtar had I been seeking emotional support. I trusted Sohan here because I was never involved in any face to face discussion with Akhtar for any serious concerns. In fact, till now we had never talked about our feelings for each other. Things happened in bed were left unspoken in bed only. That's why, when he was ignoring me, I was getting pissed off. Hence the small affection shown by the biker worked for me. I was impressed.

"My name is Gul and she is Sonia," I introduced Sonia. She was smiling after the gesture given by that man.

"Hello, I am Angad and they are my friends, Vicky and Sameer," he introduced himself and his friends.

Vicky and Sameer were cool and handsome but not like Angad. He was standing out of them. He was handsome, muscular, tall and fair. Riding gear was making him sexier.

"I can see that you are doing the journey with bikes," I said.

"Yes, we have travelled from Manali to Leh and then after local sightseeing, we are off to Pangong."

"She is very obsessed with bikes and all. From the time we had started our trip, she is continuously asking for a bike ride," Sonia tried to make things easier for me.

"Yes and a ride in this place would make me go crazy."

"Then why you are not travelling through bikes?"

"We cannot, that's a long story."

"Oh, in that case, can I have the pleasure of giving a ride to you, my lady?" he flirted with me and took my hand once again.

I looked at Sonia; she was signaling a yes to me. For few seconds I was numb. All these days I was asking for a bike ride and Angad was so easily offering me one.

"Will you really take me on a bike ride here?"

"Yes."

"That is so nice of you. Once the road gets clear, we can start," I did not want to let this opportunity go.

"Sure," he said and we proceeded towards our car.

"Sonia, I cannot imagine he asked me for a ride. I am going to die."

"I already told you, it is hard to say no to you."

***

"For once I thought that he will never leave your hand," Vikram said sarcastically as Sonia and I returned.

I could sense jealousy in his voice. Akhtar did not say anything. We explained to them the whole scene, how I initiated the conversation and how Angad asked me for the ride, taking my hand in his hand.

"Yeah, we saw that two times."

"You guys are jealous all because I will go for a bike ride."

"Don't you worry for them, Gul, go for it," Sonia said. "By the way, I must tell that he was not taking his eyes off you."

"Should I go?" I smiled and looked at Akhtar; he was also looking at me.

"Why not?" he looked away from me.

***

I was very excited and nervous at the same time. I had never gone for a bike ride with a stranger. But I wanted to have this experience. Actually, I was not afraid of strangers, but I was praying for good to happen. I sat on the front seat of our car to compose myself for the ride. Meenal and Aditya were sitting on the car roof, clicking pictures of the mountains. Hemant, Akhtar, Vikram and Sonia were sitting on the back seats. Ahmed was talking to some other drivers. I was waiting for the clearance signal. Soon we got the signal. BRO told us that the whole process of snow cutting would take around three more hours and we would take around two hours to reach Chang La, so we could start, but we might have to wait for an hour or so at Chang La. I came out of our car; Angad was waving at me from the distance. I turned towards the other people, took out my bag and applied my rose perfume. I looked at my watch which was showing 10:30 AM. Ahmed said that by 12:30 AM, we should reach Chang La. So we decided that I would join them at Chang La only. There was no signal in our mobiles for communication, so they told me to stay close to our car. Ahmed was also told by Akhtar to keep an eye on Angad's bike while driving so that we could not be missed.

"Ok, I must leave. They are starting," I took my bag.

"Enjoy, it's your day." Everyone shouted but I heard a voice saying something different.

"Stay safe. We will be around."

I looked back and found Akhtar looking at me. I looked at him for a while and felt as if I was leaving something behind. *Am I doing right?* I thought. *He must stop me from doing childish things. Maybe he doesn't care for me. Why should I think of a man who is not even talking to me properly?* I was confused. And then the feeling was replaced by excitement and thrill as I reached Angad. They were ready after wearing all the required gears and were waiting for me.

"Here, wear this," Angad handed me a set of gears.

Although it was not my size, still for safety reasons, I wore the gear set given to me and signaled an ok towards my car. And then I seated myself behind Angad and he started his bike.

"You are sitting in a wrong way."

I was holding the back side of his bike to maintain my balance on that road, full of rock, mud and wet soil. I remembered Sohan. The first time I went out on a bike ride with him, I was sitting in the same manner. *You must hold me, that is the right way of sitting on a bike,* he said. I laughed and only held his shirt from both the sides of his waist. Since then I had gone multiple times on a bike ride with him, I would never feel shy holding his shirt, resting my head and body on his shoulder and back, but I would never put my arms around his waist holding him tightly.

"What happened? Are you comfortable?" Angad asked.

"Yes, I am doing well," I put my hands around him holding him to maintain my balance.

For two hours, I forgot everything. Though it was much challenging, I enjoyed it a lot. We stopped when needed and whenever we wished to see the beautiful sight. Otherwise I would hold him tight and feel like heaven, crossing the cold breeze among the mountain series. Many times I would walk for few minutes when the ascent would go steep till the time we would find an easier section of the road. Akhtar and others were staying close. Angad and I spoke with each other throughout the journey. He told me that he was from Chennai and was working in Dubai. From Dubai they had come for this trip as they love biking. I also told him so many things about my family and friends, my likes and dislikes. He was a nice man. After talking to him I came to know that he was engaged. But as he found me attractive, he offered me this ride.

"You are daring, not every Indian girl would go out with strangers in an unknown place," he said as we reached Chang La.

Chang La was the second highest motorable road after Khardung La, maintained by the Indian Army at a height of around 17500 feet. The snow cutting process was still in progress. We were waiting for Akhtar and others to come.

I smiled. "I believe in living life the way I want it. I don't want to regret for anything later. That's it," After ten minutes Akhtar and others reached. When I saw them, I handed Angad the gears set he provided me in the start of our journey and hugged him. "Thanks for everything. I would never forget this journey, all because of you."

"Same here," he kissed me on my cheeks.

I felt his beard prickling on my cheek. Never before this time, had a man kissed me except Abbu. My heartbeat was throbbing in my ears but I did not react much. I made sure that Akhtar and others were watching me from the distance.

"Bye, we will stay in touch," I moved away from him. Akhtar and rest of the people were eagerly waiting for me to share my experience with them. While having tea, I told them my overall experience. I told them about the actual thrill and difficulty faced while riding through a bike on such roads. I also complained about the stress I felt on my back and head. They asked me about Angad, I told them that he was engaged, and then they felt bad for me.

"I was not going to marry him anyway," I cleared the doubts they were having. I still had feelings for Akhtar, though it was hidden.

"Hmm, did he ask for your number?" Sonia asked.

"Yes, we have exchanged numbers and emails. He will contact me after reaching Dubai."

"Good, at least now you will not ask for a bike ride," Akhtar said, the least I expected from him.

"Yes, I am happy; I want to reach Pangong Lake as soon as possible," I took a sip of tea.

***

We started for Pangong Lake when the roads were cleared completely. Now we were descending from Chang La entering the Changthang Plateau. The plateau was one of the most beautiful natural settings known to mankind. After some time, tarmac road started which was again maintained by the BRO. As the area was again close to the actual line of control, small Army troops could be seen after every small distance.

The temperature dropped, even when it was a bright day and we saw so many frozen water bodies on our way. And then the Lake appeared. Pangong Lake was around hundred and thirty four kilometers long extended from India to Tibet. Almost forty percent of the lake was in India and the rest was in Tibet. The lake appeared as if an artist had painted it.

The ever changing hues of the Lake made it picturesque. The serene water of the lake was bright blue, sometimes changing to green, surrounded by huge white and brown mountains, etched deep down in my memory. It was surely the best place I had ever seen. Experience of the bike ride faded away as we proceeded along the sides of the Lake. Temperature was close to zero. Ahmed told us that despite being saline water, the lake freezes in winter. After travelling around twenty kilometers beside the lake, we reached our camp.

The area was less populated by humans and was much close to nature. Similar to the camp of Nubra Valley, we were given three tents in same manner. As soon as we reached, I went to washroom to get fresh. It was the third day of my periods so I was relaxed as I did not need the sanitary pads. I was already wearing a jacket over my top but the shiver was not going. So I covered my head with a shawl and wore another jacket. And then when I came out of my tent, Meenal asked me to join them for tea and evening snacks.

We sat surrounding a hot chimney, which was placed to maintain the temperature in the small dining area, which was a few meters away from our tent. We remained seated there for around twenty minutes and decided to rest for a while before dinner. As we moved out of the dining hall, Aditya and I decided to go near lake which was around half a kilometer away from our camp. Rest of the people did not join us as it was very cold.

The sun was down and the bright blue color of lake had changed to the transparent one. The lake was clear, reflecting every single particle within. We touched its water, removing our gloves, and found the water up to frozen temperature. We sat there for some time, clicked few selfies and pictures, and returned when it was totally dark. After entering our tent we saw that others were already ready for dinner.

We had not eaten anything since morning so we hurried to grab something to eat. Hot local meal served after such an amazing day was adding into our experience. I observed that though Akhtar was behaving normal with me but, he was still continuously looking at me as if he was trying to say something. I wanted to ask him what he was feeling for me. Sometimes he would look at me and hide his smile.

I wanted to search his mind in order to find the exact thing going inside him. At this point, I was not angry on him, maybe because of the place which was so romantic. *I would ask him to sleep with me and then I would clear things between us. And I did not have the fear of periods so things could be controlled once again*, I thought. After dinner, at around eight in the evening, Hemant went to sleep in their camp. Akhtar, Aditya, Vikram, Sonia, Meenal and I rested in our camp. The caretaker of the camp provided us so many hot water bags to be placed inside our bed to make it warm. This time our bed was comfortable enough to sleep, unlike those of the Nubra Valley. We were already affected by the awesome surroundings, which reflected over our conversation. We were not making fun of each others, rather we discussed about life we had faced so far. And then the topic of discussion changed into how a girl should be in nature?

Vikram was saying that a girl like me should carry some attitude with her. "I appreciate that you are bold, but you were so easily impressed by that boy, Angad."

"What would happen, if I would show attitude to people who are not going to stay with me? He just met me for few hours. If I would have shown him attitude, don't you think that he wouldn't have given a damn to me. I don't think that carrying attitude would work in such areas."

"Even I think the same way," Sonia supported me.

"Girls should not be bounded. They are meant to fly, let them enjoy it. They would eventually understand the difference between right and wrong," Akhtar said.

"I agree. Abbu also say the same thing. After Amma passed away he never stopped me for doing anything. *If you would not fall, how you would learn to rise*, he would say. And it is applicable to my brother, Shahid too," I told them how Abbu had sacrificed his needs just to make us happy and safeguard our future. "He is our father and mother, both." I was feeling nostalgic.

"You are a brave girl. Just remember to stay the same," Akhtar said.

This time he was appreciating me for the way I was. I felt good. At least he was having some opinion about me. I felt even more emotional.

"That is why she is my darling," Aditya tried to break the emotional moment.

He and Meenal were listening to us without saying anything. And then we discussed some of the secret stories of people from our office. Even Sonia, who was not from our office, joined us enthusiastically. I don't remember how the topic changed to ghosts. Meenal started sharing some of the true stories she was aware of, followed by Aditya and Vikram. Others were listening attentively. Till midnight, we discussed so many things related to ghosts and black magic.

"Honey, let's not discuss ghosts anymore, please. I won't be able to sleep otherwise," Sonia said out of fear, looking at Vikram.

We laughed and then decided to go for sleep. Akhtar also came out of the bed to leave with Vikram and Sonia. I did not say anything to stop him. I was happy at least he was talking to me, and I did not want to ruin rest of the days, so I kept quiet. Aditya decided to sleep with Meenal and I as others went.

CHAPTER 11

Leh Trip day 9

I checked time; clock showed 5:30 in the morning. I thought to call Sohan, but finding a network in my cell phone was next to impossible. I wanted to know his progress on his cricket practice matches. I also wanted to motivate him to give his best performance, but I was helpless. Over these days, I have only heard tales of his cricket matches.

Whenever I would request him to take me to one of his match, he would simply deny. *Girls should never be involved with sports, they create pressure which effect the performance,* he would say, and I would not say anything in return. I would never let his performance degrade because of me. But yes, I would definitely call him before and after his match to know the status and then he would provide me with all the details. Details including his individual score, numbers of boundaries he had hit, numbers of catches he had taken and everything else. And most importantly about the female HR he had impressed. Sometime he would send me his picture wearing his cricket gears.

"When I wear my cricket gears, I look like Virat Kohli," he said once when he was telling me about one of his cricket matches. He knew that Virat Kohli was my favorite cricketer.

"Why you took his name? Why is he involved in the discussion?"

"He is involved here because there are some people who love Virat Kohli. They just need to watch me on ground," he referred to me as a third person.

"How would they watch you playing? You never invite them to watch you perform," I complained to him.

"Ok hmmm hmmm," he ended the conversation.

There were some rules Sohan would follow at any cost. And, *not to take any girl to see his cricket match* -was one of them. *Barber shop is another location where no girl was allowed to go with him,* I reminded myself and smiled while resting on bed.

***

It was the second to last day of our trip, tomorrow morning we were going to fly back to Delhi. I was resting on Aditya lap around eight in the morning and Meenal was lying near me. Rest of the people were busy in their tent. We were waiting for one of the care takers who was going to bring hot water for us to be used in bathroom. And while waiting for that, we were discussing about the monotonous life we were going live after this trip.

"Ten to seven work, struggling back to home, eating dinner and then going for sleep so that next day again we could start for the same schedule," Aditya complained.

He was right. That was the monotonous life of IT, unless someone was able to handle it extra ordinarily, which in most cases does not happen. Though we used to hang out a lot every weekend, but the level of satisfaction we had received in this trip was beyond compare. They might not have Wi-Fi connection here, neither could they watch a 3D movie. Their lifestyle was simple yet they were happier and delightful as compared to us, who on the other hand were well furnished with all the luxury items starting from the morning alarm set in our smartphones to the hot water shower taken before bed in the night.

"Eat sleep work repeat. It's an infinite loop," I remembered Sohan.

He would always say this phrase to me whenever I would ask him to do something special. "Nothing is special, I am in a loop- eat, sleep, work and repeat," he would complained about his tedious life.

Aditya laughed. "Well said, Gul."

"I don't want to go back," I raised my eyes and looked at Aditya. I also had to face never ending EMIs, money crunches and much more similar stories back in Pune.

"Me neither."

"But we have to," Meenal interrupted us.

Why you don't agree with us Meenal I thought. *Why did she have to make us realize that we do not have any other option?*

"Hmmm ok," I ended the conversation. Somewhere in my mind, I was happy; I was going to meet Sohan after a very long time. And then I was waiting for his cricket match too, which was scheduled a day after tomorrow.

"Let's get up and get ready," Meenal said as the caretaker brought two buckets full of hot water.

We stepped outside bed and went to get fresh, and then we had to proceed for breakfast after which we would start heading back to Leh. It was a bright day today. The brisk cold wind was blowing heavily. I looked up, sun was scintillating over the crystal blue sky and then I looked straight. I saw another sky at a distance of few hundred meters away, waving slowly along with the wind. It was much more beautiful and alive. I smiled looking at the alluring view. Akhtar and others were also out of their tent, enjoying the sunlight in cold weather.

I looked at Akhtar and smiled again. He was looking fresh and energetic. So do others. I went closer to them; they were waiting for breakfast to be served. We asked to serve it outside the dining room so that we could enjoy the few last moments of this lovely trip and adore it for rest of our life. After last night, Akhtar was not bothering me. I knew that if my feeling for him was not genuine enough, it would fade away with time. *I would not expect anything from him; let him surprise me, if he wants to.* But even though I made my mind for not running behind him and it was clear that he was definitely not after me, we were still gazing at each other having conversation through our eyes. I felt as if he wanted to say so many things to me but there was something which was holding him back. His eyes were definitely going against him.

I could see the desire in his eyes. For them, I was the one who might be distracting him again and again. But I had no option to hide myself. Breakfast was served and we were ready to roll back to Leh. Ahmed told us that before going back, we would visit the place near Pangong Lake where the last scene of the movie Three Idiots had been filmed, when Kareena Kapoor Khan kisses Aamir Khan. We took out our luggage and loaded it in the car. This time Ahmed was driving slowly along the shore of the lake. We were awe-inspired by the lake which was sometimes green, sometimes blue and some other times transparent. It was playing with our eyes. We wanted to catch every possible view of the place and the lake.

"Can you see those small shelters?" Ahmed pointed at a distance.

"Yes," we replied in unison.

"That is the place where the movie had been filmed."

"Yes, you are right," I remembered the scene. "Can you stop the car? I would like to walk from here."

"Sure," he parked the car in a safe place.

We stepped out of our car and walked around a kilometer to reach the location. There was a state of tranquility received at every step I took. Aditya and I were continuously clicking pictures of each other so that later we could upload them in Facebook. The lake was surrounded by so many ducks and gulls which were adding into its beauty. We spent around an hour sitting on the shore of the lake, and at around eleven we started our journey back to Leh. The route was similar but our feelings were changed. None of us wanted to go back this time.

***

Our last destination was Magnetic Hill which was at a distance of thirty kilometers from Leh, but to reach that location and to experience the phenomena of nature that defines gravity, we had to cross Leh, as it was on the opposite side of the city. We were traveling since last five hours and had reached the outskirts of Leh. We were hungry so we decided to stop at some local restaurant to have food, meanwhile Ahmed decided to take some rest. The sun was setting down; it was pale almost losing its radiant. Cold on the other hand felt much more familiar to us. We were now used to it. After having lunch when I returned from a hand wash, other people were already settled inside the car, Akhtar was standing outside and rest of the people were laughing.

"What happened?" I saw that Aditya was sitting on Akhtar's place with Meenal and Hemant.

Vikram laughed. "Our seats are not fixed, why only Aditya will sit with you? Let Akhtar sit with you this time."

Something was not right. Maybe they sensed the silent awkwardness which was growing between Akhtar and me.

"Yes exactly. I want to stretch my legs. It is so congested in the front seat, and then you don't allow me to sit near the window. I will sit here for rest of the trip."

They surely had planned something funny, I thought.

"I will sit in my seat," Akhtar said.

But as Ahmed was waiting for us and no one moved from their seats, Akhtar looked at me. I immediately stepped inside the car and made space for him near the window, which I never did for Aditya throughout this journey. Aditya would plead me so many times but I would always ignore his request. But this time I was not able say any word to oppose.

"This is not fair. Why don't you order Akhtar to sit inside? All these days you harassed me for the window seat and now you are not uttering a single word."

"Wow. Finally we have got someone who can command Gul,"

Meenal laughed. Everyone burst into laughter.

Akhtar and I were silent. From the corner of my eye I saw him controlling his smile so that no one could notice it; I was also blushing but not reacting over the conversation Vikram and others were creating about Akhtar and me. I had observed over these days that they would not step in middle of the conversation between Akhtar and me. They would behave as if they were not around. And now they were behaving totally opposite. They were making fun of us when our chemistry no longer remained. For rest two hours, Akhtar and I behaved as if there was no one with us in the journey. All that time Vikram, Sonia, Hemant, Meenal and Aditya teased us singing various romantic songs and making different stories related to us. It finally came to an end when we reached Magnetic Hill via Leh Kargil Srinagar Highway. The place was surrounded by huge mountains with no signs of plantation over them. The place was quiet but alert as it was close to Kargil.

Magnetic Hill – Park your vehicles in the box marked on the road and experience the phenomena that defines gravity was written on a billboard near highway. The place was known to create magnetic field high enough to attract vehicles and other metal bodies.

Eager to see the effect, we stepped out of the car and Ahmed placed it inside the box and turned off the engine. The road was plain, still we watched our car moving upside slowly. We were dumbstruck. We repeated the process so many times to record it. Finally when it was getting dark, we decide to move back to our hotel. I requested Aditya to sit with me and offered him the window seat. I did not want Akhtar to feel awkward because of me.

***

On the last night of our trip we were feeling emotional. We had to start early tomorrow morning. We packed our luggage, as the flight for Delhi was scheduled early in the morning and there was only one check in counter at the airport. Apart from feeling nostalgic, I was also feeling restless because of my chest pain which was back again. Everyone was laughing as Aditya was narrating some funny incidents from his college at the dining table, but I was not. My eyes were rolling upside. I was not able to bear the pain I was going through. It was hard for me to breathe as the pain was increasing with the intake of oxygen. I was sitting on one corner of the table, Sonia was sitting on my right side and Aditya was sitting opposite to me. Everyone was looking at his direction. I tried to take few sips of water to feel a little better, but as I was not able to hold the glass, I landed up breaking it on floor. It was then everybody turned their attention towards me.

"I am sorry," I fainted. I was in my little senses but felt very difficult to react. I saw with my almost closed eyes that they were taking me to my room. They were tensed and shocked with the sudden drop in my health. I heard them talking to each other while they gently placed me on bed.

"Does anyone know what happened? Did she complain about bad health?" Akhtar asked.

I could sense that he was worried.

"No, she did not," Meenal replied.

"My chest is hurting," I managed to speak. "I need the pain killer Hemant had given to me in Nubra Valley."

"Your chest is hurting gain?" Meenal shouted.

"What do you mean again?" Akhtar shouted as soon he heard Meenal.

Apart from Meenal no one was aware about my chest pain and that was why they were shocked. I was shocked, too, as this time the intensity of the pain was damn high.

"Can I have the medicine please?"

Hemant rushed to another room and brought the medicine, Sonia immediately handed me a glass of water and helped me to take it. They were standing surrounding me, continuously seeking for answers.

"Are you ok now?" Akhtar sat next to me.

"Better," I looked at him. "It had happened previously also, but this time it was unbearable. I was not able to breathe properly."

"Why do you get the pain?"

"I actually don't know, maybe because of physical stress."

"Have you consulted any doctor yet?"

"Not yet, but now I think I need to," I closed my eyes. The medicine was definitely strong, the pain was going, but the restlessness remained for a little while.

"After getting back to Pune, consult a good physician. Now try to take some rest."

"Hmmm."

"Let's go," Akhtar said to others.

"No," I shouted. "Stay here, please, I don't want to be alone. You won't be disturbing me."

I closed my eyes to get some sleep; I heard they were talking slowly about me. Akhtar sat next to me for a while without talking to anyone. I don't remember when they went to their rooms as I slept.

CHAPTER 12

Leh Trip day 10 – supposed to be the last day

Meenal woke me up. I refused to wake up and covered myself with the homely blanket. I was feeling relaxed and did not remember that we had to leave to Delhi today. Unlike previous time when I took medicine and had a fight with Akhtar at Nubra Valley, this time I had a sound sleep. I didn't even remember what had happened last night after I fall asleep. I felt as if I had just gone to bed and only after few minutes, they were waking me up. I wanted to sleep more.

"Are you feeling well?" Akhtar asked.

"Yes, please let me sleep," I refused to come out of the blanket. My chest pain was gone.

"Ok, then Meenal is going to use your bathroom first."

"No, I will go first," I jumped out of bed. I smiled looking at him; he was certainly handling me well. Meenal laughed standing next to Akhtar.

"Good, we would start at 07:00 AM to reach airport, finish everything on time."

"Stop laughing," I looked at Meenal when Akhtar left.

"Ok, I will not laugh, but I cannot ignore everything."

She was clever; she would not say anything until it was the right time for her to intervene.

"I don't know actually but I think I like Akhtar. I am confused actually." I was genuinely confused. I did not know if it was my love for

Akhtar or infatuation, but I certainly knew that I never had this type of feelings for any other man before. So I was excited what destiny would unfold next for me.

"Hmmm, just wait and watch."

To wait and let time turn the page of my life, was the only thing I could do, because one thing was sure, that as the time would pass, I would come to know about everything. It was possible that my feelings for Akhtar could fade away over time; on the other hand it was likely possible that it could even grow stronger. I just need not to think about it too much as Sohan had told me to think like a man. "I will pack my luggage and then I will go for bath. Is that ok with you if I take another half an hour?"

"No problem Gul. Meanwhile I will do my packing."

Apart from being clever, she was also adjusting in nature. She would always adjust herself according to the situation without even complaining. I, on the other hand, would prefer in giving my point of view over situation so that better outcome could be achieved after having a fruitful discussion. I believed in confrontation over backing down. And then I would adjust to the final decision taken. As she agreed, I took out my clothes and went to take bath. While bathing I thought about Sohan. *He must be playing in his practice match, their match is scheduled tomorrow.* I wanted him to win. He would be happy like anything, which in turn would make me happy.

***

Check in line at airport was extended outside, where family and friends see off their loved ones and wish them luck for their journey. We did not expect such a huge chaos at airport. We immediately took our place in queue to avoid any further delay. Clock was showing 07:15 AM in morning and our flight was scheduled at 09:00 AM. Earlier I thought that the chaos was because of single check in counter, but later we figured out something else.

Passengers who were close to counter were shouting and they were furious. I saw that a tall man was surrounded by many passengers who were yelling at him. He was wearing white shirt and a black trouser with a same color blazer. His clothes were neatly ironed. He was also wearing a red tie which was hanging till the second last button of his shirt just above his leather belt. Above the tie his identity card was hanging, revealing that he was one of the employees from the airport authorities. He was continuously repeating the same sentence- *we have canceled all the flights due to climatic changes,* but no one was listening to him.

They were asking him same question again and again. Akhtar and Hemant went to inquire about exact issue while we remained in queue. From some of the passengers, we heard that atmospheric pressure and density had dropped a lot, which could cause airplane to crash at the time of takeoff or landing, and hence the flights have been canceled. Akhtar and Hemant added into this information that the airport authorities were ready to arrange another flight tomorrow for each destination for which flight has been canceled. They were also ready to provide accommodation till that time. *Perfect. Another day in Leh,* I thought.

"When there is no other option, why people are shouting?" I asked. "After all, it is a matter of life and death. And more importantly it is Leh. Who doesn't wants to stay here?"

"They are angry because they have emergency. Few are not well enough to stay in this atmosphere. Others are having meetings and other important tasks to complete, so they all want to leave," Akhtar answered.

I did not imagine that there was another side of the coin as well; I was more concerned about what we could do now. I saw that people around us were disturbed; they were planning how to get back to their cities. Few were inquiring if a road journey was possible, few were blaming government; another few were sharing stories of similar incidents when their flights were canceled along with the effect it had created, and some other people, like us, were happy.

"Are we going to stay?" Sonia asked.

She was worried about our connecting flight from Delhi which was scheduled tonight.

"Let people settle down first, then we will talk to that man. In any case we are not going to Delhi today for sure," Akhtar replied.

We discussed that airport authority must provide us flight ticket from Leh to Pune, otherwise it could be problematic for us to reach Pune from Delhi with no reservations in hand. Also there should be a cab facility to and fro airport. The tall man agreed, as he had no other option but to entertain passengers. But he asked us to cancel the connecting flight from Delhi to Pune and to provide the refunded amount back to them. In return he also agreed to provide us accommodation, flight ticket to Pune and a cab service to drop us to the hotel and pick us from there tomorrow. After everything was set, we moved to the Hotel Grand Dragon.

The hotel was only few kilometers away from airport. It was an eco-friendly substitute of luxury offering so many services including coffee shop, restaurant, gardens, gym, spa, free Wi-Fi, conference hall and much more. Our cab driver told us that whenever there was some movie shooting arranged in Leh, all the celebrities would stay at this hotel. It was one of the famous hotels among celebrities and politicians. It was indeed.

Its ambiance was reflecting a grand impression of high class opulence. The halls, restaurant and gym were big enough to accommodate more than hundred people at a time. Rooms were spacious and clean up to my expectations. We were provided with two rooms, each having so many facilities including a desk with a lamp, a modern bathroom, a mini fridge, natural spring water to drink, coffee maker, telephone, hair dryer, LED TV, huge fluffy king size double bed and extra cozy blankets. The room was open from one side with a balcony facing magnificent Khardung La Pass Mountains, Leh Palace and Shanti Stupa. It acted as a cherry on top of the cake of our Leh trip.

*****

"I did not go for practice match. My whole body is hurting," Sohan replied to me on call.

As another gesture of high class living, the hotel was also providing us good network coverage so I called Sohan to ask him about his performance in his trail matches and to inform him about the climatic changes at Leh due to which our flight was canceled. I was shocked as he did not go for practice.

"Why? You have your match scheduled tomorrow. You must practice hard."

"I know that I must practice hard, but I should not over exercise my body so that it would refuse to perform tomorrow. I want to take rest to perform well."

When a human body was suddenly exposed to exercise, the muscles get stiff and refuse obvious body movements with a continuous muscle pain that does not go away easily. Sohan was involved in a physical activity after a very long time. As a result his body was hurting as it was not used to it.

"What if even after taking rest also you are not able to perform?" I realized that it was not the correct way to motivate him.

He shouted. "Gul, I have told you multiple times not to say anything bad about my cricket or my performance."

He was angry. I knew that he would never appreciate me getting too involved with his sports, the sport which meant a lot to him and was his passion.

"I did not mean it. You know, it was a slip of tongue."

"Whatever it was, Gul. You know that I am very concerned about it. You also know that I never inform anyone about anything which is important to me in advance until it is done. Be it my cricket match or my travel schedule or anything else. But I told you because I never expect anything bad from you." I listened to him silently as I knew I had hurt him. "You also know that before any cricket match or journey I only call my parents, no other human is involved. They would be the only one aware of my schedules. And then I started telling you about these things knowing that you are genuine. And you are saying like this?"

"Because I really don't wish anything bad for you. It was by mistake. I am sorry, please understand." I pleaded to him.

"Enough, Gul, I don't want any other discussion. I am feeling very bad." He disconnected.

Oh My God! What I have done, I thought. I sat on the sofa placed near reception area connecting it to the huge green and colorful garden. Akhtar and other went to take a tour of the hotel and I remained to call Sohan. But instead of motivating him, I made him angry. Apart from being handsome he was good and soft spoken. He would never appreciate anyone saying any bad words for others or even for themselves. *If you cannot speak good, at least try not to speak bad,* he told me once when I was in need of leaves and my manager was not approving it. *I will go sick and take sick leaves,* I said when he warned me for the usage of my words.

Getting sick was obviously not a good thing to wish. *You never know which part of your speech is going to be true, speak well always so that good will happen always,* he said. He was right, after that day I always try to speak well, but today it happened unintentionally. I knew that he was very protective about his family, cricket and travel. But I did not mean to hurt them in any way. Why would I? He was my best friend and I would always pray for his wellbeing but he would never understand. *Calm down, he must be angry. Call him after sometime and tell him sorry once again. He would definitely understand,* I thought. *Yes, I am also his best friend. And he himself said that he doesn't think that I would wish anything bad for him. It was my slip of tongue and nothing bad will happen to him because of this, he would surely play well resulting in their victory. He is a champion and few words cannot make him fall.*

***

That tall man had come to the hotel to collect documents and other information from passengers for whom he had to arrange flight tickets. After lunch, we went to one of the meeting rooms where he was sitting. The room was big enough to accommodate thirty people at a time. A big table made of glass was placed at the center of the room surrounded by many movable chairs. A huge white board was fixed on one wall of the room which could be used for explaining data and graphs over the meeting. The opposite wall was fixed with a big LED TV which was currently switched off. Three telephone handsets were placed over the table to entertain conference call facility and each chair was provided with a small water bottle to drink water and a notepad with a pen to note down important things related to the discussion. The man was sitting with his laptop opened to record everything he was doing, along with two of his assistants who were acting on his command. The other two were also wearing clothes similar to that of the tall men. As we entered he asked for our documents required to make the reservations, and just after we provided him required documents, he immediately went to complete the procedures. We canceled our ticket from Delhi to Pune and provided him the amount which would get refunded to us later. He, on the other hand, provided us two boarding passes each, one for the Leh to Delhi flight and another one for Delhi to Pune. He told us to reach airport before six tomorrow morning as the flight for Delhi was at 7:30 AM. He also told us to directly proceed without check in as he had already marked us checked in. *Great,* we said and greeted him goodbye.

Later in evening I called Sohan once again but he did not respond. I sent him a message asking for apology with a sad smiley, but again he did not respond. I got a little upset. Sometimes, I would fail to understand his behavior. He knew that I did not say anything intentionally; still he was avoiding me as if I have committed some crime. This was the first time he was not responding to me for such a long time, otherwise he would definitely talk to me whether it would be his mistake or mine. *Will he never speak with me? What would I do if he would be always angry? Should I call him once again?* My mind was surrounded by so many questions. I wanted to call him but I was self-bound. I knew that he would get irritated when he would be pushed for all those things he did not want to do. Calling him again and again when he was not responding was one of the things. *If I did not respond to your first call means that even if you call me a hundred times, I would not respond.* He angrily told me once when he was in a meeting and I called him three times because I was going for an appraisal discussion with my manager and I needed his words to gain more confidence. He was very busy that time, still after my third call he messaged me that he would call me back. But this time a whole day had passed and he was not responding to me at all. I surely did not want to irritate him more, so I did not call him.

I went inside one of the rooms where Aditya and Hemant were watching TV. Akhtar, Vikram, Sonia and Meenal had gone to market for shopping and I did not know what on earth they were buying which was taking so long. After three hours they arrived and started showing us things they had brought. Vikram had brought a black jacket which was looking like leather but it was made of some other fabric. Aditya also wanted the same type of jacket so he asked to go to the market again. Vikram and Sonia wanted to rest so Meenal and Hemant agreed to go with him. After Aditya, Hemant and Meenal went to the market, Vikram and Sonia went to other room to take a little rest before we could go for dinner. Akhtar and I were left alone in our room. He was sitting on one corner of the bed and I was sitting on the other corner. No one was talking to each other, trying to fully concentrate on TV, but I was sure that he was pretending as if he was watching TV like me. I was watching TV but genuinely I was thinking about him. I wanted him to talk to me, to hold me like he did on previous nights and to come closer to me, but he was doing none of it. I waited for a while just to let him take the first step. When he did nothing, out of frustration I switched off TV.

"Why you switched it off?" he looked at me.

"It was boring." Nothing could frustrate a woman more than the ignorance of her man. In that case she would do anything to grab his attention, but at the same time she would behave as if his ignorance was not bothering her. I did the same thing; I did not tell him the exact reason behind switching off TV.

"Then what is not boring?"

"We can talk with each other," I gave him an option out of the many things we could do. "I am very good at it." I got off the bed and then moved towards his corner of the bed where I sat facing him. I was wearing a tomato red color top having a V shape neck. The neck was deep so I had worn black spaghetti inside it, which was peeping out from my top covering my cleavage. I was wearing a black track pant which was covering my legs. I looked at him for a while. He was sitting on bed with his legs covered inside blanket and his upper body leaning against wall.

"I have a better option." He folded his legs and came closer to me.

I gave him an amorous glance, knowing that it was enough to express myself and that he was clever enough to understand it. He came closer and with his right hand touched my neck and gently moved it behind my ears and pulled me towards him. With the flow I went closer to him till the time there was no space between us. I closed my eyes. His right hand was now resting on my left shoulder; soon he placed his left hand on my right shoulder, holding my neck as if he was holding a newborn baby. He ran both his hands to drop my top off my shoulders and then he moved his hands over my bosom towards my waist and took them inside my top without taking his eyes off me. My whole body started to shiver and breathe with him. Then he unhooked my bra. With both hands I held him around his shoulder. He leaned towards me making me fall over bed and then he kissed me on my neck. An amatory ran through my body when he kissed me. I moved my hand on his back holding his shirt. After few kisses on my neck he looked at me.

"Gul, you are like a rose, so fresh and beautiful."

I smiled getting shy for the compliment he had made, but I maintained my eye contact with him.

"*Ladki sundar ho na ho, namak honi chahiye,*" I meant that beauty isn't enough, a girl should be the spice, the seasoning in life without which everything was bland. He laughed.

I knew he would laugh because I did the same thing when Sohan told me this. Sohan said once when a girl was playing with her hair near Kooka shop and he was impressed by the grace she was displaying. "*Ladki sundar ho na ho, namak honi chahiye.*"

"Well, then you are a perfect combination of spice and beauty."

Akhtar came closer to me to kiss me on my lips. I lifted my chin to help him. He kissed me for a long time making tingling sensation on my tummy. While he was kissing me I managed to unbutton his shirt. He was slim. His body was covered with less hair and he was much fairer from inside. He took his shirt off and then struggled with my clothes. He had already unhooked my bra so it took very short time for him to make me naked after he removed my track pants. He looked at me with orgasmic eyes. I was lying in bed almost naked in front of him. Without losing any time he again kissed me, this time more intensely. Then he started removing his jeans when Vikram knocked.

Akhtar, Gul, let's go for dinner.

CHAPTER 13

"Yes Abbu, now I will try to save money. I will not shop unnecessarily; I will not go to parties, right?" Abbu was worried that I would never be able to save money and that I would inherit his bad fortune.

"We need to my child. You will understand this later."

"I understand, Abbu. It is just like I don't want to spoil my present worrying about my future, which no one can predict. But still I would do as you would say, don't worry," I realized that there was no end of this conversation.

"Ok, take rest now."

"Tell me more," Chaudhary said the moment I disconnected my call. She had returned early from office. Throughout the time I was speaking with Abbu, she was sitting in front of me to listen more about my trip. I was sharing my experience since the time she had returned. She was listening and enjoying as if some movie was playing in front of her. She told that she could imagine the scenery and joy we had witnessed. I told her so many things from the bike ride with an unknown man to the last day stay at hotel Grand Dragon, but I did not tell her anything about Akhtar. I was not sure and nothing was official, so I thought that there was no point in revealing things. *I must wait for the right time,* I thought.

***

Last seen today at 9:00 AM. I checked Sohan's Whatsapp, he wasn't online since morning. I wanted to call him and ask him about his match, but I was upset because he did not respond to my calls and messages. Since the time I had met him this was the first time that before his match, I did not call him and wish him luck. And this was also the first time when he did not call me after his match and provided me details about his day. I was not feeling good, though Akhtar's Whatsapp messages were surely diverting me. But every second I was thinking of Sohan.

Akhtar and I were talking casually to each other, asking each other about our likes and dislikes, playing silly games and sending cute selfies to each other. He was much more talkative as compared to the days in Leh, but still he was not talking about his feelings for me. He was telling me about what had happened in office today; he was the only one who had gone to office among us who had returned from Leh. Vikram, Hemant, Meenal and I were resting at home while Aditya went to his hometown for an extended holiday. Akhtar told that our group had become famous in office just because we had made our plan a big success.

From managers to team members, everyone was asking him about our trip. He showed them so many pictures which he had taken from his mobile. He also told me that so many people were asking him about our next trip so that they could join us. He was happy while narrating all these things, I was also feeling happy as those were one of the best days of my life, and I was discussing it with a man I was falling for. My happiness increased even more when Sohan called me. It was around 10:00 PM, I looked at my mobile screen and disconnected his call, texting him, *don't talk to me*. But I did not mean that; I was just trying to gain some more attention from him.

After two minutes he messaged me on Whatsapp with an image. I opened the image he had sent and felt remorse. It was Sohan's image. He was sitting on a sofa near a reception area. The picture had been taken recently as it was dark outside window where he was sitting. He was wearing a white trouser made with some high elastic material and a long sleeved shirt of same color and fabric. He was a wicket keeper, too, other than the second opening batsman. That's why he would always prefer long sleeve shirt in order to avoid abrasion while diving for the ball. His clothes and shoes were dirty reflecting that he had dived a lot to stop the ball behind the wickets. His left hand was holding his mobile phone from which he tried to talk to me a moment earlier, and his right hand was resting on his lap covered with a plaster. Tears rolled down my cheeks because I felt that somewhere I was the reason behind his injury. It was more hurting because he was smiling on that image. Though he was injured, there was a spark on his eyes as if getting injured during a match was a matter of pride for a sportsman. Somehow I gathered all my courage to face him and made a call to him.

"I am sorry," I burst into tears the moment he picked my call. I could never imagine anything bad happening to him, especially when it had happened when I slipped my tongue and unintentionally said something bad to him. I just wanted to go back in time and change everything I had said.

"Why are you crying? It's just a small ligament tear."

Although he was furious on me yesterday, he acted normal today without blaming me for anything.

"How it happened?" He told me that his team won the toss and decided to bat first. They set a target of one hundred and eighty runs in twenty overs, out of which he had contributed with eighty five runs being not out. I was again proud of him. He was a very good batsman and I knew that though he did not practice much, he could play cricket with his eyes closed. Cricket was surely running in his blood.

"So you got fractured during the second innings."

"Yes, when we were fielding."

He said that during the twelfth over, he changed fielding for the right hand batsman who had recently came for batting after their fifth batsman got run-out. He removed the first and second slip with confidence that the batsman would not score any runs near the slips or gully, but the batsman did it in his first ball, and to save that boundary, Sohan took a dive and felt a stroke of pain on his right shoulder which almost killed him. The match was halted as he was injured but he decided to play rest of the match after taking little physiotherapy from their doctor.

"And guess what, we won the match with four wickets and fifty two runs and I was given the man of the match," his voice tone reflected the command he had on cricket.

"Love you for that," I appreciated him. "But are you mad enough to risk yourself. Why didn't you replace yourself with some other player and went to the doctor?"

"For cricket, yes I am mad. I cannot leave it in between. This is nothing, even after the match, I rode my bike back to home."

"What? Now this is insane."

"It was not hurting at that time but then it started getting swollen and it was getting difficult to move my hand, so I came to doctor."

"Why didn't you call me? I would have joined you to the hospital."

"It's ok. I came with my roommate. I cannot ride a bike."

"Hmmm, what did doctor say?"

"She said that one ligament from my shoulder joint has been torn. It could take more than eight weeks to heal properly. By that time I need to cover my shoulder with a splint and should do no physical exercise."

"*Ahaan*, you got assistance from a female doctor. Lucky you," I tried to lighten the moment, but I got worried as eight weeks would be a long period to see him like this.

"She was in her fifties." He clarified that he did not have any lucky moments with the doctor.

I laughed. "That is sad. Can I ask you something?"

"Yes, please. Go ahead,"

"Are you upset on me? Do you think I could be blamed for all that has happened to you?"

"No I would not blame you," he took no time to answer. "But I would again tell you to speak good always."

"Yes, I would definitely try. I am sorry," I felt bad for him.

"It's ok. I will hang up now. It is getting late and we need to go back home."

"Hmmm, take care and ask me if something is required from my side." But I knew that he would not ask for anything. He could take care of himself even in the worst situation of his life. I wanted to take care of him these days, maybe that way I would feel a little less guilty, but I could not force him on this until he would feel that it was required. I was lost in my thoughts about Sohan when Shikha called me; I had not spoken to her since a long time as after her marriage I was not disturbing her much. But she was a darling to me. We need not speak to each other all the time, but when we would, we would break all the limits. This was the right time to speak to her.

"Hello, how are you?" I responded to her call. My voice was still breaking.

"I am good, but what happened to you?" she realized that I was not well.

I told her everything that I said to Sohan in Leh and then what happened to him in his match. She told me to talk to her husband, Ankit. Ankit and Shikha both knew about Sohan. Ankit was also a good friend to me and he was also a cricketer, that's why Shikha would have thought that Ankit could guide me well. First, he appreciated Sohan's efforts to save few runs.

"Only a true sportsman does that."

He also told me that what happened to Sohan was not my fault but, yes, I should not speak anything bad about anyone. He was taking Sohan's side here, guiding me to be a better human being. He and Shikha then asked me about my Leh trip in order to divert my mood. I told them my overall experience. I also asked them how their married life was going. After Shikha's wedding we did not speak much, so this conversation was full of things which helped me a lot to boost myself.

***

I was waiting outside my apartment since last ten minutes when Sohan came. He was wearing a white t-shirt and black faded jeans with same slipper, which once hit that fat uncle near Kooka shop. The sleeves of his t-shirt were folded two times as usual, making a remark of his strong biceps, although one was covered with a splint. Whenever we would meet, I would observe that all the girls who would cross us would glance at him. His dress sense, fit body and cute smile would always attract people, especially girls.

Then he would also get a chance to flaunt himself and Kooka shop was one of the best places in Baner to do that as it was always full of crowd, who were mostly young. This time I was not waiting for him at the Kooka shop. A moment earlier around 08:00 PM, he asked me to wait for him outside my apartment. He mentioned that he had gone to the barber shop and while returning to his home he would meet me. His face was clean shaved and his hair was cut shorter than the usual size he would prefer. Few hair particles were still sticking on his neck making him uncomfortable. He smiled looking at me; I did not return the smile because I did not want to see him like this. Once, when his left ear was paining a lot and he wasn't able to do anything, I forcefully asked him to visit a doctor as I was unable to see him suffer. Today he was suffering because of me.

I was not feeling well, my chest pain was disturbing me again and I was feeling much weaker. I was somehow able to manage it when I was in office but since the time I returned, I was doing nothing but resting in my room. When Sohan called me, I thought to tell him that I cannot come to meet him, but then as I had not seen him since a long time, I agreed. Moreover, I would never say no to him whenever he would call me to meet him. Even if we would have a fight and I would not be speaking to him, he would call me asking to come at the Kooka shop and I would go as if nothing happened between us. Then he would make me laugh by telling various stories, buy me Kooka, make fun of me and spy on my mobile screen sometimes. Today our meeting was different; we both were seeing each other unlike other days. I was unable to talk to him because I was in pain. The pain of seeing him injured.

"I am going home tomorrow, that's why I called you to meet me."

I was not surprised; I knew that going home would be the best course of action for him. His home was the place where he would be taken utmost care. Knowing that his parents would also be tensed about him, I did not feel sad when he told me that he was going. Otherwise I would feel unhappy listening that he wanted to go to his hometown, because for that much period of time I would not see him.

"That's really nice." It was hard for me to breathe, but I did not express anything to him.

"I went to office today and my leaves are approved, so I would stay at home for a long time."

"Long time means how much time?" Although he was going home for a good reason, I wanted to know for how long I would not see him.

"It's not fixed, depends on the healing, so I can't say exactly."

"Still, you will be there for ten days, a month two months. There must be something you would have said in your office." I forced him to let me know the exact time for which he would be gone.

"Currently it's a month, but I can extend it if needed."

"You will get well soon, don't worry," I smiled. He smiled even broader. "How did you come?"

"I came walking."

"Hmmm, you should leave now. Go home and take rest."

"Yes, I have to do a lot of things. I have to pack my luggage, I have to book my ticket too."

"Oh, do you need any help?" I asked, but I knew he would say no.

"No. I will manage."

"Ok. Leave now and please take care of yourself," I got emotional. He just smiled in return. I went near parking area to call elevator, reached fifth floor, somehow managed to ring doorbell and the moment Chaudhary opened door, I collapsed. I was not able to reply anything to Chaudhary. She was continuously trying to gain my senses back but nothing was helping her. I could see that she was panicking as she was alone and she did not know what happened to me. Tears rolled down her cheeks out of tension. She was calling my name again and again.

Gul, wake up. Please wake up Gul.

***

"I don't know anything, she came back home and fell down the moment I opened door for her." When I opened my eyes Chaudhary was explaining Kishan what happened exactly.

"I am myself unable to understand what happened to her, she was doing well in office, although she was a little dull, but I thought it must be because of the exertion of their trip," Kishan replied to Chaudhary.

I figured out that I was not in my apartment; it was an unknown civil place full of lights and sterile smell. Number of people were lying in rows of beds. The room was equipped with so many modern appliances related to medical emergencies. There were numbers of windows and doors covered with light blue curtains. Many people were crying because of their pain and they were being consoled by their relatives and friends. Doctors and nurses in light blue uniform matching to the color of curtains were examining various patients. One of which was trying to read heartbeat in my chest using his stethoscope. He was concentrating hard listening to my heartbeat and was mumbling something to himself when I looked at him. He was an old man, neatly dressed with white shirt and black pant covered with a light blue apron. His head was almost bald; few gray hair present here and there on his head were combed properly. His hands were shivering while moving the stem of his stethoscope over my chest. He was changing volume and mode of the stethoscope at various locations to examine my heartbeat properly. Then he would stop for a while, think something and then he would again start listening to my heartbeat.

"How old is she?" he looked at me but asked Kishan. "Hello, I believe now you can clear some of my doubts," he removed earpiece of his stethoscope from his ears.

Kishan and Chaudhary immediately paid attention towards me. I tried to smile looking at them, my chest was still hurting and it was still hard for me to breathe.

"Yes, maybe I can."

"Is it hard to breathe?"

I nodded.

"Do you have regular chest pain when it is hard for you to breathe?"

I nodded again. Kishan and Chaudhary were trying to figure out what was going on.

"Hmmm, I see. Do you feel weak or tired after doing any activity?"

To my surprise he was asking all those things I was encountering these days. "Yes, many times and sometimes I also feel nausea," I finally complained to someone who knew how I was feeling. He patted on my head while I was lying on one of the hospital beds.

"Please get her admitted in Ruby Hall Clinic. I need to be sure of what I would speak," he looked at Kishan and Chaudhary.

They both looked at him with dumb reactions.

"Is everything alright?" Kishan asked after some time.

I also wanted to ask the same question.

"Yes, don't worry. Please get her admitted under my care and get this test done." He wrote something on his prescription pad and gave it to Kishan. "Also, buy these medicines for her, it would be helping her to sleep properly. Jyoti will explain you how to take these medicines," he gave the prescription to a nurse standing close to him. Then he looked at me. "I will see you tomorrow."

***

I had been given the medicines prescribed by that old man. One of the nurses from Ruby Hall Clinic told us that his name was Dr. Jain and he was a cardiologist. While we were coming to this hospital, I discussed with Kishan about the settlement we would need to do after getting discharged from hospital. He was aware of my financial condition so he told me that he would try his level best to get everything covered under medical insurance that was done for us by our organization. I was lying on one of the beds in casualty ward while Kishan went to make arrangements for my admission. When he returned he informed me that all the settings have been done and I would be given a private room in a while. He also told me that the lady in charge of the accounts section informed him about various schemes which were covered under our health insurance. He told me that under those schemes, I would be only paying taxes to the hospital. My tension was relieved after hearing this piece of information from him and I was ready to stay at the hospital forever. Now it was the time for us to focus on other things. He told me that everyone from office went to a shock when Chaudhary called him and informed him about my bad health.

"Were you in office when she called you?"

"Yes, I was about to leave when she called me, so I went directly to Baner from office."

"Who else did you inform about my health?" I wanted to know whether Akhtar knew about this.

"No one as of now. Hemant and others told me to inform them. Thanks for reminding me, I need to call them." He went outside the casualty ward dialing Hemant's phone number through his mobile phone.

I searched for my mobile phone but I found it nowhere. Before Kishan could return, a nurse came asking for me. They were ready to shift me to the private room. My chest pain was gone as I had taken medicines a while ago and I was feeling sleepy because of it. The nurse told me to sit down on a wheelchair so that she could take me to my room. I did as she said. I was taken out of the casualty ward towards patient elevator when Kishan joined me. He told me that Hemant and others would be coming to see me in half an hour. Then I asked him about my mobile phone and he told me that it was with Chaudhary only.

"Did you inform Abbu?" I asked him. I wanted not to tell him anything unless things were clear. He would take tension which would result in his own bad health.

"No I did not. Do you want me to call him?"

"Let's wait for tomorrow till the doctor says anything."

We entered the room which was located on ninth floor. There was a patient bed in middle touching one wall of the room, surrounded by a sofa on one side and a metal shelf with wheels on its leg on the other side. The shelf was most probably placed to keep medicines and other related stuffs of the patient. The bed was clean, covered with white bed sheet. A blue blanket and a pillow with white pillow cover were kept over it. Fourth wall of the room was occupied by a LED TV and next to it was an attached washroom. The moment we entered this room Kishan jumped over sofa and searched for TV remote and switched on one of the music channels. I lay down on bed almost ready to sleep. The maid brought dustbin and kept it on right side of my bed. She also showed me a switch which I needed to press just in case I would need something.

"You have room service on your call, madam."Kishan tried to tease me and I smiled.

"I did not want this type of service," I felt a little low. Somewhere in my mind, I knew that my pain was severe.

"Don't worry, everything will be fine."

He opened door when someone knocked it. Hemant and Meenal had come. My eyes searched everywhere for Akhtar but he was nowhere. The moment they entered, they started asking me questions about what had happened, what did the doctor say and why am I hospitalized. And when Kishan was answering them, they started making fun of me.

I laughed on one of their jokes and did not say anything. I knew that they were trying to make things easier for me. After sometime a nurse and a doctor on duty came. The nurse was holding a file with my name written on it and blood a pressure gauze. The doctor was holding a stethoscope. They both entered room to measure my blood pressure.

"Your blood pressure is normal," said the doctor looking at me and went.

The nurse noted down the figure on my file and then took out a plastic band and wrapped it around my left wrist. It had my name written on it along with my room number 902 where I was staying. We were laughing on some joke when nurse asked to bring few things from medicine counter. When asked by us she told that depending upon result of my medical tests I might undergo an operation, so we need to be prepared.

"What? I mean no one told us this thing" I shouted on her.

"What happened to her?" Hemant asked.

"Sir, she had been advised for a CT scan of her heart. After seeing the report, Dr. Jain would decide if she needs an operation or not."

"But why, what had happened? Kishan did you ask Dr. Jain about all these things?" Hemant stopped her and started asking questions.

I was also shocked, I started feeling that something bad had happened to me. Meenal came next to me holding my hand to provide me strength.

"Madam, can you please tell us in detail why is she admitted?"

"Well, as per Dr. Jain, her symptom seems like those of a patient of Coronary Artery Disorder. But he would only be sure after looking at her CT scan report. In that case she might need an operation as Dr. Jain speaks to the doctor on duty. So we hope for the best and prepare for the rest."

"Coronary, what is that?" I asked.

"Coronary Artery Disorder it is. Dr. Jain would be able to explain you that in a better way," she turned towards Kishan and Hemant. "Please bring these things from medicines counter. I need to put her on saline," she handed the prescription to them.

"Ok, we will bring these medicines."

I looked at Meenal. "Coronary Artery Disorder," I said with a sense of severity.

CHAPTER 14

"Can you see these red veins?" Dr. Jain asked us after taking out a chart describing heart anatomy in detail.

Kishan and I were sitting in his consultation room. Kishan had come from office to check on me and to meet my doctor. Ruby Hall Clinic was not far from our office. Though I was staying alone in hospital, every now and then someone from office was coming to see me except Akhtar. I did not even have my mobile phone. Chaudhary told Kishan that she would bring it today evening when she would return from office; otherwise I would have called Akhtar. I wanted to speak to him but I was scared to inquire about him from anyone. Then I was having no update about Sohan too. He would have reached Lucknow by this time. Above all these people, I was worried for Abbu. I did not know how I would tell him about my bad health. I had seen him crying like a baby during those days when Amma was ill. I surely did not want to put him on any grief again. It was afternoon when Dr. Jain called us after the result of my CT scan was ready. I was already feeling like a patient since yesterday, as I had not eaten anything, and every other nurse was either injecting something in my body or was taking out blood from every possible nerve of my body.

"*Yes*," both of us answered his question.

"These are the left coronary arteries and these are the right ones," he pointed towards the left and right side of the heart. "Their job is to supply oxygenated blood to the heart."

Kishan and I listened patiently. And then he took out my CT scan sheets. *Oh no, not these,* I thought. My heart started beating fast. I could hear the lub dub sound of my heartbeat through my ears. Suddenly my mind released a whole lot of dopamine hormone and my circulatory system started working properly as if there was no problem at all.

"It's ok, I am fine. Let's go dada," I stood up from chair. I did not want to hear anything. I was having a very strong feeling that things were not right with me. I just wanted to run away from that place. They both looked at me. Dr. Jain sympathetic though.

"Did you inform your parents that you are here?" Dr. Jain asked.

I told him that I am a single parent child and that my mother died a long back when I was small. And that it depends on the result of my test whether we should inform Abbu. My voice chocked while I told him about all these things. I remembered the time when Amma was ill. We were so helpless, still Abbu tried every possible thing to save Amma's life, but the result was not in our favor. Since then he was taking utmost care of his family so that no one would get sick. And then there I was, always ready to disappoint him.

"You should call him," he advised after listening to me.

"Is everything alright?"

"You are suffering from Coronary Artery Disorder. Your left arteries are blocked causing you problem in breathing and chest pain, because the left part of your heart is not receiving blood properly. This could also cause heart attack if not taken seriously. But don't worry, you will be alright."

I did not know how to react. I sat there without saying anything. A huge storm battered me from inside but there was no tear in my eyes. I felt as if someone was playing a double headed drum on my chest. I was not able to hear anything, not able to say anything. I was choked as if blood had stopped reaching every other part of my body.

"What should we do now, doctor?" Kishan broke the silence.

"She was already prepared for an operation as I have guided the nurse and doctors here. All her tests are done; she can be operated any time. But it will be your decision."

"Can you please tell us in detail?"

"Sure. She will undergo an angioplasty in which we will clear the blockage from her veins, and then we would discharge her in two, three days. But then she needs complete bed rest for around a month. Then she could go back to her normal routine."

I was still dumbstruck. I was only able to think about Abbu. *Why I had to put him on this situation,* I thought. *I was not able to help him financially and now this bullshit happened. Shame on me, such a bad*

98

child I am, cannot even take care of myself. Oh my god, I ruined everything. He would be so upset on me.

"Great, we have so many parties down the line to chill out. Gul, you better get well soon and get ready for the fun, dear," Kishan showed no signs of worry on his face.

I have always appreciated Kishan for being around. He would not motivate by saying any motivational quotes or putting things emotionally, but would rather crack the funniest joke ever possible. When he would be around even the darkest night would turn out to be the funniest one. He was a great helper and a great brother indeed.

I laughed. "Yes why not. But can you please make sure that I do not lose the kohl from my eyes while I am here in hospital?"

He laughed holding his stomach as if I wasn't serious about my kohl.

"Sure madam, do you need body massage and spa too? Can we leave doctor? Otherwise she would keep demanding things and then you would have to arrange whole of a beauty parlor for her here in hospital."

"Few more minutes please. I need to know her family medical history."

And then he asked me various medical questions related to me, my parents and grandparents for better understanding of my case. I was glad to have him as my doctor.

***

I held my mobile phone for around one hour but could not gather courage to call Abbu. Chaudhary was back from her office and came to meet me at hospital. She was shocked hearing about my report and hence the operation. Kishan, Hemant, Meenal, everyone had come to hospital to see me, but not Akhtar. Finally when I asked, I was told that he had gone to Mumbai for some very important business deal to represent our organization and that he was unaware about my illness. No one told him this thing otherwise he would have surely proposed someone else to attend this meeting. He had messaged me on Whatsapp though. Out of which first few were simple *Hi* and *Hello* followed by *busy?* Followed by, *please ping me once you are free, I want to talk,* again followed by *Are you upset on me?* And the last message was a sad smiley.

There were messages from other people too. Sohan did also message me the usual one he would always do while traveling home. It was just those three words describing everything about his well-being and happiness. *I am home.* He did also call me two times as usual, one before leaving Pune and another after reaching Lucknow. I knew that he would call me again late night to make me jealous, how good he had been treated at home and what other things happened during his journey. And then he would tell me that he wants to go back to Lucknow anyhow as he doesn't feel alive in Pune, and all his friends and family are there only. I would end up complaining as if I am no one to him, and he would change the topic dramatically.

"It's ok. Call him. We have to inform him anyway. Then only we can decide when you can be operated," Kishan looked at me understanding my dilemma.

We had already booked Abbu's and Shahid's bus ticket for tonight. I just needed to inform them so they could be here tomorrow morning but I was a coward to call them. I just held my mobile phone after opening Abbu's contact information. Finally, I dialed his number.

"Hello," Abbu picked up my call after four rings.

It was around 7 PM, he must be preparing dinner, and maybe that's why he responded late.

"Abbu," I burst into tears. Till now when so many people were coming to sympathize with me for my bad health and praying for my fast recovery, I held my feelings intact. I gave them a strong gesture that I was good and everything would be fine, but I had a fear of losing my control in terms of Abbu. He was my weakest link. I would do stupid things, I would not follow any of the rituals which I was supposed to follow, which would make him angry on me, but on the other hand I was ready to do anything to make him happy, to bring a pride on his heart.

"Gul, what happened? Why are you crying?"

I cried even louder. Kishan took the mobile phone from my hand and went outside our room to speak to Abbu. Chaudhary immediately came to hug me, I sobbed under her arms for a long time without saying anything. Others were trying to make me calm but it wasn't helping. I usually don't cry, especially not in front of Abbu. I knew that he would worry about me so I would always ignore him whenever I would be in a sad mood. I would mostly call Sohan all those times and cry over phone, whereas he would laugh listening to my sobbing voice.

"Do you people understand that she is a heart patient?" A nurse came in shouting. "Why this room is full of many sentiments? And do you know that only one person is allowed with the patient?"

Everyone tried to hide behind everyone else as children used to hide themselves when they were caught by the teacher or parents red handed.

"It's ok, I am fine," I wiped my tears.

"We will decide that you are fine or not. Five minutes, I want everyone out of this room." She gave us warning and went.

"So bossy she is. I don't like her," Everyone laughed after listening to me. I did too but I was worried why Kishan was taking time to return. It was around thirty minutes before when I called Abbu and Kishan went outside to speak to him. Chaudhary and others were deciding who would stay with me each night for the next two-three days and they were fighting with each other, as usual, on small things like who would bring meals for me, who would go to Baner in order to bring my clothes and other important stuff. They were also fighting discussing what we would be doing when I would get discharge from hospital.

"On top of the list, tomorrow we all will go to the Iskon temple to pray for her fast recovery," Kishan entered room.

"Sure," everyone said. He had always believed in Lord Krishna and it was obvious that he would never forget him on such occasions. Then he told us that he had fixed everything, Abbu and Shahid were ready, and they would be leaving at 10 PM and would reach Pune tomorrow at around twelve noon. He also told us that after talking to Abbu, he went to meet doctor to inform them that we were ready for the operation, and as only morning slot was available, they would operate me in morning before Abbu would arrive.

"At what time will they operate me?" I encountered mixed feelings. This was the first time when I was undergoing any operation, so I was excited but at the same time I was scared as getting operated was not a good thing to get excited about.

"At 9:30 AM. The operation will take around two hours, so by the time uncle will come, you will be still in Operation Theater, I guess," Kishan answered.

"Two hours?" Two hours seemed like an eternity to me. If someone would have asked me to get ready for a party or an event, two hours would have passed before the snap of the moment. *Turant se bhi pehle,* I thought and smiled remembering Sohan.

"Why are you smiling?" Chaudhary asked me.

"Nothing, it was just a thought."

***

I woke up at seven in morning when a nurse came in with two housekeeping staff members. The saline drip was still connected with my right hand making it difficult for me to move, which in turn was making me uncomfortable to sleep and perform any other task. In addition to this, I was feeling week to carry the weight of my own body. It was the second day when I was completely on bed, and it was the day when I was going to be operated. A fear went through me, a sudden thought of dying as if the operation would not be a success. As if it was the last day of my life. I wanted to hug Abbu and Shahid before that; I wanted to tell them that I had loved them the most in my life. I wanted to kiss Akhtar once again, to experience the feeling of being loved; I wanted to hang out with Dutta and Shikha, to discuss every crazy thought of my mind. I wanted to call Sohan and speak to him till the last breath of my life. I wanted to meet him, I wanted to laugh on his jokes, I wanted to sit on his bike, and I wanted to travel with him around the world just to feel alive.

I took a deep breath to console myself. Chaudhary was sleeping on the nearby sofa; she had taken off from her office today and was staying with me at hospital. She was studying whole night, so I did not bother her despite of the sick feeling I had. The two housekeeping staff members were cleaning my room and washroom, slowly speaking to each other in Marathi, and the nurse was checking my medicines kept on shelf on the other side of my bed. Then she looked at me with no expressions, increased speed of saline drip and went. I felt as if she did not see me. I searched for my mobile phone; it was kept on shelf only. I lifted myself a little up and extended my right hand to grab my mobile phone but it was beyond my reach.

"Madam, *kay pahije tumala?*" *what do you want?* Asked another housekeeping staff member entering my room.

She was holding a new bed sheet, pillow cover and a pair of clothes for me. Yesterday when they asked me to change to uniform of a patient, they brought an extra-large size for me. I had taken the entire hospital housekeeping staff on my head to provide me a proper size cloth.

"You should make some adjustments sometimes," Kishan said but I was not ready to wear any oversized cloth. The shirt of uniform was lengthy enough to cover my knees, and the trouser was long enough to cover double the length of my legs. I was definitely not going to wear that. Finally when I totally refused to change, they brought me a correct size which was the largest size from children section. It was exactly my size and shape.

"What size are they?" I asked her, as she passed me my mobile phone.

"Exactly the one you want. We don't want any trouble like yesterday."

Then she helped me sit so that I would change, and locked door from inside as the other two people cleaning my room left. I did not say anything to her in return.

"Do you want to take a bath?" she opened button of my shirt.

I was sitting like a small girl who couldn't even open her own shirt.

"No," I behaved like a kid.

"Why are you still wearing this bra?" she removed my shirt. "I told you yesterday only to remove all clothes and wear only this shirt and pant. Do you want me to remove it for you?"

"No."

Chaudhary woke up after listening to our conversations and laughed. "Let her save this for her husband."

"Shut up," I looked at Chaudhary getting shy as I remembered how it was unhooked by Akhtar. I got goosebumps with his thought. "I will do it by myself." Chaudhary was still laughing while entering washroom. While Chaudhary was inside washroom, that woman brought a warm wet towel along with a small kit and helped me to brush my teeth. Although I was telling her that I could brush my teeth in bathroom, she was not ready to listen. She cleaned my body with that towel, applied talcum powder on me, dressed me up, cut my long nails with a nail cutter and went. So I was ready for the operation. I took my mobile phone and called Abbu in first place. I felt so relieved after speaking to him. He was on his way to Pune. Chaudhary told me that she had informed Dutta as well and she was also on her way to reach here. After some time I called Sohan. As expected he had called me last night but I missed his call.

"Where are you? Why are you not talking to me? What have I done?"

He asked so many questions in a sleepy voice in the same way I would do, when he would not return my calls and messages. I felt so good after hearing his voice as if everything would be alright.

"I am in a hospital."

"Are you pregnant?"

Whenever I would relate myself with hospital, he would assume only one thing in return. Sometimes I would get shy when he would say it, and some other time I would feel offended for which he would laugh even more.

"This is serious Sohan," I took his name. We both barely call each other by our name but whenever we would, it would have definitely been taken for a serious cause.

"Is everything alright?" he understood that I was not joking.

"I am suffering from Coronary Artery Disorder. They are operating me today," I started crying.

"I will call you back in no time." he disconnected my call before I could say any other thing.

He would always behave like this whenever I would get emotional. Either he would cut off or laugh on me. That would piss me off most of the times, but then I would understand that he could not handle these types of emotions and that's why he would run away most of the times. *But it doesn't mean that I don't need him,* I thought. *He is so careless; whatever happens to me doesn't matter to him.*

"Hello," I said angrily after responding to Sohan's call. "Don't you think that you should take me seriously at least when I am hospitalized?"

"*Arey*, I always take you seriously, it does not depend on any other thing."

"Then why did you disconnect my call?"

"Leave it; tell me what happened to you? You were doing well when we met day before yesterday. How come this Coronary Artery Disease happened to you in one day?"

I told him everything including my chest pain which started two or three months back, how I felt when I fainted in Leh and just after we met last time. I also told him things like where I was hospitalized, when they would operate me, and every other small irrelevant thing including the size of the uniform hospital housekeeping brought for me, how the CT Scan was done, who had come from office to see me, which part of Pune I was able to see from window and where they had connected saline drip on my right hand which was making my hand movement difficult.

"Wait, I will send you a picture on Whatsapp," I said so that he would be having an exact idea where the drip had been connected. For the moment I forgot where I was or how a chest pain feels. I felt as if I was sitting at the Kooka shop with him and we were having plenty of time to discuss things that happened to us when we were not with each other. He also told me so many things like how proudly he narrated the incident of his injury to one of the air hostesses and how badly she was impressed by him.

"Now you will keep on narrating this incident to every other girl you will meet," I taunted him.

He laughed. "You know me well."

"I don't know Sohan. I am not getting any good feeling here. What if my heart stops functioning and I die in today's operation?" I told him exactly what I was feeling.

"*Chup be.*" *shut up,* he said to me.

Chup be was our expression to quieten each other, so that the other person would not feel offended and the purpose would also get solved. "Everything will be fine, science had gone far beyond thinking of mankind but still villagers believe that operations are failures."

"Bhopal is not a village." He was indirectly teasing me again by referring Bhopal as a village.

He laughed again. "I like you, even though you are from a village."

"Hmmm, I too like myself."

He laughed even louder. "Unfortunately I cannot be there, but please let me know if you need any kind of help."

"Sure, but don't worry. Kishan is already helping a lot and then Abbu will also reach today."

"Great, take care then."

"Hmmm, you too. Listen, I don't know when I would be able to speak to you again."

"Oh, yes. I will wait for your call."

I knew that he would not ask anyone about me and would wait for my call. He would never get involved with my friends no matter how much I would insist. And this was one of the reasons he would never get important information about me whenever I would not be reachable to him. He would not contact any of my friends or family to ask about me, although many times I would call his roommates or his best friends to ask about him. It was another one of his golden rules.

"Bye."

"Bye, all the best."

When I was on call with Sohan, I got Whatsapp messages from Akhtar. Kishan and Hemant had also come to hospital. They had taken leave from office today. It was just an hour before my operation, Kishan and Hemant went to complete some of the procedures and Chaudhary was watching TV with me, when I thought to message Akhtar. He was online on Whatsapp.

Me: Hey.

Akhtar: Oh hello. Is everything alright? Why are you not responding to me?

Me: How was your meeting? Is the deal finalized?

I ignored his question. I did not know up to what level he would support me emotionally, so I hesitated.

Akhtar: Deal has been finalized. Aren't you in office? Everyone there knows about it.

Me: No I am not in office.

Akhtar: Why? Is there anything I am unaware about?

Me: I am getting operated today.

Akhtar: Why? What happened?

Me: Do you remember I fainted in Leh because of chest pain?

Akhtar: Yes.

Me: It was because I am suffering from Coronary Artery Disease.

Akhtar: Let me call you.

Me: No, you can call Kishan for more details; just tell me when are you coming back?

I did not want to face him over phone; I had never done that before for personal matters.

Akhtar: I am leaving right away. When is your operation? And how long will it take?

Me: It is at 9:30, will take two hours I guess.

Akhtar: I will try my level best to be there on time.
Me: Hmmm.

As I got more and more tensed, I could feel the pressure building up inside my head. My heart started beating at a very fast rate. I was already feeling cold because of saline drip which was connected to me, but now I was shivering out of it.

Me: I am not feeling good, can we speak later?
Akhtar: Definitely yes, I will see you soon, don't you worry.

Chaudhary saw me shivering. I told her that I am scared of operation and I don't want to do any such thing in my life. I knew that I was acting childish but that was my genuine feeling. Something was biting me from inside, I just wanted to go out of hospital without any saline drip, without any medicines, without any of those pitiful faces for me, which were making me feel sicker. I wanted to go away from people who were being extra sweet to me; I definitely did not want to be treated different from others. Out of frustration, I started taking out the saline drip from my hand and without facing any problem I took it out, as if I was a perfectionist. Chaudhary panicked standing next to me.

"Are you out of your mind?" she called for Kishan.

"Please take me out from here," I pleaded to her getting off from bed. The moment I kept my foot on floor I felt weak, all things present in room started rotating around my head making me hard to realize where I was and where I have to go. By the time I was resting on bed I did not have the knowledge of my chest pain, but the moment I stood up my chest started hurting as if there was no heart at all, this time, pain was extended to my back, neck and head. I was feeling numbness in my left hand. With a dead reckoning towards the direction of gate, I lifted my left leg to move outside room and fell aimlessly on ground.

***

Lift her in three, two, one, go. One of the ward boys was guiding others when I opened my eyes as they were trying to lift me up from ground. I was not able to see anything because it was too bright and blurry for my eyes to see. I was only able to hear so many voices. I was familiar with some, though I was not in situation to understand what they were speaking. They were Chaudhary, Kishan and Dr. Jain speaking to each other. I did not hear anything from Hemant. I did not know whether he was present. I did not even know if my chest was still hurting.

***

I was lying down on a bed, a bed which was used to move patient from one place to another. They were also moving me somewhere. I saw so much of brightness on the ceiling of the hospital; three horizontal white lights separated from each other at a distance of about half meter, were crossing me again and again making it hard for me to see any other thing. I tilted my head a little towards my right to find anything sensible, but I just landed up seeing intense dark bodies moving in opposite direction to mine. I just closed my eyes to ignore the confusion of bright and dark surroundings.

CHAPTER 15

Beep, beep, beep, beep. A sound was disturbing me continuously and was not letting me sleep. It was more powerful towards my left ear making it an obvious guess for me that the origin of the sound was on my left. I opened my eyes to figure out what it was. My eyesight was blurred so it was hard for me to find out the reason. But using my common sense I assumed that it was some machine. I saw someone sitting on a stool on my left side looking at me. I signaled towards the machine to stop the irritating sound by lifting my left hand. And then I saw that the machine was connected to the index finger of my left hand through a switch. It was the machine used at hospitals to examine heart beats of patients; continuous beep sound indicated that it was normal for me.

"Have I been operated?" I gained my senses back realizing that I had been operated without my knowledge. And then I saw that the person sitting next to me on the stool was Abbu. "Abbu."

He did not say anything but looked at me with wet eyes, stood up and kissed me on my forehead. "Abbu, your beard is prickling on my nose." Abbu was a tall and skinny man, always wearing shirts and pants. Apart from shirts and pants, I have seen him on *kurta pajama*, which he would wear on festivals, and vest with a *lungi*, a long garment wrapped around his waist covering his legs, which he would wear at home. He had grown mustache and beard on his face, and in order to maintain them he would comb them multiple times a day.

"How can you be so funny even at this moment?" he smiled and wiped his tears.

"I don't have to worry when you are here," I buttered him because I was scared that he would be angry. But he did not say anything and patted me on my forehead.

"Where is Shahid?" I looked around for my little brother.

"He had gone with Kishan to buy you medicines. Kishan is a very nice man, I would always remember him for the things he had done for us."

I smiled in return. I too had the same feeling for him. Few words were not enough to describe the respect he had gained from me. Abbu told me many things doctors had advised him in order to take care of me. He also told me that they have done an incision near the left side of my groin and from there they have cleared the blockage of my arteries through a balloon type of structure, which was blown where the blockage was present.

"The incision will take around two days to recover and then you will be discharged."

"Then I will be back to my normal life."

"Yes, but no party and all. Now you have to understand that these things are not only waste of money, but are also bad for your health," he sounded a little frustrated with me. "Have a little control on yourself, and then do these things after your marriage if your husband permits."

"Abbu please, I want no marriage discussion. No one can guarantee about anyone. What else if my husband will also not allow me to do these things, to enjoy my life the way I want. I cannot live like that. I want to live as if it is the last day of my life, doing anything, traveling anywhere I want to go, talking whatever I want, and most importantly, not getting married if I don't find the suitable match." That was true. For me marriage was not an integral part of life, it was just a naming convention this society had given to the right of getting physically involved with opposite gender. It had other benefits attached to it like getting emotional support, long term commitments from your partner, stability and many other things. But I believed that all these things could also be achieved without marriage. All we need was to understand the other one, develop compatibility, offer space to them, share days and nights, provide eternal peace and respect, make them laugh, wipe their tears, and when there would be no other definition possible, one might get married.

"You are just like your mother, never listening to me. Anyway, it is not the right time to discuss these things. Your health is our first priority. We better focus on your recovery," he changed the topic.

I nodded in agreement with him. Then I saw that a tall fair man with short hair entered our room. He was wearing a white t-shirt with gray jeans. The white color of his t-shirt was complementing his complexion. His face was charming and there was soft beard and mustache on his face, showing that he had just crossed his juvenile age. He appeared as if everything was in his control, that he was matured enough to take decision and differentiate between right and wrong. He was the live image of Amma. He was Shahid, looking exactly like my mother. I felt as if Amma was smiling at me.

"Shahid, how are you, my dear brother?" I tried to lift myself up in order to hug him. He rushed towards me in order to stop me for any movements and sat next to me on my bed. We talked with each other like two friends were talking after a long time. We had not seen each other since the time he had joined his college. It was around nine months, so I asked him things from his college life, about his friends and his crush. He asked me about my Leh trip and for the period of time when we were talking to each other, we forgot everything else. By this time Abbu was resting on the sofa which was kept on my left. Shahid told me that Abbu was very tired but did not try to take some rest since the time he had heard the news of my operation. He was worrying all the time and was sitting next to me praying for my good health. And now when he had seen me and Shahid, both smiling, he would have relief. That's why he was able to sleep. We tried to maintain silence for him but as Shahid and I both were seeing each other after a very long time, we were laughing loud.

"Your smile was the thing we all missed a lot," I heard a voice out of many entering the room.

It was the voice which made me shiver each time, which would always touch my soul through my ears. The voice for which I was ready to ignore every other voice, which would made me smile from inside. It was Akhtar's voice. He entered with Kishan, Hemant and Chaudhary. They were carrying many fruits and juices for me.

"I too missed my smile." Everyone laughed. Akhtar gave a naughty smile as he understood the context of it. It was meant for him. My lips would automatically get curved when he would be around. Soon the room was filled with joy and laughter, everyone was happy, there was no room for tensions and tears. Dutta had also arrived; she had brought me flowers and chocolates to eat, which everyone else enjoyed to the fullest. I was amazed that everything was fine and I was surrounded by the people I love. I looked at everyone, they were smiling with cheer in their eyes, I saw Abbu and saw that there was a sense of satisfaction on his face when he was talking with Akhtar. Akhtar was narrating him something and Abbu was listening to him.

I thought that after they have already introduced with each other, it would be easy for me to introduce Akhtar to Abbu as my life partner. Abbu looked at me and smiled. He gave me a gesture that he was satisfied that I was surrounded with good people, so now he doesn't have to worry about me. Shahid was sitting with Kishan and Hemant, and they were providing him some tricks to impress girls from his college. Chaudhary and Dutta were sitting next to me talking to each other. Dutta was telling Chaudhary about her pre wedding shopping and other things from Mumbai. And Chaudhary was telling Dutta that she was working hard and she would try to crack the management entrance exams this year, Dutta was motivating her in return. They were also discussing about the colleges Chaudhary could opt for, none of them were near to Pune. *Once Chaudhary leaves for her studies, I will be left with no friend here,* I thought. *Except Sohan.* I reminded myself. *Yeah, he will be here till eternity.* I smiled and closed my eyes to take some nap. And then I searched for my cell phone immediately opening my eyes. I thought to call Sohan and tell him that I was not killed in the operation.

"Hello," I said in a heavy voice, as he received my call. I was resting on bed since last couple of days which made my voice heavy.

"Hello. Are you ok?"

His voice, on the other hand, was as charming as always. We limited our conversation as I had to take rest and as he was avoiding easy conversations which meant that either he was sitting with his family or was with someone else. It was around six in the evening, so chances of him to be with someone other than his family, were high.

***

Dutta and I had just finished the supper Kishan had brought for us. The saline drip was still connected to me, but apart from that intravenous solution, I was also allowed to take meals which included fruits, juices, non-spicy dishes and other related things. Abbu, Shahid and Chaudhary were sent to Baner so that they could take rest properly. Although Abbu was not ready but when I requested him, saying that I was fine and I wanted to eat something made by him in the morning, he went. Akhtar, Kishan and others also went after equipping us with all the necessary stuff. So it was only Dutta and me left at the hospital. Everyone was fighting to stay at the hospital with me, but I chose her as she was one of the best companies. And then we were meeting after a month, I wanted to tell her about Akhtar, although she taunted me many times when I was gazing at him. She would have definitely guessed something from my behavior, but still it would be fun discussing him with her. Also I was comfortable with her when it comes to medical related things like changing my dressing in front of her or peeing off in the urine drainage bag or lying down without wearing any under garments.

"How come you attract all the bad things?" she asked me as a sarcasm when the nurse inspected me and went after giving me medicines. "One month back, I was here with you and everything was normal and suddenly you are operated. Wow, what did you do?"

"I don't know. Some symptoms were there, but I ignored them and here I am."

"No, no, no, don't tell me these things. You were always dramatic since childhood. Shikha and I never got our school dress torn even while jumping off the wall or playing in the ground. But you, oh my god, you would get it torn even while standing up from the bench."

"How can you blame me for that?"

"Shut up, this is just one example. There are numerous events like it."

"That was just one incident, Dutta."

"Oh, you liar, was it just one incident? Whose email ID was hacked?" she quoted another incident, laughing about it.

"Please don't remind me that." We were in twelfth class when someone hacked my email ID and used it to send porn sites to all my contacts. The very next day in school, I was almost dead out of shame. I was also called by the principal for consultation and it was also reported to Abbu. For whole two months, I was forbidden to use internet.

"Why? We cannot ignore that."

"But it was not my fault?"

"When did I say that it was your fault? But who sets password like, *IloveRanbirKapoor*?"

"Yeah, I love Ranbir Kapoor."

"And did you forget about that fight?" she listed another funny incident.

"How can I?" There were boys divided into groups in our college based on the locations they were staying. Boys staying in Arera Colony would join the group of Arera Colony, boys from BHEL would join BHEL group and so on. None of the groups would like each other. During the third year of our college, BHEL and Lalghati group encountered a fight because of some silly reason. Almost all the people from our college were gathered when they were fighting with each other. Dutta, Shikha and I also went to watch them fighting; there were seven to eight boys, kicking, punching and smashing each other in a way as if they wanted to kill each other. The college professors and guards were trying to stop them, but the boys were so violent that after a point no one interfered and decided to call police and their parents. I was standing on the front row to catch the entire scene properly, while Dutta and Shikha did not get the place and were struggling for the view. So without informing me, they decided to move to the other side of the area where they thought would be a less crowded place to view the fight. After sometime I tried to search them behind me but they were not there. I noticed that all the other people started shouting, looking at me, because two boys had come very close to me, holding each other's neck with one hand and punching each other's faces with the other. I shouted and tried to run. But I got hit by the punch of one of the boys. It was so hard and stroked exactly near my left jaw that I fell on the ground and fainted.

"The professor tried every possible way to stop the fight, but who knew that a girl would stop it by just getting a punch on her own face," she laughed hard sitting on the sofa.

"That was jaw breaking, madam. I was bandaged for two damn weeks," I remembered the pain.

"Who told you stand at the front?" she tried to control her laughter.

"*Oye*, don't tell me this. You people left me there, you should be blamed, not me."

"I am not blaming you for anything, darling. I just want to say that you are vulnerable. It is never your fault, but the shit happens to you. You are somehow attracted to bad things," she changed her tone. She was serious.

"I know."

"Don't get me wrong, but it is true, be it some funny incidents or some serious life related issues, you are always badly caught. See this operation from nowhere. I mean can you imagine this coronary disease can happen to a girl at the age of twenty four?"

"You are right, but things are changing. Some of the very good things are also happening to me, which can be added on the list."

"For example?"

"Like *ishq wala love*." I sang one of the songs from the movie, Student of the Year. She immediately jumped next to me from the sofa to inquire more about it.

"I was a little sure about it, but then I am confused who the lucky man is."

"Confused? You can guess it right away."

"Sohan?" she did not take any time to answer.

"What?" *Why did she take his name?*

"Yeah, I mean I have never seen you with him but I can see the difference in you when you talk about him. You look so happy and extraordinary and comfortable and everything far beyond what actually you are. This is love. He is changing you."

"No Dutta. I mean, yeah that can be true, but I don't love him."

"I thought Sohan and you love each other."

"No, it is not like that. We are very good friends. I don't have those feelings for him. I never thought about having such feelings for him."

"Then, is it Akhtar?" she smiled.

I could see that her eyes were sparkling with the confidence and joy for her best friend finding the love of her life. I did not say anything but blushed out of the warmth of the feeling I had for Akhtar.

"Please tell me in detail."

I told her everything, how it started, what happened at Leh and how Akhtar and I were talking to each other these days. She listened to me as if she was living those moments with me.

"Then what about Sohan?"

"He too did not feel anything for me, Dutta. We are clear about it. In fact he knows about Akhtar."

"Good then," her voice did not reflect much charm.

"Actually, if you would ask me about Sohan, I would say that he is the best person I have ever met. I am sorry I do not want to hurt you but he means a lot to me, even more than you people. I trust him like anything; the comfort he provides me is unbeatable by anyone else. I don't think about anything else when I am with him or when I talk about him or think about him. But I have never thought about kissing him, or getting close to him. On the other hand, I have been kissed by Akhtar and I wish that he should be the only one kissing me forever."

"Are you sure? You are saying many beautiful things for Sohan and then you say that you don't want to kiss him. These are implicit feelings people find when they spend a lot of time with opposite gender."

"Yes. I am certain about it. I want to kiss Akhtar not Sohan."

"I don't understand."

"Listen carefully, I will tell you exactly what I feel, then you will understand that my feelings are different for both of them." She looked at me with eyes full of repulsion to whatever I was going to tell her. Still I tried to convince her. "Akhtar and Sohan are two different personalities, in terms of thinking, in terms of speaking and in terms of everything else. When I look at Gul as a third person, she is totally different when she is with Sohan, and she is someone else when she is with Akhtar. When she is with Sohan, she doesn't have to think before she speaks, she doesn't care about what she is wearing, she laughs madly on his jokes, and life is easier and smooth for her when he is around. On the other hand, she feels very conscious when she is with Akhtar. She is concerned about whatever she is speaking or wearing should impress Akhtar. She doesn't want him to look at any ugly side of her. Also, she wants him to appreciate her every now and then. Sohan never appreciate her for her looks or behavior and she never mind. But she wants to know what Akhtar thinks about her. She wants to improve her in way he likes. She wants to kiss him again and again."

"You want to impress Akhtar, which is why you are a little conscious when he is around. Whereas Sohan and you have taken each other for granted, that no matter what, your friendship can never be broken, so the fear of losing or dislike does not come into picture," she understood my point. "But still your definition of love is not correct, my dear."

"I don't know. I don't have to worry about Sohan. I know he is there and he will not mind if I get involved with someone else."

"Then?"

"I am worried about Akhtar."

"Why? He is good. Though I am not sure how genuine it is, but I have seen attraction for you in his eyes."

"I know. But I am not sure if it is only attraction or something more than that. We are physically involved, but he has not said anything about his feelings for me."

"You want it official?"

I blushed.

"Have patience. You have just returned from Leh and then this operation happened. He too needs time to understand his feelings, right?"

She was right. I was just worried as this was happening to me for the first time. I was too eager for his proposal. I was thinking about the day when he would propose to me and we would be together forever. And then my beautiful dream was interrupted by Shikha. Dutta had informed her about my operation. She called to enquire about my health. She scolded me first as I did not inform her, and then she, along with Dutta, started making fun of me by the name of Akhtar. They were saying that Akhtar would surely have a strong impact on me because this was the first time someone was able to steal my heart. They were also making fun of Akhtar and my timings, as each time we tried to get intimate with each other, we were interrupted by someone. *Bitches*! That was the only word I said to them and they both laughed.

CHAPTER 16

Abbu and Shahid returned home from the nearby mosque after performing Asr, the late afternoon prayer. It was the month of Ramdaan and they were fasting since last ten days. As I had been recently operated and the doctor had advised me to take utmost care of my health, I was not allowed to hold these fasts. After I was discharged, we took rest for about a week in Pune and then we came to Bhopal so that I would always be present in front of Abbu and he would be able to supervise me.

I decided not to join office until I am fully recovered and as everyone in my office was aware of my operation and Dr. Jain had already advised one month rest for me, my sick leaves were approved. Abbu was very happy with this decision and though he was fasting continuously, he was always eager to cook my favorite dishes for me. He would feed me timely, would go to the mosque with Shahid to perform prayers, and would spend his holy time narrating spiritual stories to us and doing other household works. I would ask to help him on his daily activities but he would refuse, as taking care of his children was his favorite thing to do.

He would ask me to take rest all the time and do nothing. Shahid would go to college, study for his mid semester exams, spend some of the time with me and would devote himself to the holy month performing prayers and reading Qur'an with Abbu. They were the true follower of our religion, unlike me. They would follow all the rituals without any fail. On the other hand, I would take these things lightly. This time I had an excuse for not fasting during the month of Ramadan, but Abbu was not upset on me due to this. This was not my fault. As the days were passing, I was getting bored. There was nothing for me to do.

All my friends from college were not in Bhopal as they moved to other cities to work. I would spend my time watching TV and sleeping. Sometime some of the family friends would come to visit me, some other time I would chat with my friends from Pune and with Shikha and Dutta. I was less interacting with Akhtar these days, he was also fasting and I did not want to indulge him into any romantic conversations with me which might divert him from his daily schedules. Month of Ramadan was known for composing yourself physically and mentally from all good things and giving up bad habits. It was also believed that people should avoid sexual activity with their partners to save energy and control their attachments with worldly things and relations.

So this was the time Akhtar and I maintained distance with each other. This was also the time to actually analyze our feelings for each other. From my side it was genuine; I was all the time thinking about him, I was again expecting to see him, to get ready for him and definitely to love him. But I was more concerned about getting the same feelings back from him. *When I will meet him after a long time and he gives me the same importance, then I will take this thing to next level,* I thought. Though he would ping me daily asking about my wellbeing and telling me different things from office, I would limit our conversations to the required level only. But I would never let him feel as if I was trying to avoid him.

I never wanted to do that. When he would try to flirt with me, sometime I would flirt in return and some other time I would dramatically reply to him taking the conversation to some other topic. Though my heart would not allow me to do so, but I would try to keep a control on things. Shahid and Abbu would notice me blushing while reading Akhtar's conversations, Abbu would remonstrate with me saying that I should not get this much engaged with my cell phone, these are not good habits, and Shahid would ask me about the person with whom I was talking these days. I would listen to none of them and continue blushing and smiling.

I would tell Akhtar about Abbu scolding me and Shahid asking different type of questions to me, but he would not mind them and keep messaging me. After spending around three weeks away from each other, he was definitely missing me. This was much clear from his conversations. I was missing him too and was much more eager to meet him in return. He would also ask me when I was going to return to Pune, but I would never provide him exact information.

Me: What do you want me to wear for the party?

I asked Akhtar when he informed me that after I return to Pune, we have to attend one wedding where we have been invited by one of our colleagues.

Akhtar: Don't wear anything.

Me: Chup be.

I used one of the common phrases of Sohan and mine, which Akhtar wouldn't understand.

Akhtar: You can wear anything you want, everything suits you.

Me: I may wear a saree then.

Akhtar: I don't mind. I have never seen you wearing a saree.

He said making a heart shape smiley

Me: You will soon see me wearing a saree.

***

"*Eid Mubarak*, madam," Sohan said in a pleasant voice.

"*Shukran*," I elegantly thanked him for the wishes.

"Where is my *Eidi*?" He asked me for his gift which usually elder ones give to younger ones during the festival.

"I should ask this question to you, after all *Eidi* is given to small children by other elders and you are four year elder to me."

"*Chup be*, I am just three years older than you. Do I look aged?"

I laughed. I knew his age but I acted as if he was aging. Each time we would discuss something related to our age, I would act as if he was very older to me, and then he would freak out.

"If you think that all because I am four years experienced than you, I am aging, that is not true. My parents planned everything, from my birth to my academic years. We should also plan our children accordingly"

Did he say our children? Is he talking about his and my children? I thought. "How it can be planned?" Actually I was not thinking about the question I asked. Something else was going on in my mind. I was perplexed that he said our children which could be the result if we both made love with each other.

"It can be. It is a simple calculation."

"What?"

"Yes, see, from the month of delivery, age of the children is calculated and that month of delivery can be planned. You just need to choose the month you want to give birth and then you can conceive nine or ten months before that. Simple, isn't it?"

"Ok fine, no more discussion about it," I felt shy. We had never discussed such things, this was happening for the first time when he made me feel as if we were planning our own children, which I did not want.

"What happened? This is the truth of life."

"Leave it please. I have some serious topics to discuss." I told him that I need to return a huge amount of money which I had borrowed from people. I had asked Shikha to lend me forty thousand rupees when I went to Leh. I had to return that and then due to my operation Kishan had spent around twenty thousand rupees on me which was not settled under my health insurance. I also told him that Abbu had also borrowed five thousand rupees from his friend during the same period of time when I was operated.

"A total of sixty five thousand rupees."

"Yes, I do not understand how I will return this money. I did not inform Abbu about this. I am feeling so tensed," I felt a fear of getting bankrupt.

"Enjoy."

Enjoy? What did he mean by enjoy? I thought. I really do not understand him sometime especially when he uses the word- enjoy. *Does he really want me to enjoy? Was it a sarcasm?*

"What do you mean by that?"

"*Yahi sab toh life hai.*" He meant that such ups and downs were the part of the life.

I told him when I would return to Pune and asked him when he would be joining office back, as it was already around two months since he went. He said that it was not finalized but he was recovering fast and maybe by the first week of August he would return as there would be a lot of work pending on his name.

CHAPTER 17

"Please carry on, I cannot come. It is raining heavily," I told Akhtar on call. He suggested me to go to Kishan's apartment after office, get ready and attend the wedding, but I did not agree with him and came back to Baner. The party was in Koregaon Park which was no less than fifteen kilometers from Baner. Due to heavy rainfall, there was no commute available to me to reach the venue.

"Get ready, I am coming to pick you."

"No Akhtar, this is unnecessary burden on you. I will arrange for something by myself," I had never asked Akhtar to favor me, and there was no point in asking him to travel in opposite direction just to pick me up, especially when it was raining and difficult for him to drive.

"I told you to stay at Kishan's apartment but why will you listen?"

"Don't worry, I will try to come. Just give me time to get ready and book a cab."

"Ok. Let me know if you need anything."

I, too, wanted to attend the party, after all I was getting a chance to flaunt myself after a long time, but the rain was ruining everything. I asked Chaudhary to check the availability of cabs after every five to ten minutes and book one for me the moment she would find one available. Meanwhile I adorned myself with ornaments and a beautiful saree.

***

"You are late." Aditya said, when I stepped out of the cab Chaudhary booked for me.

He and Akhtar were waiting for me at the entrance of the venue. Neither I, nor the driver, knew the location, so I asked Akhtar to come outside the hotel and guide me how to reach there. Aditya accompanied him.

"I know but it is all because of the rain." We were asked to reach by eight in the evening, but I was two hours late as it was raining.

"Let's go inside, everyone is waiting for you."

Akhtar did not say anything. He just smiled when I reached. I was a little nervous regarding my appearance, but as usual when I saw him, the feeling of love overshadowed every other thing. He was wearing a *kurta pajama*. The *kurta* was made of silk and it was the perfect turmeric yellow in color which would always fascinate me. The white color of the *pajama* was complementing it in the right way. The color combination was making him look stunning. Though everyone was dressed extraordinarily well, he was standing out from other people.

We entered the hall, I saw Kishan, Hemant and others were standing together, enjoying some kind of refreshment drinks. I saw that an old woman and a man were also standing with them, laughing at their jokes and narrating stories from their experiences. That woman was wearing a *salwar kameez*. The neck of the royal blue *kameez* was embroidered with flowers made from red silk thread. The long shiny *duppatta* of the dress was completely covered with the same type of red flowers. She had draped that *duppatta* over her head out of which her radiant face was emerging. That man was wearing *kurta pajama* which was much more similar to that of Akhtar, but it was light green in color with dark green vertical stripes on it. Akhtar looked exactly like him. Though I had never seen them before, I could easily figure it out that they were Akhtar's parents. They all smiled looking at us.

Akhtar introduced me. "Ammi she is Gul."

Why didn't he inform me that his parents are also coming? My heartbeat paced up when I went closer to them. They were my future in laws. *I will make a perfect family with them,* I thought.

"*Assalaam-o-Alaikum,*" I smiled and greeted them in Arabic.

"*Wa'alaikum Salaam,*" they both replied to me.

"You are beautiful," his mother came closer to me.

"*Shukran,*" I smiled and looked at Akhtar to see his reaction. I was wearing a synthetic saree having same color as that of her mother's dress. It was having blackish golden border with conch shell shaped design made on it with some black wire, which was giving it a little three dimensional look. The same shape was present here and there in the saree too. The saree was paired with a blouse having the same blackish golden color as that of the border. It was having short sleeves with deep back. The shoulders were tied with thin rope out of which pearl hangings were suspending on my waist. Though my hair was short I managed to make a bun from them, applied kohl on my eyes, brown shade of lipstick on my lips and a golden color earring on my ear.

"What is your full name?" his mother asked me.

"Gul, why don't you take something hot to drink?" Akhtar interrupted me before I could answer his mother.

I did not understand, but I felt as if he did not want me to answer his mother. I did as he requested. We moved to start dinner by proceeding towards various stalls offering various types of Indian dishes. We decided once we finish starters, we would go to the stage where the bride and the groom were sitting. Akhtar's mother and father went just after finishing dinner, *I will return in some time*, Akhtar said and went to drop his parents home.

"Aditya, please take a picture of mine," I pouted; the moment Akhtar's parents went.

"I thought she became sober after her operation but no, she is still the same," Kishan said and everyone laughed.

I was actually behaving sober when Akhtar's parents were present. I did not want to portray myself badly so I controlled my behavior. I was unaware of their likes and dislikes so I preferred speaking with manners, controlling my gestures, preventing myself from flaunting in any way which could look bad from their perspective. Actually I did not know about their perspective but I imagined what Abbu would like and behaved accordingly.

"Sober? Me?" I laughed. Actually that was totally unlike me. They knew that I would never change my behavior for someone. Many times Abbu would ask me to behave sober saying that too much vivacious nature was not good, but that was the real me, and I believed to behave exactly the way I was. But they did not know that the presence of Akhtar was affecting my behavior these days. I would feel nervous each time he would be around and this time he was present with his parents, so the level of nervousness was doubled. Akhtar returned after forty minutes. The function was almost over so we planned to go somewhere. As we were gathered after a very long time, everyone agreed for the after party. We decided to go to Kishan's apartment and watch a horror movie, but there was one problem, Meenal and I were wearing saree and we complained that it was difficult for us to wear the same throughout night.

"You can wear the smallest shorts and t-shirt Kishan has," Akhtar suggested.

Meenal and I nodded.

"Let's go then."

I looked at Akhtar to ask him whether I was going with him in his car, but Hemant already shouted that all the girls would come with Akhtar so I moved silently with others. I was walking downstairs with Kishan finalizing which horror movie we should watch. Other people were also coming, talking to each other on various topics. Kishan was suggesting that we should watch paranormal movies. We searched Google for the list of latest horror movies. The Conjuring was on top of the list but it was not released yet. We found trailer of the movie and started watching it in the staircase passage only. Soon we realized that other people walked ahead of us, and it was only Kishan and I present on that area watching one of the most horrifying trailers. Sound of rain striking the road and building was echoing inside the passage like one of the haunted nights of the movie; dim depressed light was playing with our eyesight, numbness of the passage was giving a cold sensation over our skin and Lorraine and Ed Warren were performing exorcism on Carolyn Perron in the trailer when I screamed, as out of nowhere something as cold as a dead man, touched me on my waist. Kishan too screamed after hearing my scream. Akhtar was laughing out loud holding his stomach. It was he who pinched me from behind.

"What are you?" I controlled my heartbeat which was running furiously. Kishan was standing without any clue of what made me scream.

Akhtar laughed. "Sorry. I did not mean that."

"I can kill you for this."

"What happened?" Kishan looked at both of us.

"Why did you scream when you don't know what happened?" I looked at Kishan.

"In the middle of nowhere when we are watching such a dreadful trailer, if you will scream what will I do? You scared me."

All three of us laughed.

***

After arranging Kishan's room, all boys were settled, whereas girls were changing in other room. We had quickly searched for two shorts and t-shirt which Meenal and I could wear whereas Akhtar, Aditya and Hemant adjusted themselves borrowing other clothes from Kishan and his roommates. Kishan was connecting his laptop with the sound system and was adjusting his laptop screen so that it could be visible to all. We did not find any good paranormal movie online, which we had not seen, so I suggested them to watch the movie, Orphan. It was one of the must watch horror thrillers. Kishan had kept the movie for buffering and they were waiting for us to join them. I went to washroom before anyone could use it so that I would get an unspoiled washroom to use. Up to my expectations their washroom was pretty clean this time.

"Gul, click on play button and settle down," Hemant said when I entered Kishan's room.

They had placed mattresses on floor and all of them were resting on it inside their blankets.

"Where do I rest?" I scanned everywhere, looking for the place they had made for me to sleep.

"Find yourself and please play the movie. It is getting late."

Rest of the people did not say anything, they were waiting for me to play the movie and to settle down.

"Please tell me."

"Here Gul, between Kishan and I," Meenal replied.

Meenal was sleeping on the corner of one row, Kishan was sleeping next to her followed by Aditya and Akhtar. Hemant and Kishan's roommates were sleeping in another row.

"I will not sleep in between two people, you know it."

Hemant and Kishan started laughing as if they planned to frustrate me.

"Kishan, Aditya, please move. Gul, come here," Akhtar made space for me next to him on the corner of the same row.

I looked at him, remembering the day in Leh when he was complaining that because of me he was not able to sleep, as I was fighting with him for the corner place to sleep and today he was sacrificing his corner of the bed for me. I played the movie, switched off lights and sat next to him leaning against wall.

"Today, I will sleep on your lap," Akhtar rested his head on my lap.

No one responded. They concentrated on movie as if nothing was said. I did not respond much but kept my hand on his forehead and started playing with his hair. They were silky in texture as if he had applied some gloss over it. I tried to tangle it within my fingers but they did not stick to one place. I felt as if his hair was playing with my fingers. Soon I started enjoying it and forgot about movie. I tangled it many times within my fingers, divided it into parts, tried to braid it, comb it with my fingers, massaged it and did every other thing which was possible.

"Why are you not checking your cell phone?" Akhtar looked at me.

"Because, I am playing with your hair."

"Check your Whatsapp once."

124

He had messaged me on Whatsapp.

Akhtar: I missed you.

I did not reply but pulled his cheeks.

Akhtar: You were looking damn sexy in saree today.

He messaged me again after some time.

Me: Now you are talking.

Akhtar: Literally, when I saw you I forgot everything. I was just amazed by your aura. I did not remember what I was supposed to do next but stood there looking at you.

Me: I adorned myself for you, it was raining heavily but still I came only for you but you did not even click a single picture with me.

Akhtar: We are always surrounded with people; it was not possible for me at that time. See even now we are talking through Whatsapp.

Me: It is ok. At least I can see you.

I sent him a heart emoticon. He replied with a kiss.

Me: Why aren't you watching the movie?

Akhtar: You are here, I cannot concentrate anywhere else.

Me: Are you blaming me?

Akhtar: No, actually I don't want to concentrate anywhere else.

Me: You know what? I missed you too.

I confessed to him that I was also missing him when I was in Bhopal. I wanted to kiss him, but unfortunately there were a lot of people around, preventing us to behave the way we wanted to. I was sure Akhtar was controlling himself too. That was the only thing we could do. I asked him to lift his head and I lay down next to him, sharing his blanket. Others were still watching the movie; they were sometime predicting the upcoming suspense and some other time were watching it silently. They were involved in it. I was enjoying being with Akhtar, I turned left facing him. He held my right hand and kept it on his chest, holding it. I was able to feel his heartbeat. It was calm and clear.

***

Hemant, Aditya and Kishan's snoring woke me up. I checked my mobile; it was showing five in the morning. Akhtar immediately turned to face me. He was already awake.

"Wake up," he came closer to me.

I cried, moving my head inside blanket. I wanted to sleep.

"Please wake up," he tickled my stomach.

"No, tell them to stop snoring."

"I will not." He came close to me, took his hands out from my grip and tickled me again.

"Let me also sleep then," I faced him away.

His hands were now resting on my stomach. He pinched my stomach but I did not react. He moved his hands on my thigh to seduce me, and when I did not react at all, he moved his hand inside my t-shirt and unhooked my bra.

"Are you mad?"

He was smiling mischievously. I stood up and moved to another room in order to hook my bra. He followed me. I took my hands back inside my t-shirt and before I could hook my bra, he placed both his hands on my waist, held me gently and pulled me towards him. I looked at him, placing my hand around his neck like a garland, playing my fingers on the back side of his head. His heartbeat was violent and demanding this time. He lifted me up to match his height and then he kissed me. I went with the flow and kissed him back. We were meeting after a very long time so something like this was expected. He took my t-shirt off while kissing me and moved his hands tenderly on my bosom. By this time we both were so sexually involved that I forgot about everything else. Where were we? What were we doing? There was no such question in my mind. I just wanted to kiss him more and more. He looked at me for few seconds and kissed me back. I pushed him back as I heard some noise from the other room. I immediately took my t-shirt and ran towards living room. He followed me again.

"Gul, don't go away from me."

"Please understand that I do not want to go away from you, but there are other people present here. My brother is here."

He looked at me for few minutes without saying anything. By this time I had hooked my bra properly, wore my t-shirt over it and stood away from him so that there would be minimum chance of getting seduced by him. But it wasn't enough; his romantic gaze was still seducing me. He came forward without saying anything, kissed me, and again tried to take my t-shirt and bra off my body.

"No," I pushed him back. Then after some time I held his hand and took him to the balcony. Clock was showing six thirty in morning. Sky was painted gray with black clouds ready to rain anytime. Wind was cold; some sparrows were sitting on electric cables connected between poles, chirping slowly as a sign to start their day. Kishan's balcony was very large; large enough to enjoy camp fire at nights, but it was wet except the part which was covered by roof. A pair of bamboo chairs was placed there for seating, but it was full of clothes which mainly consist of undergarments, leaving no space to sit. In addition to this, it was very dirty as if it was not dusted since a decade. Somehow I managed to keep all those clothes at one side, dusted the sofa and asked him to sit.

"What is going on Akhtar?"

"What?"

"What is going on between us? Is it just our physical need?"

"I like you."

It was not the thing I wanted to hear.

"Like as in what? You like me as a whole or you just like my body?"

"Are you insane? Why are you asking this thing again and again?"

He was sounding frustrated.

"Because, I don't feel as if you are emotionally attached to me. Every time you only want to touch me."

"Ok, I will not touch you then."

"Fine, as you wish," I stood at one corner of the balcony under the sky. It wasn't raining but the wind was mixed with tiny droplets of water making it very difficult for me to stand. I started feeling cold. I crossed my hands and started rubbing my arms in order to keep myself warm, but I started shivering. Though Akhtar called me two or three times I pretended that I did not hear him and looked far away towards the sky. *I will maintain distance from him.* I thought. *It was my fault, I thought he loved me. I was wrong and Abbu was right. I should not trust everyone; I am a fool to believe in everything.*

"Come here," he grabbed my hand and taking me inside when I was busy in my thoughts. "Do you understand that you just recovered from illness? Why are you doing this stupid thing, I thought you are mature."

"I am not mature, I am stupid and I do not understand anything," I did not look at him. "But I have understood one thing. I have to stay away from you."

"Gul, I have never been this close to any girl. Please understand that when I see you, I lose my mind. I do not know what I have to do, and when I touch you, I feel peaceful. I am too comfortable when you are around."

"Are you serious?"

"Yes, this feeling is new to me; I need time to understand these things. I agree that I am unable to control my physical attraction toward you, I am sorry for that, but it doesn't mean that it's not genuine."

I kept looking at him with naughty eyes. Whatever he was saying was making me feel good; my heart was ready to come out of my chest to get merged with his heart. I felt as if the birds were chirping love songs for me, the wind was mixed with tiny droplets of love potion, the sky was painted with the color of love and the dirty chairs were decorated with flowers petals.

"You know, you are the most beautiful person I have ever met. Beautiful yet down to earth, understated yet elegant, humble yet bold, intelligent yet dumb."

I laughed loudly.

"Don't laugh, I am serious."

My laughter automatically turned into a shy smile.

"When you are not around, I keep thinking about you, your dazzling smile, your naughty talks using your special quotes, your funny jokes, your humor, your way of thinking, your hair and your alluring eyes."

"My eyes," I interrupted him.

"Yes, your eyes, anyone can spend their life in them, reading them, they are your first tongue, and they speak exactly the way you feel. Like now you are feeling loved. I can see the feeling of admiration through your eyes."

I lowered my eyes. This was the first time he was praising me word by word. Before him only Abbu would speak about my appearance. *Your eyes are like a mirror of your personality,* he would say. I was actually touched when Akhtar interpreted my eyes exactly the way Abbu would do.

"And the way you put kohl on your eyes."

"Enough," I stopped him and he smiled.

CHAPTER 18

The day Akhtar expressed his feelings was one of the best days of my life. I was on cloud nine. I would talk endlessly with him. As his desk was adjacent to mine it was easy for me to communicate with him. Sometime he would bring a LAN cable, connect his laptop with the available port on my desk and sit in my cubicle. Other times I would call him regarding some issue and then he would take enough of his time to solve the issue with me.

We would go for tea breaks and lunch together. And then after office we would hang out late at night, followed by parties which would give us plenty of time to spend with each other. And for the time we were not present with each other, we would chat on Whatsapp. No other thing was present in my life; I would not talk to other people but Akhtar. I would get dressed for him. I would ask him what to wear and what not to wear.

He would reply, saying that everything suits me. He would keep track on my attire, unlike Sohan. If I would do some variations with my hairstyle, accessories or anything else, he would immediately give positive feedback. If I would wear some clothes which he had not seen, he would ask me if they were new. Whenever we would go for casual hangouts, I would sit next to him in his car.

That seat was reserved for me and everyone was aware of it. Even if I would be late, they would occupy other seats, leaving the front seat for me. Then Akhtar would tickle me here and there whenever we would stop on signals, and I would pinch him in return which he would enjoy to the fullest. He would walk with me, keeping his hand around my shoulder, without any hesitation. Other people would behave as if they were unaware of everything which was happening between us.

Akhtar would always make sure to sit in front of me whenever we would dine together so that there would be no barrier and he could gaze at me easily. He would take my pictures without my knowledge. We would exchange selfies over Whatsapp.

Sometimes, I would chat with Sohan too but it was very less as compared to how we would usually chat. And he would remain busy whenever he would go to his hometown, so I would not disturb him much. He would sometime ask me why I am not talking to him much but would never ask for details. Akhtar was unaware that Sohan, with whom all of us had a professional relationship, was actually my best friend.

Akhtar was unaware of many other things as well. He did not know about my money crises, about my friends from school or about my future plans. He was much more interested about my appearance or the fun I was to be with. He would never involve himself discussing his life goals or sharing his family details with me. But, he would definitely take care of me. On holidays, he would keep asking me if I had taken meals or not, he would remind me for medicines. If I had to go somewhere, I would complain that I do not like walking in rain, as it would be so dirty outside and then he would pamper me saying that whenever he would be around, he would never let me walk. There were many other small things where he was making me feel special, like buying shirts after asking my opinion, cuddling me whenever we would stay at Kishan's apartment, asking me to eat from his plate or sometime even feeding me from his own hands but taking me into serious matter was still missing.

***

My cell phone vibrated, I looked at screen with barely opened eyes and saw that Sohan was calling me early in the morning. *Why is he calling me so early?* I thought. And then, I silently escaped from Akhtar's embrace and moved to another room to talk to Sohan.

"Hello," I said in raspy voice.

"Are you sleeping?"

"I was sleeping," I yawned. There was a lot of disturbance coming from his background.

"With whom are you sleeping?"

"Sohan, what happened?" I rubbed my eyes. I was still in doubt why he called me.

He laughed, as I did not answer his question. "I am starting from here."

"Oh yes, I forgot. Where are you? Are you at railway station?" I questioned him and answered myself. I genuinely forgot that he was leaving for Pune today. He called me yesterday night, but I missed his call. Later I did message him on Whatsapp and he replied with a picture stating that he was packing his stuff.

He made his voice and acted as if he was crying.

"*Oye* drama queen, what happened now?" He was a tough competition to me when it came to being dramatic. Maybe that's why I would figure out when he would behave childlike.

"I don't want to leave Lucknow," he maintained crying tone.

"*Chup be*, come soon. I am waiting for you since eternity," I said to him even though I was fully occupied by Akhtar, and there was no time to think about anyone else.

"*Tum tension na lo*," he changed his tone into an excited voice. "I am sitting in locomotive with driver, so I will be the second person to reach Pune."

I laughed. He would always say that he would sit on locomotive whenever he would travel in train because that part of the train reaches first to the destination.

I told him that we are at Kishan's apartment to celebrate *Raksha bandhan*. Sohan was a single child to his parents and maybe that's why it was never important for him to be at his hometown to celebrate this festival. I never asked him anything related to this. For me it was always beyond happiness whenever he would come back to Pune.

"Ok. I will hang up now. Let me board and settle."

"Yes, please. Keep me posted and travel safe. Bye."

"Who was it?" Akhtar asked me as I rested next to him.

"A friend."

He did not ask anything else, but started checking his cell phone. Hemant, Aditya and Kishan were snoring as usual and Meenal was hidden somewhere inside her blanket. Kishan's other two roommates, Priyam and Mudit, had gone to their hometown. We were at Kishan's place since Friday night when we decided to tie *Raksha bandhan* knot to our brothers. Hemant and Aditya asked Meenal to tie *Rakhi* on their arms, which was sent by their sisters and I was going to perform the same ritual for Kishan. He was also single child to his parents and since last year I was tying this knot to him. Abbu was having no objection with this; instead he was happy because Kishan was genuinely like a brother to me and a son to him. Abbu would have surely objected if he would have come to know that I was staying at Kishan's place since last two nights.

For him we were going to gather on the festival only, to celebrate it. But it wasn't true, we were only moving to our place in order to get new clothes, or in my case to take bath. I was the only reason why Akhtar was also staying at Kishan's place. He would go to his home during dinner time and would come back making some excuses to his parents. His mother would call and scold him once or twice a day and he would listen without saying anything. Meenal would make fun of him on this. But I knew that it was difficult for him to make any excuses and did not return to home at nights when he was living with his parents. I myself did not want to disrespect his parents, but at the same time I wanted him to stay with me also. Whenever he would go to his home, before he could leave, I would confirm multiple times from him asking when he would return. I would also message him on Whatsapp reminding him that I am waiting for him, and he would reply with a kissing smiley.

***

"Gul, I am not dating anyone since a long time," Sohan replied.

He was trying to convince me that he was not dating any girl when I was asking him information about all those girls he dated when he was in Lucknow.

"I do not trust you on this."

"I cannot help then."

"What are you doing?" he asked me after few seconds when I did not say anything.

A small boy was crying in the background since the time he had called me and no one was trying to stop him.

"I am getting ready. Afternoon is the right time to tie *Raksha Bandhan* knot, so we are just…"

"This boy is irritating me like hell," he shouted before I could complete my sentence.

Sohan did not like children, particularly those of others. He would always plan to harm or haunt them in some way or the other. He would tell me how he would take children of his neighbors or relatives to kitchen and burn them with hot pliers. He would also burn them with candle wax, scaring them to hell. He would say that burning them with candle wax would be the best way to haunt children because it would solve the purpose without leaving any marks on their body. And in case he would be encountering any infant, he would bring few seeds of chilli and secretly put it inside their mouth and run away. People would keep on wondering why the baby was crying and he would silently enjoy knowing the reason behind it. I remembered, he told me that once when he was around thirteen years old, he went to some place with his father where he pushed a little boy from a stool and he got hurt. That boy's parents noticed Sohan performing this crime and complained to his father, then Sohan was punished to baby sit all of his relative's children knowing his dislike for children.

"Why is he crying?" I asked to figure out the root cause.

"He is crying for every food and items passing by him, no one can buy him everything. Let him come to my side, I will cut his skin with nail cutter."

"Sohan please calm down. Why are you saying this? What if someone does the same to your children?"

"*Chup be*. No one is allowed to say anything about my children. They will be the best and I will love them like anything," he sounded protective about his future children.

"Wait for the day; I will pull their ears."

He laughed. "You are allowed."

I remembering our last conversation about children. He was always comfortable to speak about children or any other topic with me, which I was expecting from Akhtar, who wasn't showing any such signs.

"I will hang up now, Akhtar is calling me," I tried to stop the comparison which was going inside my mind.

"Is he also there?"

"Yes, I told you, we are here since Friday."

"Ok. Enjoy."

I was again unable to identify the context behind it.

"What do you mean by enjoy?"

"Nothing, bye."

I hate him said the inner Gul to me.

***

"It is actually difficult," I said to Meenal when she came out of washroom. "I cannot wear it for the whole day."

"You have to Gul, there is no other option," she adjusted her *saree*.

We were celebrating traditional day at office on the occasion of *Raksha Bandhan* festival. Female associates were wearing *saree* and male associates were wearing *kurta pajama*. Some of the associates were wearing formals.

"The fabric of this *saree* is difficult to carry unlike my other *saree*. It is so slippery. Even though I have pinned it properly, it is not staying at its position." I was wearing a plain red *saree* with black velvet lace border. The *saree* was made of fine net which was so silky making it hectic for me to carry. Velvet blouse of the *saree,* with half sleeves, was black in color and was totally comfortable and stable. As the blouse was high neck I did an updo with my hair, wore no other jewelry but a black round *bindi* on my forehead, shined my lips with a red gloss and did a smoky eyes makeup.

"Shall we go?" she ignored my concerns.

"Shall I pin this?" I asked her to pin the loose end of the *saree* together.

"No, no, no," she did not take any time to decide. "You are looking perfect like this."

I did not say anything. I sagged my face and moved outside washroom with her. Kishan, Aditya and Akhtar were waiting for us. They were also in traditional attire. We had to go for lunch to one of the restaurants. Akhtar was wearing white cotton *kurta pajama* but he was not looking as stunning as he did few days back when we went for the wedding of a colleague. Maybe I was feeling frustrated with my own get up so did not pay much attention to him. Since morning he was flattering a lot, but I took it very lightly.

"What happened?" asked Aditya when we swiped out of office and I was not saying anything.

"This *saree* is troubling me a lot."

They started discussing that we have started partying a lot, which was causing financial imbalance to everyone and we should control our hangouts. I did agree with them, my financial condition was already bad and these daily parties were causing trouble to me. But then I was not in a state to say no because none of them knew about my problem. Now, I was feeling even more frustrated when they reminded me about my financial crises.

"Aditya, can you click one picture please?" Akhtar asked Aditya when we entered the lawn of the restaurant.

Every one of us stood at one side whereas Akhtar remained at the other side. Aditya took out his cell phone to click Akhtar.

"Gul," Akhtar signaled me to join him.

Kishan whistled loudly when I moved from one side to other and stood next to Akhtar. I felt a little nervous as Akhtar had never done anything like this before and no one had ever acknowledged us together. Akhtar lifted his left hand, stretched it towards me and kept it on my left shoulder embracing me. I took my right hand behind him, holding his waist and placed my left hand just below his chest posing like couples. I moved a little closer and touched his cheeks with my head matching his height. Aditya took many pictures of us; I was blushing from inside as I did not expect this from Akhtar. He, on the other hand, was looking happy too, he had lifted my mood by a very simple gesture he had just shown. The irritating *saree* was suddenly appealing about the charm and beauty it had given to me when I wore it. My money crises suddenly became the myth of my life. Everything was perfect.

***

"Let's meet tonight," Sohan said to me on call.

"Are you alright? I mean, I have to always ask you to meet me, but today you are asking me to meet you."

"*Koi badi baat nai hai,*" he meant that it was not a big deal if he asked me to meet him.

"At what time should I meet you then?"

"Do one thing, wait for me when you finish your work and I will pick you up from your office."

Oh god, what had happened to him? I thought. His office was in Deccan and my office was in opposite location when it comes to going towards Baner from Deccan, still he was ready to pick me up. Previously, when we both were staying at Magarpatta City, he would take the route via Koregaon Park to commute to his office. Koregaon Park was close from my office too, so he would pick me up while returning from office which would make sense. But then he would ask me to come to a place so that no one from my office would know that he used to drop me home.

"No, you will ask me to come to the square, but I cannot walk today."

"I know you are wearing *saree.*"

"How do you know that I am wearing a *saree?*" I was upset with him as last time when I was telling him about Akhtar, he abruptly disconnected the call. So I did not tell him that I was wearing *saree* today, otherwise I would have sent him my pictures for which he would have not praised me.

"Madam, we are your customer. We are paying you; we know everything happening at your end."

"*Customer hoge toh apne ghar me hoge*, do not tell me these things," I meant that he could not show his customer attitude to me. I used another of his phrases which he would use whenever he would not consider someone as superior than him. He laughed without saying anything.

"I will call you before leaving."

"Sure. Bye," I felt amazed as suddenly I was getting admiration from those two men who were most important to me after my family. It was surely a beautiful day for me, and I was getting irritated before without knowing what the day would unfold next for me.

***

"I will sit with both my legs on one side. Then you ride slowly and safely," I told Sohan before getting seated on his bike. He was waiting for me near the exit gate of our office wearing his helmet. He was wearing white slim fitting shirt, which was shining out in black cloudy weather, and gray trouser which was also slim fitting to him. His sleek black oxford formal shoes were just another quote of his fashionable attire and his black metallic chromosome watch was completing his look. He was looking way beyond handsome and attractive without even showing his face. Girls from distant were gazing at him and I saw their heart broke when they came to know that he was waiting for a girl, who could be most probably his girlfriend.

"Listen Gul, I have told you multiple times, it is not about how fast you drive but about how you drive fast," he took up the glass of his helmet and handed over his laptop bag to me.

He would always have something to tell me like this. It would just need me to doubt him in some way or the other and then he would be ready to tell me his learned lessons or his life rules, which would make me believe on his skills even more which I was missing these days; I did not say anything in return but smiled in admiration. He started his bike and we left. It was around eight in the evening and as it was not raining, everyone was out on their vehicle to reach their home. The road was full of vehicles, honking and trying to overtake each other. Even though Sohan was very good at driving, there were other factors which were making it difficult for me to sit on his bike. I was sitting one sided, holding my hand bag from one hand, his laptop bag was hanging on my back and though my right hand was free, I was trying to hold his bike so that I would not slip because of the *saree* I was wearing. *You can hold him.* Inner Gul was awake in my mind. *No I cannot.* I replied to her. *Yes, you can. What is the problem here? You are not comfortable so you can hold him, simple.*

"It is slippery, I cannot sit like this," I said to Sohan so that he would figure out some way to solve my problem apart from what inner Gul was suggesting to me.

"You are overloaded, give your hand bag to me," he pulled his bike on one side of road.

"This *saree* is slippery," I got off bike, not complaining about my hand bag but my *saree*.

"Still, give your bag to me; I will keep it on my lap," I handed my hand bag to him. "Is it fine now or should I take that laptop bag too?"

"No I can carry your bag like I always do." Every time Sohan would pick me after his office, he would hand over his laptop bag to me and I would hang it on my back. This was a default thing he would do. His bag was never a problem to me but the *saree* I was wearing was. Even after giving him my hand bag I was uncomfortable sitting behind him. I was continuously telling him that I was slipping from his bike seat. He was driving very slowly but it was not helping out much.

"Will you mind if I will hold you?" I asked him when I gave up managing myself.

He smiled. I was holding rear side of his bike with my left hand; I wrapped my right hand around his abdomen and rested my body on his back. He sped up his bike with confidence knowing that now, I would not slip. After forty minutes of bike ride, holding Sohan and resting my body on him, in a state of tranquility, we reached Baner. He parked his bike in front of Kooka shop and I got off his bike. He removed his helmet and adjusted his hair looking at rear view mirror and then looked at me.

"Let's go somewhere else, I don't want to drink Kooka today."

"Where do you want to go?"

"Sit," he said and took me to Aundh.

Aundh's ITI Road was one of the most happening places nearby. People from various age groups would come and hangout there. It was having shops of various types and ranges with a large footpath where people could sit as well. It was having huge range of restaurant serving world class food to their customers. The most popular one was Kadhai near Crossword bookstore serving Indian street food and sweets in their own way.

As we reached, Sohan started looking for parking but found none. So he parked his bike on the other side of road. Like the roads which we faced so far, this ITI Road was busy too. He was holding his helmet and my handbag from his right hand. We waited for few seconds to cross road and then he held my right hand from his left hand and started crossing road, taking me with him. I did not give any reaction but was totally awestruck by what he had done.

We have crossed roads multiple times before but he would never hold my hand even after knowing that I was poor in crossing roads, especially at night. I had told him multiple times that the shining headlights of vehicle would make me nervous, and I could not guess the distance of the vehicle from me, making it hard for me to cross the roads, but he would never help. Rather, he would make fun of me and would leave me behind running from one side to the other and then laughing on the opposite side, watching me cross the road. But today, he not only stood on my right side to protect me from the upcoming storms of vehicle, but held my hand too.

I was feeling special. As we crossed road, he handed my handbag to me and asked for his laptop bag. I adjusted the free end of my *saree* after giving him his laptop bag.

"I will eat *Pani Puri* first. Will you?" He proceeding towards Kadhai, informing me that he would eat one of the famous Indian street foods.

I smiled in confirmation and we moved towards billing counter to get our coupon. He told me many things in detail which he had done while he was in Lucknow. Dishes which his mother cooked for him, places he visited, shopping he had done and many other things, which made my day.

CHAPTER 19

"I have never been to any pub," I said when we were sitting idle at Kishan's apartment, making plans which we could possibly do tonight.

"Oh really, we can go to Area 51 tonight. It is Saturday and they have couples entry," Aditya said. "But girls are outnumbered."

We were only two girls, Meenal and I, against six boys.

"I will not make a stag entry," Kishan said.

Hemant, Priyam and Mudit nodded in agreement.

"Why are you people being a spoilsport today?" Meenal asked. "Why are we here when you don't want to go anywhere?"

"Who goes to pub with sisters?" Kishan said. "Both of you are our sisters. I am not in, ladies,"

I looked at Akhtar; he was not saying anything but was listening to everyone, playing some bubble game on his cell phone.

"Please," I requested them.

"Can any of your female friends join us?" Hemant asked.

Meenal and I looked at each other. The answer was no. I could have asked Chaudhary to come with us but she was busy in her own schedule so there was no point in asking her. Even she couldn't have solved the problem completely.

"It is fine if sometime we do not party," Kishan moved to another room.

"Akhtar," I made a sad face.

"What can I do? I am myself not here tonight."

"Where are you going?" I wasn't aware that he was going somewhere tonight.

"One of my friends has come from Delhi. I have to go and meet him."

I did not say anything but started watching TV silently. Since last weekend we were not able to plan anything. Though it was good in terms of saving money, it was quite boring when we would not do anything and stay at Kishan's apartment for no reason. Maybe I was feeling bored because Akhtar did not join us last weekend, as his mother was not well and this weekend also he was going to meet his friend. Sohan asked me to meet him two three times, and I couldn't meet him because I was in Kalyani Nagar. When I did not meet Sohan because I wanted to be with Akhtar, and Akhtar left all those time due to some situation, I was regretting why I did not meet Sohan.

"I am going to Baner then."

"Why?" Aditya asked. "Please stay, we will do something."

"If you have any plans for tomorrow I will come back, but I will leave now as I have to do other work as well," I took my hand bag. I was not at home for almost every weekend, which would leave no time for me to wash my used clothes or complete other works. I had to visit parlor too, so I thought to utilize this time.

"Are you leaving right away?" Akhtar asked.

"Yes," I rudely replied.

"If you can wait for one hour, I can drop you. I have to go near Baner only."

"Ok."

Then he went to his home to get ready. It was almost two months since Akhtar said that he liked me, I always wanted to ask him what he was thinking next. When was he going to take me officially as his girlfriend? This December I was turning twenty four years old. Abbu was already indirectly asking me about my marriage. He did not tell me, but I was sure that he was looking for some matches for me.

Before he could find any suitable match for me, I wanted to confirm Akhtar and my relationship status so that I could tell Abbu about him. But as we would always meet in group, I was not getting the right time to discuss this thing with him. I did not want to have this conversation over telephone or Whatsapp, so I thought this would be the right time to ask him about us. He was already too comfortable with me. I was seventy percent sure that he loved me. But then Dutta told me that I should wait for rest thirty percent too. She also said that I must not propose him, instead I should hold back until he proposes me.

She did not want me to turn into any grief in case Akhtar was not ready. She told me that just in case Akhtar would say no to me, it would be hard for me to overcome this feeling. She wanted me to have no expectation from him. Only then if anything good would happen, it would be a matter of great joy for me, but I was not able to control anything. I wanted to conclude fast, whatever the conclusion was. So I made up my mind to ask him about us.

When he came, I went down with my finger crossed hoping for the best. After a very long time I was feeling nervous in meeting him and unlike other time, this time the feeling of nervousness doubled when I saw him. He was wearing white t-shirt with gray jeans; the left leg of the jeans was ripped near his knee. His hair was wet and neatly combed as if his mother was sending him to school and combed his hair herself. He was looking cute and innocent like a child while talking to someone over phone roaming in parking near his car. He was planning with his friends, where they should gather and what could be done. When he saw me he disconnected his call, came close to me and touched my cheeks with his left hand. It was a fresh and cold touch.

I looked at him with brooding eyes. I was deeply engaged in thoughts of how I should ask him about things which were going inside my mind. He came closer to me, bent toward me and kissed me gently. This time I did not kiss him back. I stood still, otherwise I would either wrap my hands around his shoulder playing with his hair and he would lift me holding my waist, or I would keep my hands on his chest when he would be holding my face while kissing me.

After few seconds he sensed something was not right and stopped kissing me and looked at me. I lowered my eyes as a tear rolled down from my right cheek, the cheek which he touched from his hand. Whenever he would kiss me, he would ask me to look at him so that he could see my feelings through my eyes, and all those times he would always find me blushing out of shy. I did not want him to look into my eyes this time, as they were filled with the uncertainty of what would happen next.

"I am sorry," he moved a little away from me.

"It is not your fault," I wiped off my tear.

"Is everything alright? Do you want me to stay with you?"

"Can you drop me home?" I did not answer his question. I knew that if I would answer him, it could create a huge mess. I might ruin his evening with his friends so I thought to keep quite.

***

Tears which were coming out from my eyes were getting mixed with the water coming out of the shower. I was feeling so helpless, as if I missed the only chance of proposing Akhtar and now he would leave me behind. I was crying calling myself coward as I failed to express myself. I blamed myself. I told myself that he had asked me for time to come to a right decision. I told myself that I must wait for that time when he would accept his feelings towards me. Then I would be really happy and worthy of it. But I was not happy. I closed tap, wrapped myself with towel, came outside and found two missed calls from Sohan, followed by a Whatsapp message, *why are you not responding to me? What have I done?*

I unlocked my mobile screen and called him. The mobile screen went wet when I placed mobile on my ear.

"Hello," I said with stuffy nose when he received my phone call.

"Where are you?"

"I am at home."

"Whose home?" he accused me.

"Sohan, I am not in a good mood."

"*Koi badi baat nahi hai.*" He meant that it wasn't a big deal if my mood was not good. "Will you come to D-mart with me?" he did not gave a serious thought to what happened to me.

"When are you going to D-mart?"

"Now. I will pick you in fifteen minutes. I am starting from my place."

"I cannot get ready in fifteen minutes. I have just taken bath; I am not even wearing anything."

"Why are you talking to me without wearing anything?"

I laughed. "I am talking to you without wearing anything because you cannot see me naked."

"OK hmmm hmmm."

"Call me when you reach here," I disconnected his call. After ten minutes he called me when he was waiting outside my apartment. I was still not ready, my hair was wet and I had to apply kohl on my eyes as well. I hurried, closed my apartment door and ran towards elevator which took more than five minutes to stop at my floor, as someone else was using it. Meanwhile he called me again and asked me to hurry up. I reached him ten minutes late.

He was smoking, parking his bike near another *paan* counter, which we would rarely visit. He was wearing a dark blue t-shirt which was looking more like a shirt, as it had white buttons on it with small pockets on his chest on both side of the button. His t-shirt had half sleeves folded two times as usual, but this time his biceps were not as strong as before, maybe because he couldn't exercise due to his injury. His neck was covered with Chinese collar of the t-shirt and he had unbuttoned first two buttons which made him look cool. His t-shirt was slightly inside his black jeans, which he was wearing without belt. His batman printed slipper was adding to his coolness. He knew how to carry himself, which was one of the reason he was my favorite. He smiled looking at me. So did I. I took another five minutes to cross road while he was laughing on the other side.

"You are late, I am here since eternity."

"I don't know about eternity, but you are here earlier than the time you committed. I told you I will take time."

"Ok, ok," he started his bike.

I sat behind him and we proceeded towards D-Mart.

"Listen, I will give you thirty thousand rupees."

"What?"

"You owe money to some people right? Return it. I would have given you more, but I need money for something."

I did not expect him to say this to me. He had helped me many times before, but not like this. I did not know how to react.

"But Sohan, I will have to return it to you as well. There is no difference."

He grabbed one trolley when we reached D-Mart.

"Yes, but without any pressure. Return it to me whenever you are comfortable."

"I love you."

He smiled. He actually solved a lot of my problem. *I will return Kishan his twenty thousand rupees.* I thought. *Five thousand rupees, I will give to Abbu and rest five thousand to Shikha.* In case of Shikha, I did not have to worry because she also said the same thing which Sohan said- *I can return her money whenever I can.* She wasn't in a hurry. *But it doesn't mean that you should take it lightly.* I said to myself. *True.* Sohan was comparing *dahi* and yogurt while I was busy in my thoughts. By this time he had added some other stuff in his trolley like coffee powder, some snacks, men's deodorant, shampoo and shaving gel. After reading few details on the packaging of both *dahi* and yogurt, he ended up picking both.

"Do you want anything?" he picked few other things while I was following him to different sections.

I signaled him a no by shaking my head, I did not want to purchase anything, but I was still looking into various items they had kept for customers. When he proceeded towards men's clothes section, I left him and went to crockery section. I did not want to offend him if he wanted to look at some personal clothes. But, as far as I knew, he was the kind of person who would always think twice before doing anything. First, according to his style statement, I knew that he would always buy clothes from showrooms, and second, in case he wanted to buy any personal items, he would have never asked me to accompany him. Still to avoid any awkward scene, I did not stay with him.

"Gul," he called me after some time.

He was still in men's clothes section.

"Yes."

He was searching something under a large basket which was full of handkerchiefs.

"See this handkerchief; find me two more similar patterns, please," he showed me a sample of Van Heusen handkerchief he was holding.

I stood on the other side of the basket and started looking for one.

"Is this the one?" I picked one handkerchief from the basket after examining few.

"No. See it has only black lines in its border, yours is a different one.

The handkerchief he was holding was a solid white one with black lines on its border. The one I picked up was also solid white in color but it had red lines on its border. We searched for few minutes but found none matching the one he had picked. Moreover that basket was containing only four or five handkerchiefs from Van Heusen brand and the rest of the handkerchiefs were from a local brand.

"Can I help you, madam?" one of the attendants asked me while we were struggling to find the handkerchief of Sohan's choice.

I explained him our need. He searched for it and ended up finding nothing.

"Maybe it is out of stock, sir," he looked at Sohan.

"Can you cross check?"

"Sure." The attendant started looking for barcode of that handkerchief.

Unlike the local ones, there was no barcode present on the Van Heusen's handkerchiefs. The attendant took one sample of it and inquired some of the other attendants. By this time three of them were looking for what we were asking, or more precisely what Sohan was demanding. I looked at Sohan, he was looking pissed off. I had never seen him like this; I doubted that he was going to shout at those attendants.

"I will confirm with my manager sir," the attendant who came first to help us said to Sohan and took one of the handkerchiefs; other two attendant disappeared as he went. Sohan was still holding one handkerchief he wanted to buy.

"Why is it so urgent?"

"Stay out of this. I will screw him if he tries to mess with me."

"I will gift you a better one," I tried to calm him down. He did not reply. After some time the attendant returned with another man. The other man was his manager, I believed.

"Sir, these are Van Heusen handkerchiefs. They come in a pack of three or six, each with different color border," he took all handkerchiefs out from the basket.

"But they are open here like the other ones," Sohan was ready to argue with him.

"Someone by mistake opened them, I think."

"Then do the mistake again and get me two more handkerchiefs with black border."

The attendant and I were watching silently. Some other people crossing by noticed us.

"Sir, they come in a packet. We cannot open and sell them as they do not have individual barcode," the manager raised his voice.

Now he was also sounding angry as Sohan was asking something which was not possible.

"Don't shout, if they are open here means something illegal happened with them."

I moved from the other side of the basket towards the side where Sohan was standing. I was a little afraid, as he was losing his temper, but I placed my right hand on his left shoulder rubbing it lightly in a gesture to convey that it was ok, let it go, but he did not notice.

"We will inquire about this, but we cannot open another packet for you. If you want, you can buy a pack of three or six, which comes with different color border."

And then he showed some of the sample packets the attendant had brought when the manager said something to him in Marathi.

"I am ready to buy a packet, all I am saying is to make a packet for me which would contain all three handkerchiefs with black border."

I knew he was demanding something which was not feasible, but at this point I was unable to find a way to calm him down, and because of his anger he was being rigid.

"We cannot do any changes; you have to buy the original packet as it is."

They both were arguing with each other, and no one was ready to listen. After some point, the manager gave up and adjusted a packet as per Sohan's demand. Sohan took the packet and proceeded to pick some other things from his list. I was saying nothing to him, I was a little upset. Though he won the argument, I was not expecting such behavior from him. When we reached billing counter, the bill counterman said something to another attendant and after few seconds, the manager came to generate our bill. Sohan's face turned red out of rage. The manager was reading barcode of every item we had in our bucket. When he picked up that handkerchief packet, he did the same thing. He scanned the barcode of the packet but edited its price manually.

"Why are you editing it manually?" Sohan shouted in anger.

People standing in other queues looked at us.

"We have given you special service, sir. How can the price be normal?" the manager replied sarcastically.

His sarcasm increased Sohan's anger. D-mart price for the packet of three Van Heusen handkerchiefs was two hundred and sixty rupees, whereas the MRP of the packet was three hundred rupees. The manager had cost us the MRP of the handkerchief instead of its D-mart price.

Sohan raised his voice to a pitch I never imagined before. "Are you trying to fool me?"

"We did not want these handkerchiefs," I shouted looking at the manager and then stopping my angry eyes on Sohan. No one responded to me but agreed at the same time. I pulled Sohan's hand, signaling him to move out of the queue and asked manager to proceed with rest of the items.

When he was done, I lifted the bag, which was filled with our items, and moved out while Sohan was paying them. He was smiling naughtily coming out of the exit gate, looking at me. I was still looking at him angrily.

"Calm down. Don't scare me," he said in a naughty way.

He realized that I was genuinely angry and he would have to face the circumstances.

"Sohan what was that? You are mature and more educated than him. Still he was arguing for right thing and you were shouting unnecessarily."

"They pissed me off, I was angry enough to hit them."

"So what if you were angry? If someone is pissing you off, will you behave illiterate? What if at some time, I do something which pisses you off? Will you hit me?" I shouted on him.

"No *baboo*, I will never do that," he said innocently and I had to smile.

CHAPTER 20

Day by day Akhtar's mother was getting angrier on him due to his increased activities, which was causing him to stay away from home most nights. Rest of us were staying in rented house with other roommates, so it was not an issue for us, but on the other hand when Akhtar was staying with his parents he had to report everything to them.

He told me that his mother had started thinking that he was in bad company. She would spy on him by checking his cell phone or calling his college friends to inquire about him. His college friends would handle the situation, but would later ask him questions like where he had been. He had told them that he would hang out with friends who went to Leh with him, but they were not convinced. They also said to him that he had never behaved like this since the time they were friends, but Akhtar was not ready to accept what was going on in his life.

He would spend time with me, get intimate with me, exchange selfies, praise me, but would never commit anything to me. This was disturbing me from inside. Each time I would meet him, I would decide about asking him to marry me, and each time I would fail. This was building a lot of emotional stress on me which was one of the reasons I was getting irritated if he would tease me. I would sometime shout on him in front of others. Some other time I would demand something which was not feasible for him. I just wanted to test how different he would treat me from others. But he would always control his behavior in front of others, and would show exactly opposite gestures for me when there would be no one around. I was totally in doubt why he was behaving this way.

I remembered last time when we went for lunch, he publically asked for a picture with me, posing like a couple, and now I was nothing more than a friend to him when I was in front of others. But he would never let me feel unwanted over Whatsapp. There, I was the woman of his dreams he would always fantasize about making love with. I wasn't totally happy with his dual personality; I wanted him to be the same no matter what. That's why I would ignore our gathering many times and run to Baner if Sohan would ask to meet him, who on the other hand, would always make me feel happy.

Though he was also the one who would keep me away from his friend circles, but I would never take that offensively because I knew the reason behind it. Once when we were staying in Magarpatta City, Sohan introduced me to his roommate, Akhil. Akhil sent me a friend request on Facebook after our second meeting when Sohan took me to his apartment. I accepted his friend request without informing Sohan. It was not a problem until Akhil and I met a third time when I was moving from Baner. Sohan came with him to help me, since that day Akhil was messaging me on Facebook and we were chatting formally.

I told this thing to Sohan and he took it casually. One night when Akhil was drunk, he forcefully wanted me to chat with him and asked for my phone number. He said now that I have moved to Baner, I must not be dating Sohan so he was ready to date me. He also said that just in case I was seeing Sohan too, I need not to tell this thing to Sohan and could date both of the men together. *We can enjoy without letting Sohan know about this,* was his exact words.

I was pissed off after reading his message. I called Sohan immediately and told him that I did not want to see his face again and disconnected without listening to him. I was crying breathlessly thinking about how bad Sohan would have represented me in front of his friends, which was the reason his friend was treating me this way. Sohan called me back and asked me what had happened. I told him everything. He asked me to share screen shots so that he could read Akhil's exact word. He said that he would take care of this and explained that he had never discussed anything about me with his friends, so there was no chance that he represented me bad in anyway.

Next day, I received another message from Akhil asking for apology. I did not respond but asked Sohan what he said to Akhil. *I have spoken to him and this thing will never happen again,* he said. Since that incident, Sohan was very careful introducing me to his new friends. When another of his roommates from Baner, who was in touch with me because I wanted to plan a surprise for Sohan's birthday, did the same thing, Sohan turned very protective for me. Since then he would neither take me to his room, nor would he let me see any of his friends. He shared one of his trusted friend's contact information with me and told me to get in touch with him in case of emergency. Apart from this friend, I was in touch with Kunal and Harish only, who were gentlemen like Sohan. Still without breaching Sohan, I would never speak to them unless there would be something I would be secretly doing for him, otherwise he would always be my first point of contact.

***

Akhtar told other people that he would drop me home when we came out of a restaurant after our team dinner. I did not object because he had done this before as well. Before leaving toward parking, we brought *paan* from a local shop whose shopkeeper was about to close his shop. It was ten minutes less for eleven in the night. We greeted each other and started leaving.

As other people had to leave on two wheelers, and Akhtar and I had to leave in his car, we moved in another direction toward four wheeler parking. When we reached Akhtar's car, he asked me if I wanted to spend some more time with him. I nodded in agreement as I was waiting for such moments like never before. On the way, he told me that his parents had gone to Delhi for some reason and he was alone, so he was taking me to his home. It was the first time I was going to his home. My heart was filled with feelings of excitement and fear.

Excitement, because I knew what was going to happen. Fear, because I doubted myself to stand up to his expectations. We were quiet. Maybe he was also surrounded with similar feelings. He was driving, holding my right hand with his left hand, sometime leaving it to change gears and then holding it back. The silence was breached when he parked his car and a pet dog from his neighbor's home started barking. He opened gate and took me inside. It was dark, so I followed him to his bedroom. It was a simple room with a double bed kept below a huge window which was covered with curtains and a wooden cupboard attached with wall on the left side of the bed. Right side of the bed was attached with a washroom.

"I will get some water for you," he moved out of the room leaving me with no clue, what I was supposed to do next.

Should I take off my clothes and wait for him naked on his bed? I asked myself. *No, maybe I am overreacting. I must not act without knowing his intentions. Am I breathing well? You ate a pan stupid, go gargle first.* I ran to his washroom, gargled many times and made sure that I was not breathing badly by breathing outside my mouth and smelling my own breathe by blocking it from my hand. I came out of washroom and applied lip gloss over my lips. I lightly applied my rose perfume so that he would not come to know about it, but at the same time he would experience a good fragrance from me. I checked myself multiple times standing against the mirror which was fixed on one of the doors of the cupboard.

You can do it; you can do it, I told myself roaming around his room. I knew that this time we would definitely end up having sex with each other, as there was no interference from others. *Calm down Gul, do not expect much,* I murmured and stood on one side of the bed, opened curtains and looked outside.

After few seconds, he stood behind me, gently playing his fingers through my hair. He kissed me on my back, closed the curtains and moved his hands even more gently toward my waist. He slowly started biting me on my back, taking my hair off my shoulder. I stood blissfully, enjoying the soft pain caused by his bite.

He moved his hand lower on my back, just above the strip of my bra, touched the zip of my peach color plain georgette *kameez*, unzipped it slowly, held me through my waist and turned me toward him. I looked at his eyes while he hurriedly kissed me on my lips.

With his hands, he dropped the *kameez* off from my body and leaned towards my neck, kissing me just above my cleavage. Then he pushed me on his bed taking my white leggings out, closing lights and removing all his clothes. I had never seen a naked man before. I liked it. He moved over me to kiss me again, faster. He pressed his lips into my neck, creating a lot of pressure on my body. His hands were equally dominating over my bosom. I moved my hands over his back, he was sweating. He was continuously running his hands over my bosom, then through my stomach going towards my belly button, and then coming back towards my bosom creating a huge force which was causing me to moan in despair, which in turn encouraged him more. By this time his body was totally resting on my body, his teeth biting me slowly over my neck.

He took his hands to unhook my bra, which he tossed to the other side of the bed, dragged his lips over my bosom. He buried his face on my breast making a tight hold on both of my hands and then he took his teeth on top of my breast, I moaned again taking my head upward, exposing a lot of skin for him to tease. My body was pressurized by his manly force causing me uncomfortable breathe and warm sweat.

He was holding my hand tightly, leaving no chance for me to escape. I did not want to escape, but to be taken a little gently. He did not care and continued causing me discomfort. By this time my pleasure had turned into an unknown fear. The thing I liked earlier started scaring me. *Gently,* I screamed while he was roughly kissing me all over my bosom.

He looked at me with a wicked smile, kissed me on my lips and started moving his face towards my stomach. Then he rested on his knees on both side of my abdomen, left my hand unattended and moved his hands towards my waist through my breast, trying to take off the last piece of cloth which remained between us. A fear ran through my body. Though I was having no control over the situation, my mind was continuously telling me that I would not be able to bear the pain. His ruthlessness added onto the danger I was feeling.

"I am scared," I gasped heavily, while his right hand was inside my boy shorts. He did not listen and started taking it off. "I am scared. I do not want this," I said loudly escaping from his grip. His desperate face turned shocking.

"It will be fine," he came closer to me. "I will not harm you," he kissed me on my lips and tried to take out my boy shorts at the same time.

"I am scared," I repeated and buried my head on his chest.

"Why are you scared?" He hugged me tightly so I would not escape from his grip, his hand was again inside my boy shorts.

"I am scared it will cause a lot of pain to me," I cried taking his hand out from my shorts. Now his hands were patting me on my back.

"A little pain is expected, like this," he tried to convince me and again took his hand inside me.

"No. I do not want this," I pushed him out from me.

"Fine, I will not force you," he came closer and hugged me tightly for few minutes.

I was shivering under his arms. He held me from one hand and tried to take out one towel from his cupboard. And then he wiped off the sweat from my body, covered me with the towel, and asked me to rest while he lay down next to me. I hid my body under his arms and closed my eyes sobbing lightly.

"You have never told me anything about your likes."

This was the first time he was asking me something which was personal to me. I told him what he asked. I also told him all those unusual things I remembered I had done during my graduation. He was cross questioning me sometimes and I was answering him. I told him how I got this job and what happened in our training. I told him about Dutta, Shikha and Chaudhary by narrating many incidents we would cherish throughout our life.

"And now our friendship is even growing stronger with time." I smiled rubbing my hand on his chest. "I love you, Akhtar," I said after taking a pause. I crossed my finger and looked at him for his response, but he was already asleep.

CHAPTER 21

"Since the day you have come here you are hiccupping badly. Who is missing you?" Shahid tried to tease me.

It was one of the beliefs that if someone misses you, you get hiccups. I was in Bhopal since last couple of days and was very disturbed by the merciless hiccups. Sometimes, Akhtar would flirt with me by saying that he was missing me hence I was getting hiccups. I would blush for what he would say, but on the other hand I would feel annoyed by the hiccups. They would strike at any random time and last for hours. I did not notice how they would disappear.

"It is my boyfriend who is missing me," I laughed. I did not know why I laughed.

"And who is your boyfriend?" he tickled me.

I laughed even harder. I was joking with him. I was single. I did admit to Akhtar that I love him, but he was not awake to listen to me. Nothing had changed since the night I had spent at Akhtar's home. He would behave with me like a friend in public, but like a desperate and a true lover when we would be alone. But irrespective of the fact that we were surrounded by people or not, he would keep gazing at me with greater admiration.

Only the conversation we would have over Whatsapp had changed. He would not resist saying how desperately he wanted to love me. He would keep praising me. Now the usual *Hi* and *Hello* between us had turned into serious sexual discussions. The cute and ugly selfies had turned into nude erotic ones. We would talk less with each other and exchange many selfies which was one of the ways he would feel me around him. Before coming to Bhopal, it was easy for me to electrify him with my sexy clicks. I would take pictures while bathing, while changing clothes, and send it to him and he would ask for more. He would ask me to show which color bra and panty I would wear for the day, and then he would tease me.

He would keep track of my periods and take care of me on those days. As I was not able to satisfy him last time when we were at his home, he would suggest me to watch some porn movies so that I would gain confidence, but I would never do that. He would say that just in case he would catch me again, he would not show any mercy on me. But these things were missing since the day I was in Bhopal. He was turning restless. Though I had managed to send one selfie to him wearing bikini but he was not happy. He was asking for more nude ones which was not possible for me. I was trying to sympathize, but he was being stubborn like a small child.

**

Me: It is not possible for me Akhtar, why don't you understand.
Akhtar: But I want to see you, now.
He was awake early morning and was craving for me.
Me: You can see me in pictures I have sent to you earlier.
Akhtar: No. I want to see how you are looking right now.
I clicked one picture of me on my phone, while resting on bed, half covered with a thin blanket. I sent it to him.
Akhtar: Not like this.
He replied making angry emoticons after looking into the picture I had sent. *Why can't he control himself?* I thought. *Please,* he added after few seconds. *Men will be men,* I thought and moved towards kitchen to bring a glass of water, and to check if Abbu and Shahid were lost in their sleep or not. They were showing no signs of being awake. Abbu was snoring which was adding benefit onto Akhtar's greed. I came back to my room, locked door from inside, closed all curtains and switched on lights. Then I removed all my clothes, sat on bed and clicked one selfie posing like a goddess of love, who would sexually arouse and delight her male counterpart. I opened my Whatsapp to send the picture to Akhtar while he was sending me multiple angry emoticons. The moment he saw my picture, all his anger turned into kisses.
Akhtar: I can run all the way to Bhopal after seeing you like this.
Me: And then?

Akhtar: And then I will kiss you without wasting any time.
Me: Huh, just a kiss for such a picture.
I said as if I wasted my efforts just to get a mere kiss from him.
Akhtar: No, you will moan in pain after that.
I smiled and send two three more such pictures to him. He yearned with the pain of being away from me before getting into sleep.

***

Shahid was getting ready for his college. I was hiccupping in kitchen while making breakfast. As I warned Abbu about getting inside of kitchen, he tried to occupy himself by cleaning our house. Akhtar was very happy today, as his day started the way he wanted it. He was continuously chatting with me. No doubt he was in a very good mood. I had kept my mobile on the platform of kitchen, as I had to reply to him every now and then. I garnished one plate of *poha,* which was rice flattened into dry flakes and cooked after soaking them under water, with some freshly cut coriander leaves and came to our common room to serve it to Shahid. When I returned, Abbu was reading my Whatsapp chat with Akhtar. His face turned pale with the shame, how his only daughter had taken out clothes to make it naked in front of the world. His shivering fingers were scrolling up and down in the mobile screen trying to figure out how shameless his daughter had turned. His watery eyes trying not to believe what they had just seen.

"Abbu, I can explain," I looked at him with trembling voice. He slapped me without uttering a single word. I did not dare look at his face again. I stood in silence. I knew no words would be justifiable enough to explain to him why I did so. He slapped me again and again. I fell on ground, but he did not stop beating me. His shivering weak hands suddenly gained power to beat the hell out of me. Shahid ran towards me, trying to save me from his terror, continuously asking what had happened and crying at the same time. Abbu roared in pain, the psychological pain which I had given him, and for the physical pain which he was giving me.

He was beating me for the first time in his life. I did not protest, thinking that it might help him to forgive me. Shahid tried to control him taking some of Abbu's un-aimed punches on him, still struggling with what had caused such turmoil at his home. When Abbu got tired and saw blood on his hands, he handed over my cell phone to Shahid, so that he would unfold the disgusting face of his lovable sister. With those hands covered with blood, Abbu slapped himself multiple times on his face, sat on the most unreachable corner of kitchen and cried as if someone had killed his child. He was beating his own head realizing that the one who had killed his child was himself. I was crying, laying on ground for the trauma I had given to him. I had never seen him like this, not even when Amma died. Shahid was crying with so much anger on his face. He stood still, looking at Abbu, and then he looked at me, took his bag and went out without saying anything. After sometime, I wiped blood from my mouth and nose and went closer to Abbu. He was still sobbing looking towards the roof.

"Abbu, I am sorry." My mouth was filled with tears and blood. I touched his feet and asked for his forgiveness. He did not react. "Abbu please forgive me," I rested my head on his feet.

"Go away," he looked away from me.

His voice was firm with the order he had given.

"No Abbu. Please. Please listen to me," I cried and begged him.

"Go away. And never come back." This time he looked at me with eyes filled with hatred.

"Please Abbu I will never speak to him again," I was ready to sacrifice the love of my life for my life. He did not say anything, but grabbed my hand and dragged me out of the house. I tried to hold everything that was coming in between trying to keep myself in. He threw me out like garbage which was meant to be picked by none.

"You are not my daughter anymore," he closed door on my face.

I kept knocking it again and again to hear nothing back from him. I moved to every possible window which could have connected me to him, but I found him nowhere. I kept calling him multiple times asking for his forgiveness, until I fainted.

***

I had lost the track how long I was laying on the ground outside my own house. I opened my burning eyes. Fierce, scorching sunlight was falling on me. I tried to pick myself up but my body was hurting, making it hard to move. My head was spinning like a wheel. Dried blood coated my face. My throat was crying for water and acute hiccups tried to take my last breath. I felt nauseous so I opened my mouth to take out the acidic sensation, but there was nothing inside except the guilt of hurting Abbu. I closed my eyes trying to recollect my strength.

A cute young girl with her long hair falling over her waist was playing inside my mind. She was wearing a knee length white cotton frock. Her frock was ripped in places but she cared for nothing. Her father was calling her and she was busy combing hair of her cute little doll. *Gul, my love, don't you want to get your hair done?* Her father said coming closer to her. *First I will comb her hair and then you can comb mine.* She replied to her father winning hearts of a million people through her cuteness. Her father picked her up and kissed her multiple times on her forehead. *Abbu, your beard is pricking on my nose,* she said struggling to get away from her father's embrace. But her father did not stop and loved her even more. *You are the best thing that ever happened to me,* her father said and kissed her again.

I burst into tears. How could a cute girl who was the best thing that ever happened to her father turned out to be the worst? I was dying out of shame. *Abbu had never let money affect our upbringing. He had sacrificed a lot just to make us happy. He always believed in me.* I thought. *And what have I done? I stabbed him on his chest. I must tell him that I love Akhtar which made me do so. If he is ready to accept Akhtar, it will be well and good for me, otherwise I will do whatever he will say.*

I picked myself up and moved towards main gate of our house. It was still locked from inside. I knocked but Abbu did not respond. I knocked again and again, called out for Abbu and failed to hear anything from him. But I kept knocking until he opened the door. His eyes were red. It was a clear sign that he had cried a lot. Without saying anything, he threw all my stuff outside and closed door again. I begged to him to accept me back and cried out.

"If you do not take your filthy face from here, you will end up watching me dead," he opened door again.

His voice was filled with abomination.

"Because of you, my little boy, Shahid, will suffer. Is that what you want?" he shouted with tears running from his eyes.

"No," I moved backward. I had already seen how we suffered when Amma died. I did not want to recreate the same scene, so I silently started collecting my stuff in my bag. It contained my cell phone as well. There were lots of messages from Akhtar, but I did not find them important to read. I cursed him somewhere in my mind. He was the reason for what happened to me. I was an idiot to fall for him. I was a fool to take off my clothes for him when he did not even acknowledge his feelings for me. I covered my face with a stole so that no one would be able to see my shameful face and moved toward city to somehow get back to Pune.

***

Where are you? I messaged Chaudhary after coming back to my room. She was nowhere. *Out of boredom, I moved to my brother's place,* she replied to me after sometime. I took deep breath as a sign of relief. I did not have the courage to tell her what happened with me, or why I was back to Pune early, or why I was beaten so badly. In fact I did not have the courage to tell anyone about it. I was not replying to Akhtar, and Abbu was not replying to me. Akhtar did not even call me once to ask why I was not replying to him. But I did not lose any hopes and kept calling Abbu and Shahid every ten to fifteen minutes. I had not eaten anything since yesterday, and I was feeling weak. But my willingness to live this life was much weaker than my body. I looked at mirror and found multiple bruises over my face, but I kept wondering about the bruise Abbu's heart would have because of me. I moved inside washroom to clean my face when I heard my phone ringing. I ran to hear from Abbu, but it was Sohan who was calling me. I felt bad as it was not Abbu but at the same time I felt glad as Sohan was the only one with whom I would have thought to share my pain. He was calling me when, unknowingly, I needed him the most.

"Hello," I received his call and said in a dull voice.

"Where are you? You don't have any time for me."

I started crying over phone.

"Why are you crying?"

"I had a fight with Abbu," I sobbed. I told him everything that happened back in Bhopal, but I did not tell him that Abbu raised his hands on me. I did not want him to dislike Abbu for any reason.

"It is fine. This is every family's story, but it doesn't mean that he doesn't love you."

"He asked me to never come back to home. He also said that I am not his daughter anymore," I burst into tears.

"He must be angry. When you get angry with me, don't you say that you will never talk to me, but does it ever happen?" he laughed.

"No," I also smiled.

"When you say so, I just give you time to rethink about it. After some time, when I feel that you will be no longer upset on me, all I need is to call you back and speak like nothing ever happened."

"Maybe I will call him after sometime," I understood what he was trying to say.

"Sure."

"But what if he never speaks to me again? Where will I go?" I immediately forgot what he just told me and started losing all my hopes

"Hmmm, then I will suggest you to take transfer to Lucknow."

"Lucknow?"

"Yes, I am going back to Lucknow."

Since a very long time he was trying to go back to Lucknow, and finally the time had come for him.

"What? But I cannot stay here without you," I cried even more loudly.

"That's why I don't tell you anything in advance, because then you start crying and make things difficult for me," he got a little angry. I cried even more. "Baboo it is not fixed yet and even if I go, I will come to meet you."

"Take me with you," I requested him. It was obvious that I had a bad habit to see him every day and to talk to him every time. He was implicit part of my life.

He laughed. "I already asked you to take transfer to Lucknow. But wait for some time. Let me go first, I may go to Lucknow or Delhi and then you can come."

"Is it not fixed yet?"

"No, it is in progress. I want to go to Lucknow, but due to career point of view, Delhi is also an option."

"I will follow you wherever you will go," I wanted to follow him wherever he goes, like ants follow their trails.

He laughed even louder.

"Yes, let me know when you move and I will ask for transfer," I said without even thinking of anything else. I knew life would be better if he would be around. He did not say anything. I also kept quiet for some time thinking how he had diverted me from the trauma I was going through. A moment earlier, I was dying out of shame and then his call changed everything. I felt normal and gained a little confidence to call Abbu once again.

"I will call you in evening. We will meet then."

I did not put the phone down, standing in doubt how I would show him my abnormal face.

***

After Sohan hung up the call, I lost all my courage. I was crying and hadn't eaten or drank anything. I called Abbu and Shahid a thousand times and received a single message from Shahid. *Do not force us to change our number,* he warned me through a message. I did not call them after reading it, but I was not able to stop my tears; my eyes were swollen bulging out of my face like that of a frog, my bruises were even darker, and under such condition I was going to see Sohan. He called me and asked me to meet him. He was so innocent that I was not able to deny. I tried to clean my bruises, especially the one near my lips, so that it would be less visible. I washed my eyes with cold water but they were still burning extensively. I took out one of my cotton *kameez* to wear, draped its *dupatta* over my head and moved out of house. I kept my eyes low to avoid looking at people who were crossing me, but I had to look up to find Sohan. And when I looked up I found everyone was gazing at me as if my sin had been broadcasted. I somehow managed to pass them to find Sohan standing in front of Kooka shop where he was speaking to someone over phone. His charming eyes were looking in my direction. When I reached him, the charm from his eyes turned into repulsion. I smiled with my broken lips making an eye contact with him, but lowered my eyes when he did not return the smile.

"Shall I take you to doctor?" he disconnected his call.

His voice was dull as if he was feeling pity for me.

"No, I am good," I cleverly wiped tear from my left eye. He signaled me to sit and went to order two Kooka with crush. Before getting the order, he turned and looked at me. His eyebrows were curved towards each other making vertical wrinkles on his forehead, signaling that he was feeling stressed because of me. He gave me my Kooka and sat next to me. I focused on finishing my Kooka without saying anything. When we were done, he asked my permission to leave. I knew that it was difficult for him to stay. Whenever there would be any situation out of his control, he would not speak, but at the same time there would be numerous things going on inside his mind which would clearly reflect on his face. He would not crack any joke, he would not smile, he would not even look at me, and I had learned to silently accompany him on those situations. I remember once, for some reason his Goa trip with Kunal and Harish was cancelled at the last moment. It was the most awaited trip for him and he was desperate for it. A week before his trip I had a fight with him, and as usual I was avoiding him. On the day they were supposed to fly for Goa, Harish told me that the trip had been cancelled and Sohan was so upset that he had blocked both of them over calls and Whatsapp and had left all the common groups, leaving no chance for communication. That day when I messaged Sohan on Whatsapp he asked me to meet him. When I met him, he was very disturbed but resisted himself for saying anything against his friends. I just followed him silently for one hour from Kooka shop to *paan* counter and then to my apartment parking. I knew that my presence mattered more than my words to him.

"All because your trip is cancelled and now you are sad doesn't mean that I am not upset with you. Our fight is a different account and for that you still need to conciliate me," I said to him in order to break the silence and make him smile. He laughed after listening to me and went after talking to me for a while. Maybe I was his stress buster that day, but today I was causing him stress. That day I had to make him smile as I could not manage to see him upset, but today when I was upset, I saw him helpless. He could not have raised his voice against Abbu nor could he blame Akhtar.

CHAPTER 22

"Where were you? I was worried," Akhtar said to me after coming to my desk.

"You were worried and you did not even call me once."

I had joined office back when my face was normal. No one from office was aware that I was in Pune; I did not want to create any scene, so I did not bother anyone. But the person who had joined office back was not the same person who had left. A part of me was killed back in Bhopal. The part I thought Akhtar could bring back. I did not want to force him to accept me all because Abbu had abandoned me, so I did not tell him what had happened. It was only Sohan who knew about it. I was behaving normal with others, controlling my trauma from inside.

"So, did you get the good news," Hemant shouted coming to my desk.

"Good news?"

"Our big brother will get married soon. He is seeing girls these days," Hemant patted Akhtar on his back.

Soon Kishan and others created a chaos at my desk. I looked at Akhtar with questioning eyes. He avoided looking at me. I realized how Abbu would have felt a few days back when I did not stand up to his expectations. I was in the same place today. Now it was clear to me why he was not messaging me since last couple of days. I did not know how to react, but there was a burning sensation inside my chest which was increasing as people were laughing around me.

I wanted to run away from Akhtar. I wanted to run away from

everyone, to a place where no one could ever notice me shrieking. But all I could do was to give a fake smile in order to hide my scream of pain. Few days back I was so happy and important and today, I lost all my happiness and importance in others' lives. I lost my family for a person who was planning his own family other than me, without even informing me. I lost my family for a person who was not even sure to love me back for his entire life. I looked at everyone and felt as if they were laughing on my misfortune. *Why are they laughing, aren't they aware about Akhtar and I?* I thought. Though I was surrounded by them, I felt alone. Slowly, I turned towards my desktop to avoid their celebration, which was killing me, and eventually they moved to their desks but Akhtar remained. I behaved as if he did not exist. He moved my hand bag to one side and sat on my desk. I pretended to be busy.

"I will not lie to you," he said after some time when I was totally ignoring him. "I am seeing girls and my parents have decided to marry me this year."

I looked at him with wet eyes but did not say anything.

"Let us go outside."

His hands were shivering, and he was trying to smile in order to behave normal. Looking at his face, I understood that something even worse was yet to come. We moved outside office and reached parking, which was the perfect place to discuss personal matters.

He spoke when we reached near his car. "You already know that my parents are searching a match for me."

I did not say anything in return, but stood facing him resting my back on his car.

"Talk to me Gul. This is not easy for me," he sounded frustrated when I was playing with my fingers out of nervousness.

"Do you love me?" I looked at his eyes with a clear vision of what should be the agenda of our discussion.

"This is a big question," he smiled again, pretending that he was not breaking down.

"Of course it is a big question. Do you think that we are passing time with each other?" I interrogated him.

"No, but I cannot say that I love you," he looked at floor while I was looking at his face.

I was dumbstruck by what he just said. I felt as if I was slapped for trusting him and breaking Abbu's trust on me. But the problem was that I wasn't slapped on my face. It was my soul who was hit; it was my trust which was smashed. Somehow I felt as if I deserved it, all these days Abbu would guide me how harsh this world was, but I never listened to him. I trusted everyone. Today I was punished for not listening to him.

"You do not love me, but you were ready to have sex with me. It means you were just fulfilling your physical needs."

"That was my fault. I should have never done that," he said with tears in his eyes.

"What did you say? When you were kissing me, at that time did you feel as if you were making a mistake? And if it was a mistake since beginning, why did you do that? How can you justify it?"

"I knew that we don't have any future together, but I was helpless. I lose all my control when I see you. I just wanted to be with you. I cannot tell you how I feel when I see you smiling."

"And then you are saying that you don't love me," I turned polite as he was contradicting his own words. I knew he was lying, I have seen love in his eyes for me. I have seen how he would look at me with admiration. I have seen how happy he would turn when I would be around.

"I like you; I am comfortable with you. But I cannot commit anything false to you because I know that cannot happen," he gained his confidence.

"What is it Akhtar?" I moved closer to him, looking at his eyes and taking his hands on mine. "I know you love me. What is the problem, tell me?" I tried to melt him emotionally.

His eyes were speaking what his lips were not able to say. Somehow I knew why he was forcing himself to say that he didn't love me, but I wanted to hear it aloud. He kept looking at me with tears flowing down slowly from his right bearded cheek while he was still smiling trying to convey that he was alright.

***

Days were passing; I was only a body which was forced to live without any hopes, without any expectations, without any interest to do anything. I was just living for the sake of living. I would not talk to people, I would not laugh, and I would not go out for any social gathering. I would just go to office and return home. If money weren't important, office wouldn't have been an option I would have considered. Initially Kishan and other people were asking me what had happened, but I did not dare tell them anything.

They would ask me to join them over lunch and tea breaks, they would expect me to be a part of their gatherings, they would tease me some time to make me laugh. But nothing would change my feelings. Akhtar, on the other hand was behaving totally normal, as if nothing happened to him. He was part of every social gathering, every fun activity, which I was also doing before my life was ruined. Two three times I tried to move on and joined them when they invited me to such parties, but I ended up being a spoil sport to their good moods.

It was not possible for me to show something which was not true. I was sad. There was no other part of me, and the feeling was more intense when Akhtar was around. I would die multiple times watching him laughing on jokes, playing pranks and being the ideal person for everyone. Sometimes I would piss off and shout unnecessarily. I was not able to digest how happy Akhtar was when I was having nothing. Sometimes I would feel like telling him the cost I had paid to love him, but I knew that I was not important to him anymore and nothing could change his decision. So I started living with it, I left the entire common Whatsapp groups as they were irritating me more.

My heart would burn when Akhtar would chat in those groups but would not reply to me. He was clearly avoiding me; I, on the other hand, was avoiding everything else. So eventually everyone left me on my own. They stopped inviting me whenever they would hangout, they stopped trying to make me laugh, and they stopped noticing that I existed. Or maybe I did not exist. I was not trying to hang out with anyone, I did not want to laugh or feel happy, I was having no reason to do that.

Abbu and Shahid were not talking to me since last one month, and the person who was responsible for it was not even giving a thought to me. On the worst of my mood, when there would be nothing to console me, I would plead to Akhtar. I would beg in front of him to accept me, to talk to his family about me, to love me, to ask for my selfies and to do every other thing which he was doing earlier. But without any surprise he would ask me to move on. I was not able to make him understand that I was totally consumed by him. Same office, same friend circle was making it more difficult for me to come out of his aura. But genuinely I did not want to come out of his aura. He was an ideal man. That's why everyone was on his side. I was on his side too, that's why I was not forcing him to run away with me. I did not even ask him to do so.

I knew he was the only son of his parents who were the main reason why he was not accepting me. His parents were fanatic orthodox. He told me that they would never accept me, for I did not belong to their category. They were *Sunni* and I was *Shia* by category. This was not surprising for me. I knew that most of the love stories were incomplete because of the fight between religions and cast. The thing which was shockingly disappointing for me was that Akhtar was not even ready to try once for his love.

When love had to fight against religions and cast, the people who are in love with each other stands together, but I was standing alone fighting against the world to console my own love. I didn't know what would be the result of this fight, but at least I was ready to try. I was ready to convince his family on his behalf, I was ready to do anything they would ask. I was ready to serve them in every way.

I was ready for the change. But before his family, he himself was my first challenge. The way he was behaving with me was breaking me from inside. I was getting weaker every moment. I was finding no roads to my happiness.

I started disliking myself. I started believing that I was not meant to be loved. I would look at mirror and curse myself. I would laugh on my misfortune. I would cry feeling pity about myself. I would imagine how happy my life would turn if Akhtar would accept me, I would be lost in my imagination where I would live happily with him. Some other time I would plan to end my life. I would surf internet to find the suitable way to commit suicide. When I would walk on road, I would pray to get hit by a huge vehicle. When I would listen about anyone dying out of disease, I would wish of getting such deathly disease. But none of my prayers were coming true. Neither was Akhtar listening to me, nor the one who created this world.

***

I was resting my head on my desk trying to calm down the intractable hiccups which were causing me trouble. They were so severe that my shoulder blades were also paining which was extended to my neck. I was not able to breathe properly, so I thought to rest for a while. But there was no such thing applicable on me. Even if my body would rest, my mind would continuously suffer from stress. I was missing those good old days where people would praise me by saying that they wanted to be like me, free and happy always. But now I was no such example for anyone, I did not want to be like me. No one could have hated anything like I hated myself. I was tired of everything. Each morning I would look at pictures of Abbu, Shahid and Akhtar, praying to get back in their life, and each night I would cry tremendously because another day would have taken me far away from them. I lifted my head to find someone who could have patted consolingly on my back saying everything would be alright, but I found none. I saw Meenal and Kishan were discussing something with Vikram on his desk. I did not pay much attention on them and rested my head back feeling more than ever alone, crying slowly so that no one would get disturbed.

"Gul," A heavy concerned voice called my name.

I wiped my tears and looked in the direction of the voice. Vikram was standing on my right side. I looked at his desk, Meenal and Kishan were no more there.

"Yes Vikram," I unlocked my desktop, trying to resume my work. I did not care if he had noticed me crying, which was happening every now and then.

"Is everything alright?"

Maybe Meenal and Kishan were asking Vikram to speak to me. He was our team leader and according to the organization policy he had the right to speak to his team members about their personal issues if in case their personal issues were impacting their performance in office. In addition to being a team leader, he was my friend, which gave him another benefit.

"Please release me from this project," I burst into tears. This plea came instantly on my mind and without even thinking about it, I requested him to release me from his team so that I would look for another engagement. *New people and location might help me overcome from current situation*, I thought.

"What?" he was shocked. He wasn't expecting this.

"Yes, I feel suffocated here," I expressed myself. He was the one who could have helped me to move out from that environment. To move out from distress was still on me. He asked me to follow him to a meeting room in order to discuss the matter officially. I followed him. I told him that I want release in any case. First, he guided me through the cons of asking release during the period of time where financial appraisal was due. He told me that as I was one of the key performers, management would not agree to release me, and just in case they are ready to release me, they would not guarantee a good increment to me. But money seemed superficial to me, I was satisfied with my current income, I did not want to ruin rest of my life for the sake of just one increment, so I made my choice and told him that within few days I would send one official email to management asking for release.

***

Sohan was not happy with the email I marked to management asking for release. According to him I was being unprofessional. He advised me to think about it once again.

"You know that your yearly increment and promotion is due, Why are your personal issues important than your professional growth?" he asked me on call.

I did not reply to him. There were few people gathered at Meenal's desk to resolve one issue and I did not want to say anything in front of them. In addition to this, I was unable to explain him how stressed I was feeling to be a part of the place where Akhtar was always around yet far away, like horizon. Sohan was very busy these days as he had requested for Diwali leaves, due to which he had to work extra hours to complete his targets. It was one of the reasons he was not seeing me and was unaware that I was not seeing Akhtar. He was also unaware how depressed I was. But whenever he would call me, I would feel rejuvenated.

"I will explain everything to you when we meet," I expressed my expectations that I wanted to see him after a long time.

"I am not sure about it. I have lots of work," he regretted and abruptly kept me on hold.

I waited for two or three seconds when he took me on conference call with the person who had called him. The other person was buttering Sohan to get some work done. I kept my phone on mute and smiled in admiration of what he had done. He had taken me on conference call previously as well. Once, he asked me for dinner but unfortunately the same night he had to urgently go somewhere with his roommate. I did not believe him so he called his roommate and discussed their whole plan while I was on mute. Finally when I was convinced I went sad as I was not going to see him. He asked his roommate to wait outside their apartment, went all the way to a grocery shop and bought me chocolates. A simple dinner, which was strongly desired by me and so equally unsuccessful, remained pending ever since then. Another time, he took me on conference call with one of his colleagues when he was speaking to me on phone, and his colleague was continuously trying to reach him. They went to some serious office discussion while I was on mute for more than twenty minutes. Later, when their conversation was not ending, I left the call. Since then he had taken me on conference call with countless number of people, but not with his family or best friends. Many times he had merged my call with the call from my team only. Those calls would be the funniest ones to discuss. Some time when Akhtar would call him during my call, he would make sure to take me on conference so that later he could flaunt himself as one of the most important customers that even my Akhtar was buttering him.

"Did you notice how important I am, everyone keeps buttering me," he interrupted my thoughts when the other person disconnected call. "They know I can get their job done."

"Yeah I noticed. If I will butter you, will you meet me then?" I asked innocently from the core of my heart. He laughed loudly after listening to me. Excessive amount of dopamine was immediately released from my brain, making me feel better when I heard his laughter.

"Why not," he took deep breath after his delightful laugh.

***

Hemant and Akhtar were engaged in friendly combat. Hemant was trying to read Akhtar's messages from his mobile phone while Akhtar was trying to get it back. Others were enjoying, some of them were cheering Akhtar, while few others were on Hemant's side. I was on totally opposite side watching the end of my own happiness. According to my understanding, Akhtar was caught chatting with a girl and Hemant was trying to expose him. By the overjoyed display of their playful act, my heart was breaking every second and no one was noticing it. I silently lifted my hand bag and moved out of office with a strong decision in my mind that these people who once pretended to be my friends could never bring my happiness back.

***

Sohan said that he would reach in ten minutes but it was more than twenty minutes and he was nowhere. I kept waiting for him sitting inside the Kooka shop. A man had brought his two daughters to the shop. The elder one was around eight years old and she was scanning menu suggesting everything to order. The younger one was three or four years old and was so adorable and fair in color that everyone in the shop were admiring her. She was wearing a baby pink fairy frock made of tulle with much cuter pink ballerina.

She was totally looking like a fairy, which was not ready to stand on her legs. She was continuously requesting her father to take her on his arms while her father was busy placing an order. When he was done, he took her on his arms and searched for seats with his elder daughter, while she continued kissing his father on his cheeks with her soft red lips. Her father was smiling how her little princess was showing her affection. I smiled too looking at the young girl who reminded me of the lovable daughter once I used to be, and soon the smile turned into agony because that lovable daughter was now dying out of loneliness as her father had abandoned her.

My eyes blurred with tears, I saw that Sohan was also watching that cute little girl. He was smiling for the first time after looking at children of others. Otherwise he would always dislike them. He looked at me and his smile broadens. His laptop bag was hanging on his left shoulder, and he was holding his helmet with the same hand. His right hand was busy playing with his bike keys. He was wearing white half sleeves shirt paired with gray trouser.

Even after all day long his trouser and shirt were as clean and crisp as if he would have just picked them from his laundry. His shirt was neatly tucked inside his trouser where his black leather belt was shining, and his black formal shoes were equally competing with the shininess of his belt. I noticed that he was growing French beard which was perfectly shaped and trimmed. On contrary to his organized appearance, his hair was a little messy on his forehead. Because of that he was looking much younger and smart. And I could not ignore his gleaming eyes which were behaving as showstopper.

"Finally," he came close to me. "We are meeting after a long time."

He handed over his laptop bag and helmet to me so that I would keep them on either side of my chair. I nodded with a forceful smile on my face. The girl who was abandoned by her father was dominating me. He kept his bike keys inside the right pocket of his trouser, adjusted his hair and went to order which was already known by the shopkeeper. When the shopkeeper smiled at him, he returned and sat in front of me. I was looking at my mobile screen where nothing was flashing.

"Today your mood and your face are complementing each other," he took out his mobile phone.

I looked at running vehicles on main road. He was right. The rotten I was feeling inside was clearly reflecting over my face. I had stopped applying kohl on my eyes. It was getting difficult to manage them when my eyes were always crying. Apart from kohl, which was my default adornment, there was no other decoration I would wear. My face was as pale as my life. But the important thing which couldn't be ignored was that he had paid attention to me. Though he would never make any direct statement about it, today, somehow in some way, he had expressed that my face reflected my deficient mood, which meant that other days he was finding my face and mood perfect.

"I thought of giving you good news, but I don't think you are in a good mood to celebrate it with me," he created excitement through his talks.

"What is it?" I surprisingly looked at him. He was acting as if it was not the right time to share the news with me all because I wasn't in a good mood.

"Let it be," he tried to put more fire.

"Tell me," I grinned.

"I am buying a car," he said joyfully. His face glowed with happiness and pride.

"Are you?" I felt happy for him. He wanted to own a car here in Pune since a long time. He did not appreciate his hairstyle getting ruined because of wearing helmet, and he had to fight a lot during rainy season to keep him clean while riding bike. In addition to all this, he loved driving. He had told me many experiences of how he would go on a long drive with his friends, ending up driving all the way long from Lucknow to Nainital and returning back without taking rest. There were many other unplanned trips he had done in his car in Lucknow which he would always cherish.

"Now you don't have to struggle on my bike wearing a *saree*," he pretended as if he was buying car because of me.

"That was funny."

He laughed. He told me that if everything would go smoothly he would own a car before the festival, Diwali.

"And this time I will buy a white one," we burst into laughter.

He had shared with me pictures of his first car which was in Lucknow. It was a pitch black Santro with windows covered with equally dark films.

"Your car is looking like a mysterious kidnapping car," I said to him when I saw the pictures.

"Yeah, it is mysterious and equally mischief."

He told me that he was going to surprise me after buying the car, but as I was in a bad mood, he thought of surprising me today. He also said that as he was planning to buy a car, he was only able to help me with thirty thousand rupees; otherwise he could have given me more. I told him that his car should be his first priority before lending money to anyone. Before I returned to my apartment, he asked me if I got a chance to speak to Abbu, I told him that I was unsuccessful at every attempt.

"You are a strong girl, things will be fine."

I smiled because I did not have anything to say in return, and he went. When I entered our apartment, Chaudhary's room was closed from inside, so I directly went to my room. After some time she came and stood at my room entrance, leaning her right shoulder against wall, both her hands were crossed over her stomach and she was smiling looking at me. I looked at her and smiled back.

"What is that?" I asked her when she did not say anything but kept smiling for a long time.

"Anything special today?"

I looked at her with perplexed eyes.

"After so many days, I can see you humming a song."

When she explicitly mentioned I realized that I was actually singing the song which was playing in the Kooka shop. I pulled her rosy cheeks

She smiled. "Is it related to Akhtar?"

She knew about Akhtar. Once I was feeling so depressed and helpless and couldn't control myself from crying loud, she was the only one who consoled me. I told her everything. She suggested me to move on and do not think about Akhtar anymore. According to her, he was not a gentleman and apart from being aware about situation at his home, he got physical with me. But then she was aware of the pain I suffered from, she was aware how desperately I wanted to be with him, so some time when she would not be able to console me, she would pray for Akhtar and me to be together, so that my happiness would be back.

"No dear, Akhtar does not care for me anymore. I was with Sohan."

"Why don't you see him more frequently?"

I was confused why she was saying so.

"You cannot ignore such a drastic change he has brought in your behavior today."

"I know that I feel better when I see him, but this feeling is temporary."

"Every feeling is temporary if it is not associated with the right one. You know Akhtar is never coming back. There is no point in wasting your time for him. I know it is difficult, but at least you have to try instead of giving up. Engage yourself in other activities and meet new people."

"I don't want to meet anyone. I like it this way, alone."

"At least you can meet Sohan. Things which I was not able to do since last couple of weeks, he has done that in just one meeting. Girl, he has a magical influence over you. He can be the right one."

"No, Chaudhary. We are just friends," I did not consider Sohan as an option to love.

"Ok. Let him be your friend then. But you also agree that he uplifts your mood. So what is bad in seeking his help?"

I did not say anything but thought about what she was trying to say. I knew Sohan had good influence on me. He would always unknowingly unlock my door to happiness. But it was human tendency to run for all those things which were not meant for them. I was in need of Akhtar over Sohan because Akhtar was not present in my life, whereas Sohan was only a phone call away. So he was losing his importance when compared to Akhtar. Even when Chaudhary asked me to make a choice, I chose sorrow associated with Akhtar than ecstasy being with Sohan.

CHAPTER 23

I was waiting for Megha in one of the meeting room; Yogesh, who had taken my technical interview for their project requirement, had gone since last twenty minutes to call Megha, who was their project manager. Megha was going to assess me according to her managerial skills. I was released from my previous project. Unlike everyone else, only Sohan was upset from my release, as there was no one left who could have helped him in a way I did in the project.

He gave me an option to join his organization. If I would have accepted his proposal, Sohan and I would have spent a lot more time together, but I refused. I did not want to work with Akhtar and others. It was the main reason I asked for release, sacrificing my increment, so there was no point in joining anything which would have forced me to work with all those people I was running away from. I considered joining a different account with new set of people, a better option for me.

Since the last couple of weeks, I was reporting to group of people who were responsible to provide me a future engagement, and today they asked me to meet Yogesh in our main office which was located in Hinjewadi. This office was a huge one which was capable of accommodating thousands of associates. There were four giant buildings of which one was used for admin activities. Important client meetings and dinners, recruitment process, HR and visa related activities, resource management and all other regional work was done there. It was also having one huge theater which could be used for plays, shows and other fun related activities.

Rest three building were dedicated to project related work, each facilitated with its own library. These three buildings were having breakout area, for small tea and snack break at almost every alternate floor. Apart from these breakout areas, there were two huge cafeteria buildings with large number of stalls to accommodate maximum number of people. Anything which a person could think for eating was available there- from sugarcane juice to cold drinks, from *paratha* to pizza, from *paan* to ice-cream, from chocolate to pastries and cakes and many more. The last section of the office was sports arena. Volleyball, basketball, squash, badminton, yoga, gym and other physical activity could be done there.

The sports section also contained guest house where travelers and clients could stay. Apart from all these, rest of the thing which one could see inside that office was greenery, which was planted in a fairly large space. Bushes and flowers were arranged in various shapes and colors, trees were planted to keep the place cool and pollution free, small water bodies were created to enhance the look and feel. Rest of the space was defined by grasses. Ornamental and other types of lawn grasses were planted along pathways.

The overall appearance of the garden was like a colorful ever changing tableau. One could always find housekeeping staff maintaining the cleanliness of the garden and the edifice. Security staff was always standing in alert. There was no section available without human interference. Associates could be found discussing their serious concerns in admin building, taking a break from their busy schedules and breaking into laughter while having tea, sharing their meals with each other, engaging themselves in physical activities or talking over phone while roaming in the garden. Every place was always crowded. But it did not create any difference to me. I was still alone as my heart was looking for Akhtar's company to get sociable. I thought if I would not see him again, it would help me to overcome my feelings for him, but it did not.

Now I was always deeply lost in my thoughts. I was always thinking about him. What he would be wearing for the day, when he would be leaving from office, did he have food on time, what he would be doing other than office, was he sleeping properly and many other such questions were always remaining unanswered in my mind. I was always disturbed from the thought of a girl who would come in his life to own my position. I was always insecure that he would soon start loving someone else. I stressed thinking that soon he would kiss and touch another girl, a girl who could be his life partner unlike me. I would always feel helpless and there was no solution for my helplessness. There was no way I could have stopped my imagination about him getting involved with another girl. I was so jealous of that girl I was not even sure existed in his life. I would keep checking his Whatsapp and keep assuming things on my own. If I would find him online, I would assume that he must be chatting with his girl. If I would not find him online, I would assume that he must be speaking to her over phone. I would assume him hanging out with his girl on weekends when he would not see his Whatsapp for hours and days. And much of my assumptions were true.

He was frequently changing his Whatsapp and Facebook display picture which were taken on locations other than Pune, which meant that he was travelling a lot with his girl. Once he changed his Whatsapp display picture to his portrait. He was standing in sunlight wearing aviators, looking upward in the direction of sun. I saw shadow of a girl's hand on his face who was clicking him through a cell phone. All my hopes of getting back to his life died that day. I was sure that there was a girl other than me in his life. My insecurities were on a level beyond earth.

I was getting more and more irritated, frustrated and angry. My head was always filled with bullshit and my blood would always boil out of jealousy. I was degrading slowly but effectively. Since the day Chaudhary suggested me to seek Sohan's help to get normal, I was feeling a little hesitant to speak to him. I did not want to forget Akhtar. He was my love and he was also the one who made me stop loving myself.

***

After two days, Yogesh confirmed me that I could join their project. He introduced me with his team which was sitting in one cubicle. It was a team of four members. Apart from Yogesh, there was one boy, Shailesh and two girls, Sapna and Payal, who would work with me. Yogesh and Shailesh were a little reserved in nature unlike the boys from my previous account. After a formal introduction when Yogesh asked Sapna to brief me with basic project details, they continued with their own work. If a girl would have joined in my previous account, all the boys would have fought with each other to train her, but here they were away from these childish antics.

I grabbed one chair and sat between Sapna and Payal, who were sitting on one side of the cubicle. The other part was occupied by Yogesh and Shailesh. My seat was still not confirmed. Sapna and Payal started asking me many questions and I answered them in order, asking few questions from my end. Sapna was a tall and a fair girl with curly hair falling over her shoulder. Her eyes were dove-shaped covered with glamorous eyebrows. Her small and thin baby pink lips were looking so cute below her tall nose. She was pretty. Apart from being a Maharashtrian, she was speaking confidently in Hindi, though her Hindi was broken and spoken in Marathi accent.

Payal on the other hand was very happy as I was from her paternal place Mahdhya Pradesh. She was tall and slim. Her hair were much like her health, straight and thin, which she had tucked on the back side of her neck with the help of a clutcher. She was wearing frameless spectacles over her long nose, which made her almond shaped eyes lose their attraction. Her small dark lips were complementing her wheatish-brown complexion. She was very friendly in nature. I spend all of my day with these two pretty girls.

When I returned home, Chaudhary had already left for her hometown for her management entrance exams. I wanted to tell someone about my new project and new friends, but found none who could have felt great for me. At the end Sohan was the only name which popped inside my head so I called him but he did not receive my call. I checked Akhtar on Whatsapp and found him online. I kept his Whatsapp window open, thinking that he was present on the other side. I felt connected with him, but closed my Whatsapp after some time, realizing the bitter part about him being online.

I called Abbu and got no response from him. There was darkness all around. I closed my eyes in anguish and found that the darkness was inside me. There was no way to escape from it; it was continuously surrounding me more and more. I placed my cell phone on one side and rested on my bed, closed my eyes once again to find some peace and went asleep. After some time Sohan's call woke me up from my weak sleep.

"Hello," I picked his call. I was feeling sleepy.

"I am waiting for you outside your apartment, *turant se pehle aao*." He asked me to meet him.

"What happened?"

"My car, I bought it."

All my sleep turned into excitement.

"Did you?" I asked him equally happily. "I will be there in no time."

As I was already dressed well, I picked my apartment keys and rushed towards elevator. Within few minutes, I reached him. He was standing near one of the grocery shops on the other side of road. I did not pay much attention to him and searched for his car. A brand new white Maruti Swift was parked near him with its headlights on and indicator lights blinking in a rhythm. I looked at his car and smiled broadly at him. He was smoking, standing at a distance, looking proudly at his car.

"Why are you smoking? I have asked you many times to quit smoking, but you don't listen to me."

"Gul, instead of congratulating me, you are putting eye on my smoke. Do you know how nervous I am?"

"Are you nervous? All these days I have heard stories of your great driving skills and here you are, nervous. I knew those stories were fake." I pretend to underestimate him. That was one of my ways to motivate him and keep him going, which would work always.

"Nervous? Did you hear nervous?" he threw his cigarette away.

I looked at him with playful eyes. He was looking confident.

"Let us go then," he offered me a drive.

I signaled a yes through the smile on my lips. He unlocked his car and I sat on the seat next to him. His car smelled like a combination of some plastic, adhesive, rubber and sealers. It was the smell of a typical new car which his car perfume was not able to remove. Its seats were covered with black and red seat covers which were covered in plastic.

He switched on his car engine, AC and radio while briefing me about the interiors of the car. I listened to him with much enthusiasm. I kept looking at his glowing face while he was continuously telling me all the things that happened with him today. He told me that early morning one of the executives from showroom called him and said that he could pick his car today as every formality was done. He said that though he heard good news early morning, he had to struggle the whole day.

He had to return back through his car so he did not take his bike to office and preferred an auto over it. But as it was getting difficult to get an auto, he somehow managed to reach office by bus. And then whole day long, he was surrounded with issues which were not getting resolved. At the end of the day his colleagues asked him to leave, as they were also happy for him. They were ready to handle those issues in exchange of sweets. And then he went to the showroom with his manager to complete rest of the formalities.

"Where is my sweet?" I asked out of all the things he told me.

"Duh, do good and cast into the river." He said one of the famous proverbs, meaning that all the good things he had done for me meant nothing to me.

I looked at him confusingly.

"You care about sweets, it is so materialistic," he judged me. "I thought of sharing my first drive with you, but I guess mere sweets could have created more impact on you."

"Am I the first one to sit in your car? But you said that you went with your manager, he would be the first one to sit in your car with you."

"No. After everything was done, he went in his car and I in my own. You are the first one, Gul," he proved me wrong.

I did not say anything. I wanted to thank him and say that I was so glad for the gesture he had shown, but I did not find any suitable words to express my gratitude. I just kept looking at him with admiration while he was driving carefully and passionately over the roads of Baner.

"*Offo*, these people don't know how to ride a bike," he passed a humor when one of the bikers overtook him without waiting for his approval. We burst into laughter.

Yesterday, he was one of those bikers and today, he significantly made a difference from them. I felt proud sitting next to him and watching him move his hands over steering and gears like a driving professional.

"I want to drive."

He smiled looking at me and ignored what I said.

"I want to drive. Teach me," I held his left arm, feeling his strong biceps.

"No. Not on day one of my car."

"Why not, I will be a good student."

"No Gul, some other time," he rejected my request.

"Maybe you don't trust yourself to be a good teacher," I again underestimated him. I knew he was a good teacher. He had taught me how to ride a bike when we stayed in Magarpatta City. We used to go for bike rides after dinner; he would take me to show his office location, places which would run late inside Pune and places where couples would find their privacy. Some other time we would just ride slowly inside our residential area, visiting every road.

On one such night, I told him that I wanted to learn riding a bike and he immediately parked his bike on one side of road offering me a teaching. I hesitated for some time trying to postpone learning how to ride a bike, but when he insisted a lot, I agreed. Before I could sit and start his bike, he gave me theoretical knowledge. He told me whole bike anatomy, and I listened carefully as within few minutes I was going for a practice. He told me two or three times about how to start a bike, how to change gears, how to apply brakes and what to feel while riding a bike and cross questioned me to confirm if I was able to understand properly what he was telling me.

When he felt confident, he asked me to sit on his bike and he seated himself behind me where usually I would sit. With both my hands, I made a strong grip on his bike handle and removed it from side stand. He leaned his body over my back and held bike handle above my hand resting his chin on my right shoulder. He asked me to start bike. I gasped out of nervousness and started it as he taught me. Initially, I was not able to handle the weight of bike, so he was managing it by holding its handle, but when I started riding it straight, he left the handle. He was only guiding me to change gears and to apply clutch and break. But he was leaning over me owning the handle when turns were coming and other vehicles were passing by. After two or three rounds we both felt confident about my riding. I increased speed and asked him how was I riding?

"Good," he again leaned on me trying to hold the handle.

"Your beard is prickling on my ears."

He did not say anything but softly rubbed his cheek multiple times on my ear trying to tease me. I laughed as he was being naughty. Actually his beard was prickling on my face previously as well but out of tension and excitement of riding a bike I was not able to pay much attention on it and was fully concentrating on riding well. As he told me initially, I started feeling the ride; I was enjoying it, thus other things came into notice.

"You turn angry easily," he said when I was lost in my thoughts, assuming that I got angry when he refused to let me drive his car. I did not say anything; I was reliving that bike ride in my thoughts.

"Gul," he called my name looking straight towards road.

"Yes."

"I will handle the steering and you can handle the gears," he took out a win-win situation.

"Done," I knew handling gears was much tiny job as compared to handling steering or accelerator but I agreed with him. It was a big day for him, I did not want to ruin it. He told me about the gear system of a car and the need to change gear and then he asked me to take control. I held the gear with my right hand, attentively waiting for his command. Whenever he was asking me to change gear, I was obeying him like I would always do. Sometime he was habitually moving his left hand over my right hand to change gear, taking it back immediately as I was shouting on his interference. After some time when I felt bored I asked him to take control.

"I will stop here only," he parked his car near my apartment gate. "You have to walk from here."

"No problem," I moved out of his car understanding that it must be a tiring day for him, and sometimes it was alright, if he could not pamper me like he would always do.

CHAPTER 24

I thought that changing project and location might help me in moving on from the depression I was suffering from, but things were worse here. I was always surrounded with a number of people but I had no one to talk to. All four members of my team would use their local language, Marathi, to communicate with others. Initially, they would remember that for me they have to speak in either Hindi or English, but eventually they would start conversing in Marathi forgetting that I was also around.

They would crack some joke and laugh, whereas I would look at their faces as if I was a living dead; they would share project related details and increase their functional knowledge and interaction with clients, whereas I would feel as if I were not a part of their team; sometimes they would even forget to ask me for lunch. Then I would miss Kishan and others from my previous project. Before I took release from that account Kishan had already switched to another company, but till the time he was there I never felt alone.

It was around the time when Kishan had joined his new company, that Akhtar started ignoring me and telling me that he could not take our illicit relationship any further. After Kishan went, I was alone, here in my new project also. I turned to be an introvert by fate. I was never like this before. There was not even a single thing or person who could have controlled me from giggling here and there, but now I was always surrounded with some kind of offensive negativity.

Sometimes Saini, who was my college friend working for the same company from same location, would ask me if there was something wrong with me, and I would reply even more bitterly. Dutta and Shikha were tired of asking me what had happened, though Dutta already had a glimpse of what it could be. But she was unaware of the actual disaster that had happened to me. I was ignoring their calls and messages like Akhtar and Abbu were ignoring mine.

Chaudhary was aware about my gloominess but she was so busy that even after staying at same place, we would not see each other for days. Out of all the people who were close to me, I was speaking with Sohan only. I would reach office trying to start my day with new hopes and positivity, and when my team members would ruin my efforts, I would call Sohan and cry, saying that I don't want to work in such an environment.

Sometimes, I would even tell him that I would commit suicide if things do not change. He would somehow uplift my mood from melancholy to cheerfulness. This was happening every other day; I was calling him every morning when I would lose all my hopes and he would spread his magic over me. Though he was busy on his own schedule, sometimes out of town due to some meetings, sometimes visiting his hometown and some other time moving to other cities for his cricket tournament- he would never feel irritated with my depressed calls.

***

I was returning early from office as I was not feeling well, both physically and mentally. I was irritated and my body was feeling equally stressed. I was desperate to speak to Akhtar, so after gathering all my courage, I opened my Whatsapp and messaged him.

Me: Hi.

And then I closed my Whatsapp immediately, keeping my fingers crossed, expecting his reply from the core of my heart.

Akhtar: Hey, how are you?

On the contrary to my expectations he replied immediately. We were speaking after months. My eyes got filled with tears of joy and my heartbeat increased as if he was standing in front of me. I did not expect that he would reply.

Me: Can you meet me?

A moment later when he did not reply after reading my message, I realized that I made a mistake by bluntly asking him to meet me. He was speaking to me after a very long time and like a fool I ruined everything. My tears of joy turned into sadness, as I knew that he would never reply to such questions. Even after knowing that he was involved with another woman, I was so innocent to expect things from him. I loved him without thinking about rest of the world.

I did not even ask for any commitments, all I needed was a bare acknowledgement that he loved me. That was enough for me. Initially, I was thinking about my future with him, but when he said that whatever happened between us was wrong, I felt bad. It was alright if he was unable to hold my hand for the rest of his life, but it was unsatisfactory to raise questions against the righteousness of the moment when he held my hand. That was much more provoking and disturbing for me. I rolled to one corner of my bed while tears rolled to one corner of my face. I was feeling nauseous and my body was resisting any movement. I lay with no strength. In addition to my heart, my body was rejecting every signal from my brain. None of things were in my control. I sobbed under the narrow cover of my *dupatta,* which added to the inferiority of my own existence.

Later, when the only option left to me was to curse myself, I somehow managed to pick myself up to face the harsh realities of life. Even though I was half dead, I had to eat, sleep and work. I would try to ignore my life up to maximum extent, but at the end it would catch me like spider web catches insects. I moved to the kitchen to find something to eat. I remembered how Akhtar would message me, reminding me to take meals and medicines. Now, neither his messages were vibrating on my cell phone, nor I was taking meals and medicines on time.

I was famished and I returned equally disappointed from kitchen. I found nothing to eat. I did not have the courage to cook anything to calm down the hunger pangs going inside my stomach so I picked up my cell phone to order some food online and what I saw was serendipity. Akhtar replied to me after almost half an hour since the time I asked him to meet me.

Akhtar: Ok. I am in Aundh only; I will most probably get free by 8:30PM, so I will stop by.

I danced ignoring all the troubles I was facing a moment earlier. I danced like a peacock welcoming first shower of the rainy season. The feeling was joyful. Even though I knew that this meeting would be unlike how we used to meet, I was happy. The thought of seeing him was planting seeds of liveliness inside me. *I can live for thousand lives to capture even one single glance of his face,* I thought.

Me: I am waiting.

I replied to him after reading his message a hundred times, and then I hurried getting ready even though I had almost two hours for it. I knew he had appreciated me more in traditional attire so I picked up the most loved *kameez* from my wardrobe. It was a parrot green *kameez* whose stiff transparent cloth was crafted with small shining stars with a silky thread creating flower pattern all over it, stitched with a butter crepe lining. It was paired with red leggings and a beautiful multicolor georgette *dupatta*. I wore it and flaunted multiple times in front of mirror applying kohl and appreciating my own beauty. The feeling of getting ready for my love overshadowed the feeling of hunger. The blissfulness of face to face conversation with him healed every pain of my body. I finished applying kohl on my eyes when my phone rang. I ran for it thinking it might be Akhtar asking me to meet him early, but it was Sohan.

"Hello," I picked up and answered dramatically happy.

"Where are you?" he questioned without even noticing my happiness.

"I am at home. I am at my own home," I did not gave him a chance to cross question me.

"Good. See you at Kooka shop then, sharp 8PM."

He was confident that I would not disagree with him.

"No, I am a little busy," I replied hesitating. I had never said no to him.

"Busy?"

He knew that my life was empty. I had so much time to do anything, and this was the fixed time when we would see each other. This was the time I would certainly remain available for him.

"Yeah, Akhtar is coming to meet me."

"Oh enjoy."

There was a taunt in his tone.

"What do you mean by enjoy?" This wasn't the first time when I was pissed off with him when he used the word- *enjoy*. But this was the first time I was so aggressively asking him the actual meaning behind using the word.

"Enjoy means enjoy, why are you taking it other way?"

He was sounding annoyed.

"Yes I am taking it other way because you said it as a taunt," I replied being more annoyed than him. It was one of the special days for me which he was ruining.

"I will talk to you later."

"Well, do not talk to me ever."

"Ok," he disconnected the call.

I hated him for avoiding conversations. If I was wrong, I wanted him to correct me, but all the time he would run away from speaking things that could have solve the matter right away. I hated him for not understanding how happy I was when Akhtar agreed to meet me. I hated him because he did not deny when I asked him not to talk to me ever. I wiped my tears protecting the kohl from getting smudged. All these days, Sohan was consoling me but today he was the reason behind my tears. *I will not speak to him again, he never wants me to be happy,* I thought. I looked at my watch to calculate how much time was left for me to meet Akhtar.

Another forty minutes were required for thirty past eight. Every single minute was passing like a year. It was hard for me to wait for him. I was checking time every now and then. I looked at watch after a long time and it showed that only five minutes were passed. In addition to Sohan, I hated the watch for not running quickly. I wondered if I was dreaming. Suddenly, a feeling of uncertainty grabbed me from nowhere. *He will not meet you. He is just fooling you,* a part of me said and laughed at me. I felt insecure. *No, he is a man of his words.* I replied to myself. *If he said he will meet me, he will meet me.* I tried to convince myself but the more I happened to know him the greater were my insecurities and vulnerabilities. I knew that he was always uncomfortable in front of me since the day we kind of broke up.

Though he would try to behave normally, he could not handle my sad face, so he would simply avoid me. And apart from the fact that he said he would meet me, I knew that nothing could happen between us. Still, I was happy to meet him but, I also knew that my mood would automatically turn down when I would find him in front of me. I have tried multiple times to behave normally for him so that he would not feel offended, but it was clear to everyone that I had failed at each of those times. A kind of uneasiness was always present between us. It was the uneasiness which would disturb him from the core and it was the uneasiness which would kill my soul. I was helpless all those times. I was having expectations from him which he did not want to fulfill. I wasn't in a state to either blame him or convince him for what I was expecting, and he wasn't in a state to satisfy me anymore. I was getting more and more certain that he would not come.

I picked up my cell phone to call and confirm from him. When he disconnected my call after two rings I felt more vulnerable. *Why he did not respond?* I thought. *Is he busy? Is he avoiding me again? What could be the possibilities of not attending my call? He might be present with his girl, that's why he rejected my call. Should I call him again? He is coming to meet me in few minutes; maybe that's why he did not answer.* So many questions started running in my mind.

Sometimes, I was provoking myself whereas some other time I answered myself to allay my fears. *I am driving;* he messaged me after a minute. I took a deep breath of relief. *He did not respond because he is driving to reach my location,* I thought. As Baner was not more than fifteen minutes away from Aundh, I quickly cross checked myself in front of mirror and went to Kooka shop. I knew he would not come to my apartment so Kooka shop was the best place to wait for him.

On my way to Kooka shop I smiled and greeted everyone who crossed me. I was happy, so was the surrounding. These days moon was always darker for me, but tonight the silver tranquil moon was bright. It would hide behind clouds, emerging out quickly saying- *it's your moment. Yes, it is my moment*, I thought. *If this is the last time we are meeting, I will make it worthwhile. I will find peace for rest of my life in these moments. I will cherish it till my last breath. I will worship it.* A drop of tear rolled out of my eye, it was the reflection of serenity which I was feeling. I wiped it with a smile on my lips. As I seated myself, the shopkeeper looked at me and smiled whereas his eyes searched out for Sohan. *No it's not Sohan, its Akhtar.* I wanted to tell him that I was waiting for Akhtar, not Sohan, but I did not bother to tell him anything. I just started scanning road expecting Akhtar to reach to me at any time. I was keeping track of the time as well; as each minute was passing, I was estimating where Akhtar would have reached. My heart would beat faster and faster as the time was passing. I took deep breath to control my emotions and smiled at the change of fate, but I kept examining road and waiting for him.

He should be here anytime. I told myself when it was exactly fifteen minutes since the time he texted me. *Maybe he is stuck in traffic. Why everyone is out today?* I blamed others for creating traffic when he was ten minutes late. *Shall I call him?* I asked myself when another five minutes passed and he did not show up. By this time someone was calling me a fool from inside and my eyes, which were continuously waiting for him, experienced stress. I called him when he was another five minutes late. He disconnected like before. I aggressively called him back. He disconnected it again. I felt cheated. I called him two more times and he disconnected each of the time. *You are robbed.* The inner clever Gul was laughing out loud at me. *He tricked you like he always does,* I somehow agreed with her. I wanted to disagree but I knew she was right. Unless Akhtar was taking some longer route, Aundh was not half an hour away from Baner.

Me: I am waiting for you at one of the shops.

I ping him after checking his Whatsapp where his last seen was two minutes before. *He can check his Whatsapp but cannot pick my call.* I felt outrageous. I was breathing heavily out of anger and exasperation.

Akhtar: I cannot come, go home.

He replied immediately. I did not understand how- *ok, I will stop by,* changed to- *I cannot come.* I did not accept his fraud and called him for explanations. I called him multiple times and each time either he did not respond or disconnected my call. By this time I was walking furiously on road with no direction. I was surrounded with intense violence. I felt extremely pathetic by the way he was treating me. *Why did he commit when he did not want to meet me?* I cried out loud, but he was not close enough to hear my scream.

Me: Even if it takes whole night, I will wait for you.

I typed with shivering fingers and sent it to him. I did not want to blackmail him, but I was genuinely ready to wait for him even if he was never going to come. With so much courage and happiness, I had walked out from my home. I did not have the courage to go back and face defeat for rest of my life. I preferred dying over it.

"You said you will meet me," I did not greet him and burst into tears when he called me after reading my message.

"Yes, but I had to come for a family party. I wasn't aware of it," he was calm even after hearing me crying.

"You must come and meet me," I cried even louder. "I was only minutes away from you; if you would have wished, you could have seen me on the way. Now I don't know anything. Either you come right away or I am waiting for you whatever time you take." I gasped at every word.

"What is this obstinacy? I told you I am in a family party. I was with my cousin when you asked me to meet. Nothing was planned at that time so I confirmed you, but then this party happened all of a sudden and I could not deny. I was not responding to you when you were continuously calling me because my cousin was around. Now I had to come out of the restaurant to speak to you," his voice was soft but the way he was continuously speaking to defend him, explained everything to me. He was getting irritated.

"Where are you right now?" I was still finding it difficult to accept what he was saying, and believing that he did not want to see me.

"I am at FC Road."

"I am coming there. I want to meet you," I wasn't in my senses. I was speaking things which could have irritated him like hell.

"Are you crazy? I am not coming to meet you and you are also not coming here."

"Do not shout at me. Things cannot always be like you wish them to be. I am not your puppet." I did not know what I was speaking. The only thing I was aware of was that I was heartbroken. I was stabbed in my heart by exactly the same person who had my heart. I was not able to control my tears or my words.

"I will shout at you because you are talking insanely. And I never treated you like a puppet, that's what you think whereas there is no such thing like this."

"Then why don't you come and meet me. I swear, Akhtar, even if I die today, I am not going back," I cried to plead to him.

"I am not coming Gul. Go home," he raised his voice to a level I had never heard before.

"No." The conversation between us reached to some other level. For the first time we were yelling at each other. He was feeling irritated with me and I, on the other hand, was feeling irritated with everything.

"I am fed up with this. Do you understand the trouble I am facing? Do you even care? I am unable to find peace in office or in home, and here are you, increasing my blood pressure. All because of you my blood is boiling," he lost his temper.

"What did you say?" I did not believe what he just said. I felt the ground slipping away from my feet after hearing him.

"Yes, because of you my blood pressure is out of control."

He did not even think that he was blaming me for his bad health. I, on the other hand, was on the verge of attempting suicide, but never happened to blame him in this way.

"What did I do Akhtar? I only asked you to meet me. I am waiting for you only because you said you will come. Please come, maybe for the last time," I tried to convince him to meet me once.

"It is not possible at all. I cannot leave this function. Why are you being crazy? Why don't you let me live peacefully."

"You want to live peacefully?" I asked him as if I was genuinely going to solve his problem. "Then consider me dead," I disconnected his call.

What is my fault? I screamed in pain sitting on ground. People around me were already looking at me with disgust in their eyes, which turned extremely offensive. I picked myself up and walked in no direction. I did not have any inkling of what I was doing, but one thing was for sure, I was not going back. *How dare did he blame me for his health issues?* I thought while walking on a lonely road. *Has he lost his peace because of me? He must be true. What good I have done in my life? I am the reason why many people are suffering. He is just another person after Abbu and Shahid.* I started blaming myself. *I am not worth enough to live. I must end everyone's suffering. I must end everyone's suffering.* The sentence echoed multiple times in my mind, and I started running towards main road in order to find a way to end the suffering.

I looked here and there behaving like a psychotic. Even though it was late, the city was running normally with no room for a crazy person like me. People, who were earlier smiling at me, were now feeling some kind of threat from me. The bright moon turned frosty. There was something sinister, the way it was laughing at me. The kohl, which I wore to adorn my eyes was now smudged all over my grim face. It was the sign of how unfortunate I was. I felt something discomforting on my chest. I was losing my eyesight, my body was sweating heavily and I was also losing my breath. *I must end the suffering.* I repeated again and again when Akhtar messaged me.

Akhtar: What is this nonsense Gul? Why don't you believe that I am at my family function? Do you want to speak to my mother? Shall I send you the location? Ok wait.

He messaged me his location over Whatsapp. It was some restaurant in FC Road.

Me: I can also send my location to prove that I am still waiting for you.

I looked around to find a landmark. I laughed when I found one. It was Baner *Shamshaan Bhoomi.* Whatsapp location also showed Baner graveyard on its list of landmarks around me. *What a perfect location for me to die.* I smiled at the occurrence of events but I did not send him the exact location. Rather, I mentioned that I was near some restaurant. Even though I was mad at him, I did not want to freak him out.

"Go home Gul. Why are you behaving like this?"

"Why did you call me? I told you I am dead for you," I ignored his request.

"Stop talking insanely, Gul. You are ruining everything. My family is continuously asking me why I am looking tensed. They are worried why I am escaping outside to talk over phone. When all my family is enjoying inside, here I am, convincing you to go back to your home. I cannot come to meet you."

"If you cannot come right away to meet me I will wait for you. Even if it takes all night you will find me here, I swear."

"Why are you disturbing me like this?" his voice was full of hatred for me. "I am tired of you. I never imagined you would behave like this."

"It is just a reaction to what you are doing to me. You are treating me as if I have committed some sin."

"Please go back home Gul."

"No," I stood firm on my decision like it was written on stone. "If you are sticking to your decision, I will stick to mine. Do not show off as if you care for me; and if you do really care then come and meet me," I challenged him.

"I will not try to prove anything."

I knew he was not going to come and meet me.

'Ok. Do not call me then. Even if you will call, I will not respond. Let it be, I am ready for whatever happens to me tonight," I spoke my final words to him and disconnected his call. I knew I wasn't doing the right thing, but I was out of control. It was the limit for me. I felt defeated and cursed myself for the defeat. I looked at the heavy vehicles honking on roads and speedily passing. I thought to jump in front of them but suffered another defeat. Akhtar called me few times but as I said, I did not respond. I missed Sohan and got mad at him as well. If he wouldn't have fought with me, I would have called him at this time. *He, too, did not care Gul.* I said and gnashed my teeth. When nothing came to my mind, I called Dutta. She happily received my call and started complaining for the no-show that I was. I told her what happened and she freaked out.

"Are you mad? It is 11PM. Are you a fool to hurt yourself for a person who does not even care?"

"I don't know, Dutta. I am not going back. I will wait for him," I sobbed.

"There is no sense Gul. Do you think he is going to come?"

"No, he is not going to come."

"Then, what is the point? Rather go back home, relax, have dinner, and if he asks, tell him that you are still outside." She laughed

I laughed too, but I did not agree to what she said.

"Hmmm."

"Good. I will call you after sometime. Take deep breaths and go home. Ok?" she said softly.

I disconnected the call. I felt a little peace somewhere in the storm I was facing, but I was still disappointed and hurt. Akhtar called me again and I received his call but did not say anything.

"Gul, are you there?" he called my name after a few seconds of silence.

"Why are you calling me, Akhtar?" My voice was calm but broken.

"I want you to go home, Gul," his voice was broken. "I know you are disturbed, but I cannot come."

"I wanted to meet you Akhtar."

"I will come and meet you tomorrow before going to office. Please go home now."

"I know Akhtar you will not come. You are tricking me."

"No. I will come, but why do you want to meet so eagerly. If there is something urgent we can speak over phone," he tried to negotiate with me.

"I don't want to speak on phone. I want to see you."

"At least tell me what the urgency is?"

"It is very difficult for me to live without you. I want to live with you," I answered in a very impartial way. Neither did I propose to him, nor did I mention that I can live without him.

"It is not possible, Gul. I have told you many times," he replied irritatingly as if it was the time to raise some concern other than the concern between both of us.

"Why?" This time I wanted it to hear from him without assuming anything on my own. "At least speak to your family Akhtar."

"I can't."

"You can't or you don't want to?"

"It was very clear in my family that I have to marry according to them. It was very clear since the beginning. I cannot even ask them about this," he told me about situation at his home.

"But things can be changed."

"No, this thing can never be changed in my home. So there is no point in asking them," he was confident about his family.

"Not even if it was about Hasrat?" I knew this question would have pierced him through his heart, but I wanted to be sure how adamant his family was. Hasrat was his first girlfriend. They were very serious for each other. We had spoken multiple times about their relationship, and all those time he did admit that he still loves her, and I would burn like a candle when my love would claim to love someone else.

"Yes, not even for Hasrat or Prakhya," he gave example of both of his official girlfriends.

For the first time when I was hearing about his girlfriends I did not feel envious but sorrowful. Even though he was in a legitimate relationship with both of them, unlike me, they were left behind by him, like me.

"And don't you know how I was humiliated when I told my parents that I wanted to marry Hasrat," he said after few seconds when I was feeling pity for his girlfriends.

"At least you tried for her. Try once again please."

"No Gul, I can't."

"I do not understand this, Akhtar. Either you should say that you want to talk to them or you don't want to," I was frustrated. I was tired of hearing that he couldn't. I wanted to hear his willingness.

"We can stay friends," he ignored what I was asking.

I understood that he did not want to speak to his family. Maybe he never wanted this thing with either Hasrat or Prakhya. I was just another girl.

"No Akhtar. I cannot stay half here and half there," I sobbed on the conclusion I was going to make. "Mine is a binary state, either zero or one. If you don't want me at one, then I choose zero. From now on you will not hear anything from me."

"Why, Gul? Why you have to do it like this?" he was pissed at me. "Listen, it is getting late and everyone is calling me. Why don't you go home and we speak tomorrow when I will come to see you?"

I did not understand, when it was pretty much clear that nothing could happen between us, why he said that he would come and meet me? Maybe he did not want to end it like this.

"No Akhtar. We are not meeting tomorrow. I know you will not come. You are just trying to get an escape," I knew his nature. He would always avoid such face to face conversations.

"Trust me on this. I will meet you tomorrow before going to office. Please go home now."

I was unable to reply. He thought that I was agreeing with him so he disconnected the call, but I did not. I just ended the conversation. I wasn't in a state to convince anyone what I wanted. Explaining my own situation was equally difficult. The storm was again furious at my end. I could not see anything but smog all the way through my blurred eyes. My heart was beating in my head. My body was tossed by the frightful push through the vehicles running over road. My legs and fingers were shivering out of fear. My mouth was as dry as dust. *This is the end*, I thought and managed to welcome my demise. I was standing over the divider separating the road of Baner from the road towards Baner graveyard. I somehow looked at the upcoming vehicles towards me and decided to jump in front of one. It was a truck, which was transporting goods.

I felt sorry for the driver who would bear the guilt of my departure. Till now, I had always suffered estimating distance of any running vehicle while crossing roads but this time, I calculated it well. The driver was continuously honking at me as a sign of warning. He wasn't aware of my actions so he did not reduce his speed. I maintained eye contact with him and counted three to jump, so that there would be no chance of failure.

One, two, three, when I counted three, I felt a strong breeze which pulled me back and the truck was gone. I saw that Sohan was holding my right hand from behind and he was smiling at me. His face was shining like a star, making it difficult for me to look at him. Due to the kind of cosmic rays he was emerging, I was only able to see his face, whereas his body appeared like a shadow. His hand was holding my hand strongly like never before. I did not say anything. I looked at road to confirm my defeat and then I looked back to find no one. Sohan wasn't there. It was my imagination where he intercepted me from committing such crime. My heart pumped out of my chest and I fainted falling over road. When I was falling, a car hit me. Apart from the internal injury given by Akhtar,

I got multiple external injuries for which I wasn't aware whom to blame. I did not understand what just happened. There was pain. There was blood. There was a lot of noise. There were people shouting and running towards me. There was a vehicle escaping from the scene and there was I, lying down representing the face of failure. There was another me, who was killed again.

CHAPTER 25

When I opened my eyes, I was in a general ward. It was very early in morning and most of the patients around me were sleeping. Saline solution was running into my body through my left hand. I was feeling dizzy and hard to breathe. I remembered that I had a fight with Akhtar because he refused to meet me, and then I was hit by a car when I failed to hit the truck. I searched for Sohan as he was the last thing I could remember from last night, but I only found one nurse who was in night shift, sleeping on a chair near the entrance of the ward.

The coat she was wearing on top of her chiffon blue *saree* was almost colorless, but one could figure out that it must be gray during its early days. She wore black socks on her feet, above which her bold silver anklet was shining. Her slipper lay unattended on floor. She hurried towards me when I tried to lift myself from bed. I was not able to balance my body. She told me to rest. She was saying many things, but I was only able to understand that a couple brought me to hospital last night when I was unconscious. She also said that they were not able to contact my family as my mobile phone was broken.

I don't have any family. I murmured inside my head, which was spinning. I could not understand what damage that accident had done to me that it was so difficult for me to do anything. It was hard to breathe, it was hard to speak, it was hard to understand what someone else was speaking, it was hard to control my own body, and in addition to all these things, it was hard to exist. The nurse went away, when she noticed me crying, and returned with a doctor. Without speaking, the doctor started checking my nerves.

"Do you want to call someone? What is your name?" He handed over his mobile phone to me.

His voice was filled with some fear which I was unable to understand.
"What is it?"

"Do you have any medical history?"

I looked at him with angry eyes as it was not the right time to play questionnaire session.

"You went through a cardiac arrest last night."

A heart attack, I tried to speak, but I was choked. My tears said what I was unable to speak.

"Stop crying, it's not good for your health. Take rest instead. We have given you basic treatment but that's not enough. You must visit some cardiologist. Call your family; they can take you from here."

I closed my eyes still aghast. Life was playing with me. I did not know if I was supposed to laugh on my misfortune or cry on my suffering. I felt as if I was handpicked by the creator of this world to tease till the last breathe. Every day was tougher than the previous day and every moment depressing. I lay helplessly on the bed of hospital thinking about my life which was full of misery since my existence. Amma suffered from Anemia when she delivered me. Somehow doctors were able to save both of us, but then she couldn't survive after Shahid. Abbu had faced a lot of trouble for our survival. None of his family members supported us through those days, but they humiliated him many times asking to return all that money they had lent.

Abbu had to borrow money from other people to shut their mouth. I remembered that once he lost his job when Shahid was very ill and he couldn't make it to office. His union leader was already irritated with him, as he was borrowing money from every individual from their union and was unable to pay them back. Out of frustration he fired Abbu. But that doesn't mean he was free from all those debts. Abbu still had to return that money.

He would search for job, earn on wages sometimes but would never compromise on our education. He would stand in queues to bring home food for us. He would agree on the quality of food but would never let us sleep hungry. We have survived on the food spared on us by some of his good friends. We have survived on food sold by government for poor people, and we have also survived on food which was meant to cover Abbu's stomach. Throughout his life, even if he had seen a lot, nothing could have let him down, but I did. *I was meant to be punished,* I thought. I thanked him for all the sacrifices he had done for me and decided not to contact him ever. I knew he could live with the thought of being betrayed by his daughter, but he could not live with the illness of his daughter when all his life he had just asked for his family's good health. I agreed that whatever happened between us happened for a good reason. I did not want him to suffer again. I just wanted him to be happy forever. I sobbed and turned on my right feeling pity on myself. *I am so wretched that's why I am not a part Akhtar's life,* I thought. *I cannot be a part of anyone's life. I don't deserve to be.* I felt darkness all around. Before my life could genuinely end, I was already dead in my conscience. I just had to wait to see how dramatically it would bring non-existence to me, but I was still unable to figure out which wrong habit I was practicing due to which I was suffering from such disorders.

It was a mystery for me. *If no bad habit can still cause me heart disease, what cigarette can do to Sohan?* I thought feeling protective for him. *I will make him quit smoking. I don't want him to go through any painful situation.* Even though he fought with me, and we agreed on no further communication with each other, I was feeling concerned for him. I remembered that no matter how this life had tried to tear me apart, he was the one who had always made me smile. I remembered his eminent face smiling at me when life when life tried to pull me down.

I remembered his vivid eyes doping me with his charismatic aura. I smiled feeling his presence around me. I felt uplifted. I took deep breath and tried to stray from the bitter part of my life forgetting that I was in hospital. *Yes you are in hospital and you don't have enough money to pay their bills.* Inner Gul was talking sensible with me. I was again surrounded by the real part of life where money was superior to all. It was month end and I hardly had some hundreds of rupees. I felt like a beggar, who had already asked for money from people around her. I felt like a weakling beggar, who did not have enough courage to ask for money even when she was in a 'do or die' situation.

I realized the pain Abbu would have gone through when he would have to ask for money to look after his family. I buried my face out of shame inside the stinky pillow of the hospital. After few seconds, I checked on that nurse, she was snoring. I lifted myself slowly, balanced my body, took out the drip needle from my hand, piercing it back on the saline bottle, grabbed all my stuff and without making any noise, I escaped from the hospital.

***

I was checking time continuously, making my own assumptions. I knew that Akhtar use to reach office by ten in the morning, and as both the needles of clock were running towards ten, I was caught between the desire of meeting him and the certitude that he was just fooling me. Even though I was sure that he would not meet me as he said last night, I was still expecting his call. I was expecting that before going to office, he would come and meet me. I trusted him blindly, knowing that he had tricked me by saying that he would meet me today. My heart was so naive. Even after receiving multiple defeats it was ready for another one.

***

Saini was suggesting me to go back home and take rest. He was not aware that I suffered from a cardiac arrest last night, but still my situation was so critical that he could not ignore it. I preferred sticking at office thinking that it might help me to stay busy and not think about Akhtar, but with no surprise he was continuously playing around in my mind. I was fighting with myself, sometimes defending Akhtar, sometimes attacking him. I kept thinking how he could mislead his own words. Even if I told him that he was lying to me, he assured me that he would come and meet me.

He should have at least texted me that he cannot come. Don't I deserve to be informed? I thought. I checked his Whatsapp through the broken screen of my mobile and found it evident that he was ignoring me. For a person like Akhtar, where he was known for his commitment, be it personal or professional, I was the one who had suffered from his renege. He was behaving as if I was some kind of communicable disease which would spread to him if he would meet me. It was very sick kind of feeling I was getting from him. I was feeling despicable and riotous. I always considered him as a kind and gentle human being, but he was continuously challenging my belief.

***

Dr. Jain had gone to examine my reports. After getting salary, first thing I did was to get an appointment from him. Despite being busy, he took me on priority and scheduled my scan. He was worried, as I was already having a medical history, and I was back to consult him in the interval of some four or five months. On the other hand, I wasn't worried at all.

Last time when he called Kishan and me in his cabin, I freaked out. But this time I was prepared, as I was already going through the worst. Everything here was familiar to me; everything was in its place exactly the same way when I left this room. Nothing was changed apart from date in the digital calendar which was kept on the table beeping *December five*. I ignored it when Dr. Jain came in with a smile on his face and multiple films in his hands.

"Something is wrong," he complained, keeping those films on table and grabbing his chair to sit.

I just smiled in return. Everything was going wrong in my opinion.

"Your situation is critical Gul."

"How critical is it?"

"Almost seventy percent of your heart is not working. I don't understand if you are taking medicines properly, how this happened? And if by chance there was some problem, why didn't you consult me before?"

He was upset on me. As a patient I failed him too. I lowered my eyes as I did not have any answer for his questions. I was not taking medicines properly, nor did I complain about any health issues. I always ignored them all.

"Answer me Gul, this is something serious," He forced me to confess my faults.

"I had few issues, but I did not pay attention to it," I replied slowly still managing to not look at him.

"Are you mad? You have heart disorder, I told you to take care of your lifestyle and your health. That's the key for you."

I did not reply. He told me many things, including what possible symptoms I would have faced, what I should and shouldn't do, which medicines I should start taking, suggested me ways to healthy lifestyles, told me that other similar cases have lived long, and recommended open heart surgery through which they could clear the blocked area present in my heart.

"As almost seventy percentage of your heart is blocked, open heart surgery is the best course of action."

He was confident to cure my disease but I was not seeking for any cure. I had already made my decision. *When the soul is already dead, there is no point in struggling to keep the body alive*, I thought in my mind.

"I don't want any surgery," I finally spoke, which irritated him a lot. He fixed his eyes on me, this time examining my behavior.

"Are you going through depression?" he pierced straight into the area I was weak. My misty eyes answered him well. Yes, a deep depression it was.

***

I lay on my bed remembering my conversation with Dr. Jain after I returned to my apartment. I was feeling alone. Although that was my all-time sentiment, today it was harsher. Something was disturbing me, but I wasn't able to figure it out. I felt as if I was drowning whereas everyone else was breathing happily. I was having no idea of what I was, where I was and where I was meant to go. Out of the blue, I opened my Facebook application on my mobile phone. There were multiple notifications, but I ignored them all and started scrolling down to see posts in my wall.

Akhtar is in a relationship (Today). 55 likes. 20 comments.

After reading it, the monster inside me was provoked. With frailty heart and shivering hands, I scrolled every comment to find out who the hell that girl was, who was in a relationship with him, but apart from wishes and questions asking about the girl, I found nothing. I also visited every girl's profile I was unaware of, who had either liked or commented on his post, but I ended up with a furious bellow. I noticed that Akhtar had replied to none of the questions.

I quickly checked his Whatsapp where he had last seen it hours before. I did not understand what was happening. It was a weekend and early morning. He had updated his relationship status in Facebook and was not online in Whatsapp since hours. I couldn't picture anything out of it. *Did he propose her and she agreed? Or did his parents fix his marriage? Are they out on a date? That bitch must be sitting on my seat next to him. Oh my god, what if he kisses her?*

Many things started running inside my head increasing my heart's functioning, which Dr. Jain had already advised to be taken care of, but nothing was in my control. I felt as if everything was paralyzed for me. *Call him and ask,* was the only thing my mind was able to signal me. I called him and as usual he disconnected my call. I was very prone to disaster whenever he would disconnect my call. Going crazy, I called him multiple times and he switched off his cell phone. It was turning into a nightmare for me.

I cursed the day and thought about the date Dr. Jain's digital calendar was displaying. I thought why December five ended to bring out this miserable day for me or why I survived to witness this downcast. Even though Akhtar's number was some time switched off and some other times unavailable, I called him every second weeping, yearning and suffering. I messaged him multiple times asking to either meet or speak to me. *I am driving. I will call you once I am back. I am into something. I cannot talk-* were his replies to me, which were playing with my patience, but I did not lose any hope and called him with every breath, expecting to somehow reach him.

My eyes and face were red and swelled out of grief. I even fainted a few times, but the moment I gained consciousness I called him back. Luckily, once his mobile phone was on and he received my call.

"What is wrong with you? Why are you giving spam calls to me? And are you behaving like this after reading my Facebook status? Can't I post anything?"

He was aware that I freaked out because of his status. Even after knowing that such acts could bring out a great desolation to me, he chose to announce his love affairs publicly.

"I want to meet you, Akhtar. Please understand," I managed to speak with a heavy voice even when my throat was choked.

"I told you I will call you when I reach Pune," he did not even notice my tears and pain.

"When will you reach Pune? Where are you?" I still believed that he owes me replies to such questions.

"I will call you back in the evening."

And then in a hurry, he disconnected as if he was committing some crime and someone caught him red handed. Helplessly, I believed what he said to me and waited till evening, but like always he tricked me again. Even after knowing that he would always play with my emotions, I was so dumb to believe him. My anger had gone to some level beyond my control; I was stressed beyond my breaking point. My physical and mental situation were undergoing great trauma, and I was feeling so mad at him. I started calling him, and things started running in a defined pattern.

I would call him, his cell phone would ring and then he would switch it off after getting my calls. After some time he would switch on his mobile phone and again switch it off after getting my calls. But I would keep trying to reach him continuously. I messaged him multiple times, begging to receive my call, and all those times he just replied saying that he was driving, which was just an excuse, I knew he did not want to speak to me. I have seen him talking to people over phone while driving. He could have spoken to me once, which could have calmed me down, but he chose to make things worse.

He wasn't responding to me. I was getting irritated. I was calling him again and again, which in turn was irritating him more. I was behaving like a mental patient and he was ignoring me like I was some unknown person to him. The whole day turned into a disaster for me, and I certainly ruined his day as well, but I was uncontrollably wild. I was undoubtedly acting as a bitch in both of our lives. Even though it was evident that I was no one in his life and he was in a relationship with some other girl, I was so impatient to meet him. Whole day, I waited to hear from him without taking any meal and without drinking anything, but when the night started getting remorselessly darker, I left all my hopes and disappointedly lay on bed. I realized that there was no future for me and I should accept whatever good was happening in his life. I just imagined him happy and did not remember when blackness grasped me inside its ruse. I woke up when Akhtar called me after midnight. I received his call with first vibration.

"Are you mad? Do you want to ruin my marriage?" he shouted as soon as I received his call.

I cried in blood after suffering from another allegation. Previously, I was the reason of his bad health and now I was being the witch to break his marriage.

"Why would I do that?" I burst into tears. I knew that I was having no chance with him, and his happiness was my utmost concern, but I was unable to control the girl who was irritating him. She was the hidden but bold part of me who was always provoked by him.

"Then why did you behave so? That girl was asking me why someone is disturbing me so much. Because of you I had to keep my mobile phone in airplane mode. My family was in tension as they were not able to reach me. Each time I was switching it on; I was getting flooded with your missed calls and messages. Do you know you have called me hundreds of times?" he raised his voice.

He was very irritated and angry.

"I wanted to talk to you," I tried to justify what I did.

"I do not understand what you want to talk about?"

"Please do not shout at me."

"I will shout at you. You have made my life a living hell. Tell me, was I supposed to drive on highway or speak to you? Even if I was telling you that I was driving, you were not ready to listen. There was no chance to handle mobile phone while driving. My girl was also unhappy. Now that I have dropped her home, I have called you."

"Are you getting married?" I asked him when I did not understand how to confront him, but I couldn't ignore that he called that bitch- *his girl.*

"Yes. She is working in Pune and my parents had asked me to meet her, so I asked her to come to Lonavala with me, but she only agreed when I updated my relationship status in Facebook. Her name is Sumnah and you can check her on my Facebook profile."

"Have you reached home?" I asked a lame question because I could not hear what he was saying.

"No, I am so tired, and in the middle of nowhere I am speaking to you because you do not have any patience."

"Drive safe and go home then," I replied gently, even when he was lacking respect for me.

He disconnected call like he never wanted to speak to me.

Bye, I whispered in my head. I started realizing that he genuinely did not care about me, and it was so easy for him to move on. On the other hand, I had lost everything for him, my family, my friends, my identity and everything else, so it was very difficult for me to understand how he was behaving with me. I was irritated, but that was obvious reaction any person could have shown after breakup. I remembered once he told me how bad he felt when his first girlfriend Hasrat behaved the same way with him.

It was February and at that time his girlfriend was living in Delhi whereas he was in Pune. He asked his lead to arrange some training in Delhi so that he could celebrate Valentine's Day with her. He and his best friend went for the training. His best friend would attend the training, whereas Akhtar would spend his time with Hasrat. One day, when he thought he would propose to her, she did not respond at all and he turned insane. He told me that he called her multiple times feeling like his life was ending.

He messaged her, called her from different numbers but nothing changed. In the middle of the night, he told his best friend that he wanted to go back to Pune otherwise he would commit something wrong out of frustration. Initially, his best friend denied saying that there could be serious trouble if they leave training unattended and uninformed, but when he said he didn't care about anything, he would quit his job, his best friend agreed and same night without having any reservation they returned to Pune. He left his job after that incident as he was not able to concentrate properly on anything. He became deranged during that time and today, when I was on his position, he was blaming me. He was rejecting me even when he knew the feeling of being rejected.

I lay down with no energy in my body. My face and eyes were swelled like no one could have recognized me. I had empty stomach since last night and my chest was paining like someone had drilled a big hole inside it. My legs and palms were burning as if they had caught fire. I sensed some fluid over the part where I was resting my head. It was my nose which was bleeding. But I did not have enough strength to pick myself up or to clean it. I lay down like I was dead but my mind in contradiction to my body was alive.

I was thinking about Akhtar. I was thinking whether he had reached home. I was thinking why we were not together? And all the thoughts were turning me crazy. I was feeling violent. Though I did not have enough strength, if someone would have asked me to kill myself or someone else, I would have done that without any failure possessing maximum energy. Akhtar's continuous despicable behavior for me had turned me into a monster. I did not care for anything, I just wanted Akhtar badly, but all I could do was to lie down helplessly.

***

"I would have done something for you if I would have been there," Sohan felt sorry for me.

He was the first one to wish me on my birthday. Like always he had to participate in cricket league conducted by his father's sports organization, which would always make sure that he never be with me on my birthday.

"It is ok. Your cricket is more important than my birthday as long as you are winning trophies and titles," I consoled myself. But deep inside my heart, I had always wished him to be with me on this day. Although I had never expressed this feeling, as I did not want to stand between his dreams, today I was missing him badly.

"But this is very surprising for me that they did not plan anything for you, whereas I have seen you proactively planning their birthdays," he was talking about my ex friends.

It was surprising for him that none of them planned anything on my birthday, but I knew that this would happen.

"Time, it changes everything." I said the bitter truth. "But I don't care; I would have felt bad if you wouldn't have called me," I tried to show how important his call was. Even though I asked him not to talk to me, he ignored everything and proved that our friendship was beyond everything else. I was obliged by his gratefulness.

He smiled. "That will never happen."

I could imagine the radiant smile on his face which in turn was automatically curving my lips. I did not say anything in return, but kept imagining him smiling, whereas butterflies kept flying inside my stomach. His smile was the only thing which could have forced me to desire for a long life.

"Tell me what you want as a birthday gift?" he broke my obsession with his smile.

I was surprised because I have never seen him gifting things to anyone. He was very poor in expressing his affection. Taking out time to buy things in order to gift someone was definitely not present in his book of golden rules.

"I want a white *Lucknowi kameez*," I replied energetically, as if I was prepared.

"I will bring you one."

"Will you shop for me?" I confirmed if he was going to shop for me.

"Yes, now I will hang up. Happy birthday once again."

"Thanks," I felt overwhelmed with his presence in my life.

CHAPTER 26

"I am really very sorry," Kishan apologized to me for missing my birthday.

"*Offo*, it is alright. I know you do not remember dates."

"Yes. And you are not in any Whatsapp groups, so I missed totally.

"In fact everyone missed it."

"Really?" he understood whom I was talking about. "Everyone is busy in their own life," he defended others. "Even Akhtar changed his number, and I wasn't aware for a long time."

"What?" All these days I was stalking Akhtar over Whatsapp and was always worried why he wasn't using Whatsapp frequently. His last seen were abnormal as compared to the frequency he used to be online. I was all the time surrounded with insecurities related to him. *Is he good in health? Is he facing any difficulty?* All such types of questions would make home inside my mind. His Whatsapp was the only thing I could have used to figure out his well-being.

His profile pictures, his status, his last seen were the things which would ensure me that he was doing well in his life, but since last few days I was feeling that something wasn't right. I wanted to inquire about him but did not have enough courage to ask anyone about him, so I was living with all those insecurities. And here was the result of the amount of caress I was feeling for him. He was using some other number and I was judging his activities based on a false fact. All my tension and concerns were a waste. I was voluntarily boiling my own blood for a person who was trying every possible way to get rid of me.

"Can we talk later?"

"Ok. Bye," he disconnected call.

I felt tragically upset. My feeling for Akhtar was genuine and deep, but still I wasn't having any place in his life. It was sad and hard for me to believe that I was detached as if I was never a part of his life. He told me that we can still be friends with each other and he had changed his number so that I won't be able to trouble him again. If that was what he wanted, he should have told me not to contact him again. I did not understand why he was being so ruthless for me.

**

"You are scaring me. What happened?" Sohan asked me when I reached him half dead. My body was pale, my weakness was reflecting through my eyes and I was gasping heavily. Out of all the disturbance and storm going inside me, I felt that he could make me feel better. Even though he was returning late from office, he stopped to see me. Initially he denied meeting me, but then he sensed something was wrong and agreed. I thought of telling him everything, which I was hiding from everyone, but when I saw him panicking, I dropped the idea. His contagious smile was missing on his lips, his innocent eyes were stressed out forming vertical wrinkles on his forehead, and he was shockingly gazing at my depleted face. *I must not burden him from my pain*, I thought. *But he is your best friend*. Apart from the fact that there was nothing which was hidden from him, I decided to hide the truth of my life.

"Will you tell me?"

"I am not well," I lost my control. He looked at me attentively, asking for detailed description. "I went to doctor and he said that I have a tendency to develop polycystic ovaries," I told him the part of my life which wasn't painful at all. "Will I be healthy ever?" I referred the actual disease I was suffering. Polycystic ovaries was just another consequences of artery disorder. He looked at me with questioning eyes while a drop of tear slipped from my eye. I looked away to hide the guilt of keeping him away from the complete truth, whereas he took out his mobile phone from his pocket and started doing something.

"It is curable and very common in women of your age," he read about the syndrome." I got scared; you used a lot of jargons."

His vivacious smile was back on his lips. I looked at him with watery eyes; I was uplifted after watching him smile. He put his mobile phone back in his trouser pocket and hugged me. A shiver ran through my body in the form of goose bumps over my skin.

"Don't worry, Gul," I felt protective under his arms.

We were never this close to each other. I could smell his body odor. His arms were strong enough to assure me that I did not want anything else in my life. I wiped my eyes and took deep breathe to realize that this was the beguiled happiness I was lacking.

"I am tired of all this."

He left me from his grip. *Take me back in your arms*, I requested in my mind. I did not want to get escaped from his arms. That was the place which was making me feel alive.

"You are a brave girl."

I reflected the positivity he was spreading around me.

"What happened to your mobile?" he looked at the broken screen of my mobile phone.

"Nothing," I hid the actual reason behind the damage of my mobile phone.

"I will buy you a new one," he took my mobile from my hand checking its functionalities.

"No. I don't need any phone, this one is working fine," I wasn't in need of a new mobile phone and was shocked as he was being too sweet to me.

"I know you don't need a new mobile phone, but I will still buy you one. Harish is coming to India, so I will ask him to bring an iPhone for you," he handed over my phone to me.

Harish had gone onsite and he was coming to India on leave.

"I don't need any iPhone," I was impressed how he was thinking about me.

"*Offo*, why are you arguing with me?" he dominated me.

"Sorry, as you say," I was ready to obey everything he would ask. "By the way where is my birthday gift?"

"It is in my apartment. You called me in such a hurry that I came directly from office. I will bring it next time."

"Ok," I felt overwhelmed that he actually brought me a gift.

"I will leave now," he took out his car keys.

"No," I did not want him to leave. I was feeling perfect with him.

"It is already eleven, Gul. I have to take dinner as well. I am hungry." I gestured him to leave.

"Take care, everything will be fine." He came forward to hug me again.

Don't hug me again, I will go mad. I stood still and whispered inside my head, equally wanting to hug him back. He quickly moved his right hand toward my right shoulder, patted me twice and stepped back. I held my breath meanwhile.

"Shall I help you cross road?"

But without even waiting for my answer, he held my hand and safely landed me on other side of road. I followed him happily.

"Bye."

He ran toward his car, unlocked it and went while I was lost in his thoughts, walking inside my apartment. My pale face was blushing; my tired weak eyes were reflecting his attractiveness, and my difficulty in breathing had turned into pleasure after smelling his body odor. I was feeling derived from his magical aura. It wasn't like I wasn't impressed by him earlier, he was no doubt the best human being I had ever met. I had always praised him for being a superhero in my life, who would be my remedy for all sort of problems, but today he was giving me goosebumps. My heart was rhythmically beating. It was evident that whenever I was with him, I forgot about every other thing as if there was no problem in my life. Today, I was able to realize that no big problem would have broken me like this if I would have recognized this feeling for him earlier. I felt as if I was flying in sky like a free bird. The wind was reminding me about him. It was earlier causing his hair to flow in the opposite direction of his hair style. He was continuously adjusting it with his muscular hands. Also I must admit that I was unable to resist myself from looking at his arm's pumped up veins, which he was showing off by folding his sleeves up. The most beautiful pair of eyes, his murderous smile covered with lightly trimmed beard, everything was making me fall for him.

I remembered when Chaudhary and Dutta tried to make me understand that Sohan and I were a perfect match for each other. I realized they were right. As compared to Akhtar, Sohan was far beyond handsome and mature. No doubt, I was much happier whenever I was with Sohan; still I was so dumb to ignore him. I was so dumb to ignore the amount of caress, respect, affection and comfortableness I had with him. Even though we would fight a lot, he always understood me and was always the first one among us to persuade me. I would tell him that I hate him whenever he would shout at me and whenever he would not listen to me. But today, I realized that I had never bitterly hated him, rather, I had always romantically hated him.

I remembered all the time I had spent with Sohan while lying in my bed. The pain, the suffering, which was attached to me when I woke up today, was no more present. It was replaced with the never ending stories Sohan and I had created together. Those were the stories holding magnificent healing powers against my severe wounds. I remembered, when our every attempt of dining together was failed, he once asked me for dinner but he had to go somewhere else to meet a girl as she was in need. I had a very bad fight with him as I was waiting for him and he didn't show up. Next day when we met, I told him that I hated him and that girl too, who did this to me.

"Why didn't she ask anyone else?" I was angry enough to blame that girl for stealing my Sohan away for her need.

"She is my friend, Gul, she can ask me for help."

"If she is your friend, who am I then, who kept waiting for you since eternity?"

I cannot forget the way he smiled and then he said something which melted me like butter. "You are the only girl with whom I have spent maximum time in my life, I meet you almost every day and we talk endlessly. There is no other girl who is this close to me and still you are saying these things."

I was proud to be that girl. I was proud that, for the kind of person he was, finding it difficult to be emotional with anyone, it must be something very special which made him say that I was the only girl with whom he had spent a lot of time. One of the times we travelled together, he kept playfully taunting me throughout the journey, as I did not bring anything for him to eat. Later, when one of the co-passengers offered us chapattis and pickle to eat, I was excused. He was carrying his hard disk and I got a chance to look at his photos that night.

After looking at his pictures, I came to know why he was so charming. His eyes and smile were breathtaking since the time he was born and his hairstyle was always the same. Unlike his nose, I would have wanted to pull his cheeks if I would have met him during childhood. His great fashion sense was evident in his school uniform too, which he maintained well like his office formals. He also showed me some of the pictures of Kunal and Harish. We started making fun of Harish as he wasn't impressive during his school days. Kunal did not change since he was a teenager. We kept looking at his pictures, talking with each other while everyone, who was travelling with us, slept. Later, we realized that we should at least switch off lights for others. He made bed for both of us but I was sitting on his seat implicitly assuming that none of us wanted to sleep.

"Say something now," he whispered into my ears when it was dark and we were surrounded by few minutes of silence.

"I don't know. I did not bring any script," I whispered back when I did not find anything to speak.

We returned to the world of silence while I kept scrolling his pictures. I did not remember when he fell asleep. I noticed it when I asked him something and he did not answer. His neck was hanging in the middle of nowhere and he was sleeping like a small child. I moved closer to him and slowly rested his head on my shoulder, and then I made sure that he must not get disturbed by any cause. Now, I was able to understand how pure and divine that journey was. I got tears in my eyes and curve on my lips as I relived that journey.

There were many moments when he had filled me with utter joy. Things which he had done for me would be simple but they were the most important and memorable part of my life. My cheeks were paining as I was continuously smiling thinking about him and about the time I had spent with him. I was feeling motivated. He always had the power to drive me towards good, he had the power of turning my sorrows into joy and he had the power to mold me righteously. I was getting a feeling which I never experienced before. I wasn't feeling like myself. I only wanted to think about him and to be around him. I wanted to stop the time so that I could save this feeling for a lifetime. I was proud that I was drowning in his color and that I would never take any other form. I was happy as he was one of the most beautiful images evocatively getting crafted inside my heart.

CHAPTER 27

"Why are you wearing such a loose shirt?" I asked Sohan. He was going to meet some of his friends in Pimple Saudagar and agreed to drop me at the lab for my MRI scan.

"Do you find it loose?"

"Yes, it is loose compared to your other shirts." He wasn't aware that I was tricking him to get to know about the size of his shirt. I knew if I would offend him he would reply back with the exact size he wore.

"Madam, it is 39 slim fit, I always wear this size."

"I don't agree."

"Really, you can check by yourself."

I moved towards him in order to check the inner side of his collar. *39 cm slim fit* it said.

"Yes, you are true but it is not looking like that," I came back to my seat. His birthday was coming and I wanted to gift him a shirt, but I couldn't have asked him this question directly. Apart from the size of his shirt, I saw that he was wearing some religious thread on his neck which he would always hide. I was never able to know about his religious point of view. He would never discuss their rituals with me. He would never tell me how strongly he was a follower of such things, but I had seen him wearing religious rings and bands. I never asked him about them. Only once when he was adjusting his band on his wrist, I asked him why it was too tight and why doesn't he just remove it? It cannot be taken out was the only thing he said and changed the topic.

Since then I never tried to offend him. I also saw trimmed body hair on his chest, which would disturb him very badly, but I did not react, as he was very protective on this topic as well. Once he told me about it, but after that I did not dare to initiate such topic on my own. He told me that he had inherited every single thing from his maternal family, including his complexion, height, his eyes, nose and every other thing. The only thing which he had inherited from his paternal family was his body hair. When he told me this thing, I laughed looking at his proud but disappointed face. Proud because he was delighted that at least he had inherited something from his paternal side and disappointed as he had to go through various hardships hiding those hairs. But he was always charming for me. I never judged him anyway.

***

"Can I pay rest of the money when I come to collect reports?" I asked the lady at billing counter.

"Ok, you can collect your reports after four days."

I moved out of the lab. Four days. There was no chance I could get money in four days. I was worried. I had paid the entire amount I had with me. I was left with no money at all. I did not imagine that the MRI scan would cost me this much. I was saving money so that I could buy gifts for Sohan, but this test ruined everything. I wasn't affected or feeling shame that I had no money to pay for the test, but the thought of not being able to gift Sohan on his birthday was killing me from inside. I wasn't coming back to collect reports, but what would I do for him now, was the question of a lifetime for me. *How will you go to Baner? Think of that first.* The inside Gul asked me. She was scary at times. Suddenly the question, which seemed unanswerable for a lifetime to me, turned into a less priority. I was in a place I had never visited before and I did not know how to commute from here. Earlier, I thought that I would return through a cab, but hiring an auto was impossible at first go, which was not even allowing me to think about a cab. I checked my wallet for hidden money and found nothing. I looked around unaware of what help I could ask from people and got more scared as none of them appeared helpful. I started walking trying to remember the way Sohan had taken, but as I was not paying attention while coming here, I did not remember anything. I kept walking, looking here and there, trying to figure out something when a man approached me.

"Where is the way to Nigdi?"

He was wearing a pale white shirt and a black trouser. His shirt was looking like he had not washed it since days and his trouser was touching ground covering almost all his feet. His hair was brown in color and he was dirty like he had not taken bath since the time he was born. His dark complexion under the sodium street lights was making him look like a beggar. He was holding a small polythene bag from one hand and a mobile phone from other, which was forcing me to believe that he wasn't a beggar. I wasn't getting a genuine feeling from him so I avoided him and continued walking.

"Madam, where is Nigdi?" he asked again, coming closer.

This time he was giving a fishy smile to me, which scared me to death.

"I don't know," I walked away. Now I was walking to get rid of him without even noticing that I was walking in opposite direction of Baner. I looked back after few minutes and found that he was still walking behind me. *Is he following me?* I thought. I made a tight grip on my wallet though it had nothing to protect. I looked around out of nervousness, Dr. Jain had already advised me to avoid any physical activity and still I was walking. I wanted to run but I did not have any strength to run away from the situation.

I was sweating badly and my heartbeat was rising, giving me acute chest pain. When nothing came into my mind, I signaled one auto to stop and without thinking about anything, I sat inside and asked him to drop me at Baner. After some time, when I was able to catch my breath, I got surrounded by another problem. *How will I pay him?* I thought looking at the meter which was running with a speed more than the speed of the auto. I started crying, feeling pity on myself, moving to one corner of the seat so that the driver could not notice me. I remembered last time when I did not have money, and I choose to escape from the hospital, but this time I couldn't even run. I started practicing in my mind how I would ask him to forgive me for not being able to pay him. Each time I was thinking about some way to make him believe that I genuinely did not have any money, I was getting buried under the ground out of shame.

I had never felt such humiliation in my entire life. When I lost every power of finding out a way, I remembered Sohan. But before making a call to him I thought hundred times what he would think about me? Genuinely, I knew that he wasn't going to judge me like this. It was my own feeling towards myself which was causing me to believe that Sohan would think the same way. *She always needs money. Am I her cashier? Before asking for it, doesn't she realize that I have already given her a lot of money?* Such questions were running inside my mind which I was thinking on behalf of Sohan. But ultimately I called him, as he was the first and last option for me.

I called him two times and both the times he did not respond. I looked at my watch which was showing eight in the evening and thought of all those reasons why he wasn't receiving my call. *Maybe he is driving. Maybe he is in the loo.* I thought. *I shall wait for his call. If I call him multiple times, he can get irritated.* After a couple of minutes when he did not respond, neither through calls nor by message, I called him again as the road started seeming familiar, which meant that Baner was closer. Luckily he received.

"Hello," he breathed heavily.

"What happened?" I got worried and forgot my own problem.

"I am at gym. I just saw your missed calls."

"Oh." I did not say anything and lost all my courage to speak about my problem.

"Tell me why you called?"

"Sohan," I took a pause. "I need money."

"How much?" he said in a very polite tone.

The way he asked me how much money I needed without even enquiring the reason behind it, not even caring when would I be able to return him the lend amount, broke me from inside. *How he can be so nice?* I thought. His big heart was turning me into his devotee.

"I don't know," I felt chocked from inside, whereas tears started running from my eyes like a waterfall.

"*Arey,* maybe I will see you tomorrow, so I will give you the money then."

"No, I need it right now."

"Now? What happened?"

"I am returning from the lab, and I don't have any money to pay the auto driver," I sobbed. The auto driver looked at me through rear view mirror.

"Are you at Baner? How much time do you have?"

"Maybe half an hour."

"Ok, don't worry. I will finish one set of exercise and then I will reach you by that time."

I disconnected call, taking a breath of relief. I thought that it would take around thirty minutes to reach my apartment, but it hardly took twenty minutes. When the auto driver stopped his auto, I came out of it and told him that one of my friends was coming with cash and he needed to wait.

"Madam it is Ok, please don't cry. I will wait," he gave a proof that he was another good person like Sohan. I smiled in return and called Sohan.

"You said you will take time. I was exercising accordingly." He did not expect me to reach early. "I am leaving from here, I need to go home as I did not carry my wallet with me, and then I will pick my bike and come to you."

I kept waiting for him. My head was spinning like a wheel, and I wasn't able to feel my heartbeat. I felt as if I would collapse, but somehow I managed to stand there waiting for Sohan. After fifteen minutes, through my blurred eyes, I saw one motorcycle skillfully overtaking other vehicles and coming towards me. I smiled as I knew it was Sohan. He came at a greater speed, parked his bike and with even greater speed took out his wallet, paid the auto driver and then turned to face me. I moved behind him, buried my head on his wet shoulder and started crying. He remained still for few minutes and then turned toward me. I looked at ground as I did not have the courage to look at him.

"Take this," he took out five hundred rupees from his wallet.

I signaled a no, still looking at ground.

"Take this Gul. Almost half of the month is pending, how will you survive?"

"I don't want to survive," I looked at him.

"*Chup be*." He asked me to shut up. "Take this; I will give you more if required."

I signaled a no again. He was being so nice to me, which was making me feel more humiliated.

"Do one thing," he placed the cash back on his wallet and handing it over to me. "Take out the amount as per your need."

"No Sohan," I smiled.

"Take it," he ordered me. "Let's have Kooka now."

I took out the same five hundred rupees note.

"No. I don't want you to spend your money on me like this."

He laughed loudly and started walking towards the Kooka shop. I followed him blindly.

***

It was a sunny and a hot day outside and as Sohan and I had to travel to the other end of the city, I wore a cotton *kameez*. I was unable to bear the heat, waiting for him standing outside my apartment. We were going to meet one of his friends, who was hospitalized. When he came I freaked out.

"Where is your car?" He had come on his bike. I shouted because I was ill and could not manage to travel more than twenty five kilometers directly under the sunlight. I was feeling drained.

"We will go by bike. A car will take too long to reach there."

He was right, but I did not want to go on his bike. With frowning face, I sat behind him and when he told me that we would stop at his office for some time, as he had some work, I started getting irritated.

"Why didn't you tell me in advance that we are going through your bike? Why you have to go to your office? Do you care that it is hot and I am not feeling well?" I was asking him many questions from behind and he was just making fun of me.

"I will show you my office," he did not give attention to the complaints I was making.

I did not say anything further, and sat quietly till we reached his office. I had seen his office from outside, which happened when we used to go for late night bike rides, but today I was going to enter it. He told me that he would introduce me to some people who knew that Sohan and I were friends. He was trying to calm me down, but things were getting piled up making me furious. He introduced me to two or three people. We spoke to each other for few minutes and then they went inside their workplace, leaving me to wait at the reception for more than forty minutes. I called Sohan and each time he said that he would finish his work in five minutes, but did not return for a long time. When I warned him that I would leave from his office alone, he came.

"I did not finish my work," he came towards me.

I looked at him with steaming eyes and did not say anything, but he kept speaking to me. While we were walking out of his office, he continuously was telling me funny things trying to make me laugh. From one topic of conversation, he was initiating another topic and then some other topic. I knew he was doing it on purpose, but I was actually furious because we were going to meet someone who was not well, and he was having a lot of work, delaying our main purpose. When we came outside, without any further delay, he sat on his bike, started it and signaled me to sit.

"I told you not to park your bike in an open area, but you never listen to me," I complained that it was difficult to sit on his bike as it was burning, but he did not want to waste his time to find a parking area.

"I am taking an auto."

He looked at me and did not say anything as I was uncontrollably angry and it was his fault. First, he did not bring his car. Second, he took a long time to complete his work, and now his bike seat was burning.

"I will do something," he dragged his bike under a tree, putting it on a side stand. "Why don't you come here and stand under the shadow."

I moved under the tree with angrier expression. He immediately went to a cigarette shop, asked for a bottle of water and came back. Then he searched for a cloth which he could use to cool the seat. I saw him putting a lot of effort by pouring water on the seat and then cooling it down with a piece of cloth, which he had brought after searching a bike which was parked nearby. He repeated the process two or three times, checked the seat and then signaled me that I could now sit.

"It is still burning out of heat. But I will manage," I had to because he had shown great efforts.

"I am not sure about the seat, but yes, you are definitely burning out of anger."

I laughed. As of now he was knowingly trying every possible way to make me laugh, but his innocent act did the magic on me.

"That is because you never listen to me. We started at eleven thirty, now it is one in the afternoon but still we are here. It will take another hour to reach to the hospital. I don't want to face sunlight for such a long period," I rested my head on his shoulder. There was no option for me to tell him how bad I was feeling from inside. He raised speed of his bike as we started speaking about various things. Though our conversations were always unlimited, conversing on his bike while travelling was close to my heart. I remembered, once when he picked me from my office and we were returning to Magarpatta City. We were not able to hear each other properly as it was very noisy due to huge traffic. But we had to speak to each other, so he asked me to plug in my ear phone and then he called me through his mobile phone wearing his ear piece. I was sitting behind him on his bike and we were speaking over phones. We had done such strange things which I could remember for our life. Today he was telling me many things, sometime making fun of me. Other times I was making fun of him, and then he started making fun of Akhtar.

"Don't say anything about Akhtar." I pinched him from my left hand on his waist.

"Someone is getting possessive," he held my hand from his left hand.

"Yes, I lob him," I said childlike while he did not leave my hand. After few seconds, I removed my hand from his grip and wrapped it around his waist, went closer to him, rested my head again on his shoulder and closed my eyes, hugging him from behind. He did not resist and continued riding his bike without saying anything further. I told him that I loved Akhtar but I was finding the actual meaning of love, on Sohan's shoulder. A place where I was never hurt, which was always serene for me. I imagined life as a never ending journey of bike rides with him, where we could start for no reason and go wherever we wanted. We had never thought of why or for what reason we should meet. We had never thought of why we should go to so and so place and why not, until we were together.

**

When we entered the hospital, everyone looked at us as if we were aliens.

"That's why I don't visit hospitals with a girl. Maximum people here will be thinking that we are expecting." He tried to crack a joke.

"Do I look pregnant?"

"No. Do I look pregnant?" We laughed.

He was always good at cracking such jokes which would sometimes embarrass me. One of our mutual friends, Mangesh, was already present at the hospital. Mangesh was here because patient's family member had gone for some work. He told us to come to fifth floor. As visitors elevator was over crowded, Sohan asked me if we could use staircase. Initially, I denied, but as the elevator was taking too long, I agreed. After we reached third floor, I handed over my handbag to Sohan, as it was getting very difficult for me to carry. Sohan took my handbag, but was unable to understand why I was weak. He was looking at me after every two steps, which seemed like a mountain to me. I was not able to see anything, my legs were shivering and I was feeling darkness all around but somehow I managed to reach the fifth floor where Mangesh was already waiting for us. Apart from Mangesh, there was a fat man guarding the place through an iron gate.

"Only two visitors are allowed," Mangesh said.

We looked at that fat man who rudely agreed to what Mangesh said. We requested him to let three of us in, but he did not listen at all. Finally we agreed that Mangesh and Sohan would visit first and then Sohan and me.

"Keep my bag inside the room," I requested Sohan. I did not want to be alone, or more specifically, I wanted to be with him for every possible second. The guard closed the gate as soon as Sohan and Mangesh crossed it.

"I am only going upstairs for some time, and look at you. What will you do if I leave forever to Lucknow?" he teased me from other side of the gate.

I looked at him with watery eyes. I could not imagine my life at Pune after him. In fact, I could not imagine my life without him at any place. I did not care if I was sad or happy as long as he was around. But he had already informed me that he would leave to Lucknow. It was a reality for me scarier than death. I held the gate, went closer and kept looking at him. I got a feeling that he was genuinely leaving me and would never come back. Numbness scattered all around. I started losing my heartbeat as if it was emanated from him. I felt every other thing moving forward, but I stood still as if someone had pressed pause button for me. There was no going forward without him.

"I am not going anywhere. I was kidding."

And then he opened the gate and came on my side. Then he requested the guard to let three of us in. I looked at the guard with pleading eyes. If he would have disagreed, I would have burst into tears, but he allowed us and I mischievously smiled with tears in my eyes.

***

"Wow, it will rain." Such unpredictable was Pune weather. On winters, when we started it was a hot and sunny day, and when we were returning it was cloudy and dark.

"I have told you multiple times to think before you speak. How will we return if it rains? I have pending work in office," he shouted as if I planned such weather.

"Sohan, you always blame me for things where I am not responsible."

"I am not blaming you, *baboo*," he changed his tone.

"Yes, you are blaming me. How can you think that if I ask for rain it will start raining?" And then I was lost in my thoughts. *If that is the case, if my tongue is so powerful, then I ask to live a long life with you*, I thought.

"Don't get upset now," he interrupted my thoughts.

I did not say anything because I was feeling sad. I knew I had no control over things; I could not make things happen all because I wanted it to happen. But I could not explain how desperately I wanted to see him smiling every day. How badly I wanted to see his sparkling eyes all the time. I wanted to fight with him on silly topics, and then I wanted to laugh with him till my stomach hurt. I wanted to go on long bike rides with him where our conversations would never end. I wanted to watch him helplessly falling asleep. I wanted to hear his real life stories multiple times and respond as if I was listening to them for the first time. I wanted to learn from him. I wanted to serve him and his family. I wanted to make him happy. I wanted to praise him. I wanted to see him winning trophies in cricket. I wanted to motivate him and watch him being successful in personal and professional life as well. I wanted to have Kooka with him every night. I wanted to wait for him and then shout at him for being late. I wanted to caress him. I wanted to travel around the world with him. I wanted to click his pictures multiple times. I just wanted to be with him till eternity could get defined.

CHAPTER 28

"What is this?" Sohan asked when I handed him a basket full of chocolates.

I knew he loved chocolates more than anything else. That's why I thought they could be one of the best options to make him happy on his birthday. Since last one week, I was meeting him every night and gifting him various things. I had asked Shikha to lend me some more money. She was another gem of my life like my family, Dutta and Sohan. Without inquiring about the reason, she helped me. And then I had also saved a lot of money by avoiding my medicines.

As I wasn't getting improved on health, there was no point in wasting money on them. Till now I had gifted Sohan things related to his likes. He was a big fan of Joker, so I gifted him a poster with Joker quotes written on it. I also designed a poster for him written with some bad boy bedroom rules. I gifted him a mug painted with Batman's bike, as he was a bike lover. He also loved collecting badges so I crafted one for him. I made a bicycle out of paper for him and a musical card listing some of his favorite Johnny Bravo's quotes.

A pen drive, a key chain, a transformer's car magnet and a tie were some other gifts I have purchased to make him feel special. I had wrapped all these things inside one basket, and I had filled that basket with many colorful paper strips rolled to make it curly. Yesterday, I gifted him one album made of canvas boards. The album was designed with pictures from his childhood, his friends and family. I had decorated it with cigarettes and wrote dialogs which he and I would use. I could not explain the epitome of happiness I saw on his face when he opened it.

"Yes, another favorite thing of yours," I wanted to tell him that making him happy by doing things he liked was the only thing I ever wanted to do. He smiled scanning inside basket. "Leave now."

"Yes, I have to go to the barber shop."

Tomorrow was his birthday and he had to look good, but more importantly I had to run to his apartment, that's why I wanted him to leave, otherwise I wouldn't have ever let him go. I had invited some of his friends for dinner at his apartment. His roommate had already purchased things which I asked him to buy and had given me his apartment keys.

"Bye."

He left and I went to his apartment without his knowledge. I was cooking when someone knocked on door. Sohan's roommate had informed me that he wouldn't return from office before ten, so according to the pattern in which the door bell was ringed, I figured out that it must be Sohan. He and his roommate had defined a pattern to ring the bell in order to inform each other that they were at the door. Apart from both of them, I was the one using that pattern.

"Welcome," I happily opened door for him.

"How are you here?"

He was happy and surprised to find me at his apartment.

"Is Nikhil around?" He asked for his roommate.

And then while he was setting down, I told him how I planned everything. I also told him that I was cooking, as I had invited his friends who would reach by eleven. After getting fresh, he helped me in kitchen by cleaning utensils, but went to his room as his roommate and friends arrived. They were talking loudly, laughing at jokes and discussing some of the serious current affairs when I called them for dinner. After dinner, at sharp midnight, I served the cake. We cheered Sohan when he cut the cake, and then his friends charged at him with the cream of cake to apply it on his face. From one corner of room, I watched them creating chaos. I watched Sohan feeling delighted and laughing loudly from the core of his heart, which was directly reflecting through his eyes. I closed my eyes, captured the scene for a lifetime, joined my hands and prayed for him. I asked for all his sorrows and failures to be mine and prayed to return all my happiness to him. I asked for all type of misfortune to stay away from him always. I asked for his life to be filled with beautiful surprises and grand success. I asked for his good health and long life. His phone started ringing when they were eating his birthday cake. That was another surprise for him. I had asked Kunal and Harish to take him on a conference call and wish him together. I knew they were the integral part of his life. Without them none of his moments were complete, so they were going to wish him, but I also knew that he would have turned jubilant if they would have done something special too. After disconnecting their call, Sohan looked at me with glistening eyes. I smiled in return. I was content after watching him happy, and I couldn't wait for the next day which was full of even more such wonderful elements. When everyone went, Sohan asked to drop me home. First he was teasing me that as he was very tired, his roommate would drop me, and I was showing him tantrums. Later, when I playfully agreed saying that whomsoever would drop me, would receive more gifts tomorrow, he quickly agreed to drop me home.

"Do you have more gifts for me?"

I could sense excitement and charm on his voice.

"No. I said that because I wanted you to drop me." His face turned plain after hearing to me. "Wait and watch," I said after some time to make him enthusiastic. His ardent smile returned on his face. I started feeling nervous when my apartment came near. I wanted to hug him, but unlike him, I was so shy to do that. He would have done it so skillfully, but I was feeling numbness in my hand and feet imagining going towards him in order to hug him. I started thinking how I would approach him. *It is simple, wish him and give him a big hug*, Inner Gul said as if it was as simple as hugging a child, but how much courage I required to do that wasn't measurable. We stood in silence for few minutes when we reached my apartment. As it was late, he had come inside to drop me safely. I was looking here and there trying to find out a way to hug him.

"I will leave now. I have to catch my beauty nap."

"Happy birthday once again," I took his hand with trembling fingers and wished him, realizing from inside that I was shy to hug him.

***

I asked Sohan to come to my apartment after his office. I had collapsed early morning, so I did not go to office. I had to do few more things on his birthday and one another gift was pending, so somehow I made him to stop by. I had asked my friends to send birthday wishes to Sohan. Throughout the day, they were telling me that Sohan had thanked them in return for their wishes. I had also asked one of his female colleagues to buy a chocolate cake on my behalf and tell the delivery boy to call Sohan and deliver it to him with a special birthday message written on it. When they had celebrated his birthday at office, she messaged me pictures of Sohan cutting the cake. Later, this evening

Sohan had called me to tell what had happened at office. He had already guessed that the surprise cake was sent by me. He informed me that he would reach my place by eight in the evening, so I was preparing to hide my illness. My face and body were looking depleted. I wore a full length pajama and a loose t-shirt in order to hide how thin I had turned. I applied gloss over my lips, as they were looking dark, and wore a large black frame anti glare so that he could not see the paleness in my eyes. I combed and opened my falling hair which could add into my fakeness. I opened gate with a smile when he knocked, and my smile broadened when I saw him smiling in return.

"Why you did not go to office today?" he entered my apartment and sat on a chair.

"I wasn't feeling well," I sat in front of him.

"Are you taking medicines?"

I just smiled in return. I wanted to tell him that those medicines were not working for me, my actual treatment started and ended with him, but I chose to stay silent. This was second time when Sohan had come to my apartment. First was when I was staying in Magarpatta city. On one weekend, when we both were working, he dropped me home after office and I asked him to come inside.

"Is anybody home?"

"Yes. Everyone is at home. Why would I invite you if I would be alone?" I mischievously played with my hair. He smiled, and the very next holiday when I was alone, I called him. He agreed to come but asked for a cup of tea. It was he, who brought the packet of milk. I made tea for him and then we spoke with each other for hours. Those were the early days of our friendship, and it was the first day when he told me everything about his life. I kept listening to him as if someone fond of music listens to songs. His magnetic voice was attracting me since then.

"Do you remember that the box containing your gifts was filled with many paper strips?"

"Yes."

"Did you throw them away?"

"No. Why?"

He was sounding eager and confused.

"Well, do not throw them, they have a purpose."

"What?"

"I have written a message for you on those strips," I gave him a clever smile.

"No, they are plain."

I was happy that he had paid attention to every detail of things I had gifted him.

"No, they are not. Instead, they are invisible. You have to find out a way to read them," I looked at him like a genius.

He looked at me as if I had done some magic and then I asked him to be seated for a while, and I went inside to bring the shirt which I had purchased for him. When I returned he was playing with a tennis ball which was kept near our television.

"I told you to be seated," I ordered him to sit again. Then I gave him the bag containing his shirt. He opened it with utter joy. I was looking at his face, which was filled with amazement and a sweet smile.

"Do you like it?" He smiled answering my question. "Now will you take me out for dinner?" Even though I was energy less, I asked him to take me out.

"Not today, I am already going out with my friends. But I will surely take you out for dinner soon, and it will be a very nice place. I promise."

"You never take me out," I made a crying face. I was waiting for a dinner with him since eternity.

"It will happen soon. For now, I have to leave," he picked up his stuff.

"Hmm. Bye," I greeted him with a heavy heart.

***

"Size forty?" I shouted as soon as I saw the size of *kameez* Sohan had brought for me. He and his roommate had come for some work, so he asked me to collect it. "Do you think I am fat?"

"I don't know. When I was purchasing it, I thought it will fit you, but now you are looking much slim. One can never understand a girl's figure," he laughed playfully.

"But forty is too much, even you can fit under it," I got upset. The *kameez* he had purchased was beautiful. It was a type of *anarkali* but a little less in circumference. Beautiful small flowers were embroidered over it with silky woolen white thread. He had brought a pretty *kameez* for me, which wasn't my size.

"I will get it altered for you," he looked at my sad face. "I will ask tailor to stitch two lines, one from here and another from here," he referred to either side of the *kameez*.

I laughed loudly looking at his innocent face. "It's not that easy." And then I told him how it needed to be altered. I told him that the shoulders were falling, sleeves were loose, neck was wide and it should be body fitting below chest.

"I told you, girl's clothes are full of curves," he made a naughty face.

I smiled getting shy. Later, I tried the *kameez* and messaged him pictures, then he genuinely agreed that it was loose. He asked me to return it so that he could exchange it with a proper size.

***

My managers were not satisfied with my performance. According to them, I was taking many leaves, and I had not done anything extraordinary which could overcome my drawbacks so they had declared me an under performer. I was already facing financial crises, and now I had a big question how I would survive with a decrease in my salary. These were the toughest days of my life.

I had lost my dignity in front of Abbu and Shahid, I almost reached the situation of a beggar, I was abandoned by Akhtar and his friends and Akhtar had also treated me like a filthy face, I started hating myself turning from a jolly girl to a depressed, negative introvert. I had been operated and now I was starving for death. I was suffering every day, begging salvation from this painful life, but I believed that more suffering was planned for me, that's why I was living to die even more mercilessly.

After my salary was decreased, I wasn't going to office much. I was already feeling suffocated in that surrounding, and then this thing happened. If I would go to office, they would send me back in ambulance advising me to visit a doctor. I would lie down in bed throughout the day and later faint. And then I would wake up restlessly, try to eat something and then faint again.

I did not have enough energy to pick up even a glass of water and take medicines which were left. Sometimes my biological system would work properly and I would feel good. I would cook; sometimes I would watch TV and some other times I would go to office. But all those times, it doesn't matter if I was good or in a bad situation, I would try to find my tranquility. And these days, I was certainly able to find it near Sohan. After his birthday, I did not have anything to do for him. I had a glimpse of how I would celebrate his next birthday, but I wasn't sure I that I would be present to wish him next year.

On the other hand it was certain that he was going to celebrate his next birthday in a place other than Pune. I would pray to leave this life before he could leave Pune. I couldn't bear separation from him until it was caused by my demise. In that case I would be helpless, but I couldn't manage to pass from the Kooka shop when he wouldn't be around to make me laugh through his high skilled speech.

I couldn't manage to cross roads when he wouldn't be there to leave me on one side laughing from the other end. I couldn't manage to watch any bike on road when he wouldn't be there to take me on a ride on his bike. I couldn't manage to watch any person driving perfectly when he wouldn't be there to criticize them. I couldn't manage to buy vegetables from the shop near *paan* counter when he wouldn't be there to buy me a *paan*.

There were many things I couldn't even imagine without him. He wasn't a part of my life, he was my entire life. I had a very bad habit of thinking about him in every situation. If I would be happy, I would think about sharing the happiness with him. If I would be sad, I would pray and request god to take away all his misfortunes. That was the ultimate goal of my life, to watch him beatifically smiling throughout his life.

***

Why don't you take medicines? You will feel better. My chest was hurting like never before and my body was beating in sync with my heart. I was able to feel it loud through my ears, but my head was causing me trouble greater than anything else. It was hurting as if someone had exploded it with some grenade, and then every piece was grounded to powder by continuously crushing it with a stone. I wasn't able to orient myself properly with such a heavy head. Somehow by holding walls, I went to kitchen to bring food, take medicine and then rest. My jaw movement was hurting me even more, so I was eating slowly. I had taken few bites when Sohan called me.

"Hello," I said in a dead voice.

"I have met with an accident," he sounded disturbed and restless.

"What? How? Are you alright?" I asked without taking any breath. A high energy was suddenly supplied to me.

"I am near Balewadi Phata, come here."

I immediately went. I was worried if he was all right. I couldn't even care that I was having dinner, which was important for me as I had to take medicines. He might need me was the only thought running inside my mind blocking every other concerns. I had to reach him as he had asked me to do. Even if I would be dying and he would ask me to do something, I would give first priority to whatever he would ask and then I would die happily.

"Are you all right?" I asked, as soon as I stepped outside auto. He was changing his car tire.

"Yes, I am all right. But look, my car got hit," he made a sad face.

His car was hit. There was a dent above its front right tyre. I could imagine how bad he must be feeling. His car was very precious to him.

"How did your car get hit?" I touched the dent from my hand. He told me that while he was driving, suddenly a dog came, and to save him, his car hit the divider of road. The tyre burst and he was unsure how the dent came. He called me first and while I reached him, he searched for any mechanic who could help him fix the damage but found none. He did not even find anyone who could have helped him to take his car on one side of road. After struggling for a few minutes, a good man helped him and they collectively parked his car in a safe place so that he could change the tyre.

"Why you want to be the hero all the time? Thank god you are not hurt," I said a little angrily, trying to help him through the tools. But asking him this question wasn't right in the first place. He was genuinely a great man for whom saving a dog was a small thing; I had seen him risking his own life just to make sure that things were fine.

Once he was driving late from office and he saw that four boys were bullying two girls on road. The girls were on a scooter and they were on bike. Initially, he thought that they were together and were misbehaving with each other after getting drunk, but when he crossed them he did not feel good. Still as it was late and he could not find anyone else on road, he decided to ignore it. After going a little ahead, he thought that he would be equally guilty if he would hear anything bad related to this incident in news. Then he immediately took a turn, deciding that as he was outnumbered, he would not come out of his car but help those girls by driving parallel with them. When he reached them, he asked if they needed any help. They refrained to tell him anything as the boys started shouting loudly out of anger and drunkenness.

They started abusing Sohan and blocking his way, but he did not leave until he was sure the girls were fine. Later, the girls told him that two of the boys were their boyfriends and they were creating a scene because they had a breakup a few hours ago. Sohan left them as they told him that things were under their control. Next day, he bravely told me about what happened. He was proud that though the situation was under control he tried to help those girls. I was also proud that he was being responsible, but I warned him to confirm his own safety first before taking any such actions.

"What else I could have done?"

"I know you did the right thing, but I just want you to be safe. You know that I am worried for you."

"I know, *baboo*."

While he was dropping me off, he told me that he had called the car service center. They told him to bring his car early in the morning so they could fix and return it the same day. He also told me that he would use his bike to commute to office tomorrow.

"Manage for one day."

"Yes. You want Kooka?"

I smiled because I would never say no to Kooka, as I would get more time to spend with him. He parked his car safely, cross checking it multiple times, and then held my hand to help me cross road. We were standing over divider, waiting to reach other side when he quickly asked me to follow him, tried to fetch my hand but unfortunately did not get it. In a fraction of few seconds, he was standing on the other side, helplessly looking at me. I felt as if he was trying to say that he tried but couldn't take me with him. I kept looking at him while my eyesight started blurring. A giant hammer was beating my chest trying to crush me down. I stood still, but from inside, my body was falling. My head was spinning and so were the surroundings. Vehicles, their lights, buildings, roads and so many people started rotating around me with a high speed. I wanted to shout aloud for Sohan, but I was only able to stretch my hands outward trying to find him. After sometime things started rotating with even higher speed, and I started collapsing when Sohan held my stretched hand firmly with his strong hand.

CHAPTER 29

"We don't have much work today. Everyone is relaxing."

Sohan had called me and was talking to me since last twenty minutes. I, on the other hand was unaware what work was going on in my team, so I preferred talking to him. He was in a very good mood today. People sitting around my cubicle were looking at me because I was continuously laughing over phone, listening to Sohan's humors. My jaw and stomach were hurting as I was continuously laughing, but he wasn't ready to stop.

"That's why you are talking to me."

"No, I am talking to you because it feels good to talk to you."

I blushed.

"So? Don't you go to meet Akhtar and other people from your last project?"

I did not expect that he would ask about Akhtar. Every time when I had tried to tell Sohan about Akhtar and me, he had refused to hear me. And now all of a sudden he was asking about Akhtar when nothing was left between us.

"No, I have broken every personal, professional and oral relationship with Akhtar."

"You are funny," He laughed very loudly and then the call got abruptly disconnected.

"Hello? What happened?" I called him back. He was still laughing.

"I fell from chair after listening to you. I only talk about personal and professional relationship not oral. Don't you have anyone near you? How can you talk such thing publicly?"

"There are people around me but I don't care."

He started laughing again as if I was genuinely having oral relationships with Akhtar.

"I, too, don't talk about that," I realized that few people around my desk were also silently smiling after hearing me.

"Now that you don't see him, what do you want to do?'

"I don't know. Maybe I can move in an apartment with a man," I was giving this hint to him that if he was ready, I could move in with him. "Do you know any man who wants to live-in with a woman?"

"Gul, are you alright?"

"Yes, I am serious."

"I know one person who wants to live in with a girl. I think he is good for you."

He was much enthusiastic than me.

"Tell me more."

"I will send you his picture over Whatsapp, check it."

I disconnected his call and checked Whatsapp. He had sent me a picture of a man. He was dark, fat and old.

Me: You have found this match for me?

I said with angry emoticon.

Sohan: Yeah, what is the problem? He is rich.

Me: No. He is old.

Sohan: But I thought you like old and rich men.

He said as a taunt to me, referring to Akhtar, as he was rich and elder to me.

Me: Can I block you?

I asked his permission to block him over Whatsapp. Whenever Sohan would try to tease me, I would ask his permission to block him over Whatsapp, but obviously he would not grant me the permission, rather he would request me so that I would not do anything like that. It was strange that whenever I would ask his permission, he would not behave like a master to me, but rather he would request in return like I was superior to him.

Sohan: No please.

Sohan: What about this one.

He messaged me picture of another man who was old, dark but thin this time. He was trying to make fun of me.

Me: No. Someone else, please.

Sohan: Am I a pimp who can arrange clients for you?

I burned from anger after reading what he messaged.

Me: Pimp? Are you insane? By saying that, do you mean that I am a whore?

    Sohan: I just used it as a metaphor. I didn't mean that.

    Me: Such words can never be used in any way. I am hurt.

And then I blocked him over Whatsapp. I was feeling sad because I did not expect Sohan to use such words for me. I had known him as a very polite and civilized human, and I wasn't able to bear what he just said. I remember once he was telling me about girls, who were easily available for dating and one night stands.

"I don't think that such types of girls exist," I wasn't agreeing with him that girls were bitch and they don't have any emotions.

"No. I have seen such girls, who are ready to have sex just after their first date."

I did not say anything in return, as I did not understand what to say.

"In fact I have been on date with such girls. But only on date, then they were expecting more which I couldn't fulfill so I started avoiding them."

"At least they have been asked for a date. Look at me, no one ever asked me out for a date," I felt pity on myself.

"Because you are a good girl, a man like me will never hurt you."

He said he would never hurt me and today, he was giving me metaphor related to a pimp and a whore. I kept my head down and tried to convince myself that he would never do anything to hurt me and it was a bad metaphor he just happened to use while he kept me calling. I disconnected every call but he kept calling me again and again.

"I don't want to speak to you. Don't call me again," I responded to his sixth call.

"Gul, listen to me, please. I did not want to hurt you," he sounded disturbed.

"I am very hurt and disappointed. I really do not want to talk to anyone. I will call you back myself."

"Ok. I will wait for your call."

I disconnected. That's how we were with each other, laughing at one moment and fighting the other.

***

"Hello," Sohan responded to my call.

I had called him while returning from office. He received my call before it could even complete its first ring.

"Hmmm." Even though I was upset, I still called him because I knew that he was the only one who could have cheered me up.

"Are you alright now?" I did not reply. "*Yaar*, I did not mean what you thought. I did not say it to you," I did not say anything again. "Where are you?"

"I am returning from office." This was the question I could answer easily.

"Where are you? I have started from my office, I will pick you."

I told him where to come. Even when I was sitting next to him, I wasn't interacting much. He was asking me questions and I was answering them. He was trying to have more conversations, but I was limiting them by either answering through one word or just saying *hmmm*. He was initiating other topics thinking that I might interact actively, but I wasn't in a mood to turn any of his attempts into a success. He kept trying until we reached my apartment.

"Talk to me, Gul."

He parked his car and I remained seated inside for a couple of minutes.

"Why? So you will get a chance and call me a whore," I started crying.

"Shut up, Gul. You know I did not mean that. Why would I call you so? In fact I can never say anything bad for you," I kept crying. "I just used that word; I did not even imagine that you will take it some other way. Ok *baboo*, I am sorry," he added when I wasn't able to control my tears.

"I am not asking you to apologize to me. I know that you cannot address me that way, but I just felt bad that you used such a word. I wasn't serious at that time when I asked you to suggest someone to live with me," I sobbed and wiped my tears. Sohan was one of those people who would rarely apologize, not because they had done something wrong and they had ego problems, but because they would never do something which would cause them to apologize. If he was apologizing to me it meant that he genuinely had that feeling. He kept looking at me without saying anything, whereas I was still weeping without making any eye contact with him.

"I will take you to my room," he changed the conversation. "I will show you how I have installed your posters."

I looked at him with amazement while he started his car and took me to his apartment.

"I will take the stairs,"

"Why?"

"You have told me to avoid using elevators alone with any boy," I mischievously smiled. There was a boy who was living in my building. He used to talk to me whenever he would see me. Even if I wasn't interested to speak to him, he would stop me in parking area, elevators and garden, and he would try to have a conversation with me. I had told Sohan about him, and the type of conversations he would try to have with me, and Sohan, after judging him based on his conversation, suggested me to avoid using elevators and other isolated areas whenever only he would be present with me. He also suggested me to be careful anyway.

"You can trust me."

That's the problem, I trust that you will not do anything with me, I thought in my mind. I wanted him to come closer and do something with me. After we reached his apartment, I felt enchanted when he was explaining to me how he had adjusted interiors of his room only because he wanted the posters I had gifted him to look even better. He told me that the collage I had made for him was the best gift he had ever received. He told me that one of his friends was getting married and he would wear the tie I had gifted him on the occasion of his friend's wedding. But he did not tell me when he would wear the shirt even when I asked him to send me his picture after wearing it. He asked me how I had made the musical card and bicycle toy for him. He also asked me how I had coordinated with his roommate and friends to invite them on his birthday. He asked me whether he should keep the coffee mug safely or start using it. He asked me many other questions and I answered them even more enthusiastically. I asked him whether he was able to figure out how to read those paper strips, and in return he started asking me ways to read them.

"At least you should do something; I had worked so hard for your birthday," I wasn't ready to help him here.

"Should I burn them so that the ashes will speak out what you have written for me?" He tried to find some funny way to read them.

"I will kill you before that."

He started laughing.

"Let's go. I will drop you home."

I started following him out of his room.

"How is your mood now?"

He asked me to confirm if I was still upset for what happened today.

"First, you make me upset and then you make me happy. Then why did you make me upset in the first place?'

He smiled irresistibly.

***

"Here are your medicines." Sohan handed me the medicines I had asked him to purchase.

Since last week I was in home as I was not feeling well. I had called my manager and informed him that I would not be able to join office back. Initially, he frowned as I started explaining my situation to him but ended up crying. He asked me to get well soon and said that we would discuss this thing later. I did not tell him that probably I would not have any discussion with him after this.

"Thank you. I was in need of them," I tried to hold myself in front of Sohan while he took out a cigarette out of his pocket.

"Do you have a matchstick?"

I liked it that he was comfortable to smoke at my apartment, but I did not want him to smoke. I thought to again ask him to quit smoking, but remained quiet, as I did not want to be pushy. I gave him a matchstick and a bowl full of water to put the ashes of cigarette in. He smiled.

"Do you know someone who wants to purchase a used bike?"

"No. Why?" I watched him enjoying the smoke.

"I want to sell my bike."

"What?" I frowned. "Why do you want to sell your bike?"

"I don't need it anymore. I have a car, my bike remains parked always."

"Who said you don't need it anymore? Don't you use your bike when you give your car for servicing? Didn't you use it when your car was hit? There are many other things for which you don't take your car with you, and now you are saying that you don't need it." I freaked out. Actually I did not want him to sell his bike. It had created very precious memories for me. A very beautiful and mischievous part of my life was attached to it. I did not want him to abandon his bike all because he had preceded a step ahead in his life and his bike was not much in use.

"I use it because it is there. If I will not use it at all, it will start decaying. But actually I don't need it anymore. I cannot take care of it."

"I will take care of it, give it to me. Now you are saying that you don't need it anymore, but later you will come to know that it was useful." I tried to convince him not to sell his bike.

"If I need a bike, I will ask my roommate, He will give me his bike."

He had already made a decision and it was difficult for me to manipulate it.

"Please don't sell it," I requested him when I found myself failing at convincing him.

"I want to tell you one more thing," he did not consider my request. I looked at him with perplexed eyes. "It is final; I am going back to Lucknow," he added slowly so that I would not freak out.

A million wishes crushed inside my heart when I heard him. When Abbu and Akhtar abandoned me, I ran to Sohan. When Sohan was leaving, I did not find anyone who could have protected me from destruction. I wasn't able to bear the thought that I would not get to see his face whenever I would wish. I wasn't able to imagine that our conversations would get limited to calls and messages. I wasn't able to figure out that when I was totally consumed by his charismatic aura, and when I was dying, why I was needing his physical presence so badly. And I wasn't able to understand why none of my wishes were heard.

"When are you leaving?" I held my emotions, but I was badly choked from inside.

"Next month."

Surety in his voice explained that everything was final, but till now he wasn't informing me about it.

"Don't worry; I will come regularly to meet you," he understood my concern.

"Can't you take me with you?" My voice broke. He did not answer. I knew handling too many emotions was difficult for him. He would either shout at me or remain silent at those times. Today, he chose to remain silent, as it was a hard time we both had to encounter. I, too, did not say anything further, as I did not want to make it even worse for both of us.

***

I was calm and composed when Sohan was present, but since the time he had left. I was unable to hold myself. I was continuously praying for some magic which could make it happen for me to be with him all the time. I was apologizing for every bad thing I had done, but I did not want to get punished like this. He was the only one who was completing me in every sense. He was the only one who had defined my beginning and my end and now that he was leaving, I was feeling so insecure about myself. I had no one to talk to other than Sohan; I had no one to visit; I had no one who could have turned my numb face into a delighted one; I had no one with whom I could have shared my sorrows. I was filled with many sentiments which were getting piled up as every moment was passing. When they started breaking me completely, I called him.

"Hello."

"I cannot live without you," I burst into tears. He did not say anything at all while I kept crying loudly. "Please take me with you, I will die without you," I was crying as if someone was killing the most exquisite part of my life. My weeping was filled with profound request and helplessness. I kept crying and saying that I could not live without him, but he wasn't speaking a single word. Neither he was asking me to stop crying, nor was he disconnecting call.

"Come outside, I am coming to see you."

I quickly hung up the call and ran outside to see him. When I came out from the elevator, I vomited two or three times. It was rotten and filled with blood, but I did not care. I picked myself up, took the help of pillars and parked vehicles, and reached outside. My eyes had turned blood red and they were burning like fire, but I kept searching for him through my blurred vision. My body was shivering, as if it was kept over ice, but I remained firm as I had to meet him. And then I saw him coming out of his car. I gathered all the energy left within me, ran towards him, and gave him a hug without thinking. *I cannot live without you.* I kept repeating this sentence and sobbing at the same time while he held me tightly within his arms.

***

Sohan told me that once he settled down, he would try to make some adjustments for me so that I could move to his city. I told him that till the time he wasn't going, I want to spend every day with him. I wanted to wander around with him, without worrying about the place and time. I told him that I would not listen to any excuses that he had work or anything like that. He smiled and agreed. He told me that he would take me to places in and around Pune. He told me that he would recreate the time when we had met, when we had talked and wandered without any barriers.

"Yes, we will to go places on your bike as well," I said enthusiastically, taking a glass of Kooka from him.

"I have sold it."

"Why did you, Sohan? You did not even tell me about it. You know it was important for me."

"That's why I did not tell you. I knew you will not feel good."

I did not say anything and turned my face in opposite direction to him. I looked at people who were enjoying their bike rides outside. I was so jealous of them. I missed the time when Sohan would come to pick me up on his bike. I missed the conversations we would have on rides after dinner. I missed the last time when I sat on his bike.

"Now don't be materialistic, Gul."

"I am not being materialistic, Sohan," I looked at him. "I cannot even tell you how special it was for me. It was my bike. It was my first bike which you have taught me how to ride. It has many wonderful memories attached to it, memories related to you and me. I just cannot digest the fact that someone else will now be creating their memories through it. I just cannot share anything with anyone which was related to us, just like

I cannot accept you to share the thing, which I had given you, with someone else."

"But I have sold it already."

"When did you sell it?"

"Last week."

He had posted one ad for it and a person had purchased it the very next day. The person was happy that he got a bike in a very good condition.

"You should have at least taken me out for a ride before selling it," I was sad that I did not even get a chance to see his bike for the last time.

"I will ask my roommate for his bike and take you out."

"No. I did not want to go anywhere on anyone's bike."

"Don't get upset now. One of my friends wants to sell his Royal Enfield bullet. I will purchase that and then take you out for a ride. Bullet is your favorite bike, right?"

"Are you serious?" I looked at him happily. I knew he wanted to lift my mood, that's why, even though he was moving from Pune, he told me that he would buy another bike and take me out for a ride.

CHAPTER 30

I was scanning my cupboard for half an hour; I took out every piece of cloth but did not find anything to wear. I was very excited as Sohan had asked me for dinner. This was the time I was waiting since eternity. Until today every attempt of going out for dinner was failed due to some reasons. I was praying that this time it wouldn't turn out to be a failure. I could not manage to lose it this time. I confirmed from Sohan multiple times and asked if he would give priority to any other thing over this dinner. He told me that he had especially taken out time so that he could take me out for dinner, and no other thing could interrupt us.

I took shower from slightly warm water as it tends to reduce pain of my body. And then I took out a black *saree*, which I had never worn before. I chose it, not only because it was beautiful, but also because its blouse was almost backless. I remembered, once after looking at one of my pictures in Facebook where I was flaunting my back, Sohan told me that it could have created more magic if the back would have been backless. I wanted to flaunt once again and create the magic but this time only for him. I looked at my pale face in mirror; it was glowing for a change. I looked at my forlorn eyes and turned them twinkling by applying a lot of kohl. I had abandoned it because of Akhtar, but I was overjoyed that I was applying it back for Sohan. I applied rose red lipstick over my dark lips and pouted multiple times in front of mirror, praising myself a hundred times. I combed my hair and checked its length on my back. When I had the haircut, Sohan told me not to cut them again. I was happy that even though they were decaying, they were long enough to impress him. I applied anti tangle lotion over them and made a bun so that they would add to my appearance.

Once I was ready, I applied ample amount of rose perfume and waited for him. I wasn't able to figure out if my chest was paining or if it was my heart beating fast out of excitement. I wasn't able to understand if my body was hurting or if it was the sensation of happiness running through my veins. Unlike other days, I was able to breathe freely today. It was deep and calm, but when Sohan called and asked me come down, it changed its pace. I quickly checked myself once again in mirror, smiled and went.

How I am looking and will Sohan appreciate me? -was the thought running inside my mind. But every thought disappeared when my eyes met his eyes and my heart skipped a beat. I kept looking at him as tears rolled down from my eyes out of happiness. He was wearing the shirt I had gifted him. That was the surprise of a lifetime for me. He had mesmerized me by the way he had acknowledged my efforts. He was looking stunning on that air blue color shirt. It was fitting him like it was crafted for him. His strong biceps and chest were a sign that he had taken his fitness and exercising to another level. His hair were wet and neatly combed and his adorable face was looking much more attractive. As the color of the button was black, he had complemented the shirt with a black trouser and a black formal shoe. His black chronograph watch was equally classy. He was, no doubt, giving me inferiority, but I was satisfactory for me as I wanted him to be superior.

I did not look away from him. Every memory and every feeling attached with him was flashing back inside my mind. It was a beautiful tale I wanted to admire throughout the existence of life. I was able to find my heartbeat after losing everything for him. I was able to find the meaning of my life after being his devotee. The moment when I was standing in front of him was teaching me how beautiful a life could be.

"You shouldn't have dressed yourself so well. We are only going to your favorite restaurant," Sohan said.

I was standing a little away from him, gazing at him continuously. He was trying to tease me. He himself was overdressed according to the venue he had mentioned, and I was again disappointed that like always he wasn't exactly expressing his feelings toward my appearance. He just called me groomed, whereas he could have chosen more romantic words to praise me.

"Place doesn't matter to me, I am groomed for you, where ever you take me," I tried to seduce him. He smiled and won my heart once again. His smile was my joy and my treasure. I was gaining my strength as he was smiling soulfully. No matter how outrageous this world was for me, I was always happy when he was smiling.

"There is something missing on your face," I moved closer to him.

"What is missing?"

Then he checked his face in the rear view mirror of his car.

"Show me." I held his face in my hand and kissed him on his cheek. "A kiss, a kiss was missing," I whispered in his ear. A shiver ran through my body. I did not know how I gained such courage to kiss him. I looked at him from the corner of my eye, I was shy and he was blushing.

As we moved I kept thanking god for what had come true. This was the time I never wanted to end. I wanted to pause it forever and live it repeatedly. As compared to the usual days we would meet, we were not talking endlessly this time. Those meetings were beatific in their own way and this moment was euphoric in its own manner. I was carefree whenever I was with him, but today I was nervous. I was feeling something which was difficult to explain. I wasn't feeling like myself. It was as if I was evolving out of the darkness. His every word and gaze on me was giving me goosebumps, and my feelings and memories were perfectly getting tangled around him. The way he was smiling, the way he was talking, the way he was treating me, and every other thing he was doing was driving me towards him. I was so glad that I was with him, and at the same time I was so surprised how divine he was. I had totally turned into his devotee, but the only problem was that I did not have enough time to worship him for long.

***

"Now will you taunt me that I did not take you out for dinner?" Sohan tried to crack the silence when we reached my apartment.

"No, now I can die peacefully," I smiled at him.

"*Chup be.*"

We moved out of his car. Again, he held my hand and helped me cross road, but this time he held it tight enough so that no other force or miscommunication could take it apart.

"It is late, I will drop you inside your apartment," he walked inside my apartment with me.

He did not leave my hand at all, and I followed him silently. I was nervous and sad at the same time as the most beautiful part of my life was coming to an end, not only the part when he had taken me out for dinner but also the part when he was with me in Pune. He was leaving the day after tomorrow. I did not want him to leave, neither today nor any other day.

"Don't go," We reached the parking area near elevator and stood there for a while without saying anything. "Please don't go," I moved closer to him, resting my head on his muscular chest. A storm was going inside my heart. I wanted to hold him tight so that no one could ever separate us. But I was helpless. I did not have any option other than begging him.

"I have to," he wrapped his arms around me.

His voice was equally helpless and his face was dull unlike other times.

"Then take me with you."

"It is not that easy," he had already thought about all the options.

"Take me with you at least for tonight," I proposed an easier way. I wasn't in my senses; I just wanted to be with him forever.

He smiled looking at me for a while. My face radiated. At first, I did not believe what he meant, but when I looked at him, I happened to believe him. His face was sparkling too. He took me back to his car. I followed him silently but my heart was jumping inside. It was full of the joys of spring. I was smiling, getting shy all the way to his apartment, I saw that his lips were curved too, but after looking at him once, I did not dare look at him again. I was feeling so nervous that I crossed my arms together so that he would not hold them. I was breathing heavily, biting my lips out of curiosity while he kept driving without saying anything. Ten minutes journey to his apartment seemed like a never ending road to me, but as it started coming closer, my heart started beating so fast that I was able to hear its sound from my ears. I was lost in my own thoughts, my mind was diving inside the lake of love which was turning me amorous, but I got worried. I wasn't able to believe that life had turned so kind for me. I closed my eyes and prayed everything to remain as beautiful as it was.

His apartment was dark when we entered. He escorted me to his room and switched on lights. His room was empty, apart from basic things. Everything was packed. The posters I had gifted him were down from walls, his utility table, his luggage, his clothes, everything was wrapped properly.

I moved to one corner and leaned myself against wall, banging my back on it in a slow motion and keeping my eyesight low on floor. I had an idea that he was looking at me. I, was hesitating, but managed to meet his eyes. I was feeling so attracted towards him. My life was alluringly smiling, but still my eyes turned wet. I wasn't able to understand them. They were wet when I was sad, and they were wet when I was blissfully happy. Though my eyes were wet, I smiled as he was passionately smiling through his bow shaped lips.

His almond shaped eyes were darning affection straight into my heart. His oval face was radiant like never before. I moved closer to him and placed my head gently over his chest. I was feeling so helpless and out of control, I wanted to get broken inside his arms in order to fulfill every desire I had. I wanted to get touched by him in such a way that I could not find my existence without him. I wanted to get merged in him. I wanted to wear his name, adorn myself with him in such a way that even the night would get jealous, but I did not understand what should I do, I did not understand how to calm the burning inside my heart and gain peace.

He affectionately held my hands through his warm hands, touching my fingers and nails and tangling them around his own fingers. He was breathing heavily and I could hear his heartbeat as if he was too burning from the same flame which was turning me anxious. I lifted my head while my eyes were still closed and he rested his head on mine.

I moved closer while he kept exerting a gentle pressure on me. We were breathing deeper and deeper. He moved his hand, untangled my hair and combed them through his fingers. I looked at him with pleading eyes. Without speaking a single word, I requested him to color me in his own color. I requested him to accept me as his belonging. I requested him to fill my empty life with his presence.

His eyes were enticing as he was looking straight into my eyes, and then he kissed me on my forehead, holding my face through his hands as if he was holding a bunch of flowers on his palm. I felt gratitude how purely he had accepted me. I smiled and kissed him on his lips. I kissed him once, I kissed him twice and then I kissed him for a long time. He too indulged himself by kissing me back.

After a few seconds we were madly kissing each other as if we did not have any other purpose in our life. The burning sensation we both had inside us seemed to turn quiet as we kept kissing each other. I moved my hands to undo his belt and unbuttoned his shirt and trouser without any hesitation. His muscular fit body was sweating, making patterns on his slightly trimmed body hair.

Like he had mentioned, his body was full of hair, but unlike he had expected, they were looking attractive, forcing me to love him more. As he was a fitness freak, I was able to see the results of his exercising. The ripples on his body were perfectly dividing his muscles from each other. As I happened to unclothe him, he untied the single thread which was holding my blouse over my body and undraped my *saree*.

I was living a dream through my open eyes. We both were tangled with each other, twisted like a tree and a vine. We were burning together, breathing together, shivering together and moaning together. We were unstoppable, inseparable, probable and adorable. He would talk something in between, I would answer him and then we would laugh together. He would stop in between, look at my face intimately. I would erotically look at him and smile shyly, and then he would love me again like he was doing it for the first time. He was creating some kind of magic that I craved even more. The way he was looking at me was turning me intoxicated. The way he was touching me made me spellbound to him. The way he was delicately teasing me, I was lasciviously moaning for more such pain. We loved each other without any fear. Now that he was inside me, I did not want to get separated by him. I did not want the night to ever turn into a day. I did not want to face the world again; I just wanted to get disappeared with him. I wanted to stay connected with him in such a way that there could be no coming back alone.

***

He held me tight throughout night. Even though I was moving, even though he was snoring, he did not let me go, but I when things turned uncontrollable for me, I escaped from his grip and went to washroom. My nose was bleeding and my heart was beating in a much unidentified pattern. There was a harsh burning sensation around my chest and I was feeling nauseous. When my head started bursting out of pain, I vomited. It was full of rotten blood. I washed my mouth from water and looked at mirror. My face was red like a tomato, ready to blast at any time and my eyes were rolled up. I burped badly and before I could control myself, I vomited even more blood. I was rubbing my chest to calm the burning which was killing me when Sohan knocked door.

"Gul, are you alright?"

I quickly cleaned his washroom so he would not find any blood stains and moved out. When I opened gate, I fainted and fell on ground. He lifted me and rested me safely on his bed. He was continuously calling my name trying to gain my consciousness back.

"Gul, Gul? Talk to me."

Although I was able to hear him, I wasn't able to respond. I opened my eyes and saw nothing. I stretched my hands so that he could hold it. He held my hand and gave me a hug. He was kissing my forehead and was rubbing my hands so that I would respond to him. Even though I had no energy, I held his arms as tightly as possible and tried to speak to him. After few minutes of panic, I was able to feel his warm body. I was able to see his face. I was able to realize that I was holding him tight enough to cause him pain.

"I am all right," I whispered slowly.

"Gul, what happened?"

He was very restless and scared. I looked at him and kissed him on his forehead.

"Nothing, it was my first time. I freaked out," I hid the actual problem.

"You scared me." He smiled, kissed me again on my forehead and gave me a hug even more tightly. "And you are talking as if I am experienced," he added, smiling through his eyes.

I looked at him, smiled and kissed him gently. He kept holding me while I rested my head on his shoulder and tried to ignore the pain I was going through. My heart beat was increasing as I was feeling his heartbeat. The sound of his breath was making me lose myself. My life was so lonely, and I had always been thirsty for such accompany. I was glad that it was him who had changed my life the way no one could have ever done. I knew that it was my end, but I was feeling so right inside his arms that even death wasn't able to turn me down. The moment I had spent with him was so important to me, like I was born to get touched by him, like I was never belonging to anyone else. It was such a divine feeling that he had embraced me when there was no one, and when everyone had forced me to believe that I was unfit for the world. After a very long time, I was feeling as if I had returned to home. A home where everything was as pure as a *sufi* prayer. A home where there was no give and take. A home where there was nothing wrong and nothing right. His protective arm wrapped around me was everything for me. It was my life, it was my destiny, and it was also the most beautiful end for me.

***

I lay helplessly on floor. After returning from Sohan's apartment I had vomited more. The last few ones were on the floor only. My body was swollen and it wasn't working so I had vomited wherever I was. I was only able to breathe once or twice in a minute and my heartbeat was lost. I wasn't able to see anything, but I kept my eyes open. I wanted to live. I wanted to go back to Bhopal and apologize to Abbu. I wanted to call and speak to him, but I was worried that he would not respond. I was already dead for him months ago; I did not want to put him on same grief again. I wanted to speak to Shikha, but I was so embarrassed that I wasn't going to return the money which she had given me. Although she was very kind, and our friendship was beyond all these terms. Money was making me weak in front of her. I wanted to speak to Dutta, but I was scared that I would burst into tears when she would ask me what happened. I just messaged her because I knew she would not check her messages frequently.

I wanted to go back to Sohan and see him smiling. He was calling me madly, but I wasn't responding. He had sent me messages to reply, but I ignored them. He had sent me messages asking for apology if he had done something wrong, whereas I was asking for his apology, as I was going to leave him behind.

His calls and messages came to end after hours when my cell phone switched off due to low battery. I never wanted to hurt him, but I knew that I was hurting him when he was the most important person of my life. I knew he would never forgive me for hiding such a big thing from him, but I was happy that he was going back to his hometown.

I was happy that finally he had solved the purpose of my life. Out of all the happiness and sweet memories he had given to me I was only upset that he wasn't able to bring a proper sized *kameez* for me. I regretted that even though the *kameez* he had given me wasn't my size, I returned it. I wanted to wear it and dance from the core of my heart. I wanted to wear it so that it could turn my demise even more beautiful. When I wasn't able to see anything through my eyes, I closed them so that I could see through my eternal eye. Even though I did not have any picture with Sohan, I was able to craft him properly in every moment of my life.

The time we had spent together, the time we had fought with each other, the time when he had made me feel special, the time when he had made me upset, and every other time when we were not together, we were still connected through our hearts. I was smiling slowly as I was able to find him everywhere. I was smiling as his soulfully smiling face was the only image that remained imprinted on me.

--END--

Ankita handed me a piece of paper with her trembling hands. It was covered with blood stains.

"She left it for you."

I took the paper from her and looked at her with helpless feeling. Her voice was heavy out of crying. She was carrying a handkerchief to wipe her tears which had created bruises around her eyes and nose. I moved to one corner, holding the paper in my hand so that I could read it, but I was feeling coward that I couldn't open it at all. I looked around, everyone was weeping. Gul's father was crying because he didn't even get a chance to speak to her. A shiver ran through my body and I opened her letter to find out what she wanted to say.

Hey,

I know it is weird and I don't know why I am writing this even after knowing that I will be dead when you will read this but I want you to listen to me for the last time. I want you to know what I have felt for you.

Few years back I met one person. He was charming, handsome and equally gentle. He was genuine, practical, naughty and sometimes stupid. I happened to discover a great friendship with him. I happened to talk to him about whatever I felt. He made me laugh, he made me cry, he took me out on various bike rides, he motivated me through my bad times, and most importantly, he never left my hand. I feel immense pleasure to tell you that the person I am talking about is none other than you. How it can be? You always had some magical influence on me, you always had something sparkling in your eyes which had always attracted me towards you, and you always had something so powerful in your voice that I had always felt mesmeric.

You know, I was a big failure in my life. I have never achieved anything, and I have always struggled for things which were my rights, be it money or family. And if I will look at my life, I will agree to it until I see you. I feel like I was the most successful person when I see you. I feel like having you present in my life was my biggest achievement. I did not care about life being difficult or sad as long as you were there. I did not care for my problems, I did not care if I was alone, and I did not care about anything else as long as I was with you. All I cared about was to see you smiling and to see the charm in your eyes. That was what actually defined my success or happiness.

Whenever you smiled, life turned blissful for me. Whenever you looked at me, every scar disappeared. Whenever you were with me, I felt like I was in home. I cannot thank you enough for being there in my ups and downs. I cannot even express how grateful I am for the things you have done for me. I cannot even tell you how it feels to die happily calling myself completely yours.

I am so happy that I have turned into the color of vermilion when you have painted me. I feel so touched by your fragrance, but I also feel sad that I will not be able to see you again. I feel helpless. I want to see you. I want to see your naughty smile, I want to see your innocent face, I want to see the brightness in your eyes, I want to go to Kooka shop with you, I want to go on a ride with you holding you tight from behind, I want to wait for you and then I want to shout at you for being late. I want to get angry on you, I want to get upset from you so that you will persuade me, I want to call you and talk to you infinitely, I want to walk with you holding your hands. I just want to live with you.

I feel sad that I will not be able to do any of these ever again but I don't want you to be sad. Even if I am not there, I want you to continue gracefully. Even if I never got a chance to watch you playing cricket, I want you to impressively make this sport as your forte. Even if I am not there to walk with you, I want you to cover every distance and reach heights.

Even if I am not there to laugh with you, I want you to vivaciously spread the joy. I want you to exercise a lot and look handsome. I want you to always flaunt your hotness in white shirts, and I want you to quit smoking; it is very bad for health, so I insist you to stay away from such bad things. Now that I am not there, I hope you will buy an ultraviolet torch and read those paper strips under them.

Actually I wanted to tell you everything face to face when I was alive so that I could capture your reaction, but I was coward to confess myself, so I wrote them on those strips. But now I am not scared, and I will not leave this chance to tell you that no matter what, I have always loved you, and I will always love you, since eternity till eternity.

#LOVE

ABOUT THE AUTHOR

Geet, or, Gitanjali Nanda is an IT professional residing in Pune. She writes about topics that are close to her heart and resonate with the youth of today. She is unabashed to put forth her opinion and enjoys life as it presents itself. A total romantic at heart, with "Since Eternity, til' Eternity", her debut novel, she connects with a generation that believes in love and heartbreaks alike and moving on or not is a choice that they are not afraid to make.

Connect with Gitanjali on Facebook at:
https://www.facebook.com/nandagitanjali/
twitter @geetnanda
instagram @geet_nanda

www.ingramcontent.com/pod-product-compliance
Lightning Source LLC
Chambersburg PA
CBHW020559180626
46810CB00007B/2571